RIVALRY AT PLAY

NADINE GONZALEZ

THEIR MARRIAGE BARGAIN

SHANNON McKENNA

MILLS & BOON

First Published in Great Britain 2022
by Mills & Boon, an imprint of HarperCollins*Publishers* Ltd
1 London Bridge Street, London, SE1 9GF

www.harpercollins.co.uk

HarperCollins*Publishers*
1st Floor, Watermarque Building,
Ringsend Road, Dublin 4, Ireland

Rivalry at Play © 2022 Harlequin Enterprises ULC
Their Marriage Bargain © 2022 Shannon McKenna

Special thanks and acknowledgement are given to Nadine Gonzalez for her
contribution to the *Texas Catelleman's Club: Ranchers and Rivals* series.

ISBN: 978-0-263-30383-4

0722

MIX
Paper from
responsible sources
FSC™ C007454

This book is produced from independently certified FSC™
paper to ensure responsible forest management.

For more information visit: www.harpercollins.co.uk/green

Printed and Bound in Spain using 100% Renewable electricity at
CPI Black Print, Barcelona

RIVALRY AT PLAY

NADINE GONZALEZ

For Ariel and Nathaniel. Always.

One

"A bottle of Prosecco for Ms. Alexandra Lattimore."

"On the table, please."

"Very well, Miss."

The poolside attendant's voice had roused Alexa from a heat-induced slumber. It had that sweet, syrupy drawl that might have charmed her—if she were easily charmed. She yawned and stretched and felt around for her tote bag. The August heat was relentless. A bottle of water might have been a smarter choice, but she needed something light and bubbly to lift her mood. She'd only been back in her hometown a few days, and already she had to attend a country club fundraiser. Such was life in Royal, Texas. In a move that fooled no one, her mother had purchased the admission ticket, feigned a migraine and insisted Alexa attend in her place. But that didn't mean she couldn't do things her way: Prosecco, gelato, a couple of podcasts cued up on her phone and a cabana all to herself.

Upon learning of her plans, her sister, Caitlyn, had chastised her for dropping five hundred dollars on a glorified tent.

"It's for charity," Alexa said in her defense. "It's the right thing to do."

Caitlyn accused her of being antisocial. "Everyone will be there. It's a great opportunity to connect with old friends or make new ones. Every time you've come home, you've stayed here at the ranch unless we've dragged you out. Don't wall yourself off. You just never know."

It was the sort of bland advice that people in love doled out to anyone who'd listen. Caitlyn—who would swan dive into the pool party on the arm of her new fiancé, flashing a smile brighter than her engagement ring—was sick and sloppy in love. Jonathan and Jayden, her single brothers, weren't coming until later, so she couldn't even hang out with them.

"Here's what I know," she'd replied. "If anyone wants to connect or reconnect with me, they'll have to put in the work and find me first."

Alexa was a prima donna of the highest order, and she was okay with it.

"What if you run into an old flame?"

"Please, Caitlyn," Alexa huffed. "I was seventeen when I left for college. The boys I knew couldn't start a flame with a box of matches and lighter fluid."

Even now, Alexa bristled at the thought. If she encountered an old flame, she'd stomp on it. No one had time for that.

Eyes still half-closed behind dark sunglasses, she found her tote under her lounge chair, drew it onto her lap and rummaged for her money clip. "Wait a minute. I have something for you."

"No cash. A smile will do."

Oh? So the Texas Cattleman's Club attendants were cheeky now. That was new. She'd been away from home awhile, but customer service at the country club had always been world class.

Alexa slid her sunglasses down the length of her nose with the tip of her index finger. She expected to lock eyes with a cocky college student, some kid picking up shifts at the club over the summer. The man towering over her was no kid: tall, Black and built, in a fitted white tee and swim trunks. He had just enough facial hair to define his jaw and draw attention to a teasing smile.

Wait… Oh, God…wait! Oh, God… *No!*

Alexa's mind whirled through the seven stages of disbelief before finally rolling to a stop. A name slipped from her lips. "Jackson Strom."

His smile widened. "At your service."

Caitlyn had had it right. Just about *everyone* was here. "I haven't seen you since…"

"High school," he supplied.

"Sure."

Actually, the last time she'd laid eyes on him was the day after graduation, in the parking lot of a convenience store. She was on her way in, and he was heading to his car with a paper bag overflowing with snacks. She'd said "hi," he'd said "hey," and that was that.

One month later, she'd moved to New York City for college and law school. Presently, she lived in Miami and worked for a prestigious law firm. This wasn't her first time back in town. After years away, her recent trips had started in May for the funeral of a lifelong neighbor and family friend. But her visits were short and, for the most part, she stuck close to home. Alexa wouldn't admit this to anyone, but she'd broken into a cold sweat at the thought of coming to the Texas Cattleman's Club—the beating heart of Royal's society—alone, hence the cabana.

Jackson welcomed her back in town.

"Thanks. Are you the official welcome wagon?"

"Kind of, but they only trot me out for very important people."

"I'm flattered."

"I'm flattered you remember my name."

"How could I forget? It was listed second in rank to mine everywhere."

He cut her a glance. The mischievous look confirmed that

the boy she once knew and the man before her now were one and the same. His appearance had thrown her off. Her old high school nemesis had looked nothing like this. He'd been good-looking then. Lanky and all limbs, he played basketball. The girls liked him, but "cute" was the word often used to describe him. All that cuteness had burned away in ten years. Jackson was handsome. His youthful cockiness had been honed into confidence. And yet he still had a dimple in his left cheek. The well-trimmed beard didn't hide it.

"What brings you back to Royal, Alexa?"

"I'm handling a matter for my family."

That was an excessively watered-down version of the truth. The "matter" was a complex legal issue regarding the family ranch's oil rights. They were fighting an aggressive claim brought forward by a local rancher. There was no way to drop that casually into conversation, so she'd deliberately kept her answer vague.

"Ever the dutiful daughter."

"Some things don't change."

She was a Lattimore, and Lattimores stuck together even if it drained them of their lifeblood.

Jackson took a good look around the cabana while she got a good look at him. Some things *had* changed. He had the toned, chiseled body of a professional athlete, but Alexa knew better than most that his best asset was and always would be his sharp mind. Jackson Strom had been the smartest boy in her class. Alexa had been the smartest—period.

"This is a nice setup," he said.

"I like it." The canvas-covered hideaway offered a respite from the August heat. At the same time, it offered a full view of the party. If anything important happened, she wouldn't miss it. Later, she'd have something to report to her mother, some bit of gossip to satisfy and please her, and all would be well. "Join me for a drink?"

"Call me boring," he said, already uncorking the bottle, "but on a hot day, I prefer a cold beer."

She squinted and studied him a moment. Who would ever call him boring? Back when they were just kids in school, he had always been the fun, easygoing one who got along with just about everyone. "We could order beer if you like."

"This'll do," he said. "Do you really think I'd pass on the chance to have a drink with Alexandra the First?"

Alexa flinched at the old nickname. Alexandra the First... at everything. Top of the class, best of the best, honorable mention, Dean's list, on and on. She'd been crowned the class intellectual snob. Like any label, it was unfair and unearned. She'd done nothing to deserve it except excel at everything but track and field. But every high school drama needed a villain, and she'd assumed the role. What was the alternative? Make nice and try to fit in? Never. She was the odd peg that didn't fit anywhere, not even with her own rock-solid nuclear family. While she read quietly in her room or immersed herself in foreign languages for hours, her siblings got their kicks fishing, hiking, horseback riding and swinging through any and all trees.

"That's 'Stuck-Up Queen Alexandra the First,' mind you," she said. "I dropped the title and go by Alexa now. It was a mouthful."

His laugh was rolling thunder. "You were always quick with a comeback."

"We all have our gifts."

He lifted the bottle of sparkling wine from the ice bucket and poured and filled two glasses. For a beer drinker, he had the moves of a master sommelier. He handed her a glass. "I spotted you in the lobby, but you breezed by."

She'd *sped* by everyone, avoiding eye contact. An attendant had directed her to the reserved cabana, and she'd been hiding out ever since. It didn't matter that she was an accomplished attorney. Here, she would forever be the odd one out.

"Sorry about that," she said breezily. "Have a seat."

He eyed the empty lounge chair next to hers. "Were you expecting anyone?"

"I wasn't expecting you, that's for sure."

Jackson set the bottle in the ice bucket and stretched out his long legs on the lounge chair. He had always moved like that, smooth and unhurried. "You were always good on your own, weren't you?"

"Not really."

She hadn't been a loner by choice. The girl who ranked first in academics often ranked dead last in everything that mattered, such as making friends or finding a date to prom.

He frowned. "Tell me more."

"Never mind. I've worked it all out with my therapist."

Whatever pedestal she had been placed on during high school, Jackson had been determined to knock her off it. For four years straight, they'd gone head-to-head for every medal, every prize, every scrap of recognition the education system had to offer. He tried his best, but he never outpaced her. But she often wondered why he'd been so intent on ruining her life. Being the best was all she'd had. Without that distinction, she was no one and had nothing to fall back on. It wasn't like she was going to take up cheerleading or join the glee club.

"You make it sound like it was a hardship. You left us all in the dust."

"Can you blame me?"

"Honestly? Yeah," he said. "You were the coolest girl in class. I would've killed to be your friend."

Alexa tossed her head back and laughed.

"What's so funny?"

"Excuse me." She stifled a giggle. "I find that hard to believe."

He took a long sip from his glass. "What was up with us?"

Now *that* was a loaded question. "It started sophomore year—"

"No," he said flatly. "It started way before that."

They'd been in the same class ever since kindergarten. Their rivalry hadn't begun in earnest until first semester sophomore year. Jackson had placed second at the local science fair. Usually, a girl named Stephanie Davies placed second in these types of competitions, but she had moved away. That day, Alexa saw Jackson with new eyes. She caught his cocky grin as he raised his smaller trophy over his stupid head. The urge to slap that grin off his face was irresistible.

"I can only speak for myself," Alexa said. "Our tenth-grade science fair kicked it off for me. I wanted to rip that trophy out of your hands."

Jackson settled more comfortably and bit into a smile. "Sounds hot. I would've liked that."

Suddenly, Alexa was hot. "Well, when do you think it started?"

"Eighth-grade chess tournament."

"What?"

"Ms. Thomson's math-class special project."

"I remember," she said, hazy on the details. Their math teacher had organized an in-class chess tournament as an extra-credit activity. Alexa had never played chess before then, but a few quick online tutorials had gotten her up to speed. She'd won, but... "I don't remember playing you."

"Not surprised. You wiped me out in twelve moves."

Maybe it was the heavy August heat or the light sparkling wine, but the past was soup. It took a while before she remembered. "Ah! You left your queen vulnerable. Who does that?"

"Not you, Queen Alexandra."

"Hmm." Outside the cocoon of the cabana, the party was picking up. Music and laughter and conversation tangled in a distracting mess. Alexa's mind went quiet. "It was you, wasn't it? You started the whole Queen Alexandra the First stuff."

Jackson took another sip from his glass. "I won't confirm or deny it."

"All this because of Ms. Thomson's extra-credit chess tournament?"

"I've wanted to beat you ever since."

"I'll take you up whenever."

Jackson flagged over a poolside attendant with whom he seemed pretty chummy and whom he'd likely bribed to confiscate her order from the bar. Instead of ordering a craft beer, he asked where he might find a chessboard.

"Right here." The attendant lifted the lid off a wicker basket tucked in a corner. It held a collection of board games, puzzles and toys for kids. "We have chess, checkers, Scrabble…"

"Chess, please."

He slipped the man a crisp twenty-dollar bill and set up the board on the round cocktail table between them.

Alexa sat up straight. "Are you serious? We're not playing chess at a pool party."

"Would you rather play volleyball?"

"I'd rather nap."

"You've got to give me a chance to redeem myself. It's the only way to save this budding friendship."

"Fine." It had been a while since she'd played chess. This might be his lucky day.

He arranged the white pawns nearest her. "Are you really here alone?"

"My siblings will show up at some point." Caitlyn was prancing about with Dev. Her brothers, Jonathan and Jayden, would swing by eventually.

"That's not what I meant." His focus was on the board,

lining up the plastic pawns in neat rows. She wasn't fooled. He was waiting for an answer.

"Are you asking if I'm single?"

He glanced up. "Are you?"

"There's no ring on my finger."

"If there had been one, I would have gotten word. Whatever the Lattimores do is news."

"Only in Royal."

"Only Royal matters."

"I beg to differ. There's a big world out there."

"And I've seen most of it. It doesn't change the fact that I know where home is."

She admired his self-awareness. They were about the same age, twenty-eight. Most of their peers were scattered to the winds. But Jackson knew where he belonged, where best to plant roots and grow. She hadn't yet figured that out.

"And you're a lawyer in Miami?"

"That's right." Alexa took a healthy sip of Prosecco to ease down a ball of anxiety that had formed in her throat. She didn't want to talk about her job. "I guess everything we Lattimores do really is news."

"I told you."

"Is it my mother? Is she boring everyone to death with updates on my so-called adventures?"

"Your brothers, too."

"Damn it."

The board was set. He leaned back and folded his arms over his head. "Your move."

"Okay." Alexa took a sip of Prosecco. "Are *you* single?"

A slow smile drew out his lips. "That's not what I meant, but that's fine."

Alexa was burning hot again. Still, she fixed him with a cool gaze. "Just answer the question."

"I'm single. No rings. No commitments."

"That's catchy." She glanced down at the board and moved a rook. "You should get it in needlepoint."

Laughing, he reached over and advanced a pawn. "Alexa… I missed you."

He'd missed her because of her sharp tongue and not despite it. Interesting. What was even more interesting was that she'd missed him, too. It hadn't occurred to her until now. Alexa had actively erased her high school memories. She did not attend reunions or accept online friendship requests. Finally, she'd done her best to stomp out old flames. He fell into that last category. Like the other girls, she'd found him cute, very cute. He was the only boy to have held her attention—a good thing, too, because none of the others had spared her the time of day. Their rivalry had kept her on her toes. Honestly, it had kept her on the Dean's list right up until she graduated as valedictorian. It had probably gotten her into her dream school. Even so, Alexa hadn't thought for a minute that he'd seen her as anything other than a moving target.

"He likes you," a girl had pointed out one day after English class. Alexa had aced an oral presentation even though Jackson had raised his hand a dozen times to ask questions and poke holes in her argument. "Can't you tell?" Her classmate had delivered that last bit with a hair flip. The subtext was clear: the smartest girl in school wasn't necessarily the brightest. Alexa had laughed in her face. Now, though, she wondered. Meanwhile, she captured two of Jackson's pawns and a rook.

Two

Growing up, Jackson Strom had heard about the Lattimore legend. The clan was of solid Royal stock going several generations back. Augustus Lattimore had earned the title of patriarch by establishing the family ranch and running it for decades. He'd since passed the reins to Ben, his eldest son. Ben and wife, Barbara, had four children, including Alexandra. The one thing more intimidating than one Lattimore kid was all four of them clustered together. They roamed the earth as if descendants of titans. On a good day, Jonathan and Jayden were cool enough. The youngest daughter, Caitlyn, had always seemed shy. But Alexa *was* a queen, regal and elegant in all things. She was a beauty, too. Dark chestnut skin, coffee-black hair and the most incredible brown eyes fringed with thick lashes—all the better to look down her long nose at the world. One look from Alexa could turn a guy's insides into jelly. At least, that had been his experience, as far back as kindergarten.

She and Jackson had sat side by side throughout third grade. But he didn't think she noticed him—an attitude he reciprocated. Then came the eighth-grade chess tournament. Alexa beat him handily and dismissed him with a nod, as if he were nothing more than a waste of time. From that day, he made it his mission to beat her at something, anything. He failed. As he matured, he adjusted his goal. He tried gaining her respect and failed at that, too. By senior year, he set his sights on asking her out. The school year ended, and he'd never worked up the nerve.

He'd last laid eyes on her outside a convenience store. He'd said, "Hey," and kept it moving. Her valedictorian speech was still fresh in his mind. Crisp and concise, it had touched on the issues of the day and presented a realistic outlook for the future. Basically, it had put them all to shame. None of them could have come up with anything half as good. Had he known that was the last time he'd come in contact with her in a decade, he would've played it differently.

Since he'd seen her last, he'd enrolled in UT, met a girl, fallen in love, fallen out of love, moved on, earned his degree, started a business and been crowned with success. He'd kept tabs on her, though. Her family was eager to brag about her successes: law school, a job in a high-powered Manhattan firm and, recently, the move to Miami.

For the most part, Jackson was over his childish infatuation. Then she'd breezed past him in the lobby of the Texas Cattleman's Club, looking like a movie star with her hair sleeked back, dark glasses, bustier top and high-waisted shorts. As always, she'd brushed past him, her long, shapely legs taking long, purposeful strides. Jackson couldn't stomach it. This time, he would get her to notice him. The way she'd looked at him made him think he wouldn't have to work that hard. Now she was killing him at chess, and he truly didn't mind.

Caitlyn Lattimore stormed the cabana, trailed by a friend. She stopped abruptly, eyed their setup and declared, "Well, isn't this cozy?"

Alexa advanced a bishop. "You found me. Yoo-hoo."

"Checking in. That's all."

"You've checked in and I'm fine. Now run along."

Caitlyn plopped down beside her sister on the chaise.

"Not a chance! Dev is playing volleyball, so I'm free for a while."

The friend stepped forward, whipped out her phone and snapped a photo. "Sorry, I had to document this," she said. "A-JACKS is back at it!"

"Wait. What?" Caitlyn screeched. Petite with long, wavy brown hair, a sandy-brown complexion and big brown eyes, she'd always been reserved. This was the most animated Jackson had ever seen her. She clutched a frozen margarita in one hand. It was more slush than anything else, but that could explain things.

Her friend filled her in. "These two were legends in high school, always competing for blue ribbons and dollar-store trophies and stuff."

Alexa kept her eyes on the board. "Blue ribbons? You make us sound like a couple of racehorses."

Caitlyn snorted. "If the horseshoe fits! Get it?"

Alexa pinched the bridge of her nose. "And people wonder why I don't come home more often."

"Anyway," Caitlyn's friend continued, "Russ attended their private high school. I went to the regular high school, so I had to learn about Royal's young elite through Russ. Apparently, your sister and Jackson were a power couple."

"This is illuminating," Caitlyn said. "I didn't know my big sister was one-half of a high school power couple. How did you immortalize it? Carve 'A-JACKS 4 EVER' on an oak tree?"

"We were *not* a couple of any kind," Alexa said frostily. "And we're not back at anything. This is a friendly game."

"If it's so friendly, why are you going for blood?" Jackson asked.

Alexa moved her rook straight and across, capturing Jackson's last remaining pawn. "It's my nature. Get used to it."

Jackson gave up. Instead of the board, he studied Caitlyn's know-it-all friend. She had blond hair, blue eyes and a little smirk that very much reminded him of his old buddy. "Of course. You're *Russ*'s little sister."

Her smile broadened. "You can call me Alice. And I'm not that little. If you're into chess, I'm willing to learn. Call me."

Caitlyn's eyes cut to her. "Excuse me. He's found a partner."

"Your sister doesn't live here. She's probably leaving soon."

"You don't know that," Caitlyn hissed.

Alexa clasped her hands together. "You both need to go."

"So rude!" Caitlyn cried. "I went out of my way to find you."

"You've found me and I'm fine."

"You're more than fine! You're rekindling an old flame, just as I predicted."

Jackson laughed. Drunk Caitlyn was a trip.

"Jackson isn't an old flame," Alexa asserted.

"He might be a new one!" Alice chimed.

Caitlin raised her glass. "To new beginnings!"

Alexa buried her face in her hands. Jackson couldn't remember the last time he'd had so much fun.

"A-JACKS," Caitlyn said. "It's kind of cute."

"Thanks," Jackson said. "I came up with it."

Alexa glared at him. "Are you kidding me? You came up with that, too? Didn't you have any hobbies?"

Jackson grinned at her. "When you put it that way, it does sound juvenile."

"It sounds juvenile any way you put it."

"Come on!" Caitlyn protested. "It has a good ring to it."

Alice sought his eyes. "It's no wonder you're in PR. You're a natural."

Alexa reached for a pawn. "You're in PR?"

Jackson's reaction surprised him. He would have liked her to follow his career as closely as he had followed hers.

Alice answered on his behalf. "He's the owner and CEO of Strom Management. It's a well-known public relations firm."

"I'm sure it is."

Caitlyn draped an arm over Alexa's shoulders and squeezed. "Don't get snippy."

Finally, it was the aroma of barbecue that put an end to Alexa's torture.

Caitlyn hopped to her feet. "The cook-off! Come on, Alice. We can't miss it!"

Alexa waved goodbye. "I won't miss you!"

Caitlyn blew her a kiss and promised to return. Jackson had no doubt she'd make good on her promise, but he had no intention of sticking around to find out.

He stood and extended a hand. "Come on. Let's go."

"Where are we going?"

"To the cook-off."

"Oh, no," she said. "I'm not a cook-off type of girl."

"You are when you're with me," he said. "There are ribs calling my name."

"Can't we just order some?"

"You've been away from Texas too long, lady," Jackson said. "Barbecue has to be hot off the grill."

"What about the game?"

He studied the board. "It's your move. Go ahead and finish me."

Her gaze flickered from the board to his face. "I take no pleasure in this."

"Like hell you don't."

With a swift hand, she moved her queen across the board in a diagonal line and checked his king. Jackson clapped. She may not take pleasure in this, but he most certainly did.

Three

Standing in the heat with barbecue smoke wafting in the air, eating meat off the bone and fingers sticky with sauce just wasn't Alexa's idea of fun. Somehow, she was enjoying herself. She'd rather choke on a rib than admit it, though. Jackson played a big part. Eating off his loaded plate, a frozen margarita in one hand, and laughing at his inane observations felt like the most natural thing in the world.

"My favorite so far is number two." He noted his preference on a scorecard.

Number two was an entry called Bourbon Lovers. "Don't be ridiculous. You just love bourbon."

"Exactly."

"The flavor profile isn't complex enough."

"Alexa, we're talking ribs."

"It's a competition. They ought to aim higher."

"Which is your favorite?"

"Not sure. Let's try the one with papaya sauce."

"You couldn't pay me to. Tropical fruit and meat don't mix."

"But bourbon does?"

Jackson gave a low and dirty laugh. "Bourbon mixes with everything."

Alexa laughed, too.

A country band was covering a classic rock song. The music drowned out her laughter and the party din. There were no strangers here. Every face in the crowd was familiar. Each person she'd bumped into brought back a memory, and not all were unpleasant. Her siblings were here, scattered about. Her oldest brother, Jonathan, had come around to say hello. Not one to ever take a day off from the ranch, it was nice to see him out and about. He'd bumped fists with Jackson and chatted about football before taking off. A while later, her brother Jayden's grinning face had appeared on a jumbotron. One of the day's features had been a prerecorded video series. TCC members shared their thoughts on the meaning of charity. Jayden's contribution was exceptionally uninspiring. Alexa would have strong words for him later.

From somewhere deep in the crowd, someone hollered, "Woo-hoo! A-JACKS is back at it!"

Alexa shook her head. "If we're not careful, they'll think we're a couple."

"They'll think what they want whether we're careful or not."

"True." In Royal, rumors took flight without a drop of truth to fuel them.

"Stop worrying and try this one. Number five. Tell me it's not the best you've ever had."

He held out a rib, and Alexa bit from it. She chewed without tasting, a hunger of another kind taking over her.

"It's good. Right?"

She nodded. "So good."

"No papaya. That's smoked paprika."

The full flavor exploded in her mouth. "I think this might be my favorite."

Jackson winked. To fight off the urge to kiss him, Alexa cooled down with a sip of frozen margarita and looked away.

Caitlyn waved to her from the dance floor. She and Dev were laughing and twirling. Dev was handsome: black hair, brown skin and gleaming eyes. Caitlyn was radiant, laughing uncontrollably at something Dev had whispered in her ear.

Screw them both.

The band took a break, and the jumbotron lit up for another short episode of "What Charity Means to Me." The lavish pool party was a fundraiser, after all.

"Will I have the pleasure of seeing your face on the big screen?" Alexa asked Jackson.

His eyes lingered on her face. "You have the pleasure of seeing my face up close and personal. Isn't that enough?"

Alexa had stopped breathing, but she did not flinch. A sharp negotiator, both in her personal and professional life, she didn't banter about. When she wanted something, she asked for it in a direct manner, outlining clear terms. But did she want this? She had a lot on her mind. Her career had taken an unsavory turn. Her family was fighting off a legal challenge that could upend all their lives. Today was fun, sure. Tomorrow, she had to get back to work.

As it turned out, no face was projected on screen. Instead of yet another earnest speech on the virtues of giving back or paying it forward, they were treated to a woman's anguished confession of love.

"Jonathan is amazing. He just is... I can't explain it, but I can see myself with him. He would make a great husband and has father material written all over him."

A hush fell over the crowd, followed by whispered conversation carrying wild speculation. Alexa reached out and grabbed Jackson's arm. "Did I hear correctly?"

"You and everybody else here, I bet."

Well, they'd been treated to an episode of "What Jonathan Means to Me." The woman couldn't be talking about her brother. There had to be more than one Jonathan in all of Royal. "You don't think she meant my Jonathan, do you?"

"Oh, Alexa." He wiped at a smudge of sauce on her cheek with the pad of his thumb. "I've never seen this side of you."

Alexa swatted his hand away and looked around for Jonathan. Wherever he was, he must be the subject of tons of unwanted attention. Jayden would've *loved* this, but Jonathan was a quirky one. Divorced and, frankly, still pissed off about the divorce, he'd been single for a while now.

Jackson looked around for a waiter. The paprika had finally gotten to him. He needed a cold drink. Alexa offered him her frozen margarita and, only ever wanting to be helpful, brought her glass to his lips. Their eyes locked as he took that first sip. She noticed how deep those brown eyes were. A girl could swim in them.

Jackson slipped her mind...until Caitlyn scurried over and crashed into them both. Ice-cold margarita splashed and spilled down Jackson's shirt and the bodice of her bustier top.

"Sorry, guys!" Caitlyn grabbed a fistful of cocktail napkins from a passing waiter's tray and shoved them into their hands. "I came as fast as I could. Did you hear what that woman said?"

The poor girl was hyperventilating. Alexa urged her to take a breath and calm down. "I'm sure she wasn't talking about our Jonathan. He hasn't seen any action since the last administration."

Jackson peeled off his wet shirt. The man's chest was solid granite.

Caitlyn dismissed Alexa's comment. "It sounded like Natalie Hastings. I've *seen* her make eyes at Jonathan."

Alexa bit back a laugh. "Like...heart eyes?"

"Shut up. You know what I mean."

All Alexa knew was that Jackson was half-naked, thanks to Caitlyn. Seriously, she was grateful to her sister. So much so, her head was spinning.

The jumbotron went dark, and Aubrey Collins, the emcee, rushed onto the elevated wooden podium set up for the band. She tapped on the microphone. "This is exciting, huh?" The crowd was too busy gossiping to respond. "Quick announcement. The cook-off is nearing a close. Now is a good time to turn in your scorecards."

Jackson went away to turn in their votes. He returned

with a confirmation. "The general consensus is Natalie Hastings is carrying a torch for Jonathan. *Your* Jonathan."

"Good work," Caitlyn said. "What did you think about the bourbon ribs?"

"Top of my list. Smoked paprika comes second."

"I agree. It was too spicy."

Alexa would not be distracted by barbecue sauce. "Someone tell that poor woman she's wasting her time. Jonathan is happily single."

"He's stuck in a rut," Caitlyn said. "It's not the same thing. For sure he'll hate all this attention, though."

"Is he still here?"

"I don't know. I'll check."

"I'll come with you."

"Don't even think about it!" Caitlyn snapped. "You stay here with him."

Alexa watched Caitlyn dash off, then turned to Jackson. He shrugged. "You're stuck with me."

"It feels like a lot is going on."

"Want to give the bourbon ribs another chance?"

"Are you kidding?"

"I don't kid about barbecue."

Alexa pinched the bridge of her nose. "If I agree, could we go back to the cabana to cool off?"

"We'll do whatever you like."

She signed heavily. It came out sounding imperious, even to her ears. "Fine. I'll do it."

Alexa gave the ribs a second chance. They weren't half-bad. She wiped her fingers clean. "Happy now?"

His handsome face cracked open with a smile. "I can't remember a time I've been happier."

The emcee returned to the microphone. "Ladies and gentlemen! Your attention, please! It's time to announce the results of the annual TCC rib cook-off!"

"My money's on Bourbon," Alexa said.

Jackson peeled away from her. "No way! I made you a believer?"

"Not a chance, but I know better than to bet against it."

"Okay. We'll see."

The emcee cleared her throat. "This year's winner is—"

A crack, a crash and a crazy commotion—the podium caved, swallowing Aubrey Collins whole. Alexa gasped. Next thing, Jackson was telling her to stay back. Then he tore off to assist. Alexa had no intention of staying back. She took off in search of Caitlyn. Had her sister been anywhere near the podium when it collapsed? Or was she safe with Dev? And where were Jonathan and Jayden?

She found all four back at her cabana. They'd been looking for her. There were her people: her aggravating brothers, her annoying sister and her nice-enough, about-to-be brother-in-law. Alexa rushed to them, and they all started talking at the same time, sharing what they'd witnessed and from where. Jackson returned with news that the emcee was okay. Paramedics were on-site, and Aubrey was receiving medical attention. There was nothing more to be done.

One by one, her siblings peeled away to check in on friends. Alexa reached out to Jackson. He folded her in his arms and whispered, "Are you okay?"

She smiled up at him. "I like you, Jackson Strom."

"Not what I asked, but I'll take it."

She liked how easygoing he was. She liked that he liked bourbon ribs. She liked the way he'd run toward danger, not away from it. And she liked how gracefully he'd lost at chess. So, yes, A-JACKS was back at it.

"Let me take you home," he said.

She glanced down at the chessboard. "Don't you want a rematch?"

"Never mind that," he said. "I've already won."

Four

The following morning, Alexa woke up with a sharp headache. By contrast, her memories were fluid and hazy. Had she dreamed the previous day's events? Had she really attended a wild pool party with love declared on a jumbotron and a collapsing podium that sent a poor woman plunging to her peril? What about Jackson Strom? Had she fantasized about him showing up at her cabana with a chilled bottle of Prosecco and smoldering hot smile?

She stumbled to the bathroom and splashed cold water on her face. There was no time to waste. A hot shower, coffee, toast and more coffee should take care of it. Alexa had work to do and a small window of opportunity to do it. She was not in town to frolic at the country club, flirt with men or sip cocktails at pool parties. She was tasked with a serious mission. And the sooner she was done with it, the sooner she could return to Miami and deal with the unfinished business there. With so much to deal with, stress had her cornered. At times, she had to rely on special relaxation apps just to regulate her breathing. It was no wonder she'd let loose yesterday.

Her family and the Grandins had recruited her to handle a crucial matter. In the shower, she massaged shampoo into her hair and worked through the details in her mind. It was her mental process, start from the beginning and work through, catching holes in her hypotheses and any missing links. It started with Jackson—*Damn it!* It started with Heath Thurston. Shampoo stung her eyes, and as she rinsed it out, she repeated the name. *Heath Thurston. Heath Thurston.*

She had to get it together.

Heath Thurston, a local upstart rancher, had delivered legal documents to the Grandins, asserting ownership of the oil rights to the Grandins' and the Lattimores' ranches. Sadly, this sort of checked out. The Grandins had hired an investigator, who discovered that Victor Grandin had conferred the oil rights to Heath's mother, Cynthia Thurston. To top it off, Alexa's grandfather Augustus had signed off as a witness to the transaction. It had happened a long time ago. Her grandfather and Victor Grandin were the only two men who could clear this up. But Victor was dead and her grandfather's memory was impaired due to age.

Why would they do this? Why would these smart, savvy businessmen hand over rights of inestimable value to a total stranger? Well, as it turned out, Cynthia Thurston wasn't a stranger, at least not to Victor's son, David. She'd given birth to his love child, and that made her family. However, turning over oil rights to avoid a little child support and a lot of scandal was rather extreme.

Alexa was an environmental lawyer with some experience in litigating land use, but nothing had ever been as convoluted as this. The Grandins had hired her to represent their interests. She would have done it for free. The families had been neighbors and best friends for decades. If this proved to be true—if Heath Thurston had a rightful claim to the oil beneath the properties—he would not prove to be as patient as the late Cynthia. He would act on it, and where would that leave them?

Alexa may not be involved in the family business, but she understood that ranching was grueling, backbreaking work that often came at great personal cost. The hope was that one generation would hand the lands on to the next, creating generational wealth and stability. No one in his right mind would jeopardize it so thoughtlessly. The question remained: What was her grandfather thinking?

Alexa found her brothers in the dining room, already dressed and ready for work. Jayden was at the breakfast bar, scooping scrambled eggs onto a plate. "Well, look who's here," he said. "The belle of the ball."

Alexa ignored him. The room smelled of coffee. She poured herself a generous cup. "Where's Mom?"

"Farmers market."

"For real?" She tried and failed to imagine her mother perusing the stalls in designer sandals and sunglasses, sampling local cheeses.

"I caught her on the way out," Jonathan said. "She said something about heirloom tomatoes."

Jayden approached and nudged her in the ribs. "So about last night?"

"What about it?"

"Don't hold back. Give us the details."

"I'd rather talk about Jonathan's night and the very public declaration of love made over the loudspeaker."

Jonathan groaned. Jayden folded over with laughter. "Alexa, you go straight for the jugular! I love having you home."

Jonathan stood up from the table. "Can't do this now. I've got work to do."

Alexa did not back down. "A woman declares her undying love for you. What's your next move?"

"Nothing."

"Nothing?" she and Jayden cried in unison.

"Nothing at all. Like it never even happened."

"That is some weak sauce game, if you ask me," Jayden said.

"No one's asking you," Jonathan retorted. "It's sweet she thinks I'm amazing, but it ends there."

"The woman wants you to father her children, Jonathan," Alexa said. "That's your cue to make a move."

"What's your next move with Jackson Strom?" Jonathan asked.

Just the mention of Jackson's name and she was in his arms again, feeling protected and safe. Alexa cleared her throat. "He's just an old high school friend, guys."

"Wow!" Jayden exclaimed. "That's how you're going to play it?"

Jonathan laughed. "You're at risk of committing perjury, Counselor."

"It's the truth!"

"I know what I saw," Jayden said. "You two were fire!"

Alexa called his bluff. "Give me a break. You were no-where near us yesterday."

"True," he conceded. "But I had eyes on the ground."

"You mean Caitlyn?"

"Exactly."

Alexa topped off her coffee cup. "Caitlyn is wearing rose-colored glasses. You can't take her word for anything. Jackson and I were just catching up."

Jayden turned to Jonathan. "They used to call them A-JACKS, you know. They had a thing going."

"A-JACKS…" Jonathan raked his fingers through his morning stubble. "I kind of like it. Has a nice ring to it."

"I thought you were too busy to chat," Alexa said.

"I'm already out the door," he said. "Have a good day!"

Jonathan left the dining room. In jeans, boots and a rum-pled T-shirt, he was dressed for a day's work on the ranch. It was his whole life. The thought that some outsider could wave a piece of paper laying claim on their property enraged Alexa. It wasn't fair.

"For what it's worth," Jayden said, "I approve. You and Jackson have my blessing."

As if she needed his approval. "Save your blessings

for Caitlyn and Dev. I'm only in town for a few weeks this time, and I'm not looking to complicate my life with a local boy."

"I wouldn't be so cocky," Jayden said. "Us local boys have our ways."

Augustus was in his favorite rocking chair on the back patio. At ninety-four, he was always neatly dressed and expertly groomed.

His best friend, Victor Grandin, had died a few short months ago. Heath Thurston hadn't waited to start brandishing about the deed to the oil rights. In fact, he got things going by having papers delivered the day of the man's funeral, as one does. The jerk! With Victor gone, only one living witness remained: Augustus. Although Alexa's family had a vested interest in discovering the truth, she was cautioned by her grandmother Hazel to "go easy" on her husband. Still physically strong, his memory was fading.

"Good morning, Grandpa!"

"Good morning to you, darling girl!"

Hmm… Did he know she was Alexa? "Would you like to go for a walk?"

"I'd love it."

She offered him her hand. If given a choice, he would rather sit in his chair until lunch and, after lunch, return to his chair and sit there until dinner. His doctor had recommended daily exercise. Alexa gladly took her turn to give her grandmother a break in watching over Augustus.

"Come on," she said encouragingly.

He grasped her hand and allowed himself to be lifted off the chair. She assisted him down the single step to the yard, and they strolled the stone path that wound around her mother's rose garden.

"It's a fine morning," Augustus observed.

The day was still fresh, the oppressive summer heat held at bay. Her mother's roses perfumed the air. She'd forgotten how much she loved mornings in Royal.

Her grandfather chuckled. "Do you remember when Jayden chased you down this path? You tripped and landed in the rose bushes. You cried and cried."

So he did know who she was. She smiled. "It was Easter Sunday. Jayden went to bed without dessert."

"It was peach cobbler. His favorite."

"Every dessert is his favorite."

"That's true."

"Do you remember a man named Heath Thurston?"

Her grandfather made a face. The abrupt transition had taken him off guard. Alexa was a shrewd interrogator. She wasn't exactly known for her light touch. The first day she'd questioned him, they'd met in his study. He sat in his worn leather recliner, and she settled behind his imposing wood desk. The formal setting quickly worked against her. Augustus got defensive. So now they met on the back porch. She went over the same questions every day, trying to catch a detail here or there that he'd omitted the previous day. It was a long and tedious process, but there were no other alternatives. Her grandfather would not allow just anyone to harass him like this, so it fell on her lap to do it.

"I can't say that I do."

"Are you sure the name doesn't ring a bell?"

"I'm sure."

It frustrated Alexa to no end that her grandfather remembered every detail about their domestic life, down to the dessert served on the Easter Sunday his granddaughter fell into a rose bush, and nothing about signing away millions of dollars' worth of oil rights.

"What about Cynthia Thurston?" she continued. "Surely you've heard of her?"

"I haven't. Is she a friend you met at school?"

"Hold on," she said. "Maybe a photo will help refresh your memory."

If he couldn't remember Cynthia, how could he possibly remember any obscure transactions they'd engaged in?

Alexa reached for her phone to search for a photo of the late Cynthia Thurston online. She tapped on the internet browser. The results of her last search were still there to haunt her: Strom-Management.com. She'd looked him up while in bed last night. He was quite a successful entrepreneur. She quickly closed the browser, a blush spreading across her cheeks.

"You know what? Let's just enjoy our walk."

Her grandfather eyed her with curiosity. "What has gotten into you this morning, young lady?"

"Nothing. A little tired from yesterday."

"If you're tired, it doesn't show. You're glowing."

Alexa doubted that very much. Still, she thanked her grandfather.

"You look happier than I've ever seen you."

"Do I?"

"Would I lie?"

By omission? Yes. She was sure of it.

"I attended a pool party yesterday and got a little sun. Maybe that's it."

"Whatever it is, keep at it," he said. "It's nice seeing you like this. When you graduate at the top of your class, you'll have the whole world at your feet."

They paused by the stone birdbath. Augustus took a seat on a nearby bench.

"Grandpa, I'm a lawyer with a big firm in Miami."

"Yes, of course!"

She might be losing him.

"Are they treating you okay at work?"

She joined him on the bench and took his hand. For a man with poor eyesight and memory deficits, how did he know where to find her soft spots? "I couldn't ask for better. Don't worry about me. I'm a little tired. That's all."

"You're a Lattimore. We don't tire easily."

No lies were detected there! Her grandfather had worked well into his nineties and turned over the ranch to Alexa's father only after his faltering memory proved to be a problem.

"Are you happy in your personal life?"

It warmed Alexa's heart that her grandfather was concerned about her. She had always felt like an outsider in her own home. When she left for college, her family had not worried about her, certain that she was doing well.

"Are you?" Augustus repeated.

"Absolutely happy!" she replied. "Besides, I'm here to get answers out of you, not the other way around."

"I'm sorry I haven't been more helpful, Barbara. I just don't know what all the fuss is about."

Yes, she'd lost him. He thought Alexa was her mother. "I love spending time with you," Alexa replied before kissing him on the cheek.

Her grandmother came walking down the path. "There you are, Augustus. It's time for your medication."

Alexa helped her grandfather onto his feet, and Hazel escorted him back into the house. She sank down onto the bench and watched them go. The day ahead was as wide and open as the unencumbered lands of the ranch. The private investigator on the case had not yet returned with news. Until he did, there wasn't much for her to do. Maybe she'd visit with Layla Grandin and catch up with her.

Her phone chimed with a text message alert, the number saved under JACKSON STROM_DO NOT ANSWER ON

FIRST RING. Clearly she was a bit tipsy when they'd ex-changed numbers at her door last night. There were no in-structions as to what to do if and when he texted, so she stared at the phone and read the short message over and over, searching for hidden meanings and subtext.

You owe me a rematch.

Five

You forfeited your rematch. Besides, you owe me a meal that is not ribs.

Jackson dropped his phone onto his desk. *Okay, game on.* He'd spent last night plotting, trying to come up with ways to see Alexa again. He couldn't afford to play it cool. Who knew how long she'd be in town? Back when they were kids in school, he'd missed out on the opportunity to get to know her. Instead, he'd baited and challenged her at every turn. He didn't regret it necessarily. He'd had fun with it; plus, it had upped his game. But he wasn't a kid anymore.

He texted back. *Dinner tomorrow?*

Her reply came right away. *Lunch today. Pick a spot and I'll meet you there.*

He sent her an address, and they agreed on a time.

If she thought he couldn't make a simple friendly lunch into something special, she didn't know him very well.

Alexa had arrived at the restaurant before him and was waiting at their table. Dressed for a business meeting in a tailored cream blazer worn over a silky cream blouse, with her dark hair swept up in a bun and eyes narrowed on her phone, she was stunning but intimidating. For the length of a heartbeat, he was that insecure kid again. It took courage to take the next step.

He joined her at the table. It was one of the best, removed from the business on the main floor and close to a large window with a view of a water feature in the courtyard.

"Jackson," she said without looking up. "Have a seat. I've been looking over your résumé."

Had he been summoned to HR?

He sat across from her. "Have you?"

She glanced up. Her gaze swept over him appreciatively for a hot second. "It's all here on your website."

"I'm sitting right here and you're looking me up?"

"I would have done it behind your back, but why bother hiding it?" she said. "I'm curious about you. You're actually quite accomplished."

He took a sip from his water glass. "I like to think so."

"I see you've won quite a few awards for your work."

"What else do you see?"

She set the phone down. "I'm trying to say that I'm proud of you."

He leaned forward. "Well, just say it."

"You did good. Now don't let that go to your head."

"Oh, too late. My head is as big as all of Texas."

"You're such a Texas boy."

"And proud of it."

The waiter arrived with the lunch menu and a separate wine list. Alexa reviewed both and selected a crisp sauvignon blanc and mini crab cakes without a second's hesitation. She knew her mind. It was one of the things he loved about her. Correction: it was one of the things he *liked*. Jackson went for the wine and held off on an appetizer.

"You know," she said, "when I ruled out ribs, I wasn't requesting foie gras. We could have gone for burgers."

"You're not dressed for burgers."

She looked down at her outfit, the corners of her mouth turned down in the cutest little frown. "This is just how I dress."

"Do you ever take a day off?"

"Sure. Once a month, I treat myself to a spa day."

Jackson nodded. "That sounds about right."

"What do *you* do to relax?" she asked, suddenly defensive.

"I drive out to my cabin and unplug."

"Tell me more. How does Jackson Strom 'unplug,' exactly?"

"I swim, go for long runs, fish, grill, pour a bourbon, play records at night, sleep under the stars…"

She looked down at her tightly clasped hands. "That sounds nice, actually."

"It's like a spa getaway, but without the candles and moody music."

"Well, now you've ruined it for me. I need candles."

"Candles are hit or miss with me. I'm not into strong floral scents."

"Not all candles smell like a rose garden."

"Which are your favorites?"

"Lavender is my all-time favorite," she said. "I love a fresh lavender scent."

Jackson felt the stirrings of a new idea. "If I filled the place with lavender-scented candles, would you come with me to my cabin for a few days?"

"You wouldn't have to fill the place," she said. "One or two pillars would be enough. But my answer is no."

"Any particular reason?"

"I don't need a reason to say no."

"So this is a knee-jerk sort of rejection?"

"I'm here to work, not to wander in the woods."

The Grandins had recruited her to fight off a claim against their property's oil rights—that much he knew. It was the sort of thing that could start a war in their small corner of the world. Apparently, they were going after the oil under Alexa's family's ranch as well. He didn't blame her for taking the job seriously.

"What's the status of the case?" he asked.

"We're waiting for a PI's next report. When we know more, we'll take action."

"So you're in a holding pattern. Just waiting around."

She shifted in her seat. "That's right."

"Couldn't you wait at my cabin?" he suggested.

"No offense. I prefer to enjoy running water and a couple streaming apps while I wait."

He blinked, not understanding. Then he broke out in laughter that was louder than acceptable at the intimate French restaurant.

She pursed her full lips, trying hard to suppress a smile. "I'm just saying."

"The cabin has all the conveniences of the modern world, including Wi-Fi, satellite TV and cell service," Jackson said. "You won't miss a call or an episode of a show. And it has the most perfect firepit by the lake. You can have a glass of wine while looking at the stars."

"How far away is it?"

"About a three-hour drive. That's not so bad, right?"

She measured it out in her mind. "That's about the distance of Miami to Orlando."

"Let's forget Florida and focus on our great state. I want you to see the beauty of living in Royal."

"You're not going to sell me a time-share, are you?"

"I couldn't sell you iced lemonade in the Sahara."

"That's not really a compliment," she said. "Okay. Let's say I agree. Hypothetically, of course."

"Of course."

"Because I haven't agreed to anything."

"Understood." Jackson was ready for a fight. Alexa was so smart, yet she couldn't walk through an open door without a hypothetical swift kick in the ass.

"How long would we be gone?"

"We could leave on Friday and make a weekend of it," he said. "I like to enjoy my Sundays, so we could take the road early Monday morning."

"Monday morning? Don't you have a business to run?"

"Let me worry about that," Jackson said. "What do you think?"

"Under normal circumstances, I'd turn you down flat," she said. "You know that, right?"

"Absolutely." He was under no illusions. Still, he was curious. "What circumstances are we working under?"

"My sister is driving me crazy."

"Little Caitlyn?" He balked. "Come on! She's adorable."

"She's sugar and spice and a pain in the ass ever since she's found love with Dev."

"Are you closer to your brothers, then?"

She hesitated, considered her answer. "Not really."

Jackson couldn't believe it. "Isn't that the point of having a bunch of siblings? To have this big ready-made clan?"

"We're just so different," she said. "They would have loved roughing it at your cabin."

"Again, we won't be roughing it."

The cabin had been in his family for generations, and he stood to inherit it. Over the decades, it had been renovated several times. The property bordered a lake, and each room offered a view of the surrounding woods. The bedrooms were spacious; the kitchen, state of the art; and the backyard was fitted with a grill and a pizza oven no one ever used.

The waiter placed her appetizer before her, giving her the excuse to ignore his question. She picked up a fork and sliced a golden crab cake in two. "Want to try this?" she said. "It looks delicious."

"No, thank you. I'm allergic to shellfish."

She dropped the fork onto the plate. "You are?"

"Yes, I am," he said. "Don't let that stop you. It does look delicious."

She shook her head in wonder. "There's so much I don't know about you."

"Here's your chance to find out," he said. "Come away with me."

"So…what's in it for you?"

"Excuse me?"

"I get a peaceful retreat, but you get stuck with me. How's that a fair exchange?"

Behind the bite of her words, Jackson detected something new. She was insecure. That was not a word he would have ever associated with the great Alexandra Lattimore. He'd thought her impervious to what people thought or said about her, a true ice queen. But what did he know about human nature at sixteen? Back then, he took people at face value, never guessing at any hidden depths. He tried to reassure her. "Getting stuck with you is the best part."

The waiter returned to take their orders. While he selected a bottle of wine for their meal, she looked at him coolly from across the table. He was so aware of her. At all times, he was aware of her shifts in mood and how they played out on her face. The waiter moved to another table. She picked up her fork and twirled it. "In order for me to consider your offer—and I am considering it—I need clear terms and conditions."

"Alexa, you're not leasing a mobile phone. Can't a friend take you on a trip without drafting legal papers?"

"Apparently not."

"Okay. Shoot."

"I may have to leave at a moment's notice for work or other family obligations. If that happens, I apologize in advance. Please don't try to make me feel guilty. I'll book an Uber and be on my way."

Jackson nodded. He could work with that. "One—there's

no Uber. We're going to a lake cabin, not the Cattleman's Club. Two—I'll drive you back to town, no questions asked."

"I'll need my own room."

"That's a given. You'll have a suite to yourself."

She nodded and took a sip of water.

"Are you done?" Jackson asked. "Because I have some conditions of my own."

"Which are?"

"We stop all this talk about conditions," he said. "I propose we spend a weekend at my lake cabin to chill out and get to know each other better. That's the offer. Either you accept it or reject it wholesale. I won't have you controlling every little thing."

He searched her face for a reaction. There was none. Alexa was giving him award-winning poker face.

The waiter brought their wine, poured a bit in a glass for her to try. She did so robotically, nodding her approval. He filled both their glasses and left.

"All right," she said. "No terms. No conditions. But if there's fishing—"

"Oh, there'll be fishing."

"I won't be handling any live bait. That's my bottom line."

Jackson tore a piece of bread and popped it in his mouth. "What's your stance on midnight swims?"

"I don't have one," she said. "I'll be exhausted from all the needless fishing, so I'll be dead asleep by midnight."

Six

Jackson Strom was just as attractive in a deep blue business suit as in a T-shirt and swim shorts. That was an equation she couldn't puzzle out. It was the swagger. She'd spotted him as he made his way across the restaurant floor. The way he carried himself—head high, back straight, strides long and sure—had been enough to give her a mini-stroke. Her brain froze midthought, and nothing went right after that. She'd agreed to go away with him for a weekend at a… On the drive home, Alexa paused to check her mental notes. She'd agreed to go away with him for a weekend at his *cabin*, where they would hike, fish, grill and go for midnight swims. That couldn't be right.

Was it too late to get out of it? No. Never. She was a Lattimore. It was her prerogative to change her mind. If she didn't want to go on a fishing trip with her old high school nemesis, no one could make her. She'd call Jackson and tell him… Tell him what? Hmm… Her grandfather needed her for…huh…

Her phone rang. The caller ID flashed on the dashboard monitor of her father's old Mercedes: JACKSON CALLING_ DO NOT ANSWER ON FIRST RING.

Damn it!

She answered on the first ring. "Hello."

"Hey. I'm arranging for them to stock up the fridge in advance of our arrival. Is there anything you need? A specific type of coffee or milk?"

"Actually, Jackson…"

"Yes?"

"Actually…"

"Go on. I'm listening."

"I don't know what got into me back there in the restaurant."

"The crab cakes, maybe?"

"They were delicious. Too bad you're allergic."

Why was she stuck on that small point? He had an allergy. So what? It struck her as the tip of the iceberg made of all the things she did not know about Jackson Strom. She didn't know this person. The Jackson who lived rent free in her memories was a figment of her imagination. Unknowable. The person who had invited her to lunch had a sense of humor, food allergies and strong opinions on candles. The question remained: Did she want to get to know this person better? Was it worth her time? Yes or no?

"You can talk to me, Alexa," he said. "What's troubling you?"

She gripped the leather steering wheel. That question had depths that she did not want to explore. Alexa pulled into the parking lot of the nearest big-box store and cut the engine. "I'm not a lakeside cabin–type of girl," she blurted. "There! I said it. I'm not that girl and I don't think I'd be much fun, so really what I'm saying is—"

"You're chickening out."

"That's not what I'm doing." Adults didn't "chicken out." They made sound decisions taking into account their fears and anxieties. It wasn't the same thing. "It's just, I'm a city girl. I don't like anything outside the urban core. I need museums, shops, bistros, theaters, all of it."

"Alexa, take a breath," he said. "You're freaking out."

"Exactly!" she snapped. "I'm freaking out!"

"Well, don't. If anything, I'm in the vulnerable spot."

"How do you figure?"

"I'm trying to share an experience with you. What if you hate it as much as you say?"

Alexa hadn't even considered this or factored in his feelings in any way. She'd figured it was all fun and games on his part.

"I won't hate it," she admitted. "It all sounded dreamy until you roped me into it."

"Okay. That's a start."

"What if it gets all weird and awkward and tense? You and I don't have the best track record."

"We don't have to spend every waking hour antagonizing each other," he said. "How about we set aside chunks of time to be alone?"

"That could work."

Alexa mulled it over. He could take a hike and she could listen to podcasts or read undistracted, preferably by the firepit that he'd described earlier.

"For it to work, we only have to want it to."

He had a point. There was no reason to argue against it. She let out a dramatic huff.

"Listen," he said. "I have a confession."

"You don't know the first thing about playing chess," she offered.

"Which is why you can beat me so easily," he said. "You're no grand master."

Alexa was teary with laughter. "True!"

Jackson's laughter poured through the speakers. He was always quick to laugh at life—and at himself. It was one of the things that had endeared him to her. But the laughter stopped abruptly, and his tone turned serious. "I want to get to know you."

"Since when?" she asked.

"Since always," he replied. "I screwed up with you. I know."

"Generally, it takes two to screw."

His low laughter tumbled through the car speakers. "Alexa… I'm starting to think there's lava under all that ice."

"Don't tell anyone. I have a reputation to uphold."

He laughed and warmth spread throughout her chest. She switched on the ignition and cranked up the AC. The seats had a massage function, and she switched it on, too.

"Do you want to get to know me?" he asked.

She had been wrestling with that question for over twenty-four hours now. "Yes. I do."

"Then let's head out to the cabin," he said. "During the day, we'll do our own thing. At night, I'll light a fire, we'll sip whiskey, stay up late and talk."

"I'll have a white wine spritzer, but everything else sounds good."

"I'll add 'white wine spritzer' to the shopping list. What else?"

She completed her list, and they agreed on a time for him to pick her up on Friday. They were about to end the call when Alexa thought of one last point that needed revisiting. "How single are you really, Jackson? I don't want some angry woman showing up at the cabin, demanding to know why you're spending all this quality time with your former high school nemesis. It'll disturb my peaceful resting time."

"I'm very single. You don't have to worry about that."

"Good." A wave of relief washed over her. He was single and she was single, and they were free to get to know each other. How neat.

"And I never thought of you as my nemesis."

"Oh, really?"

"Really."

"What, then?" She was curious. The evidence hinted otherwise. Alexandra the First. A-JACKS. These were not terms of endearment.

"My better half."

He said it without a hiccup, without a moment's hesitation. Alexa was too stunned to say anything. Jackson said goodbye and promised to call her on Thursday.

Seven

On Thursday afternoon, Alexa sought out her mother. She checked the den, the kitchen and a sunroom that had been converted into a greenhouse. There, she found Caitlyn curled up on a rattan chair, sipping from a porcelain teacup.

"Hey, you," she said. "Where's Mom?"

"Yoga class."

"Mom does yoga?"

"Yep," Caitlyn said. "I know her schedule and arrange to take my afternoon breaks here while she's away. It's nice and quiet."

It was disconcerting to learn about her family's little routines. Alexa had no idea. She spoke to her mother regularly, and never once had she mentioned outings to the farmers market or yoga class. She would have never guessed that Caitlyn liked to sip tea alone, surrounded by potted plants. Alexa brushed off a bit of potting soil from a wrought-iron ottoman and sat down.

"I like your jeans," Caitlyn said.

"Thanks. It's part of a limited edition collaboration between two Italian design houses."

"I was wondering why you'd have them professionally pressed. That crease is sharp!"

Alexa didn't wear jeans. She wore tailored denim trousers. Her style philosophy was simple: she invested in quality pieces and took good care of them. "You don't expect me to toss them into the spin cycle, do you?"

"Heaven forbid," Caitlyn said. "Did you need Mom for something specific or just to talk?"

Alexa rarely sought out her mother just to talk. That might explain why she wasn't clued in. She added *talk to Mom* on her running mental to-do list.

"I need to borrow a weekender bag or carry-on case," Alexa said. "Anything light and compact."

"Going somewhere?"

This was the conversation she'd been dreading all week. She couldn't postpone it any longer.

"I'm going away with Jackson for the weekend."

Caitlyn dropped her porcelain teacup in its saucer with a clang. "Do you mind repeating that?"

"I think you heard me."

"Oh my God! A weekend getaway?" Her sister was screeching now. "How romantic!"

"Caitlyn, settle down. He invited me to his cabin to unwind."

"Unwind? Is that what the kids are calling it?"

"You're a kid. You tell me."

"Hold on one sec." Caitlyn reached for her phone. Her thumbs were flying over the keyboard.

"Who are you texting?"

"Jayden, obviously."

"Please don't."

The swoosh sound of the sent text message sealed her fate.

"This is a huge development, and we have to discuss, analyze, strategize."

Caitlyn's phone rang midsentence. She answered and Jayden's voice rushed through the phone's speaker. "Are you okay? What's the emergency?"

"I hope you're sitting down," she said, breathless. "Alexa and Jackson are going camping for the weekend."

This was how false information got disseminated. She

corrected her sister. "We're going to his lake cabin. I hear it's very comfortable and spacious."

"I bet it is!" Jayden quipped.

Jayden and Caitlyn burst out laughing. Alexa smoothed back her hair and willed herself to stay calm. She had expected to get roasted, but this was next-level madness.

"Sit tight," Jayden said between bouts of laughter. "I'll be right in."

Alexa bristled. "Don't you have anything more important to do?"

"Not really!"

Caitlyn ended the call and tossed her phone aside. "You can't blame us," she said. "This is big news."

"I have no trouble blaming you."

"Come on! You two went from flirty banter at the TCC to a weekend getaway in all of five minutes. We need to know the details."

"There's not much to tell. We had lunch the other day and—"

"Stop!" Caitlyn held up a hand. "Wait for the guys."

Alexa shrugged. "Whatever."

Jayden couldn't really ditch work just to torment her, and she was confident Jonathan was above these foolish games.

Right then, the door to the sunroom flung open and her older, wiser, serious and steadfast brother Jonathan charged in. He was wearing his usual work shirt, jeans, boots and a Stetson to shield him from the sun. "Jayden called. I came as fast as I could." He grabbed a chair in a corner and dragged it over to where she and Caitlyn sat. "Tell me everything."

That night, when Jackson called to confirm their plans, Alexa asked if they could set out a bit earlier. Her siblings had been dragging her all afternoon, texting her memes, and her mother had cross-examined her when she returned from yoga. Alexa wanted to slip out early before the household awakened, ready to do their worst. He agreed. "We'll leave at six."

"I'll be ready."

"Alexa, one more thing."

"What is it?"

"I can't wait," he said. "I can't wait to be alone with you."

Alexa replayed those words in her mind until she fell asleep. When she awoke hours later to the bedside alarm, it was the first thing that ran through her mind. *I can't wait to be alone with you.*

At six, Alexa was ready and waiting. She stood out on the porch, her back against one of the two Greek-style pillars that served no purpose but to prop up her father's tremendous pride. She gripped the handle of her mother's small suitcase. Five minutes later, Jackson pulled up to the gate. She disarmed the security system with her phone app and let him through. Her heart pounded as the black SUV sped up the drive. It was a lavender morning. The sky was still dusted with stars. Jackson stepped out. In a white T-shirt and faded blue jeans, he was as fresh as dawn.

"Mornin'," he said, as jovial at 6:00 a.m. as he was at noon. He loaded her bag into the trunk and held open the passenger door for her. "Let's get out of here."

Alexa hesitated. Within the blink of an eye, she'd slipped back in time. She was seventeen and Jackson was her prom date, holding open the door to a tacky rental limo. There he was, the object of her every teenage dream. She went over and touched him, just to make sure he was real.

"Are you okay?" he asked.

"No," she said. "I was thinking… If things were different back in high school—"

"Different how?"

"If I were nicer."

"Nicer?"

"Or just plain nice," she said. "Do you think you might have asked me to prom or homecoming or whatever?"

Jackson went still, but something moved in his eyes. Alexa panicked. What was she doing stirring things up at dawn?

"Forget it!" She backed away from him. "I don't know why I said that. It's early and I haven't had coffee. Do you mind stopping for coffee along the way?"

He reached out and caught her by the waist. He pulled her close. The air between them was charged. "I didn't want *nice*. I wanted Alexandra Lattimore, the one girl who was anything but nice and who ran circles around me."

"Why didn't you say anything?"

"I was scared."

"You thought I'd reject you?"

"If I had asked you to prom or whatever, would you have said yes?"

"I don't know," she admitted. "Maybe not… Or I could have changed my mind. Only it would have been too late. You would have found yourself a less-complicated date."

"And end up having a forgettable night?"

"You would have had fun," she said. "I would have ended up hating myself."

Alexa wanted to be that person that he'd imagined, imperious and unimpressed by her peers or her surroundings, but she wasn't. She never had been. She'd lived her whole life in a self-protective mode, rejecting others before they could reject or dismiss her. She now saw it for what it was: a coward's device.

His hand fell from her waist. He stepped back and held open the car door even wider. "Aren't you happy we're not those stupid kids anymore?"

Alexa leaned forward and kissed him lightly on the lips. "You have no idea," she whispered, and slid into the waiting seat.

Eight

The cabin was Jackson's family vacation spot but also his private sanctuary—a hideout when life gave him hell. It was the one place he could go to and heal after disappointments and failures. He'd invited Alexa because he thought she might need some healing, too. Jackson couldn't put a finger on it, but he knew something was troubling her. She was stressed out. He'd seen her under pressure, and this was different. True, a pop quiz was not similar to having to protect and defend your family's estate holdings. Maybe she was afraid of letting them down. The consequences could be devastating. It was a lot to drop on her shoulders, as capable as they were. He had planned on asking her about it on the long drive through the quiet, tree-lined roads leading to the lakeside cabin. Then she'd kissed him, brushed her full lips against his, and his mind had gone blank. He could think of nothing else.

The drive had gone smoothly. Alexa sat angled toward him, hands curled around a jumbo cup of coffee, looking soft and relaxed. She was willing to talk about anything and everything except herself. For long stretches, she stared out the window, soaking in the ever-changing scenery. "So beautiful," she'd let out in a breath.

Jackson pulled over to the side of the road.

"Is something wrong? Why are we stopping? Are we there yet?"

"Almost. I want to show you something first. Let's go for a walk."

She fit the coffee cup into a holder and released her seat belt. "Let's do it."

They stepped out of the car. The heat made the air feel solid. Alexa stripped off her zippered jacket, balled it and tossed it into the back seat. She wore a fitted cream-colored tank underneath. Her shoulders were bare. Jackson reached out his hand. When she took it, he couldn't believe his luck.

They walked down a path leading to the old dock. It was obscured by overgrown weeds and wildflowers, but he knew the way. It was a popular hangout spot for local kids. His memories of summer holidays and winter breaks—days filled with swimming, fishing and long naps in the sun—all looped around this spot. The weathered dock had been restored. It wasn't as rickety as in his memory. Alexa followed him down to the edge. She offered her face up to the sun like a sunflower.

So beautiful...

"What do I have to say to convince you to go for a dip?"

She turned to him, brows furrowed. He didn't know whether she was repulsed or intrigued. When she unzipped her denim shorts and wiggled them down her long, toned legs, he had his answer.

"Try and stop me!" she cried.

Just like that, she was off. She leaped into the water, arms stretched to the sky and ponytail flapping behind her. Jackson was transfixed. *So damn beautiful!* Then he snapped out of it, ripped off his T-shirt, kicked off his sneakers and, heart pounding, dove in.

With a kitchen stocked with the best of everything, they'd opted for grilled cheese sandwiches for dinner. When Jackson pointed this out, Alexa balked. "This is fine dining!

We're using two types of cheddar and sourdough bread. I'd serve this on my best china."

"Good point," he said. "This grilled cheese ain't for kids."

She was tossing a salad that had come pre-tossed in a container. Her expression clouded suddenly. Was it something he'd said?

I wonder if she wants kids. Her focus was squarely on the baby spinach leaves, even though his mind was on babies. *I should ask.*

The objective of this trip was to get to know each other. There was no need to be coy about it. Naturally, she beat him to the punch.

"May I ask you something?" she said.

"Ask me whatever you want." He slid a bottle of white wine out of the special cooler. He didn't know what paired well with grilled cheese. However, he knew she liked her wines on the crisp, fruity side, and he had stocked up accordingly. "It doesn't have to be awkward."

She lowered the salad prongs to the countertop. "I don't want to pry."

Her lips were slightly parted. When could he kiss her again? Was that a question he could ask? The kiss they'd shared earlier while swimming in the lake had left his body humming. Instead, he joined her at the kitchen island and saddled onto the bar stool next to hers. "Pry. Do your worst."

"All right," she said. "How about this. Let's make a game of it. Rapid-fire questions. You can skip one or two but no more than that."

"A game?" Jackson pensively rubbed the stubble on his chin. "You realize most people would think it strange that we need a game to communicate openly."

She shrugged one shoulder. "I don't care about most people."

They were birds of a feather. "Neither do I."

Alexa grinned. "Let's do this."

"Hold on," Jackson said, excitement working through him. "Let's make it a drinking game. Anyone who skips a question has to take a sip."

Her fast smile faltered. "Not sure about that. This could go off the rails pretty quick."

"Let's hope so."

"We need rules."

He got up to fill their wineglasses. "That's just what the world needs—more rules."

"I'm serious," she said. "We have to make sure that the information gathered here today is not misused when we're back in the real world."

"There's no chance of that." He set a glass before her. "We have a long-standing 'What Happens in the Cabin Stays in the Cabin' rule."

She rolled her eyes. "That's not specific enough. Get me a pen and paper, please."

"Alexa, really?" Jackson said, incredulous. Then he remembered who he was dealing with, and his incredulity fell away. Of course she wanted to codify this in writing. She'd probably want to call up a notary public, too.

"Pen and paper," she repeated.

"Yes, ma'am." He rummaged through a drawer and found a pad designed for grocery shopping lists with illustrated vegetables and milk cartons in the margins. He found a ballpoint pen with a missing cap in a terra-cotta pot on the counter. "Here you are."

Alexa got busy writing. When she was done, she reviewed her work, ripped the page from the pad and handed it to him. "Here *you* are."

"Wow…" Jackson's voice trailed off as he read what could very well be a legally binding document.

"Just sign on the line, initial each clause and don't forget to date."

Jackson read aloud. "This nondisclosure agreement (the

'Agreement') is entered into by and between Alexandra B. Lattimore and Jackson T. Strom for the purpose of preventing the unauthorized disclosure of confidential information. The parties shall hold and maintain confidential information in strict confidence. This Agreement may not be amended except in a writing signed by both parties." Jackson slapped the page down on the counter. "Lady, you are out of your mind."

"What? It's boilerplate."

"Are you going to confess to murder? Is that it?"

"No!" she protested, laughing.

"Are you living some double life in Miami?" he asked. "Do you have a whole other family stashed away there?"

"Nothing that exciting. I promise."

"Then what is it?"

"I'm not answering any questions. You're going to have to sign on the dotted line to find out."

His heart melted at her assertive tone. Jackson signed and dated the document and handed her the pen. Alexa signed and tossed the pen aside. She then proceeded with the game. "First topic—relationships."

That was easy enough. "Hit me. I've got nothing to hide."

"Who is your first love?"

Jackson's cool demeanor cracked. He had an answer, but he couldn't bring himself to say it. Paula Colby was a college student he'd met at a party his freshman year at UT. They'd dated for three semesters before she transferred out of state. Women moving out of Texas, and out of his life, was a recurring pattern. That wasn't what had him by the throat. For all his affection for Paula, she was not his first love. "Skip."

"You've got to be kidding!" Alexa cried. "Right out of the gate? I threw you a softball!"

"Mixing your sports metaphors," Jackson observed. "You've lost your edge."

"Do you...still love her?" she asked. "Is that it?"

He had no answer for that. "I'll skip that one, too."

"Fine!" she said. "I guess you better drink up."

Jackson raised his wineglass and winked. "Cheers."

He was good at hiding his true feelings behind a smoke screen of charm.

"Guess it's my turn," she said.

"Same question," Jackson said. "Who is your first love?"

"Gregory Milford. Some friends set us up. We texted each other for months leading up to our first date—dinner and a show. It was a very New York courtship."

"What else did you do?" he said dryly. "Stroll through Central Park? Kiss in the back of cabs?"

"Kissing in the back of cabs is a rite of passage in Manhattan," Alexa said. "Anyway, we can't all have grand and mysterious love affairs with mystery women."

"Did Greg break your heart?"

Alexa avoided his eyes. She picked up her fork and stabbed at her salad. Jackson had his answer. "He broke your heart."

"Nope," she said, and bit into a slice of cucumber. "I broke his."

Jackson clapped. "Hey now!"

"It wasn't like that. We got on very well, and then things changed."

"Changed how?" he asked. Jackson wanted to know everything about this specimen of a man who had gotten Alexandra Lattimore to fall in love with him, even if it hadn't worked out.

"I don't know..." Her voice trailed off. "He wanted more than I could give. Time, energy... I was still in school, and it got to be too much. Maybe I really am made of ice."

"Don't say that. It's not true."

"Eighty-seven high school seniors can't be wrong."

"Oh, yes, they can."

"Back to you," she said. "Did your mystery woman break your heart?"

"No." He plucked a cherry tomato from the salad and popped it in his mouth.

"Is that all you're going to say?"

"Yep."

"Why are you so tight-lipped?" she demanded. "Is she rich and famous? Are you protecting her identity? Maybe she got you to sign a real NDA?"

Jackson tapped the notepad sheet. "Wait a minute. This isn't real?"

"For us it's as real as real gets."

"Okay." He made a show of relaxing his shoulders. "I'll say this—I didn't break her heart and she didn't break mine. We went our separate ways, but I've never stopped thinking about her."

His words landed on padded silence. Alexa scooped her sandwich off the plate, the melted cheese stretching thin as she pulled the halves apart. By the way she avoided his eyes, he just knew the gears of her beautiful mind were churning.

"Jackson."

"Yes?"

"Is there something you're not telling me?"

"You're the genius. You figure it out."

She dropped the sandwich onto the plate and pushed it away. "If I were a genius, I'd have life figured out."

"You don't?"

She shook her head. "Do you?"

"I try not to overthink it."

She pressed her lips together, nodding slowly. After their impromptu swim, she'd slipped on a loose-fitting white T-shirt that looked expensive and soft to the touch. She had gathered her damp hair in a braid down her back. Her face was scrubbed clean. He longed to run a fingertip along her jawline, down her neck to the dip of her collarbone. "In the spirit of not overthinking things," she said, "I've thought about you, too."

Jackson dropped his fork with a clang and reached for her. Their kiss in the lake had been scorching hot. This one was sweet and syrupy. Her tongue swept against his, turning his blood thick. He cupped the nape of her neck and tried to draw her to him, but she broke away, leaving him panting.

She pressed her palms to his chest. "I broke up with every man I ever dated."

Okay, that was worth the interruption. "How many men are we talking about?"

She did not reply. Instead, she reached for her wineglass and took a healthy sip.

Jackson pressed a fist to his mouth to keep from bursting in laughter. "We should have made this a kissing game. Think how much more fun that would have been."

She set down her glass. "There's always tomorrow."

"All right." Jackson leaned back and folded his arms across his chest. "I have a follow-up question for you."

"Go on."

"Any clue why?"

She shrugged. "No idea."

"I reckon you were scared."

"You *reckon*? Really?"

Jackson raised his hands. "You can take the boy out of Texas—"

"No, you can't," she interrupted. "You'll never leave Royal."

"Why should I? I'm happy here," Jackson replied. "Are you happy?"

She held his gaze a long while. He'd touched at something; he knew it. She reached for her glass and took a long sip.

Jackson looked away. "Next topic?"

"Sure," she said. "Do you want a family?"

"Not right away." Jackson was clear about that.

"Same," she said. "Do you have a time line in mind?"

"Somewhere in my thirties," he said. "You?"

She let out a sigh that betrayed her frustration. "No clue. It's not something I can leave to chance, but I don't even want to think about it."

"Then don't."

"It's not that easy," she said. "My family already thinks I'm a lost cause."

It was the tradition in Jackson's family, and likely hers, to marry early and have kids while still young. His mother had started to increase the pressure, moving from subtle hints to straight-up demands. It didn't help that his younger brother was engaged and expected to set a date for the next year. Jackson didn't care. He had a very clear vision of his future. He had a list of goals and experiences he wanted to have before settling down.

"Same," he said. "Screw 'em."

She offered him a conspiratorial smile that went straight to his head. "Agreed. Screw 'em."

After dinner, Jackson gave her a tour of the property. The grounds extended to the lake. His dad's boat was tethered to the dock. They competed at tossing pebbles. He won handily. She tossed her hands up in defeat. "Fine! You win!" she cried, as she jumped into the lake. He watched Alexa floating on her back, her face to the setting sun.

He quickly joined her. They splashed around for a while until he noticed that she was trembling cold. The lake was warm enough, but she was used to heated pools. "Come. I'll keep you warm." She glided toward him and snaked her arms around his neck. Fire sparked within him at the feel of her wet body. She kissed the corner of his mouth. Jackson knew the world hadn't gone silent. A small aircraft buzzed overhead, the water lapped against the dock, a dog barked madly in the distance. Still, he heard none of it. He lowered his head and kissed her full on the mouth. She parted her lips, drawing him in. He tasted her for the first time, savored her. Her kiss was languid and unhurried, but he could not prolong it without taking this too far.

Jackson released her.

Alexa startled. "Oh, God," she uttered between sharp intakes of breath. She smoothed back her hair with shaky hands and pushed out a laugh. "That got heated fast!"

That was an understatement. He dipped below surface to cool off. There was no way he could climb out of this lake otherwise. When he resurfaced, she reached for him before he could slip away again. Their fingers interlaced with ease.

"Just wanted you to know that I'm open to the possibility," she said. "Just not…right away."

"I'm open to anything," he said, and he meant it. He was open to a platonic friendship, a hookup, a full-on love affair—it was her choice. He would not pressure her for more than she could give. That was the promise he'd made to himself on the drive over to her house early this morning. He wanted her, but he was willing to seal that door shut if she didn't feel the same. Meanwhile, she had been doing the opposite work, leaving herself open to possibilities.

All those possibilities were swimming in his head now.

"I need a shower."

This was his cue. It had been a long day. It was time to give her the space she'd asked for. She went upstairs, and he remained out on the deck to light a fire in the pit. Hunched low to study the flames, he saw the last of the sunlight twinkling on the lake's sterling surface.

Jackson heard Alexa's bare feet on the wood stairs leading to the deck. He rose and turned to find her standing at the doorway, wearing nothing but a towel. Her hair was in a knot on top of her head. She looked upset. What could

have gone wrong already? Had the hot water stopped working midshower?

"Everything okay?" he asked.

"There are candles in the bathroom." It was not a statement, rather an accusation. "And on my bedside table."

He didn't deny it. "Is that unusual?"

"Lavender-scented candles."

"Okay."

"My favorite."

"So you've said."

"You got them for me."

Well…he'd arranged for *someone* to get them. "I wanted
you to feel welcome."

She tightened her grip on the knot of her towel. "Thank
you."

"You're welcome."

"No," she said, raising her free hand to better make her
point. "I'm serious. Thank you for arranging this getaway
and taking the time to make it special."

"You're welcome, Alexa."

Her gaze skidded away from him. "You've lit a fire."

He glanced over his shoulder at the leaping flames. "I'll
put it out if it makes you uncomfortable."

"No, I like it."

"So do I."

Jackson was still rattled by her reaction to the candles.
Such a small gesture had provoked an outsize emotional re-
sponse. She could have waited until morning to say thanks.
Instead, she'd stormed down the stairs, demanding answers.
Was she so unaccustomed to being pampered without the
hefty price of a premium spa?

"Will you be roasting marshmallows?"

"If you like," he said. "We'll make s'mores."

"I'd like that." She took a few steps backward. "I'll just go and finish up…"

"And I'll set up."

"Don't start without me!" She dashed back into the house.

Nine

Alexa hated s'mores. She hated anything sticky and sweet that could potentially stain her expensive clothes. She loved the idea of spending an evening with Jackson by a crackling fire with a glass of wine. If she had to fake love for charred marshmallows, so be it.

Oh, God! Who was she? What had she become? From dawn to dusk, she had not been herself. Tomorrow she'd regret every stupid move she'd made, from reminiscing about prom to declaring herself open to future possibilities. And why had she unraveled at the first whiff of a lavender-scented candle? Over the years, she'd offered and received candles on all sorts of occasions. It wasn't that big of a deal. It just meant that he was thoughtful, likely one of the most thoughtful people she'd ever met. Was that any reason to go charging through the house, barefoot and wrapped in a bath towel, to express her gratitude?

She dropped the towel onto the bathroom floor and turned on the shower. It was a warm, sticky night. She would likely need another shower to cool off following their fireside chat. Actually, she needed to cool off, period. Alexa promised herself the night would end with her back in her room, tucked in bed and browsing social media, as per usual. The night was *not* going to end with her tumbling into bed with Jackson.

Refreshed after showering, she was debating whether to wear shorts or a summer dress when her phone rang. It was Layla Grandin. She was calling with an update from the private investigator, Jonas Shaw. In brief, there was nothing to report.

"Sorry this is dragging," she said. "I thought there would be more for you to do."

It was Layla who'd first said they needed her to take on the case, narrowly beating out her family. For that reason, she likely felt personally responsible for Alexa's comfort and well-being. In truth, Alexa would have returned regardless. She had her own reasons, not least of which was that her family's oil rights were also in peril. Her father wasn't pleased with the current lawyer. He was an outsider who wasn't invested in the case. But for her entire life, Alexa had been her clan's outsider. Now here she was, the center of attention. It was strange.

"I'm fine," Alexa reassured Layla. "Jackson took me out to his cabin. If anything should—"

"Whoa!" Layla cried. "Mind backing up and repeating those last few words?"

Shit! She should be more discreet. Judging by her siblings' reaction, her relationship with Jackson was scorching-hot gossip. They hadn't discussed how they would handle this. Given that he was in PR, she'd let him take the lead.

"Do you remember Jackson Strom from high school?" Alexa asked.

"What do you mean, 'Do I remember Jackson Strom from high school?' I remember Jackson from just two weeks ago. We get our cars serviced at the same dealership. We grab coffee and chat while we wait. I've been trying to get him to try a chai latte. My point is, I don't need a trip down Memory Lane to remember Jackson Strom. And why is this the first I'm hearing about this? I'm one of your closest friends."

What Layla was describing was so damn pleasant. How lovely to have a standing appointment with your old high school friend, to go through the trouble of arranging appointments at the dealership just to grab a coffee and catch up. It was the sort of thing that might only happen in Royal. She cleared her throat before speaking. "My point is, we're just hanging out. It's no big deal."

"Have you gotten a good look at him?"

"Yes."

"Like, really?"

"Yes!"

"I say this with respect—he's hot."

Alexa sank down to the edge of her bed and covered her eyes with the palm of her hand. "I *know*."

She relived that moment on the old dock. She'd caught sight of him just before he dove in after her. He was breathtakingly beautiful, with the sun pouring gold on his brown skin.

"Honestly, I can't believe he's still single."

Honestly, neither could Alexa.

"You can hang out with just about anyone," Layla said. "But I'd keep my eye on Jackson. I always thought you two would make a cute couple."

"I don't know." Alexa didn't like making moves if she couldn't see straight through to the end game. It was the quality that made her a natural at chess. What chance did they have at a future? Her life was waiting elsewhere.

"I bet big money he'd ask you out to senior prom and lost big. You owe me five bucks and a chocolate bar."

Alexa was heartened her lifelong neighbor hadn't bet against her. "Who was taking bets?"

"Never mind that. It was a long time ago."

"Honestly, I keep going back and forth with this. There's no way to keep it casual. Why bother starting something if I can't see it through? I'm leaving soon enough."

She didn't want to add Jackson to the long list of men with whom she'd used her career as an excuse to brush aside.

"Your heart will know what to do."

Her *heart* would know what to do? "Oh, God," Alexa moaned. "I forgot. You're one of those people."

"What people?"

"People in love. You're like Caitlyn."

"You make it sound as if I've been infected with a zombie virus."

"I couldn't have put it better."

"Well, Josh and I are very happy. Thank you very much. I want my friends to be happy, too. Or maybe it's the stress of the case that's getting to me. I need a distraction."

Alexa wished she could reassure Layla that everything would work out in the end. However, in her experience, when so much money was involved, the moral arc of the universe bent toward greed. Heath Thurston was hunting for oil. He would stop at nothing. Alexa was not an optimist, but she wasn't a quitter. She'd made her professional reputation by being methodical and thorough. If there were loopholes to be found, even a single one, she would find it and leap through it.

Layla wished her a goodnight. "Say hi to Jackson for me!"

"I will. And I'd like to try that chai latte."

"Absolutely! We'll meet up soon."

Alexa set the phone on its charger. She decided on a dusty-rose halter dress and, after a short debate, left her room barefoot. For some reason, the rest of the house had plunged into darkness. She called out Jackson's name as she tentatively made her way down the hall and stairs. Hearing no response, Alexa stopped to assess her situation. She was a single woman, alone with a man in a dark cabin deep in the woods: the premise of every slasher film.

Suddenly…a flash of light! Alexa squeezed her eyes shut and screamed.

Jackson called out her name. A moment later, he was charging up the stairs. "Alexa! What's wrong?"

"I don't know! The house was dark and…"

"I'm setting up. Did I scare you?"

"Hell yes, you scared me!"

He took her in his arms. "Sorry, babe. God, you're shaking."

He was shaking, too, but with laughter. He had the nerve to find this funny. "Why is it dark in here? What are you setting up for?"

Jackson released her and presented her with what looked like a pink carnation snapped from its stem and secured to a bit of ribbon with a safety pin.

"What's that?" she asked.

"A corsage."

He fastened the flower to her wrist with the ribbon. Then he took her hand in his. "Alexandra Lattimore, will you be my date for prom?"

Alexa looked past Jackson's broad shoulders. There was a disco ball hanging from the ceiling over the coffee table and sending shards of silver light onto every wall. A punch bowl was set up on the kitchen island. Finally, she looked up at him. His eyes had the luster of honey. She burst into tears.

"Oh, babe…" Jackson held her close, stroking her back until she calmed down. She might have been vacillating with this a while ago, but that was done. She was swinging forward. There was no going back.

Alexa straightened up and offered him her hand. "Take me to prom."

Ten

The idea had come to Jackson in a flash. They could talk by the fire any old time, but tonight was prom night. He snipped a flower from the back garden and fastened it to a bit of ribbon. He dug out the old disco ball, a holiday staple, from a storage bin. Then he had dimmed the lights, lit a few candles and quickly downloaded a few power ballads from their high school years. That was when she'd come down the stairs and screamed. He'd nearly had a heart attack.

For the second time in a day, he was holding her quivering body close. She smelled fresh from the shower, and her deep brown skin was dewy soft. And then he'd gone and made her cry.

How had it all gone so wrong? He could've waited until their second night before scaring her to death. Jackson was about to call the whole thing off when her breathing steadied. She straightened up and swiped at the tears rolling down her cheeks. Alexa was Alexa again. Head high, she offered him her hand.

Jackson hit Play on his phone, and a power ballad that had dominated the airways their senior year rumbled through the sound system.

He turned to her. "May I have this dance?"

She arched a brow. "Were you really that smooth?"

"My dad gave me a handful of phrases," Jackson explained. "It was that or 'What's your sign?'"

She grinned, a glint of mischief in her eyes. "I'm an Aries, and my boyfriend is parking the car. He'll be back in five."

"That's all I need."

They came together, laughing. They swayed to the sound of the electric guitar. She looked up at him, her eyes bright. "You made punch?"

"It's just spiked lemonade."

The singer crooned, *"Baby, you make me crazy."*

"I bet this song had plenty of girls in tears by the end of the night."

Jackson felt uneasy. He hoped to God that tonight was the first and only time he'd made her cry. "Alexa, I've been meaning to ask…"

"What is it?"

She kept her head on his chest, and they swayed together. He stroked her back. "Did I break your heart?"

She stiffened in his arms. "You mean, back in high school?"

He nodded, his jaw rubbing her hair. Of course. When else?

She jerked away, red-faced. Jackson hoped to God she wouldn't cry again. That was before she laughed in his face. "Get over yourself! It wasn't like that."

Relief shot through him. His crush had kept him humming all those years. Even so, their relationship had been rooted in mutual contempt. It wasn't ideal, but it balanced them out. Neither one of them had seemed eager to mess with the equilibrium.

Jackson cupped her face. "Hey, beautiful, you can stop laughing now."

Her laughter died. She drifted back into his arms. "You may not have broken my heart, but you had me wondering what if."

He brushed his nose against hers. "Same."

The ballad gave way to a pop song that was only slightly

more upbeat. Alexa closed her eyes and dropped her head back. "I remember this one."

Jackson closed his eyes, too. He loved the way they moved together. He loved the feel of her in his arms. He loved her fresh scent. He loved the way she was looking at him now.

The next song on the playlist was a raging dance hit. Alexa cupped a hand over his ear and spoke over the music. "In the spirit of prom, we should grab a couple of beers and go make out in your car."

Jackson liked her thinking, but he had other plans. "In a minute. I've got a lock on prom king."

"Fool! Kiss me."

His hands moved from her waist to the sides of her face. He swept the pad of a thumb along her lower lip and waited. The air between them was charged. His heartbeat drove faster than the music. He teased her with a shallow kiss. She whimpered and he kissed her deeply. It went to his head like whiskey, but her words bobbed to the surface of his mind: *I'm open to the possibility. Just not right away.* She didn't want to rush things. Neither did he, Jackson realized.

It took everything he had to break the kiss. "Let's get you that beer."

She brought a shaky hand to her swollen lips. "Okay."

Half a beer later, Alexa was dancing on the couch.

Eleven

Fishing while managing a hangover was cruel and unusual punishment. Jackson had knocked on her bedroom door at dawn. He'd ignored her pleas for leniency and sentenced her to four hours of outdoor activities. Stretched out on his boat, legs crossed at the ankles, sunglasses on to block the harmful sun, Alexa's line dipped listlessly into the glassy lake. "This is unethical," she moaned.

"Write about it in the *New England Journal of Who Gives a Damn*."

"Hey!" she fired back. "That's a venerable publication. Show some respect!"

He laughed. "It's not so bad, is it?"

"Whoa!" There was a sharp tug on her line. She gripped the handle of her rod.

Jackson made a face. "That bad?"

"I got a bite!" Alexa scrambled to her feet and widened her stance for better control.

Jackson was immediately at her side. "I'll help!"

"Back off. I got this."

He dropped his hands on his hips. "Let's see what you got, then."

"Just watch."

Alexa widened her stance and reeled in a largemouth bass with minimal effort. Its slick silver body flopped restlessly. Satisfied, she handed the rod to Jackson. He could take over now. She'd done her part.

Jackson was dumbstruck. "I thought you didn't fish."

Alexa shrugged and settled down on the floor of the boat. She joined her hands behind her head. "I know *how* to fish. I just don't see the point in it. There are easier ways to enjoy seafood."

"True," he said. "But no one will hand you a trophy at the end of the day."

"That little guppy is not going to earn us any trophies."

Her catch was larger than a sardine, but not by much.

Jackson studied it and turned to her. "Should we release it? Give it a fighting chance?"

"Please."

Jackson unhooked the fish and tossed it back into the water. He set down his rod and crossed the length of the boat to where she was lounging. There was no other word for it. She was lounging on a rowboat in the gentle hours of the morning. If her head weren't pounding, it would be delightful. Jackson crawled over her and rested his head on her chest. "Tell me how bad it is."

This was the one tangible benefit of their wild night partying to club music from the early 2000s under a '70s-era disco ball: they were no longer shy around each other. Jackson touched her every chance he got. Now he was resting on her, his weight pressing into her, his words vibrating through her, and suddenly everything was so, so good.

She raked her fingers through his thick, wavy hair. "Let's just stay like this, and everything will be all right."

"Now you're getting it." He tugged at the hem of her T-shirt. "May I?"

"May you what?"

"Touch you."

He slipped a hand underneath it, the rough palm grating against her skin. Alexa shivered. He laughed quietly. "Is that a yes?"

"That's a yes, *please*."

"Such good manners."

She shifted to face him. They were so close, the tips of their noses brushed. "I've been thinking," she said.

"Go on."

"When are we going to…" Her voice trailed off. "You know."

"Sorry. I don't."

She cringed for having to say it. "Get busy."

"Ah." He raised his eyebrows. "You mean, 'go all the way?'"

"I mean sex, Jackson," she said plainly. Exasperation crept into her voice. "When are we going to have sex?"

Jackson winked. "There you go."

"Hey," Alexa said. "I know men are intimidated by strong, accomplished women, but I wouldn't have counted you among them."

"Thanks for the vote of confidence, babe."

"Are we doing this or not?"

"What's the hurry?"

"I know I said I wanted to wait, but I've changed my mind. We have a limited amount of time. We shouldn't waste it."

"We just got here yesterday."

She traced an index finger along his jawline, enjoying the feel of scruff. "If you're trying to be a gentleman, don't bother."

He brushed the tip of his nose against hers. "I'm not going to let you do it."

"Do what?" she said, as innocently as possible.

He kissed the corner of her mouth. "Micromanage this."

Alexa held his face between her hands, keeping him close. "That's not what I'm doing."

"Isn't it?"

The boat rocked, tilting to one side. She reached out and

grabbed hold of him before he rolled away. His body pressed against hers opened a well of longing. For as long as she could remember, she'd longed for Jackson. It hadn't consumed her. It was a soft drumbeat barely audible under life's blaring horns. Deep inside, Alexa knew very well that she'd marched to that beat, allowed it to dictate her steps. No man had ever been brilliant, witty or charming enough to hold her attention for long. She had never outright compared the men in her life to the boy she'd crushed on through school, but now that she'd held him close, felt his body, tasted his kiss, all the pieces fit in place.

"I want to seize the day," she said. "Opportunities like this don't come around too often, Jackson."

"Alexa, you're not calling the plays on this."

"Why not? I'm so good at it."

"You want to cross me off your list, and I have other plans for us."

"What plans?"

"I want to take my time and see where this goes."

This goes nowhere! Alexa had come close to shouting the words. Nothing more could come of this. He lived in Royal, and she did not. Why should that stop them from enjoying the present?

Jackson pushed back onto his heels, sat in place and picked up the oars. He started to row them to shore with rhythmic smooth strokes.

Alexa propped herself up on her elbows. *For as long as you want it...* She was beginning to understand. He thought she was toying with him or that maybe she just wanted to hit it and quit it. Even after last night, he still thought that way.

When they made it back to the house, she followed him up the beach and along the granular path leading straight up to the deck.

"Hungry?" he said. It was the first he'd spoken in the last twenty minutes. She had started to worry.

"Starving."

"I'll make us breakfast. Waffles sound good?"

"Sounds amazing."

They entered the house. Alexa was feeling grimy and was desperate for a shower. She kicked off her flip-flops and followed him into the great room on bare feet. "Well, this wasn't a very productive fishing trip," she said with manufactured joviality. "We have nothing to show for it."

He darted a look her way. "Better luck next time?"

"There won't be a next time." She headed up the stairs, her back stiff. "I've crossed it off my list and now I'm done with it. Isn't that my MO?"

"Hey." He moved to the foot of the stairs. "Did I upset you?"

Alexa slowed to a stop. She gripped the rail but did not turn around. "If I had feelings, sure. Since you've concluded I don't…"

"I never said that."

"You didn't have to."

"Look at me."

She turned to face him. His brown eyes held the universe.

He climbed a step and stopped, hesitant. "This means something to me. I wouldn't have invited you here if it didn't. It doesn't matter how long it lasts. The memory is going to stay with me forever. We can't botch this."

Every day, this man revealed a new layer. He was nothing like the person she'd imagined. Alexa had to do away with all the crap she'd projected onto him, do away with the boy who lived in her imagination, if she were to have any chance at getting to know the man before her now.

"It already means something. Jackson, *you* mean something to me."

The faintest of smiles curled his lips. "I make you feel things."

"You do." She did not want to botch this, either. If he wanted to slow down, they would. "Now go and make me breakfast."

Twelve

After breakfast, Jackson left Alexa on the back porch with her laptop and a stack of books. He walked over to the neighbor's house. Earlier, he'd noticed their truck parked out front. If he did not go over to say hello, they'd show up at his doorstep with a crate of produce from their garden or a freshly baked pie. They'd likely turn up at the most inopportune time, like when he and Alexa were kissing in a messy kitchen with mouths filled with whipped cream. It was anyone's guess how they'd managed to sit for breakfast just now.

Loretta Baker came to the door. The petite Black woman in her sixties had the long limbs of a lifelong dancer. She used to wear her silver hair long. Recently, she'd cut it short to the scalp. She greeted him with a wide smile, then called out to her husband. "Honey, it's little Jack."

There was nothing Jackson could do to get Loretta to acknowledge that he was a grown man and not the boy she'd first met. For decades, the Bakers and the Stroms had been the only Black homeowners for miles around. Even though that was no longer the case, the bond between the families was strong.

She motioned for Jackson to come inside. "It's insanely hot. I swear this planet is going to spontaneously combust."

She led him into the kitchen and, without asking, poured him a glass of lemonade. Her husband, Raymond, joined them. Where she was lean, he was round and soft, and appeared to be five years Loretta's senior even though they were exactly the same age.

"When did you guys drive up?" Jackson asked.

"Last night," Raymond replied. "We noticed your lights were on and were going to stop by today, but—"

"But we see you have a very special guest," Loretta interrupted.

"How did you see that?"

"You took her out on the lake this morning."

"Right." Damn! They were good.

"Is that the Lattimore girl?" Loretta asked. "The lawyer?"

"She's not a girl. I'm not a boy. We're both adults."

Ray slapped the countertop. "I bet!"

"She's an old friend."

"Uh-huh." Loretta said. "The Lattimores are in a bind. They stand to lose the oil under their land. Has she mentioned it?"

"We're here to relax," Jackson replied.

He was only beginning to appreciate the amount of stress Alexa was under. His role was to relieve her of it.

"That's right," Ray said. "You two just relax. Forget the outside world."

Loretta nodded approvingly. "She's very pretty, favors her mother. Have you met Barbara Lattimore?"

Jackson tried changing the subject. "I see you've worked on the fence. Looks good."

Ray launched into a review of every company from which he'd obtained a free quote. This bought Jackson some time. He finished his lemonade. The older man would have to pause for a breath at some point. He would make up an excuse to leave.

Jackson was itching to get back to Alexa. He would miss her when they got back to town and had to part ways. No more drawn-out lunches, spontaneous swims or even late-night dance parties. He would miss her like crazy when she returned to Florida. So why was he stalling? For the first time in his life, he was asking a woman to take it slow. What did it matter if it didn't work out? When had he ever worried about that? Sometimes, his love affairs did not last the night. Other times, they stretched out for years. He'd always recovered. Jackson sensed this time would be different. He would not recover so easily. When you get what you want, what you've always wanted, losing it was a devastating blow.

"Anyway," Raymond was saying, "it turned out beautifully."

"Not just the fence," Loretta said. "The deck, too. Just in time for tomorrow's barbecue."

"We're celebrating our thirty-fifth anniversary," Raymond said.

Jackson let out a low whistle. "Congratulations. You two lovebirds make it look easy."

Loretta reached for her husband's hand. "It's easy when you're with the right person."

"You and Ms. Lattimore should come by," Raymond said. "Tomorrow at five."

"We sent an invitation to your parents," Loretta said. "They couldn't make it out this weekend, but you're here. It would mean so much if you would come."

Jackson wasn't sure if he could submit Alexa to the Bakers' intense scrutiny. "I'll let you know."

"You do that." Loretta slipped an arm around his and led him to the foyer. She had impeccable timing and understood intuitively that the visit had come to its natural end. She opened the front door. "One more thing about the Lattimores."

Jackson didn't want to hear it, whatever it was.

"Oil or no, they're a well-respected and powerful family."

"I know that, Lo."

"Okay, well, don't sleep on it."

"What does that mean?"

"It means the girl is a catch. And from what I hear, she's single. You'd make her a fine husband."

"Is that right?"

"Oh, yes." She patted his shoulder this time. "You're a smart boy. Play your cards right."

It stormed later that night. Jackson and Alexa sat facing each other across a travel-sized chessboard. The pawns were tiny and felt like toy soldiers in his hands. They passed a bowl of warm popcorn back and forth while they studied the board. It was Alexa's turn, but she seemed distracted.

"Before I forget," he said, "my neighbors are celebrating their thirty-fifth wedding anniversary tomorrow with a barbecue. We're invited but if you're not up to it, we don't have to go."

She advanced her knight. "I'd love to go."

He moved his bishop without thought. As always, when it came to her, he did not have a winning strategy. "You don't have to."

"I want to."

"If I remember right, barbecues are not your thing."

"I've acquired a taste for it. You think there'll be ribs?"

"I know it."

"Let's go," she said. "Unless *you* don't want to."

Jackson leaned back in the well-loved leather armchair, cradling the bowl of popcorn to his chest. "There's something you should know."

She studied the board, but she was faking. He knew when she was engaged in something, and this wasn't it. "What's that?"

"My neighbors got it in their mind that I'd make you an excellent trophy husband."

A giggle bubbled up inside of her. "What?"

"You heard me."

The rain was slapping against the windows, but all Jackson heard was her melodious laugh. "I always knew you were out of my league," he said. "But damn."

"The position is open, you know," she said.

"Really?" He munched on popcorn, taking his time. "Didn't know you were recruiting."

"You know what they say—behind every great woman is a man with great abs."

"Glad you noticed," he said. "I put in the work."

"And you make good pancakes."

"Waffles," he corrected. "My pancakes are dry."

"Your coffee isn't bad."

"And I'm good with my hands."

"I wouldn't know." She drummed the wood tabletop with her fingertips. Her dark-coffee hair was wavy and loose. He had never seen her quite like this, happy and relaxed. "You've yet to demonstrate these skills."

He winked and popped a popcorn into his mouth.

"If it helps to rebuild your self-esteem, Layla thinks you're a catch."

"Layla G.?"

"Uh-huh," she said. "She ranks you among Royal's most eligible bachelors."

Jackson made a face. "Please don't tell me she used those words."

"No." She reached for her glass of wine and sipped. "I believe her exact words were 'He's a catch.' She wants me to catch you."

"Love that girl."

"You *are* that most elusive creature—young, handsome, single, successful. Why hasn't anyone tied you down?"

"I'm more cautious since starting my own business," he replied. "I've learned to take calculated risks."

"Really?"

They locked eyes. Jackson nodded. "I need…something."

"Collateral?"

"Skin in the game."

She swirled the wine in her glass. "I didn't peg you for one to play it safe."

"Not safe," he said. "Smart."

Jackson wanted something from Alexa, some reassurance that she would take him seriously. If it didn't work out between them, fine. He could live with that. But it wouldn't be because they hadn't tried.

Alexa returned her attention to the board. For a long while, she sat still, calculating her next move. Whether it was with the match or with him, he wasn't quite sure. She extended a hand, letting it hover over the pieces before withdrawing.

"What's the hesitation?" he asked.

"Quiet. I'm thinking."

No one ever made the act of thinking so elegant, so elevated. But if she wouldn't make a move, he would. He was eager to break past this holding pattern.

Alexa picked up her queen and set it down next to his king. It happened so swiftly, he thought he'd imagined it. Jackson was no chess master, but he knew the move didn't make sense. And wasn't that the rookie move she'd accused him of making back in the eighth grade?

"What did you do?" he asked.

She glanced up at him. "I sacrificed my queen."

"May I ask why?" There was no strategic reason to do it, nothing to gain.

"You win," she said. "You were going to win anyway. I'm too distracted tonight. This way is faster."

"But you've robbed me of the thrill."

Alexa did not reply. Her gaze was a caress, and Jackson felt a thrill of another kind.

Thirteen

Jackson was distractingly handsome—sitting across from her, reclined in a battered leather chair, in a loose cotton shirt and faded jeans. Distracted or not, Alexa had the game on lock. She was poised to win but could afford to lose. What better way to drive her point home? She was through with games—not that Jackson had given her any reason to believe that he was playing around. Maybe that was the problem. He was serious, way too serious. That quip about her being out of his league had made her wonder. Would he have been this careful if he were here with another woman, someone less complicated and uptight? Someone not named Lattimore. Or was it their long and storied history? Was it slowing them down?

If that were the case, he had to snap out of it, and preferably in the next hour or so. She was facing another sleepless night. But the way he was looking at her gave her hope. She never felt more beautiful than when pinned by his stare.

He extended a hand. "Come to me."

Alexa launched forward, knocking over the table. The chessboard and pieces scattered onto the Turkish rug. The bowl of popcorn followed. She was on top of him, straddling him, and could confirm to all interested parties that he was very good with his hands. They were everywhere, roaming, exploring. Alexa gripped the hem of his T-shirt and raised it over his head. A moan escaped her when she touched skin. She lowered her lips to his chest and tasted him. A shiver ran through her.

"Let's get rid of this."

He mimicked her gesture, gathering her loose linen dress and lifting it over her head effortlessly. He brought the bundled fabric to his nose and inhaled her scent. She eased it away and leaned forward for him to nestle his nose in the dip of her neck. His hands skimmed the curves of her waist, settling on her hips. She gasped when he dug his fingers into her flesh and drew her closer to him. The rough jeans rubbed her inner thighs. She furiously worked on the button and the zipper. But Jackson was in no particular hurry. He cupped her breasts, delighting in them. He teased one nipple with his mouth and the other with his thumb. Outside, the storm raged. Need sliced through her like lightning.

Alexa pulled away and somehow managed to stand on wobbly legs. She lowered her underwear down over her hips. Jackson protested. "You're doing it again."

She froze. "Doing what?"

"Robbing me of the thrill."

"That's not what I'm doing! I'm trying to get us to the good part."

He reached out and pulled her close. "Alexa," he whispered against her skin, "this is the good part."

It only got better. Jackson sank down to his knees. He inched her silk panties down, slipped a hand between her legs and stroked her with his thumb. He started off gently, then gradually added pressure and speed. Alexa cupped his upturned face and lowered her head to kiss him. He slipped a finger inside her. She tightened around him. Leaning into him, she drove their kiss even deeper. Then, with a sudden growl of impatience, Jackson pulled back, lifted her up and sent her toppling onto the nearby sofa. His wallet and keys were on the coffee table. He grabbed the wallet and rummaged through it until he found the foil packet of a condom.

Alexa propped herself up on her elbows. She questioned him with a raised eyebrow.

"Time to get to the good part," he said, kicking off his jeans.

She watched him undress. He was a beautiful man: long and solid, finely sculpted. She could not tear her gaze away.

It had stopped raining at some point. Yet when he stretched out on top of Alexa, a flash of lightning startled her. She wrapped her arms and legs around him.

"Don't worry. I'm here," he whispered against the damp skin of her temple.

Jackson eased inside of her. Finally, they were one, rivals no more. His hands were lost in her hair again. His lips dragged down her throat. She arched her back to welcome him deeper. Pleasure rippled through her, but it was a sudden flash of insight that blew her mind. She and Jackson had to be two of the most stupid people on earth. All the time wasted antagonizing each other, baiting each other, and they could have been doing this. They were lovers at their core, better together than working against each other.

That was her last thought before a thrill took her under.

At some point, they'd rolled clumsily onto the floor. Jackson had grabbed a couple of throw pillows and a blanket off the couch. Alexa pressed her cheek to Jackson's chest, shivering as he stroked her back. Thunder rolled in the distance. She felt his heartbeat, followed the slow unwinding of his breath. She was breathing freely, too—no special app or techniques required. The house was silent except for the soft rustle of rain-soaked trees.

Her phone rang. It lay among the scattered popcorn. She reached for it and checked the caller ID. Two words flashed on the display: *Office HR*.

"Make it stop," Jackson murmured against her temple.

His stubble scraped her skin and sent a shiver of delight down her spine.

"Sorry. It's my office. I have to take the call."

His arms circled tighter around her. "This late on a Saturday?"

"Justice doesn't sleep," she said. "Don't get up. I'll take the call upstairs. It won't be long."

Pulling away from his body, his warmth, was hard to do. For a brief moment, she was tempted to follow his recommendation and toss the phone out the window herself. She couldn't. The knots in her stomach warned her that this was not a casual call.

With her dress pressed to her torso, she raced up the stairs. By the time she reached her room, the phone had stopped ringing. She dialed the number and fell backward into her bed. As she waited for an answer, she wondered if Jackson would join her here tonight or ask her to his room.

The receptionist answered. "The Law Offices of Anderson and Carmichael. This is Patricia. How may I direct your call?"

Alexa had joined Anderson and Carmichael—A & C for short—just two years ago with the goal of making partner in the coming year. That plan was falling apart, crumbling under her every step. The quality of her work was excellent. There was no doubt about that. However, the interpersonal relationships had her caught in a bind. For one thing, she had never warmed up to the senior partners…or the other way around. Either way, their interactions remained cool, and they kept their distance.

"Hello, Patricia," she said. "It's Alexandra Lattimore. I missed a call. Who's in this late?"

Patricia was the long-standing receptionist who practically lived in the office. Some of Alexa's colleagues called her "Patty Cake," which she seemed to enjoy. Alexa had never dared. It was taxing enough to refrain from addressing the older woman as "ma'am." Her upbringing had instilled in her a stiff formality that she couldn't shake.

"It's been a while. How are you?"

Patricia's tone was gentle. She was the firm's mother hen. Her desk was a designated safe space where employees could stop by for coffee and vent or pick up a little gossip. She kept a well-stocked coffee bar behind her desk and served American roast in the mornings and espresso with pound cake or chocolate between 1:00 and 2:00 p.m. Her nickname was well deserved.

"I'm well," Alexa said. "You know...visiting family."

"Does Arthur know?" she asked.

That was a funny question. Arthur Garrett was the head of the HR department. "Of course he knows. I'm on a leave of absence."

"He left me a note asking me to reach out and ask how long you planned on staying away."

"One month," Alexa said. "Arthur knows this."

Arthur had been the one to suggest she take time off.

"Hey now! Don't shoot the messenger."

There was a slight edge to Patricia's voice. Alexa settled down. She was aware of her reputation at the firm. Rigid. Demanding. Exacting. Once, in the elevator, she'd heard someone whisper, "Troublemaker." The only thing she'd demanded was respect. It seemed that was too much to ask. The average law firm remained the last refuge of the classic boys' club, but A & C was worse.

Alexa did not understand it. She had come to the firm with high hopes. A string of bitter New York winters had forced her to seek a warmer climate. Well before a headhunter reached out with a partner-track position in Miami, she'd studied and passed the Florida bar. She hadn't realized her mistake until it was too late. The senior partners of the firm had little interest in her. She'd recruited clients and won cases. They'd praise her work in staff meetings, reward her with a bonus and go on ignoring her.

Early on, a fellow attorney had invited her to lunch and asked how she was getting on. His name was Theo Redmond. Alexa had quickly gathered that he was the golden boy of the firm. Every office had one: the tall, blond and handsome type who might've failed the bar a few times and still managed to land at a top firm. Theo was trading on his looks and his pedigree. Alexa didn't mind it, certain that in the end, the legal profession valued substance over style. She'd been wrong.

That afternoon, Theo ordered cocktails and encouraged her to open up to him. "I know how you feel," he said. She was sure that he didn't. "They can be such a cold bunch."

"Aren't you dating Carmichael's daughter?"

Theo was in with the in crowd, and everybody knew it. Things seemed serious with him and the daughter of one of the firm's most senior partners. She was young and pretty and seemed poised to move up the ranks.

"*Dating* is a strong word," he said with a coy smile. "We're involved."

"Well, I'm not involved with anyone," she mocked. "I don't have that privilege."

"You could, if you were…open to it."

Was he suggesting she sleep with Carmichael himself? Before she could ask, Theo had placed a hand on her knee under the table. It lay there, like a dead fish, until she sat up straight and shifted her knees away from him. Not one to take a subtle hint, Theo had later pinned her to the rough concrete wall in the public parking lot and kissed her. His mouth was hot and tasted rank of black truffle sauce. She pushed him away and warned him never to try that again. Except he had tried, again and again, once when they'd found themselves alone in an elevator and another time by the vending machine where she routinely purchased a midmorning granola bar to tide her over until lunch. She'd avoided him, but he knew where to find her. At her wit's end, she'd visited HR and filed an official complaint with Arthur Garrett. Her encounters with Theo abruptly came to an end. She could finally get back to the business of winning cases and cashing her bonus checks. Yet one afternoon, she found herself alone in the elevator with Carmichael's daughter. The woman gave her the dirtiest look. A pit formed in Alexa's stomach. She knew it wasn't over. She'd been naive to think so.

The following week, she was removed from a committee. The week after, she was dropped as second chair from a major trial case in which Theo was third chair. That had prompted another trip to HR. "This is starting to look like retaliation."

Alexa had the firepower to strike back. Her family name had weight and her connections extended far, but she refused to call in favors. She was a professional. She could handle this on her own. Even if she'd asked her father to call on a junior congressman or another, what good could that do? This was a delicate situation. Even a Lattimore couldn't snatch victory out of the jaw of every single defeat.

Arthur Garrett stood from behind his imposing desk. "Cool down, Alexa. Don't toss that word about."

"I'm not the one who needs to cool down," Alexa said. "I've done nothing wrong."

"It's my job to put out fires. Let me do my job."

"What do you suggest?"

"Take some well-deserved time off," he said. "While you're away, I'll meet with the others and get to the bottom of this."

His suggestion was ill-advised but well timed. Her family wanted her home to spearhead the legal defense against Heath Thurston's claim on their property's oil rights. Instead of flying home for short visits, she could be home longer.

"I'll go," she said. "Only because my family needs me right now. I'll take a month."

Arthur brightened. "It's a win-win!"

That wasn't true—not even close. Something inside her cried out at the injustice of it all.

Alexa regretted having left New York for Florida. Her last firm had worked her to the bone, but they'd valued her efforts. It was very much an ironclad boys' club, but there were a few powerful women at the table, and she'd always been treated with respect.

Anger and frustration formed a knot in her chest. Never had she felt so impotent. She could quit. She could just walk out. Starting over again at yet another firm didn't appeal to her. She'd left New York before making partner. If she didn't stick it out at A & C, her résumé would start to look thin. The best thing to do was to keep taking high profile cases, keep winning and building on her successes until she was recruited elsewhere. That didn't mean she had to suffer in silence in Miami. A & C had four offices nationwide, including one in Dallas. Alexa had never considered transferring to Texas. She had never before wanted to be that close to home. Things were different now. She had an added incentive to consider returning to her home state.

Fourteen

In the time it took for Alexa to wrap up her call, Jackson had swept up the popcorn, straightened out the living room, put on a moody jazz record, and splashed whiskey into tumbler glasses. She came down the stairs and accepted a drink with a shy smile. "Thanks. I needed that."

"Tough phone call?"

"Not really. Confusing more than anything else."

"Want to talk about it?"

She smiled at him over the rim of the glass. "I can't think of anything I'd enjoy less."

"I'm your friend, Alexa." It occurred to him that she might not have too much experience in the friendship department. Maybe she needed a primer. "You can talk to me."

"Technically, we're more than friends." There was a soft purr to her voice. "And we've talked enough."

Her playful teasing was a distraction; he knew it damn well. Jackson wanted to keep on asking questions until he hit the bedrock of truth. Why had a shadow of worry passed over her face when she'd picked up her phone? Why was it necessary to lock herself in her bedroom to take a simple work call? And why was she trying so hard to stonewall him now?

Alexa was looking at him with a pleasantly blank expression, just waiting for him to fold. She took another sip from her glass and swiped at a bead of whiskey on her full lower lip with her pink tongue. Without too much thought, he reached out and cupped her jaw, bringing her in for a kiss. She let the glass skid onto the counter and threaded her arms around his neck. Jackson pulled away and studied her pretty face. Her expression was open; the cool mask had fallen away. He grazed her jawline with his fingertips, silently imploring her to open up to him. Her brown eyes glazed with tears. It was enough to send him reeling.

Something was very wrong. Alexa was struggling under a tremendous weight. Initially, he'd thought it had something to do with her family's legal troubles. Now he wasn't so sure. But as she'd said, they were much more than friends. He did not need to badger her. The truth would come. It was rising to the surface now. He trusted that she would confide in him at the right time.

Jackson kissed her again, this time with ferocious urgency. He was in his boxers and, earlier, she had slipped on her dress to better slip away from him. Jackson tugged it over her head again and sent it flying. She hopped onto a nearby barstool and drew him close. He trailed kisses down her throat, all the while whispering against her warm skin, "No more hiding from me."

She took his face between her hands. "I'm not. I promise. Things are just…messy now."

"Messy? In what way?"

"Work stuff," she said. "Nothing to worry about."

"Then why do you look so—"

She silenced him with a kiss. "Make me forget."

He could do that for her, take her to the brink of pleasure and erase the last half hour from her mind. He could do it handily, but it would only be a temporary fix. Jackson would not leave it at that. He would find a way to ease her burden and rid her of her troubles for good.

It took only a minute to grab a condom off the coffee table. He was soon back in her arms, but it seemed like too long a separation. She wrapped her legs around his waist and repeated her request in his ear. "Make me forget."

Jackson buried himself inside her. The contours of her body were familiar to him now, but the sensation that spread through him was new. They moved at a frenetic pace, pushing each other to new heights—as they'd always done. He tangled his fingers in her hair. Her name slipped from his lips. "Alexa…"

They climaxed together and clung to each other as passion swept through them. Jackson closed his eyes and pressed his forehead to hers. Their sharp intakes of breath softened, then synchronized. She swept her hands down his back. Their bodies were slick with sweat. They'd been rolling on the floor and other places. They needed a warm shower and a warm bed. Jackson scooped her up. She laughed freely as he carried her up the stairs.

On Sunday afternoon, Loretta greeted Jackson and Alexa at the door. Actually, she nearly knocked Jackson out of her way to get to Alexa. "Don't just stand there! Come in! Come in!"

Alexa presented her with a bottle of wine, a gift picked up at the last minute. She'd refused to show up empty-handed. Loretta smiled approvingly and made eyes with Jackson, reminding him of her earlier advice. *Play your cards right.*

Dinner was served on picnic tables set up on the grass. There were ribs. Also, there were champagne cocktails, lobster salad, fresh corn and mini lemon-custard pies topped with the number 35 in gold.

"That's a long time to commit to anything." Alexa frowned down at her mini lemon custard.

"I wouldn't mind it."

She arched a brow. "Should I refresh your memory, sir? In previous statements, you asserted with no ambiguity that you were in no hurry to get married. The record is clear."

Jackson folded his arms and nodded, considering. "I don't deny it. However, I would like to amend the record to reflect my desire to marry eventually and reach a significant milestone, if not thirty-five than twenty-five will do."

"Ah," she said solemnly. "The amendment is recorded and certified."

"Seriously, though," he continued. "I would like something like this. It's nice. Celebrating a lifetime with your love in a home you created, together with good food and good friends. I can't think of anything better."

Alexa just looked at him, wide-eyed. Her curls caught the light of the afternoon sun, and her brown skin had a golden glow to it. She was so beautiful. He wanted to kiss her, but not here. Too many nosy people around.

"You must think I'm some country boy," he murmured.

She reached under the picnic table to squeeze his hand. "You're no country boy, Jackson. You're a successful entrepreneur and one of the smartest people I know."

"I'm a country boy at heart."

"I love your heart, so I guess it's okay."

Those words washed over him. Without thinking, he reached into the pocket of his jeans for a green velvet pouch. While in town that morning, a necklace on display in the window of a vintage shop had caught his eye. He wasn't one to buy jewelry on a whim, but he had instantly thought of her and wanted her to have it.

"What's that?" she said.

He struggled a minute with the ties before emptying the pouch into his cupped hand. She took his hand in hers for a closer look at the gold charm on a thin necklace. It was a miniature chess piece.

"A queen?"

"The most powerful piece in the game."

Alexa's face softened, but only for a second. "It's about

time you recognized my greatness." She plucked the necklace from his palm and held it up.

"Like it?"

He was desperate for her to like it, to like *him*. He wanted
to please her, challenge her, fight her battles and keep her
safe. He had never felt this way about anyone. It made him
swoon. It made him giddy. But it freaked him out. This was
the sort of thing that only worked out if two people felt the
same way. It was no good on its own.

Alexa did not answer his question. Instead, she gathered
her hair to one side and asked him to fasten the necklace
around her neck. Afterward, he let his fingertips graze her
nape. She leaned forward and kissed him, right there, in
front of everyone.

A live band set on a podium started to play a blues favorite. Couples poured onto the dance floor and swayed under a
canopy of string lights. Above them, a quarter moon peeked
through the last tuft of clouds still visible in the evening sky.

Alexa turned to him. "Do you sometimes wonder about
the woman who fell through the podium at the TCC pool
party?"

The question came out of nowhere. Jackson tossed his
head back and laughed. "Sorry to say, I don't."

"She has a solid personal injury claim."

"If you ever want to start chasing ambulances, let me
know. I'll hook you up with an ad firm, and we'll tape a few
commercials. Maybe erect a few billboards on the highway."

"It's just…everything about that day was so surreal."

"Finding you there was the biggest shock of all. Everything else pales."

"I felt so awkward and out of place until you showed up,"
she said. "If I could book your services for all future TCC
engagements, that would be great."

He took her hand to his lips and pressed a kiss on her
curled fingers. "I'm only just a phone call away."

"I may take you up on that."

If you only would, Jackson thought.

"What about the woman who professed her undying love for your brother?" he asked, doing his part to keep the conversation light.

"I tried to get him to talk about it, but he stonewalled me. I'm not giving up, though."

"Report back when you do."

"If you don't ask me to dance soon, our host is going to poke you with his grill tongs."

Jackson stood and bowed low, a hand on his heart. "Ma'am, will you do me the honors?"

"No, thanks! I'm good."

"Alexa!"

"Just kidding!" She slipped her hand in his. "Take me for a spin, country boy."

They swirled around the dance floor. They danced as the other guests watched them and laughed at the most brazen, the ones who couldn't help but point and stare. She whispered into his ear, "This is odd. We're not the guests of honor, so why do they care? Are you some kind of celebrity in these parts?"

"No, beautiful," he said. "You're the star."

Fifteen

They walked home under a cloudy night sky, hand in hand, gravel crunching under their feet. Alexa was dreaming of the night ahead. Before leaving for the neighbors' anniversary barbecue, they'd made sure they had a quart of ice cream stashed in the freezer for "later." If it rained, they'd put on a record and stretch out on the couch. If the weather held, Jackson would light a fire. She might even try her hand at s'mores.

They rounded a bend and walked up the driveway. The porch light was on, and it cast a glow on the painted-brick facade. The cat stretched out on the porch step was a stray. He gave them the once-over and slinked off. While Jackson unlocked the front door, Alexa noticed that the plants in the flower bed looked limp. She'd snap a photo in the morning and send it to her mother. Barbara would know what to do.

Alexa followed Jackson into the house, wondering who she'd become in these few short days. Apparently, she was the sort of person who sought out her mother for gardening tips. She would have never guessed it.

Jackson locked the door behind them. "We should pack."

Those three words fell at her feet and nearly tripped her. He caught her by the elbow. "Are you okay?"

"I'm fine."

Alexa had forgotten they were heading back to Royal in the morning. The dream was over.

Jackson switched on a few lights. The room glowed.

They'd had their first real conversation at the kitchen island and their first dance on the living room floor. They'd made love for the first time on the soft leather couch. She did not want to leave this place—not this soon.

Jackson circled back to find her leaning against the locked door. "What's the matter?" he asked. "Do you need me to carry you upstairs again?"

Alexa felt as if she might burst. "I don't want to go."

"Go where? Up to our room?"

"I don't want to go home," she said. "Let's stay here a few more days."

Jackson did not say a word. Alexa panicked. How could she fix this? Play it off as a joke? She let out a shaky laugh, but it died down within seconds.

Jackson's expression was serious. "You want to stay... *here*?"

She nodded, her throat tight. She must have started playing with the golden chess piece pendant at the base of her neck, because he nudged her fingers away and planted a kiss there. A torrent of butterflies filled her chest.

"You want to stay here with *me*," he said.

Alexa nodded again. "Just, you know, tossing it out there."

His shoulders relaxed. Only then did she appreciate how much tension he'd been carrying. He'd wanted her to enjoy the weekend and would have been disappointed if she hadn't. "I figured you couldn't get out of here fast enough. I thought for sure you were counting the hours."

"Just the opposite. It's been a nice change of pace."

"Uh-huh."

He stepped back. The growing space between them made her uneasy. She reached for him by a belt loop. "Where are you going?"

"I need a minute to process this," he said. "Just days ago, I had to twist your arm to get you to come out here with me, and now you can't get enough."

"Forget it. I'm going to pack."

"Not so fast." He pressed his hands to the door, bracketing her shoulders, locking her in place. "Let me savor this moment."

In her effort to get away, Alexa banged her head on the door.

"Oh, babe." Jackson cradled the back of her head in the palm of his hand. "Does it hurt?"

It didn't hurt. Instead of crying, she started to laugh. She laughed so hard, tears rolled down her cheeks. Jackson wrapped her in his arms. He likely thought she was coming undone, which wasn't far from the truth.

Alexa couldn't wipe away the tears fast enough. "I'm okay," she said between sharp intakes of breath. "I don't know what's the matter with me."

"Nothing is the matter with you," he said. "If anything, I'm in awe. You're under so much stress and handling it beautifully. Don't worry. We can stay for as long as you like."

"Just a couple more days," she said. "Let's not get crazy."

"Done."

Now that it was settled, Alexa wondered why simply asking for what she wanted—in this case, more time with him— had rattled her to the core. She had a reputation for being demanding, yet she rarely ever made demands of anyone. This was a lifelong habit. In class, she only ever raised her hand to supply answers, never to ask questions or for help. God help her if she'd ever had to make her needs known. And yet, she'd done it with him. She'd asked for more time. Jackson was eager to accommodate her.

Alexa ran her hands along his broad shoulders. "Don't let this go to your head, but I think I like you. I mean, *really* like you."

He cocked his head. "You think? On a scale of one to ten, how confident are you?"

"Seven. Maybe eight."

"I like those numbers."

"How about you?"

"Every action has an equal and opposite reaction."

"God!" she exclaimed with a laugh. "You're taking me back to Mrs. Sanchez's chemistry class."

"Actually, it was Mr. Washington's physics."

"Right," she said. "I've got butterflies in my stomach. I can't think."

He took her hand and placed it over his heart. "Do you feel that?"

His heartbeat was steady and sure. "I do."

"Good," he said. "Because it's yours. All you have to do is take it."

The next morning, while the day was still fresh, Jackson went into town to pick up extra supplies for their extended stay, namely bread, cheese, wine and ground beef for burgers. Alexa snapped a photo of the sad flower beds and went to the back shed to rummage for gardening tools. A moment later, her mother called. She answered the call on speaker and went on rummaging. So far, she'd found a half bag of potting soil and a pair of shears. "Good morning!"

"Alexa, this is your mother."

"I know, Mom."

"Are you all right, darling?"

"Sure. How are you?"

"Are you in a safe space?"

Her mother's voice was spiked with alarm. Alexa straightened up too quickly and wacked her head on an open shelf. A few rusty paint cans rolled off the shelf and fell to the floor with a clamor, undermining her response. "Yes, I'm in a safe space. What kind of question is that?"

Her mother wouldn't drop her line of questions. "Where has Jackson Strom taken you?"

"To his lake cabin. You *know* this, Mother."

"That photo you sent—was that a cry for help?"

"The photo of the *plants*?"

"The *dead* plants."

Okay. This was officially nuts. "Mother! Get yourself together."

"What would you have me think? We don't hear from you for ages, and you send a photo of dead flowers."

"I'm fine, Mom," Alexa said. "The plants are half-dead and I need advice. Should I water them? Prune them? Repot them?"

"Who are you and what have you done with my daughter?"

"Ugh! I'm hanging up."

"You know better than to hang up on me, young lady!" her mother warned. "You can understand if I'm a little disturbed. You've never once showed the slightest interest in gardening."

"I've spent loads of time in your garden this trip, but you wouldn't know. You're never around. You're either at yoga, tai chi or pottery class."

"I'm enjoying my summer!" Barbara Lattimore cried, indignant.

"As am I!"

"That's the issue. I've never known you to enjoy anything."

Alexa massaged her temples. "I regret reaching out to you for help."

"Don't say that! You can always count on my help. I'm never too busy for my oldest daughter. I can power walk and chew gum at the same time."

"All right." Alexa lowered herself onto a wooden footstool. "Tell me how to save the plants. Jackson is the only one in his family who comes out here on a regular basis, but he hasn't touched them. They look a little sad."

"Those are not plants worth saving, my dear. Those are weeds."

"That's not true." Even dried up and wilting, the plants had interesting shapes.

"They're weeds. Pull them up by the roots and get rid of them. Find some hearty perennials and start again."

Well, damn. "Thank you, Mother."

"You're welcome, darling. Now, don't hang up. Your sister is here, and she wants to talk to you."

Caitlyn's voice came through the line, bright and sunny. "How's life in the love shack?"

"It's not a shack. It's a very beautiful lakefront cabin."

"But have you fallen in love yet?"

It was the sort of question that would normally make her throw up her breakfast. Instead, Alexa fell silent, even while she heard her mother and sister cackling like hyenas. They were only poking fun, but the innocent dart hit dead in the bull's eye. Last night, she'd admitted to having feelings, but that was a far cry from love. Had she gone and fallen in love with Jackson? No. Her love for him had always been there, a small seed in her heart. It was growing now under proper care and devotion.

Alexa lowered her head between her knees and took shallow breaths. She had to be careful here. The wrong word, the wrong response, would give too much away. But no response would give away just as much. The best defense was offense. Right? *Here goes nothing.*

"Not everyone is obsessed with love, Caitlyn!"

Alexa cringed. She'd struck the wrong tone. That was over the top.

"Uh-huh," Caitlyn said, unmoved.

Her mother jumped in. "When are you coming back? We are expecting you tonight for dinner."

"We decided to stay a couple more days," she said flatly. "There's no rush, really."

Much better. Detached, slightly bored—that was her baseline. Anything more and she'd come across as unhinged to the women who knew her best. Already, the photo of the dead flowers and/or weeds had been a dead giveaway.

"I'm surprised Jackson doesn't have to come back and—I don't know—run his company," Caitlyn replied.

Alexa wasn't surprised. They'd promised each other to make the most of these few days, forgetting the demands of work or even family obligations. They'd made love the whole night to seal that promise. Of course, her sister didn't need to know that.

"It's a slow workweek."

"Mom thinks he's kidnapped you. Could we switch to video to make sure you're okay?"

"Rather not." Alexa looked around her. She was in a dingy shed that let in no sunlight. They would think for sure that he'd trapped her in a dungeon.

"Mom, should we conference in the guys just in case?"

Caitlyn had whispered the question. Alexa hadn't missed a word. "Don't you dare!"

"Okay, girl. Settle down," her sister cooed, as if she were trying to calm a wild horse. "It's all good. We're family."

Alexa switched topics. "How's Grandpa doing? Has he remembered anything?"

She heard her mother sigh. "Your grandfather is the same—clear as day one moment, partly cloudy the next. He only remembers what he cares to remember."

The weariness in her mother's tone was new. She was growing tired of this sordid affair. The matter was too important to be swept aside. Maybe the tai chi and the new classes were her way to cope with the stress. If his claim on their property turned out to be valid, Heath Thurston would have the power to upend their lives. In essence, they would lose their life's work. It would upset her mother to no end. It would upset them all.

Alexa sat in the shed long after she'd gotten off the phone with her mother and sister. She turned her mother's words over in her mind. *He only remembers what he cares to re-*

member. She'd long noticed that her grandfather's memory loss was oddly selective. She didn't know what to make of it. He wouldn't voluntarily withhold information. Right? That would be such a low-down, devious—

The door to the shed flew open, and sunlight splashed in. Alexa squinted and turned away just as Jackson filled the doorway. He stepped inside. "What are you doing in here?"

She held up a small rake. "Looking for gardening tools."

He looked concerned. "If you've found everything you need, I'll help you carry it back."

"No need," she said. "I just got off the phone with my mother. She said there's no salvaging the front flower beds. The plants are good and dead. What's left are weeds."

"I could have told you that." When she didn't budge from the little stool, he said, "Are you that upset about it? I can get a gardener up here."

"Don't bother."

He hunched low before her. "What's really bothering you, darling?"

"This sordid affair with my family's ranch is stressing my mother out. I can't believe I hadn't realized until now. She seemed to be holding up fine. I thought her oblivious, to be honest. But she was only looking for ways to cope."

He took her hands. "And how are you coping?"

Alexa admitted that she'd be glad when she could finally put the whole mess behind her. "I want the whole thing to go away. I know… I know… It's wishful thinking, and that's not what they hired me to do."

"They should not have hired you at all," Jackson said. "The Lattimores and the Grandins can afford to hire outside counsel."

"They wanted someone they could trust, someone wholly invested in the case."

"Pay them right and any lawyer will make the case their top priority," he said. "It's different for you. It's personal.

Now you face the prospect of letting your family down. That's not fair."

Alexa nodded. "My mother wouldn't make my favorite Thanksgiving sides ever again. My brothers would likely never let it go. Thank God for Caitlyn. She'll always be on my side."

Caitlyn had been adopted into their clan as an infant. Alexa seldom thought about it. Only today, the rickety doors to her heart were wide open, and a flood of emotions were pouring out. Where would she be without Caitlyn ever pushing her to prioritize love? Most likely she'd be in the same position. She and Jackson seemed destined to link up. Except it was a little sweeter knowing that Caitlyn was rooting for her.

"Alexa. I'm serious."

"Don't be," she said. "I distinctively remember us promising not to let the outside world interfere these next few days. I even promised not to open my laptop or do any work."

"That doesn't mean hiding or pretending everything is okay when they're not."

"I'm not hiding anything!" she blurted. Again, she should've moderated her tone. Jackson gave her a quizzical look. She kissed the space between his brows to ease away the crease there.

"All right," he said. "Now, are we going to get out of this shed, or should I order a picnic lunch?"

"Let's stay and make love on the floor."

"Oh, darling." He cupped her face with one hand. "We'll get tetanus if we do."

"Darn. There goes that fantasy."

"There's a hammock on the south end of the property. That's a fantasy of mine."

"Sounds fun." Lying naked in his arms while swinging lazily in a soft hammock, the breeze teasing their warm bodies. Nothing could be better.

He straightened up and helped her onto her feet. "Let's do it."

"Sure," she said. "But first, lunch."

In the days that followed—six in total—Alexa's life mirrored a dream. On the best days, the August sun bore down on them and bleached the horizon white. There was less fishing, more lazy mornings with books and coffee on the back deck, a ride to town for fresh bread and produce, an afternoon swim, a game of chess with rules made up on the fly, meals prepared while debating the news stories of the day, arguing, more arguing and then settling at the table with glasses of wine to a meal that bore little resemblance to the recipe pulled from a local blogger's website. At some point, either before the swim or after lunch, Jackson would look at her in such a way, she'd drop the book, phone, celery stalk or whatever was in her hand and go to him. They did not make love in the hammock. That had turned out to be a logistical nightmare. Instead, she'd taken him up to her room. They spent their nights in his bedroom, which left her bedroom fresh for afternoon naps. They made love with the windows open, the breeze aided along by the whirl of a ceiling fan.

It was heaven. Miami could keep its palm trees and sandy beaches; she'd found heaven in a rustic lakeside cabin in her home state of Texas. "I never want to leave," she let slip one day. They were cooking with the television on to the local news. Jackson was obsessed with the story of the mayor's missing pet cat, June Bug. The cat had been reported stolen even though there was little evidence. However, expert reporting had revealed that June Bug, a Persian, was worth over five thousand dollars and purchased with public funds. "Catgate" was an example of public corruption of the highest scale. Jackson's running commentary had Alexa doubled over in laughter. He was certain the cat was out to sabotage the mayor's political career. "How much do you want to bet she's hiding under the porch?"

Alexa chopped shapely cloves of garlic into shapeless chunks. "I wouldn't put it past her."

"June Bug is no fool," Jackson said. "She's going to expose the mayor. When she's done with him, he'll have no career left."

"I'd love to see it."

"Nixon had tapes. Mayor Callahan has a smart-ass cat."

Alexa set the knife down to wipe at the tears at the corner of her eyes. "Do you think he'd be in this mess if he'd bought a fancy dog?"

"Not a chance." Jackson was munching on the carrots he'd attempted to julienne. "Serves him right."

"I wish I could stay to watch the whole thing unfold." Alexa resumed chopping. "I wish I never had to leave."

Jackson didn't reply. Alexa glanced up to find him staring at her. He reached for the television remote and muted the sound. The house went silent around them. "How long do you plan on staying in Texas?"

Alexa set the knife down again. She sensed that this was serious. "The plan was to stay one month. I'm approaching the halfway mark."

"And then what?"

"I go back to Miami, with short trips back here when I'm needed on the Thurston case."

"And then what?"

She knew what he was asking. It wasn't as if she hadn't agonized over the question. How do you walk away from happiness? There was a time she would not have allowed anyone or anything to interfere with her career. She placed career over everything. Her perspective had since shifted. Firstly, her career was in shambles anyway. Fighting for justice in court while suffering injustice at her workplace made the victories ring hollow. Secondly, she'd witnessed firsthand the pitfalls of placing work over all else. Her grandfather was a cautionary tale. Augustus had managed the family ranch until the age of ninety. Most people looked forward to retirement—not her grandfather. He was praised for his grit. Alexa suspected that underneath his steely determination was a reservoir of fear. Augustus's life was his work, and he didn't know how to live without it.

In the end, he'd been forced to surrender the reins when his failing memory became an issue. That was just four short years ago. Her father ran things now, but he'd had to wait his turn for far longer than reasonable. Alexa knew she had a lot of Augustus in her. She had to be careful not to repeat his mistakes, clinging to work just to avoid life.

"What would you like me to do?" she asked.

He leaned against the kitchen island, arms folded across his chest. He wore a heather-gray T-shirt and a pair of soft sweatpants that she'd figured was his favorite. "I can't ask you to do anything I wouldn't consider myself."

Alexa tried to puzzle out his meaning. He would not consider moving to Florida and therefore thought it unfair to ask her to stay in Texas. Without realizing, she touched the golden queen pendant at her throat. It helped her feel centered. Texas was home. New York, Miami—those places had quickly lost their appeal. She put more effort in staying away from Royal rather than making those new cities home. Life in Royal wasn't perfect. It wasn't all country clubs and barbecues. However, her family was here, her legacy was here and now it seemed the man she loved was rooted here, too.

"We have some things to sort out," she said. "I don't have any answers just now. Will you give me time?"

"I'm not trying to rush you into anything," he said. "I just want you to know that I'm an option."

Alexa moved away from the cutting board and took Jackson's face between her hands. "May I kiss you?"

His eyes went soft. "Do you have to ask?"

"I smell like garlic."

"Your fingers may smell like garlic." He took her hands to his lips and pressed a kiss on her fingertips. "*You* smell like lavender, always."

"And you feel warm and familiar to me. I've never been more comfortable, more myself, with anyone."

He kissed her open palm, slid his lips down to the sensitive side of her wrist, all the while his gaze never left her face.

Alexa knew that look. "We're never going to cook this dish, are we?"

"It's too hot to cook. We can toss the veggies into the composter."

She glanced away at her mashed-up garlic. "That's probably where they belong."

It was too hot to go upstairs. Instead, they grabbed a bottle of rosé, a blanket, a bag of chips and a jar of spinach dip and headed outside.

Come Sunday morning, they locked up the house and were gone.

Sixteen

Jackson swung by a coffee shop on his way to the downtown headquarters of Strom Management. He kept a list of his employees' preferences in his phone. His selection of specialty coffees and breakfast pastries would not disappoint. He had a lot to make up for—coffee might not cut it. After all, he'd disappeared for a week with little-to-no notice, leaving his office manager in charge of daily operations and his associates up to their own devices.

They welcomed him back with catcalls and derision—it was that kind of office.

"Settle down, kids. I bought treats."

The office suite occupied the third floor of an old factory building. There were a few conference rooms, a file room and a break room, but the otherwise open–floor plan meant Jackson could not get to his office without running the obstacle course of his employees' workstations. He went from desk to desk and dropped off a "please forgive me for abandoning you" gift set.

First up: Jo-Ann Lindsey, account specialist.

"Here you go, Jo. A medium latte made with oat milk and two pumps of vanilla."

"You never answered my emails, but hey, thanks, boss."

"Sorry about that. Will a chocolate éclair make up for it?"

"Hand it over."

Next: Matthew Johnson, tech guy.

Jackson delivered a large black coffee. No sugar, no cream. "Here you go, buddy."

"Tell me you watched the game. Tell me that, at least."

"Didn't. Sorry."

"And you think coffee is going to make up for that?"

"No…but coffee *and* a cinnamon roll might do it."

Matt snatched the roll. "This isn't over."

"I didn't think so."

Two down, two to go. Next: Cecily Barns, social media coordinator.

She turned down his croissant and macchiato offering. "I'm on a low-carb diet and off dairy for now."

"Sorry to hear it."

"What can I say? A lot can change in one week."

"Apparently."

His last stop was the office of his office manager, Karla Andrews. She waved him in from behind her cluttered desk. "I'll take Cecily's croissant, too."

"Here you go." Jackson handed over her iced latte and blueberry muffin, plus the butter croissant. "Good to see some things haven't changed."

"I'm actually glad when you're gone. Much quieter."

"Ouch. Can't you pretend you've missed me?"

"I'll do you one better," Karla said, leaning back in her leather chair. "I hear one of Royal's oldest companies is looking for a PR firm to reshape their image."

"Go on."

Rising from receptionist to office manager, Karla had been with Jackson since day one. She kept the business running like clockwork and never missed an opportunity to help grow the client list. Clever, resourceful and barely twenty-five, she had a double life. After she left the office, she worked at a tattoo parlor down the street.

Karla had his full attention until his phone chimed with a text message.

Alexandra the First: News update: June Bug was found three towns over in an abandoned barn.

Jackson: Good morning to you, too, darling. How was your night?

Alexandra the First: Don't act like you're not obsessed with this story.

Jackson: Weirdly enough, I am. How the hell did she end up so far away?

Alexandra the First: Local authorities suspect foul play. The mayor vows to track the culprits.

Jackson: Wanna bet he stashed that cat. She knows too much.

Alexandra the First: For sure.

Jackson: God I miss you. No one here will appreciate the complexity of Catgate.

Alexandra the First: I'm here for you. All you have to do is call. Now let's get to sexting.

She sent him a selfie. She wore nothing but black Spandex and running shoes. Her hair was gathered in a braided ponytail. Her rich cognac skin was covered in a soft sheen of sweat. Jackson noticed the golden queen pendent gleaming at her throat. She was radiant and sexy. Jackson felt a knot in his throat. He'd been good for her. He hadn't just shown her a good time—he'd taken care of her, nursed and loved her back to her true self. Still, he hadn't dared ask for the thing he wanted most of all. He wanted her to stay—ditch

Miami and come back home, come back to him. Logically, he was in no position to make such demands after just a few short days, even if those days had stretched out to eternity. Now he wasn't so sure holding back had been the best strategy. She should know how he felt and decide accordingly.

Jackson: I want to do bad things to you.

Alexandra the First: Hmm... Some other time? Gotta run!

Jackson groaned with frustration as he typed. He'd dropped her off at her family's ranch early yesterday afternoon. He was eager to see her again. Meet me later. After work drinks?

Alexandra the First: So long as I get to pick the spot.

He would meet her anywhere. Not a problem, darling.

Jackson sat grinning at his phone like a teenage fool. Karla cleared her throat. Jackson looked up at her, blinking. He'd forgotten where he was. He had not yet made it to his office. "Karla, have you heard about Catgate?"

"No." She sipped her latte. "Should I have?"

"Look into it. Fascinating stuff."

"Why don't you go ahead and take another week? Your head is not in the game."

He got up and backed out the door. "Don't tempt me. I've got one foot out the door as it is."

Of all the places in Royal, Alexa chose North Cove Park, a scenic nature preserve. A trail that led to a cliff with views of a dome of pink granite in the distance. At sunset, the massive rock glistened and revealed all its colors. In other words, she'd chosen Royal's official make-out point.

Jackson put his Mustang in Park. Good thing it was a convertible, the only appropriate car for an excursion deep into North Cove.

"Really, Alexa?" he said. "Of all the places we could have gone, you chose here."

"I've never been. This is special for me."

"You've *never* been to North Cove?" How was that possible? The camping grounds were a popular school field trip destination. "I'm pretty sure we all came up here in the seventh grade, the eighth, ninth, tenth—"

She gripped his hand and squeezed. "You don't get it. I've never been up here in a car with a guy on a date."

"You've *never* been—"

"No! Get it now?"

"Got it." Jackson released his seat belt, turned and looked her dead in the eye. "You just want to live out all your teenage fantasies with me."

"You started it!" She mirrored his gesture, releasing her seat belt with a snap and twisting in her seat to face him. "Why did you have to take me to the prom?"

"That was a stroke of genius, wasn't it?"

"Yep!"

She looked stylish yet relaxed in a body-skimming halter dress and sandals. Her hair was in the same braided ponytail as earlier. She wore no jewelry except for his queen pendant. As always, he couldn't get over how beautiful she was.

"What else didn't you get around to doing?" he asked. "Let's make a list."

"Really?"

"I'm at your service."

"Let's see… There was prom, dates that ended at North Cove and road trips senior year. We've done all of that. That takes care of it, really."

"What sort of dates? Bowling?"

"Don't even think about it. I'm glad I dodged that."

"How about a movie? We usually came up here on big opening nights. You haven't lived until you've made out in the back row of Royal Adventure Cinemas until your lips are chapped to the score of a blockbuster."

Alexa clapped. "Yes to all of that. I'm down!"

"Let's do the movie this Friday night. I'll pick you up at eight."

"It's a date," she said. "Now, we're going to fool around in your car. Maybe you can give me a hickey."

"Sure. But not a word of this to anyone! I've got a reputation to uphold."

"Not one word."

Jackson winked and reached in the back seat of the car for a cooler. A few ice packs kept everything inside nice and chilled.

"What's that?"

He opened the cooler and showed her the contents: a bottle of champagne and fresh fruit. Alexa let out a soundless cry.

"This is not standard North Cove fare," he said. "Back then, we smuggled beer from home and drank it warm. But there's only so much I'm willing to do to fulfill your fantasies."

"Jackson Strom," she said, "will you go steady with me?"

"Steady? How old are we? You're throwing it back to the 1950s."

"Okay. How about this?" She cleared her throat and started again. "So, hey. Wanna be my BF?"

They were only kidding around, but Jackson was suddenly overcome. Yes, he wanted to be her boyfriend. It was all he'd ever wanted since the ripe age of fifteen.

"Well?" she said. "Don't leave me hanging."

"I think we're ready to take it to the next level."

Her smile widened, more dazzling than pink granite at dusk. "Yeah."

"For sure. I feel this amazing connection between us," he continued, lifting phrases straight from his high school playbook. "You know what I mean?"

"I do."

"We vibe."

"Totally."

"I'd like to see where this is going."

"I'd like that, too."

"So we're on for a movie on Friday?"

"I'll have to ask my dad, but sure."

"Cool. But we're going to the new dine-in theater." Jackson ripped the foil off the bottle of champagne. "You couldn't pay me to go back to Royal Adventure Cinemas. I have standards now."

"I don't care where we go."

He popped the cork, poured two glasses and proposed a toast. "We're officially high school sweethearts."

"Awesome," Alexa said. "To us!"

He set his glass in the cup holder. "Now, let's make out."

Seventeen

Two days later, Alexa met with private investigator Jonas Shaw. She would rather be sipping champagne with Jackson at sunset, but duty called. Over the past few weeks, Shaw had been following a trail of old money. He'd combed through bank records, notes and ledgers in search for any scrap of information. After weeks of silence, he'd finally reached out. It appeared that he'd found something major. Alexa agreed to meet him at Royal Diner.

Shaw fit his long, wiry frame into the red booth and ordered a black coffee. When that was taken care of, he delivered the unsettling news in his blunt way. "Augustus Lattimore had the properties surveyed for oil."

Alexa was confused. "*Properties*. Plural?"

"Both your family ranch and the Grandin property."

"When?"

"About a year before he signed the oil rights over to Cynthia."

"But why?"

"It's worth knowing if your land is sitting on oil."

"Maybe, but what interest is it of his if the Grandin ranch has oil or not?"

"It's possible the Grandins were looking to sell or strike a deal."

"It's not possible." Alexa stirred sugar in her coffee. "The Grandins would never sell or strike any kind of deal. Neither would my grandfather, for that matter."

Jonas ran his long, thin fingers through his salt-and-pepper hair. "The paper trail tells a different story. Try filling in the blanks. Sit your grandfather down and ask—"

"That's a waste of time," Alexa interrupted. "His memory is slipping."

Shaw nodded gravely. "My mother is the same. Still, she has her moments. Flashes of lucidity. It's like a light bulb will go off in her head. Keep trying."

"Sure."

If a light bulb went off in Augustus's head, he'd flip the switch and turn it off. When it came to this matter, it appeared he preferred to leave things in the dark. She wasn't comfortable discussing this with a stranger or even Layla. Wouldn't Layla suspect the worst if it were proved Augustus was withholding information? Maybe she could confide in Jackson?

Since they got back from the lake, they'd been spending all their free time together. Jackson was fun and easy to talk to. She couldn't imagine being away from him for too long or resuming her life as before. Late last night, she'd settled on a working solution: the Dallas office. Jackson's business wasn't portable. His contacts and network were local. He couldn't afford to uproot and start over elsewhere. She, on the other hand, was eligible for admission to the Texas Bar by reciprocity and employed by a firm with offices nationwide, including a location in Dallas. They'd be carrying on long distance, but the distance would be manageable. There was no reason to stay in Miami. Things hadn't worked out as hoped. Rather than remain there and waste energy trying to sort things out or put out fires, she would walk away.

"Having your property surveyed for oil is standard practice," Jonas said. "But it's a bit odd to lump in your neighbor's property while you're at it. It tells me that Lattimore and Grandin were working together, plain and simple. Probably went in for a two-for-one type deal with the surveyor.

Augustus and Victor Senior were best friends, so maybe
that explains it?"

"I'd like to see the surveyor's report."

"So would I, but it can't be found. That's why it has taken
me so long to get in touch with updates. I've been searching."

Alexa pushed away her coffee cup, scraping the linoleum
tabletop. Archeologists had better luck unearthing the secrets
of ancient tombs than they'd had with this case.

"Now, settle down," Jonas said. "I have a lead."

"You do? Let's hear it."

"Does the name Sylvia Stewart ring any bells?"

The name was familiar. For years, she and Caitlyn had
been tasked with helping their mother assemble gift baskets
for the office employees. Sylvia Stewart was top of the list.
Every year, her mother made sure to stuff her basket with
her favorite Belgian chocolates.

"She worked with my grandfather."

"Correct. She was his secretary at the time and handled
your grandfather's paperwork and the like. If anyone can
shine a light on this, it would be her."

Alexa brightened. "That sounds promising."

"Not so fast," Jonas said. "She's retired now and an ac-
tive world traveler. It's taking a while to track her down."

"Great."

She reached for her cup. It was back to waiting, then.
What was she supposed to do in the meantime? Just sit
around? Well, maybe not… This might be the perfect time
for a quick trip to Miami. She could speak with HR and put
in a formal request for a transfer.

"I know we're in the weeds now, but things will turn
around," Jonas said. "They always do."

Shaw insisted on paying for the coffees. Alexa watched
him leave the diner and walk briskly across the street. Dusk
was settling. All at once, the streetlights flashed on. Alexa's

coffee had gone cold, and still she lingered at the table. She thought it best to update her siblings and Layla on the progress of the case right away and schedule a formal meeting with the Lattimores and the Grandins in the morning. As usual, her father would get her mother up to speed, or not. It wasn't clear her mother wanted to be in the loop.

She slipped her phone out of her purse and tapped on the group chat for her siblings. It had last been updated with a series of hilarious memes and cat videos. Her next contribution to the chat was not so upbeat. She hated to be a downer, but that was her assigned role in her family.

Alexa's phone to Lattimore4thewin: Just a quick update, guys. It seems granddad had the ranch and the Grandins' lots surveyed prior to assigning away the oil/mineral rights.

After a pause, the responses poured in:

Caitlyn: Why would he do that? I'm so confused.

Jayden: That man was up to something. I just know it.

Jonathan: He probably had his reasons. Have you tried asking him?

Alexa: Uh…no, actually. Wonder why I hadn't thought of that?

Caitlyn: That's sarcasm. BTW.

Jayden: I know it when I hear it.

Caitlyn: Alexa is doing all she can.

Alexa: I've done everything except lock him in a room and cuff him to a table.

Caitlyn: No need to go there.

Jayden: Why not? I'm willing to try.

Jonathan: I'm on a call with a supplier. Will catch up with y'all later. Good work, Alexa. Thanks for keeping us informed.

Caitlyn: Dev says hi...and good night.

Jayden: Hold up! Are we seriously not going to discuss Alexa's hickey?!

Alexa flushed. She slipped the phone back in her purse and stood to leave. All the while, the hated device buzzed and buzzed.

Alexa returned home and sought out her grandfather. After an early dinner, her grandmother told her he had retreated to his study. She found him in his worn leather recliner, a glass of liquor in hand. He was listening to a recording of an old bluegrass concert. Augustus had worked hard his whole life and hadn't devoted much time to recreation. Alexa wondered if this was his way of catching up.

He greeted her as if he hadn't seen her in days. They'd gone on their usual walk just this morning. "Come in, Alexa. It's good to see you."

She moved a pile of books off an ottoman and sat down. "Good to see you, too."

"What brings you around?"

"I had a conversation with Jonas Shaw."

"Who's that?"

Alexa took a breath before responding. Her words came

out in a dry monotone. "The private investigator we hired to look into Heath Thurston's claim to the oil under our land."

"Ah. Right."

"He has evidence that you had our land *and* the Grandins' ranch surveyed for oil and other minerals."

Her grandfather straightened up in his recliner. "I'm sure I did no such thing."

Alexa suppressed the urge to cross-examine her grandfather. *Sir, under penalty of perjury, is it your testimony that you did not have the land surveyed?*

"Are you sure? He has receipts."

"I don't care what he has!" he snapped.

Alexa caught a glimpse of the powerful man that he once was. But she had a lot of Augustus in her, and she didn't cower easily. She reached for the sound system's remote control and cut the volume. "Nothing happened on this ranch without your knowledge and approval. Now answer the question. Did you or did you not have the properties surveyed?"

Augustus averted his eyes. "I don't know. I'm not sure, dammit!"

"Grandpa, this isn't a minor thing."

There was one more thing that bothered Alexa. Her grandfather was a shrewd businessman. She didn't believe for one minute that he'd sit on a resource that could potentially make him millions. Neither would the late Victor Grandin. Everyone would have her believe that they went to the trouble to have the properties surveyed just for kicks? It didn't make sense.

"Ask Victor. He'll remember," he said.

Alexa softened. Maybe that was enough cross-examination for tonight. Augustus didn't remember Victor was dead. Or maybe he knew Victor was dead and couldn't answer? Argh! She could start again in the morning. She pressed the mute button on the remote, and music poured out of the speakers embedded in the walls. "What are you drinking?"

"Nothing but the finest whiskey from Tennessee."

She got up and went to the liquor cabinet. There was ice in a bucket and a crystal decanter filled with amber liquid. She poured herself a nightcap.

Eighteen

Jackson had no idea which movie they'd just sat through. It was a foreign film with subtitles, but that wasn't the issue. The bluesy score had set the right mood. He'd kept Alexa close to him with a hand tucked under her soft blouse. They kissed straight through the end credits—every kiss deeper, messier—until the theater lights cut on.

Squinting, she pulled away from him and smoothed her clothes. "How do I look?"

"Delicious."

"Come on," she said. "Let's get out of here."

They left the theater and found his car in the garage. Jackson leaned against the hood, and she stepped into the space between his legs. They hadn't discussed how the night would end. Since their return to town, she'd spent her nights at home. They'd talked on the phone for hours as if they really were back in high school. It was fun and all, but he didn't want to go back to that tonight.

"Want to get a coffee?" he asked.

She rubbed her smooth cheek against his stubble. He loved it when she did that. "I don't know. It depends."

"On what?"

"On whether you have an espresso machine at your place."

Jackson laughed. They were always on the same page. "As a matter of fact, I've got a top-of-the-line espresso machine."

"Is that right?" She dragged a finger down his jaw. "Does it froth milk?"

"I can't say for sure. But it has all the bells and whistles."

She made a face. "You don't know how to use it?"

"I've never touched the thing," he confessed. "There's a coffee shop just steps away from my building, and they get all my money. I believe in supporting small businesses."

Alexa's mouth twitched as she fought back a smile. "Small businesses are the backbone of our economy."

"That's what I always say."

She shrugged. "I don't need coffee, just an excuse to see your place."

"You don't need an excuse, either. I've been dropping hints all week."

"It's been an odd week," she said. "I had a tough meeting with the PI on our case, followed by an even tougher meeting with the two families. I suspect my grandfather is withholding information, but I don't know if it's on purpose or if he can't access the information because of the dementia." She waved her hands before her face as if to wipe away her last statements from an imaginary whiteboard. "Never mind all that. I'm killing the mood."

Jackson cupped her face and drew circles on her cheeks with his thumbs. "I don't want a mood. I only want what's real."

She rested her head on his chest. "This feels real to me."

He wrapped her in his arms. "Let me tell you about my week."

"Okay."

"When I wasn't busy responding to a week's worth of emails, I've been thinking about making love to you in my bed. It's killing me."

Alexa nodded. "Same here."

"Really? My bed, not yours?"

"Mine still has the same floral bedspread my grand-mother gave me when I was fifteen. It's not the vibe."

"My bed it is! Let's go."

He moved to hold the passenger door open for her. Just before slipping in, she paused to kiss him. "We've exhausted my list of unfulfilled teen fantasies."

"Already?" he said. "Don't cut it short on my account. I'm down for it."

"I didn't have much of an imagination back then," she said. "Don't look so disappointed. Now we can move on to other things."

"What things?"

"This whole experiment has been one-sided, don't you think? I figure we could make some of your wishes come true."

He was down for that, too. So much so, he was glad the open passenger door was wedged between them. He kissed her and whispered into her mouth. "Alexa, get in the car."

He switched on the light in his foyer. Alexa immediately cut it off. There was enough moonlight pouring in from the wall of windows in his living room to light the way. Moon-light touched every reflective surface, making the every-day appliances sparkle. He'd lived in this condo for three years, and it had never taken on this magical, dreamy qual-ity. Alexa made everything special. She'd made an ordinary stay at the lake cabin into something grand, a memory that would never fade in his mind. He had a feeling that tonight would mark him as well, and he was ready for it.

She dropped her purse onto the console table. "You can give me the grand tour in the morning."

"Before or after a coffee run?"

"We'll work out the logistics later." She kicked off her heels and ventured into his space and reached the spiral stairs that lead to the loft. "Up here, I'm guessing?"

She'd guessed wrong. The upper level was command central. It housed his home office and the huge TV reserved exclusively for sports. It was a chaotic mess. His bedroom was on the main floor, hidden from view by pocket doors. Jackson went over and slid the doors open. She approached, but he stepped in her way.

"This is my fantasy," he said. "I should run things."

"You know… I'm beginning to think your ultimate fantasy is beating me at chess."

Jackson did not disagree. "That's high on the list, but we can leave it for tomorrow," he said. "Tonight, I want you to do exactly what you're told."

Her eyes raked over his face. He could tell she was teetering between caution and curiosity. "I don't know about that."

"I suggest you make up your mind."

Surrendering control was not something that she was predisposed to do, but Jackson had a suspicion she was aching to do it. The weight of the world was on her shoulders. Surrendering was the easiest way to unburden herself.

"How do I know you're not going to do something crazy?" she asked. "Like cuff me to a bedpost?"

Actually, that sounded kind of fun. "Is that really so crazy?"

"Okay. Bad example."

"You won't know either way. That's part of the thrill."

"For you, maybe."

He leaned against the doorframe. "For you, too. I promise."

"All right. What do you want me to do?"

"Undress."

She glared at him. "Out here?"

"Why not?" It wasn't as if they were out in the lobby.

Alexa squared her shoulders and raised her chin. He geared himself up for some major pushback. Instead, their standoff lasted all of two seconds. She reached for the zipper of her jeans, yanked it down and stepped out of them. Her willingness to play along was ushering in a new era. They were no longer locked in an endless power struggle. They'd moved past all that. Even so, he read a silent promise in her eyes to make him pay for everything she allowed him to get away with tonight. That was his Alexa.

He watched as she stripped away her silky blouse and underthings. When she stood before him, naked, Jackson had to ball his hands into fists to keep from touching her.

He stepped aside to let her through.

Alexa's breath caught when she took in his wide custom bed. The headboard was upholstered in Belgian linen. He couldn't tie her to it if he wanted to.

"It's beautiful."

Jackson unbuttoned his shirt. "Thank you."

"So…" She turned to him. "What do you want from me?"

Only Alexa could make that question sound like a command.

Jackson tossed his clothes, and they landed in the heap just outside his door. He slid it shut. "Now you tell me what you want."

She arched a brow. "I'm not sure that's how this game is played."

"Do you want me to lick you, touch you, bite you…? Tell me. What do you want?"

Alexa's brown eyes glowed hot. She caught two fingertips between her teeth and just stared at him.

"Don't tell me you're at a loss for words."

She could not, under any circumstances, back down from a challenge. He knew that about her.

"I want your mouth all over me."

"All over? Or a more focused exploration?"

"Jackson! Stop making me wait."

"Get in bed."

With a sigh of relief, she fell onto her back with her arms

outstretched over her head. She was magnificent. Jackson could not hold back. He explored her with his mouth, his hands, sucked and licked her until her back arched with pleasure. A jagged sigh escaped her. "God! I've missed this."

It had only been a few days, but those days were too long. He had missed this, too. It had been all he could do to keep from driving to her house in the middle of the night.

There were condoms in each drawer of the bedside tables. He grabbed one and she helped him with it. Then he slipped a hand between her legs to bring her right back to the brink of pleasure. Alexa twisted and moaned and whispered, "I don't want this to end."

Those words swirled in his mind as he made love to her. He didn't want this to end, either. If they were on the same page on this as well, there was hope for them yet.

Later, when they collapsed in each other's arms, happiness grew wild inside of him. If he had Alexa, he had everything.

Her breathing steadied and Jackson was sure that she'd fallen asleep. He nestled closer, burying his nose in the nape of her neck. Alexa spoke up in the dark.

"Jackson?"

"Yes, babe?"

"I'm leaving for Miami soon."

Nineteen

Arguably, Alexa's timing was awful. Jackson pulled away from her and rolled onto his back. She immediately suffered withdrawal and cuddled closer to him, looped a leg over his to keep him at her side. "Don't worry," she said. "It's not for long. I'll be back in a few days."

"Why do you have to go at all? You just got here."

"I have some things I'd like to take care of."

"Like what?"

Alexa eased away from him. She sat up and drew her knees to her chest. This was the moment to come clean. As in chess, she tried to envision how this would play out. Step one: tell Jackson that she'd been sexually harassed at work. Step two: urge him to trust her to take care of the matter herself. Step three: request that he keep the whole sordid affair a secret. In three moves, she could ruin their night.

She started rambling. "You know how it is. Demanding clients need reassuring. The firm represents some major players. Owen Black & Co., Southbound Airlines, ETT, Blue Moon Beer—"

"ETT?"

"Evergreen Tractors and Tailors."

"We've done work for them. Southbound, too."

"What a small world!"

"Those companies are incorporated in Texas."

"That's right. And so are you."

She leaned over and kissed the tip of his nose, hoping

they could put the awkwardness behind them. He slipped a hand under the sheets. His fingers lingered on her waist, but his hold on her was firm.

"Basically, what you're saying is that you could handle the bulk of your work from Texas."

There was no putting anything past Jackson. She was heading back to Florida to officially request a transfer. It was settled in her mind. It wasn't as easy as packing up her things. The request might take months to get approved. She would have to tie a lot of loose ends with her Florida-based clients. She was willing to go through the trouble. It was worth it. Jackson was worth it. However, she did not want to get his hopes up. She would share the good news with him once the transfer was approved and she had an office set up in the Dallas location.

"Who knows?" she said evasively. "Maybe someday, I will."

Jackson's expression clouded. "Are you sure you have to go back?"

"Yes, I'm sure! We don't all have the luxury of being our own bosses. Some of us have to report back to the office from time to time. It's not unusual."

"Are you sure you're not just putting distance between us for the sake of putting distance between us?"

Alexa's heart fell. That was the last thing she wanted. Being with him felt so natural, and yet it was never boring. Each day brought a new thrill. No one got her like he did. No one had ever tried. She was not going to jeopardize this.

Instead of saying any of this, she made a joke. "What if I promised to bring you back key lime pie?"

Jackson closed his eyes. Her chest tightened in response. All her emotions were compressed inside her. Alexa wanted to reassure him, but she couldn't open up without her secrets popping out.

She stretched out over him, propped her chin on his

chest. Her nose brushed against his trim beard. "Does it feel like I want to put distance between us?" He looked at her through thick lashes. His mouth was pressed into a hard line. She reached up and traced a finger along its curve. "Well, does it?"

"Sometimes I can't read you."

This was when most people would say, "I'm an open book." But she wasn't. She was an ancient text locked in a display case. She was exhausting. It was time she clean up her messes before he gave up on her.

Alexa sought out her brother Jonathan when she returned home late the next morning. He was at the barn. She found him by the back gate, overseeing the delivery of organic fertilizer. "There you are! I looked all over for you."

He straightened up. With the black Stetson, he was even taller and more imposing than usual. No wonder women were intimidated by him. He whipped off his gloves and approached her with long, confident strides. "Is anything wrong?"

"Nothing is wrong," she said. "I need a favor. Could you give me a ride to the airport on Monday?"

Earlier that morning, while Jackson was on a coffee run, Alexa purchased the airline ticket online. She had no intention of dwelling in Miami. After meeting with the head of HR and checking in with her supervising attorney, she would head out for a shopping spree. Apart from a few sundresses, her wardrobe was pretty basic and utilitarian. If she and Jackson were going to carry on as they were, she needed fun and flirty outfits and tons of lingerie.

"You're leaving? Where are you off to?"

"Back to Miami for a couple of days. I have some business to take care of. Work stuff. You won't even notice I'm gone. Jonas Shaw is still coming up empty, so I have a few free days before I'm needed back here."

"Bet you Jackson will notice."

"Jackson will be fine. He's a strong man."

"That might be true, but he is weak in the knees for you."

Alexa peered up at him, shielding her eyes from the sun with a hand. "You're a love guru now? Let's talk about you and Natalie Hastings."

"There's nothing to talk about."

"You sure about that? Have you reached out to her?"

"No need."

No need? Alexa couldn't believe her oldest brother—the good one, the serious one, the favorite by all regards—was acting like this. At the very least, he should call the woman and clear the air. It was the gentlemanly thing to do. She was probably mortified. Even their recalcitrant private investigator had had the grace to look her in the eye and deliver crappy news in person and over coffee.

"Don't leave her twisting in the wind," Alexa scolded. "You're better than that. Ask her out for a drink. Even if it doesn't amount to anything, you'll give her a chance to laugh it off."

Jonathan rolled his shoulders back, a sure sign that he had reached peak frustration. "It won't amount to anything, so why bother?"

"Who's to say?"

"I say! I'm not interested in anything."

"Do you hear yourself? Sounds to me you're not interested in living your life. You're too young, too smart and too good-looking to live like this!"

She was hollering now. The ranch hands had definitely heard her. They tossed curious glances their way. Alexa took her brother by the arm and marched him up the brick path back to the main residence. She decided that he needed a break.

Jonathan came along, walking stiffly beside her, grumbling all the way. "I expect this kind of talk from Caitlyn, not you."

"Caitlyn was brave enough to fight for her happiness. There's a lot we can learn from her."

Jonathan stopped dead in his tracks. "What has Jackson done to you?"

"Never mind Jackson. This is about you."

"Well, I'm fine."

"No, you're not. You're dodging and deflecting." Alexa didn't stop there. "You're burying yourself in work to avoid life. You're still hurting and, possibly, still hung up on the past."

Jonathan had married young. He'd barely been out of college, still in his early twenties, and was not yet ready for marriage. Alexa hadn't approved of that blessed union. She wore a scowl in every single wedding photo. So much so, she'd been edited out of the wedding video. The marriage failed, which came as no surprise to her. Her former sister-in-law hadn't been ready for marriage, either. Anne was pretty but also needy, clingy and sort of whiny. Alexa had not thought her a good match for her Jonathan. It had been difficult watching her older brother, her idol, use all his energy to placate his young wife. She privately rejoiced when their divorce was finalized. Jonathan did not. He took it hard. He'd failed at something meaningful and at such a young age. It had marked him. Ever since, he'd buried himself in work. Someday he would take over the ranch. He was the heir apparent. That didn't mean he had to devote himself to this land like Augustus had.

Jonathan removed his hat and looked up to the sky. He was probably praying for restraint. She poked him in the ribs. "Did you know Natalie had a crush on you all this time?"

"Crush? Are we back in high school?"

Point taken. Not everyone wanted to throw it back to freshman year like she and Jackson had. Having said that,

Jonathan was deflecting once again. "Very well. I'll rephrase that." Alexa cleared her throat. "Mr. Lattimore, at the time of the public disclosure of Ms. Hastings's feelings toward you, were you or were you not aware of said feelings?"

"What was that, Counselor? Could you repeat the question?"

"Just answer me!"

Jonathan was laughing. Alexa had succeeded at something. She'd made her oh-so-serious brother laugh. His answer, though, made her sad.

"Natalie doesn't have a crush on me. She doesn't know me."

"You live in the same small town. Of course she knows you."

"She only thinks she does."

"Hmm… How can I say this without hurting your feelings?" She looped her arm through his and continued along the path. "You're being a patronizing ass."

"Alexa, I know what I'm talking about."

"Your hidden depths are pretty shallow, Jonathan. She took a look at you and sized you up. It probably took her all of five minutes."

They passed the bench where she and her grandfather sat for their morning chats, passed her mother's rose garden and newly installed terrazzo birdbath, and climbed the steps to the back porch. From there, they had a view of the neighboring ranch. The roof of the Grandin home peeked out from beyond a tuft of oak trees. She anguished over all that they stood to lose. Alexa did not know how much she loved her home until that moment. Suddenly, even Dallas seemed too far, too distant a place. The truth sparked in her heart. She'd been gone too long. She wanted to come home.

Alexa turned away from her brother. She did not want him to see her in her emotional state. As it turned out, Jonathan couldn't get away from her fast enough. He yanked open the screen door. "I'll take you to the airport. Send me your flight info."

"Sure. Meanwhile, you'll think about what I said?"

His grip tightened on the doorknob. "I'm not going to call her, Alexa."

Alexa raised her hands in surrender. Was there anything more stubborn than a Lattimore? Jonathan was an adult, and she couldn't force him to do anything he didn't want to do.

"I've known about Natalie's *crush* for a while now," he continued. "We've crossed paths a few times, and there's always been sparks."

Sparks? What a bombshell revelation this was! For once in her life, she wished she could conference in her siblings. She had to get Jonathan on the record.

"Sparks fade sooner or later."

"Not always!"

"In my case, they do."

"You don't know that."

"I know me."

"So do I. And I think you're talking crazy. Any woman would be lucky to have you." He gave her a pointed look. "Well, any woman except the one you married. She was an enigma inside a riddle, and honestly, I'll never understand her."

"I'll never understand women, period."

"One bad marriage doesn't disqualify you from the Love Olympics. You've got to get back up on the balance beam and try again. The sooner you move on from the past, the better."

"I *have* moved on!" Jonathan cried out. "Life is good now. *I'm* good. And I'm not going down that path again. The sooner you all get that, the better."

Alexa remained impassive in the face of her brother's outburst. She'd drop it for now. Later, she'd come at it from another angle. But she couldn't let him have the last word. "Give love a second chance, Jonathan."

Her brother shut the door and leaned against it with folded arms. "Give love a second chance?"

"It's a cheesy line, I know." She'd officially joined the ranks of people who said sappy things in the name of love. Heaven help her. "Just open your heart and give love a second chance, okay? I promise you won't regret it."

"Oh yeah?" He narrowed his eyes, studying her. "How can you be so sure?"

"I'm not sure of anything. It may not work out. That doesn't mean you don't try."

Jonathan let out a low whistle. "Jackson must have done a number on you for you to be talking this way."

"Oh, shut up!" Alexa pushed past him, yanked open the screen door and entered the house. Jonathan's bighearted laughter bounced off the walls and followed her inside.

Miami welcomed Alexa home with a torrential downpour. She was lucky her plane was able to land. Her neighborhood was flooded. The taxi driver refused to drop her off at her building, and she ruined a pair of three-hundred-dollar shoes trekking one block in ankle-deep water. She caught a glimpse of herself in the mirrored elevator and recoiled. She looked like a drenched poodle. She felt wretched. The dark clouds that blocked the sun made her feel unwanted. And for whatever reason, she hated everything about her home. The rented condo had a hotel vibe, which she'd loved up until a day ago. Jackson's bedroom had been a heavenly retreat. He'd hired a designer to achieve that dreamy look. Meanwhile, Alexa had moved into her fully furnished space over a year ago and had yet to add a houseplant.

Alexa peeled off her destroyed designer ballerina flats and left them in the foyer with her travel bag. In the living room, she fell back on the stiff leather sofa and took in the rain-blurred views framed by the wall of windows. Jackson had timidly offered to travel with her. She had declined, mostly because she felt bad that he'd lost so much time at work because of her. He shouldn't have to disrupt his entire life. That was the reason why she'd gotten her brother to take her to the airport. Besides, she could handle this on her own. Still, she missed him. She would have liked to get his take on her impersonal space. The couch would be so much more inviting with him stretched out on it.

Their last conversation came back to her. He'd texted her late last night. Alexa was pouring a bath when she'd heard her phone chime with the message. Because of the nature of her work, her phone was always within arm's reach. He'd sent her a selfie. He was at the office, catching up on work, and was scruffier than usual. She shivered at the memory of those soft hairs scratching the skin between her breasts. And then there was the trail his lips forged when he had dragged them from her knee to the tip of her toes.

A message followed. Admit you'll miss me.

She immediately typed a reply. I miss you right now.

He called her. The phone rang in her hand, and she answered without a second's hesitation. "Hey, you."

"Hey," he said. "If I were insecure—"

"Which you're not, obviously."

"Not at all."

His voice was gruff with fatigue, but how she loved it! He was preparing for a meeting with a big client that he'd neglected, partly because she'd taken up so much of his time. "Go on. I didn't mean to interrupt."

"If I were insecure, I'd think you were skipping town when things were getting good between us."

"Hmm… That would make me a coward."

"Or human."

Alexa sat on the edge of the claw-foot tub. She turned off the faucet and cut the water so she could hear him better. Her thoughts bubbled up in the silence that followed. "This is good, this thing between us. Isn't it?"

"Honestly?"

"Yes."

"You're the lover I've been waiting for."

She closed her eyes. More than anything, she wanted to reassure him. It might not seem like it, but she was running toward him, not away. There were too many strings tying her to Miami. She had to snip them loose.

"Alexa, are you still there?"

"When I come back, we'll discuss the future. We have more options than you know."

When Jackson didn't respond right away, Alexa bent forward and pressed her head against the cool, wet subway tile. She hadn't meant to come across as a college recruiter. Could this really be what he'd been waiting for? A woman so locked up in herself, she broke down at every turn?

"Is that so?" he said, finally. "Enlighten me. What are these options?"

"You'll know more when I get back," she said. "You're going to have to trust me on this. Can you do that?"

"I trust you, darling."

A lump formed in her throat. Alexa couldn't believe it. At long last, she was pulling first in a race that actually mattered to her.

"Good night," he said. "And don't forget my key lime pie."

The next morning, Alexa was staring at the same water-stained view, only this time from a slightly different angle and from much higher up. She lived three blocks away from her office building, which gave her a short commute—a rare luxury in Miami. Arthur Garrett had agreed to a meeting. She was ushered into the HR director's office without delay but was kept waiting a good quarter hour. First, he took a call; then another, saying only, "I see," and "I understand," while staring blankly at an open file on his desk.

Alexa studied her cuticles and tapped her foot. She wanted to jump out the window.

When he finally ended the call, he was pink around the ears and looked as if he had a lot to say. Alexa didn't want to hear any of it—not the hollow apology for having kept her waiting or the phony interest in her welfare. With her back ramrod straight, she raised her hand the way she did in school when she demanded a professor's attention. "I'm here to formally request a transfer to our Dallas office. Any time is fine, but the sooner the better. I want to be closer to my family."

Arthur leaned back in his massive leather chair. The wall behind him was entirely glass. He looked as if he were tipping into the bay. "Ms. Lattimore, I regret to say we cannot accept your request."

Alexa's hand dropped onto her lap. "I beg your pardon?"

"Your request is denied."

Arthur Garrett was a practical man who lacked vision. Alexa would have to draw him a picture. "A good number of our clients are based in Texas. With my contacts, my family's contacts, I can easily draw in more."

"The answer is still no."

Alexa's stomach had gone sour. He was enjoying this. His thin lips were straining back a smile. She was the one who lacked vision here. There was something else at play, and she didn't see it.

"Any reason why?" she asked. "I've done good work for this firm. My record speaks for itself. There's no reason I can't continue to be an asset in Dallas."

"If we believed that, we'd rush it through. Unfortunately, we don't."

We *are going to lose our shit.* "I don't understand."

"I'll explain." Arthur joined his fingertips in a steeple. "There was a time we could count on you to deliver. Not anymore. Your commitment to the firm is in question."

Alexa could not muster a word. Outrage clamped her throat. Arthur took advantage to press the intercom. He let his assistant know that he was ready. Ready for what? Alexa wasn't sure. She was reeling. Her head was foggy. Although this was the absolute wrong time to indulge in an existential crisis, there was no fighting it. She'd been the golden girl, the one to beat, the best of the best, and on and on, forever! She had never been demoted, passed over for a plum promotion or, heaven help her, fired. That was what was happening. She had no doubt.

The door swung open, and Richard Carmichael walked in. Actually, he sailed in. He wore a navy suit and a wolfish smile. His tan was a shade of terra-cotta more suited to pottery. His teeth gleamed white. "Alexandra, it's been a while."

"Not that long. I'm on leave and visiting family." She awarded herself bonus points for managing to sound coherent.

"Ah, yes. Meanwhile, the rest of us are hard at work."

"I don't understand. Arthur approved my leave."

"I urged you to take some time off because you were not having the best time," Arthur said. "A couple of days at most."

Not having the best time? He had to be kidding her. Alexa labored to get a grip on herself before she lost it. *Breathe in. Breathe out.* Negotiations were over. *Breathe in. Breathe out.* She needed a cool head for battle.

"Richard, Arthur, we're all busy people. If you have something you want to say to me, I would appreciate a direct approach."

Arthur cleared his throat. "We understand you have other priorities now. A transfer to Dallas won't solve the problem."

"What other priorities? I've always put my clients first."

"You're a fine attorney," Richard said. "No one is disputing that. We wouldn't have recruited you otherwise. But it has to be said—you are no longer one hundred percent committed to this firm. We expect our attorneys to work as a team, quash petty squabbles, keep the firm's best interest first place."

"You're firing me because I lodged a complaint against Theo Redmond."

"You're not fired, Alexandra."

Now she was more confused than ever. "Then what are we doing here?"

"We're asking for your resignation," Richard said. "It's simpler that way."

"Like this, you'll be free to pursue employment opportunities in Dallas or wherever life takes you," Arthur added.

Alexa was trembling with rage. Hot tears stung her eyes. She would rather die than break down here. She was a Lattimore, Royal born and bred. These men would not take her down. It was time to end this game. "I had such high hopes when I took this job. A & C had a stellar reputation. I was flattered when you recruited me. God, you had me fooled. Theo Redmond is a walking liability. You know this, and yet you've chosen to let go of a *stellar* attorney to placate a lazy and frankly useless one—or worse, to please the senior partner's daughter. It's embarrassing."

"You're blowing this out of proportion," Arthur stammered.

"Am I? Let's see what my friends at the Equal Employment Opportunity Commission have to say about that."

Richard Carmichael settled in the chair next to hers. He crossed his legs and made a grand show of appearing unruffled. The taut muscles of his neck told a different story. "Go ahead," he said. "Go make some noise at the EEOC. You may have some resources and a few contacts back in Texas. We have the full force of the fifth-largest law offices in the Southeast. We can drag this out for years."

Alexa felt for the golden pendent underneath her silk blouse and was instantly calmed. The moment called for a

tactical move. She wasn't sure she wanted to pursue legal
action. It was well known that Richard Carmichael planned
on retiring in eighteen months. He would be off living his
best life in Nantucket while she was languishing in the court
system. It would trash her reputation and might jeopardize
her career. But she couldn't let them off so easily. Some way
or another, they would pay. Right now, though, she wanted
nothing more than to get as far away as possible from these
two men, this toxic office and this city that held nothing
more for her.

Twenty

"There's just something about the way she picked up and left. It's a work trip. I know. I get it. No one works harder than me. But there's something going on there. She's hiding something. I can feel it."

"Have you asked her what's going on?"

"She won't answer a direct question. It's driving me nuts."

"Sounds like there's a communication gap. If it's making you uncomfortable, you have to address it."

"I don't want to come off as clingy. I'm not that guy. I respect boundaries."

"There's no way to build a healthy relationship without solid communication. I understand she's not as open as you'd like. But you have to learn to make your needs known. You talk about respecting the boundaries of others and that's good. However, you have to teach others to respect you. If you're coming into a new, budding relationship with an open heart, it's not too much to ask for your partner to do the same. Does that make sense to you?"

Jackson sat up on the bench on which he'd been reclining. It made all the sense in the world. He was walking on eggshells around Alexa, afraid to do or say anything to upset her. And it was only because he wanted her so badly. That approach wasn't going to work. It was making him feel a little desperate and a lot insecure.

"It does. Thanks for seeing me last minute."

"Absolutely, dude. You're a valued client." Russell, his

lumberjack of a personal trainer, had been holding a plank
position the entire time. He hopped onto his feet and slapped
Jackson on the back. "Now, that's enough talk. Fifty push-
ups. Get going. I want to see you work."

Jackson was gathering his equipment, stuffing his gloves
and sweat-damp towels into his gym bag, when Russell offered one last bit of advice. "Send her flowers!"

"What kind of basic advice is that?" He sent flowers to
his mother on Mother's Day. "My first gift to her was a gold
pendant in the shape of a—"

"Flowers!" Russell bellowed. "It never fails. Send a big
fat bouquet to her office. She'll melt."

Outside, the sky was thick and heavy. A storm was
headed their way. Jackson sprinted back to his car. Once
behind the wheel, he scrolled through his phone's contact
list. He had the florist on speed dial.

"Mr. Strom, good to hear from you. What can I do for
you today?"

"I'd like to send a bouquet of roses to Miami."

"Very nice. We are running a special on white roses."

"Not interested." He was only interested in long-stem,
red-hot I-can't-wait-to-get-you-naked roses. "That's not the
vibe we're going for."

"I recommend Obsession. Gorgeous crimson blooms."

"Sounds right."

"I recommend three dozen."

"Send me the bill."

"The address?"

"Hold on." He hit the browser icon and searched for Alexa's law firm. He read the address to the florist.

"I'll need a suite number. Do you have one?"

"I can give you the name of the office building."

"Not enough. You won't believe how many people with
the same names work in the same buildings. Next thing you

know, the wrong person walks away with your gorgeous
flowers. You don't want that."

"No, I don't," Jackson said. "Give me a minute."

He switched lines and called the Law Offices of Anderson
and Carmichael. A woman answered with a giddy tilt to her
voice. Jackson wondered if he had the wrong number until
she said the name of the firm. "How may I direct your call?"

"Hello, my name is Jackson Strom. I'm looking to mail a
package to my attorney, Alexandra Lattimore. I need a suite
number to ensure the documents get into the right hands."

"I'm sorry to inform you that Ms. Lattimore is no longer
a member of A & C."

"I'm sorry… What?"

"Ms. Lattimore has parted ways with the firm."

"As of when?"

"As of now."

Jackson gripped the steering wheel. The car was parked
in the lot behind Russell's gym, and still he felt as if he were
crashing. "Could you…tell me why?"

"That's confidential, sir."

Jackson was sweating again. Why would she quit her job
and not tell him? Was that what she'd gone off to do? He
drew in a long breath. The air around him had gone stale, and
he stifled a cough. Back when they were in school, whenever he was going up against her, he would try to think as
she would to anticipate her next move and to gain a com-
petitive edge. Alexa had quit her job. Why? To come home
and give them a chance? Hardly. That was wishful thinking, at best. As much as he would have loved it, Alexa was
not impulsive or rash. She wouldn't upend her career for his
handsome face. What was it, then? What was he missing?

"I don't know who will handle Ms. Lattimore's cases,"
the receptionist continued. "If you're willing to hold, I can
find out."

"That won't be necessary. This was a sensitive matter."

"I should transfer your call to a senior attorney, anyway," she said. "If only to advise you on your options."

He didn't want to speak to any other attorney. Still, he managed to control his voice and lean hard on his southern accent. It always worked like a charm. "I'm just gutted, you understand? Ms. Lattimore has an impeccable reputation. She came highly recommended. I knew I was in capable hands. Any hint on where she'll be heading next?"

The receptionist huffed. "She doesn't have a good reputation around here."

"Is that right?"

"Uh-huh," she whispered. "She's something of a trouble-maker. Trust me on this, you dodged a bullet with that one."

And there it was: the missing piece. He'd been right this whole fucking time. Something had been eating at her. He knew it. He knew she wasn't okay. He'd assumed her family's legal troubles were the root of the problem and had not dug further. Things had gone south at work. Okay. Fine. Shit happens all day. Why hadn't she confided in him?

By the time he'd gotten off the phone with Miami, he'd forgotten all about the flowers. The florist called him back, and he arranged for the roses to be delivered to her home in Royal instead.

"I got news!" Karla called out from her desk when he got back to his office.

Jackson strode past her door. "Not now!"

The benefits of the workout had faded. He was fuming. *She's something of a troublemaker.* The words chased after him like angry bees. Alexa was a genius, an ace. They were lucky to have her. They should have put her in charge of the whole place. What kind of shortsighted, narrow-minded, backward people was she working with? He was going to find out.

Karla trotted after him. "Sorry. This can't wait."

Jackson fell into his desk chair and fired up the computer. "What is it?"

Karla hovered in the doorway. "I'll make it short. Claire Kennedy of Kennedy & Sons has requested a meeting."

Jackson looked up from his computer screen. His fingers hovered over the keyboard. He'd been typing *Anderson and Carmichael* into a search engine. This news was worth the minor interruption in his quest to take down one of the top law offices in the country and avenge the love of his life. And there it was: the thing he'd been dancing around for days. Alexa was the love of his life. He had to protect her.

Although she came from a large family, he knew she often felt alone. She was probably accustomed to fighting her battles alone, too. But that was no longer the case. He was here for her—if she could only learn to rely on him.

"Did you hear me?" Karla snapped. "Claire Kennedy is a big effing deal!"

Claire Kennedy was the heir to a family-owned home-improvement-store empire. In addition, she sat on the board of a few influential nonprofit organizations. If she'd requested a meeting, he would have to jump on it. It was likely she was meeting with the competition as well. "Absolutely. Set it up."

"She suggested a lunch."

"Of course. Anytime she likes."

"More enthusiasm, please."

"Sorry. I'm having a crisis."

"I'll close your door."

He thanked her and apologized again. Jackson sat alone in the quiet space. For the first time in his adult life, his work was no longer his top priority.

He was in love with Alexa.

His pulse steadied and he let the feeling flow through him. There had never been another woman for him, no one with such a hold on his heart. She'd been his first and only love. It was time he proved it.

Twenty-One

Alexa showed up at the door of her childhood home with the entire contents of her condo packed up in four suitcases and three boxes. Their longtime housekeeper, Josie, helped her haul the luggage in from the porch. In a deliberate attempt to delay the moment she'd face her loved ones, Alexa had not bothered to call on her brothers, Jackson, Caitlyn or anyone for a ride from the airport. She'd ordered a ride from a driver with a truck.

Her mother rushed to the door. The look on her face was so comical, Alexa would have burst out laughing if the circumstances weren't so dire. She felt like a loser, and there was no worse feeling in the world.

After she'd stormed out of the meeting with Richard Carmichael and Arthur Garrett, there'd been a humiliating trek down the hall to her office. Every head had turned, but no one met her eyes. The air was electric with gossip. The news had gone around and back. She even heard muffled laughter. There were empty boxes already piled up on her desk. Trembling with rage, Alexa rummaged through her desk drawers for the few personal items she had, stuffed them in her structured tote bag. She exited the office with her head high only to fall apart on the sidewalk.

Jackson kept calling. She was dying to speak with him, but he would know that she'd been crying. There was no way to hide it in her voice. She texted him a string of lies:

Can't talk right now. Still in a meeting.

Heading out to dinner with a coworker. Will call later.

Miss you, but this dinner is running late. I'll call before bed.

She never called. That night, she got busy packing her stuff. She reached out to her landlord and paid the penalty to break the lease. She arranged for the dealer to pick up the sports car she rarely drove. She was done with Miami and vowed not to return for a long time. But now she was back in Royal with no plan, no job, nothing to do except wallow. Just the thought of enlisting a headhunter gave her a headache. She wanted to curl up in bed and cry. And yet, when her mother came to the door, she had to paste a smile on her face.

"What is going on here? I wasn't expecting you until the end of the week."

"Well… Surprise! I'm back."

She carelessly tossed her bulging carry-on suitcase into the foyer. It bumped up against the marble-top console table. A bouquet of red roses tipped over, and her mother rushed to catch it. "Careful!" she cried. "You'll destroy your flowers."

"Is that for me?"

"Yes! Jackson had it delivered this morning," her mother explained. "You should read the card. It's lovely."

Alexa ruffled through the roses, which were stunning, and found the rectangular envelope with the note addressed to her that her mother had already opened and read.

Alexa, first of my heart, we need to talk.
Patiently waiting.
Love,
Jack

Alexa's vision blurred. She forgot her mother and everything around her. She could feel the pressure of Jackson's hand on the small of her back and the ghost of a kiss under her ear. She reached for the golden queen pendent and pressed it to her lips. Jackson Strom had to be the sweetest man she'd ever known. She strongly doubted he was "patiently" waiting for anything, but it was the thought that counted.

"We have to talk, too," her mother said. She eyed the boxes piled up in the foyer. "Just how long do you plan on staying?"

"Why?" Alexa fished her phone out of the back pocket of her jeans. "Are you planning on converting my bedroom into a yoga studio?"

"Darling, this is your home, and you are always welcome. But you left in a hurry, and now you return with all this *stuff*. You look as if you haven't slept in days… This is the sort of behavior I expect from Jayden, not you."

"Uh-huh." Alexa typed a brief message to Jackson to let him know that she was back and eager to talk. She pocketed the phone. "I live a fast-paced life, Mother. Try to keep up."

"What's your plan, exactly?"

Her mother stood with her hands on her hips, her feet spread wide. She was not going to allow Alexa passage until she gave some sort of an explanation. Alexa blurted the first thing that came to mind. "I'm here to stand by my friends and family. I plan to stay for as long as it takes and see this business with the oil rights to the end. This ranch is my home, and I will defend it tooth and nail."

Her mother did not seem convinced, but she stepped aside and let Josie sweep past and up the stairs, hauling a suitcase. Alexa grabbed a box and followed. Her mother did not pick up a thing and hounded them all the way to the second floor. "Are you sure this has nothing to do with the man who sent those roses?"

"You think I'm going through all this trouble for a man? Does that even sound like me?"

"I wouldn't be against it if it were the case. Jackson Strom grew up to be a fine man with an impeccable reputation. You two would be a perfect match. We could have the wedding right here on the property. But I've never seen you act irrationally. Now is not the time to start."

Here she thought her mother would jump for joy because she'd finally found "a good man." There truly was no pleasing that woman.

In her bedroom, her mother sat at the window bench while Alexa and Josie made several trips to bring up the rest of the boxes and things. Barbara looked pretty in a pair of linen palazzo pants and a coordinating blouse. She seldom wore makeup, but lately she'd taken to dusting golden-peach blush on her cheeks to brighten up her deep mocha complexion. Alexa had inherited her high cheekbones and, some would say, her imperial air.

Josie arranged the boxes neatly in Alexa's walk-in closet. "All done! I'll find the box cutter and set it aside for you."

"Thanks, Josie."

"It's no bother," she said. "I'm glad to have you back."

"I appreciate that."

"Will you be joining the others for lunch?"

"Others?"

"The whole family is here," her mother replied.

A family lunch on a Wednesday? "What's the occasion?"

"It's Dev's birthday," her mother replied.

"Oh…"

"Everyone is here."

"Oh…"

"Your vocabulary is severely limited."

"It's just that I'm exhausted," she said. "I'll skip it. No one was expecting me, so I won't be missed."

"Nonsense! Come join us for dessert, at least."

"Mom, look at me. I'm a mess."

"Who cares, darling? We're family. And you can explain to everyone why you packed up and fled Florida as if there's a warrant out for your arrest."

Alexa smirked. "Nice."

Her mother stood and smoothed out the wrinkles in her linen pants. Clearly she cared about her own appearance.

Her mother and Josie left, shutting the door behind them. Alexa sank into her ancient four-poster bed and wondered if she should even bother unpacking. How could she possibly live here? If she didn't join the others for lunch, they'd call her antisocial. It didn't matter that she was cranky and sleep deprived. And to top it all, she wasn't even hungry. She'd wolfed down a burrito bowl at the airport between connecting flights.

All Alexa wanted was to speak with Jackson. He would be upset with her for dodging his calls, but she'd decided on the plane to come clean. She would tell him the truth. Not the whole truth, of course—a version of it. He didn't have to know *all* the sordid details. It would just upset him, and for what? There wasn't much he could do. It was better to leave that mess in the past. She was not going to sue A & C. There was no way to go about it discretely. Her family would learn about it and wage a war, seeking to destroy the thirty-year-old law firm. Her mother would never shut up about it. All of Royal would learn how Alexandra Lattimore had not been able to cut it in the big city. Would another firm hire her after that? Did she even want to work for another firm? Maybe it was time she branched out on her own. She had so many decisions to make, all of them equally pressing. For the moment, she had to freshen up and face the firing squad.

Twenty-Two

After some back-and-forth with Claire Kennedy, she and Jackson had agreed to meet for lunch on Wednesday at the Texas Cattleman's Club. Jackson wished he could cancel. He had not heard from Alexa in twenty-four hours and was in no mood to sit through an indulgent three-course executive lunch. Nonetheless, he set out early, hoping to make a good first impression and wrap up the encounter. On the drive to the TCC, a message from Alexa flashed on the dashboard monitor, turning his plans upside down.

Back in town. Thanks for the beautiful flowers. We've so much to talk about. Can't wait to see you.

At the first traffic light, Jackson executed a U-turn and sped down the causeway in the direction of the Lattimore ranch. So much for making a good first impression… He would rather be late than not check in on Alexa and make sure she was okay.

He arrived at the ranch; several cars were parked in the drive. A housekeeper let him in and asked him to wait in the entryway, where the bouquet of red roses was on display. Raucous conversation and laughter rattled through the house. Jackson realized that he was interrupting a gathering of some sort, but it was too late to duck out. Barbara Lattimore was gliding toward him, arms outstretched.

"Jackson! Welcome!" Mrs. Lattimore cried. "Is this your first time here?"

"Yes, ma'am," he said. "I believe it is. It's lovely."

"Alexa should have invited you ages ago. We'd love to have you for dinner someday."

"Is now a bad time?"

"No, of course not. It's my future son-in-law's birthday. We've cut the cake, so you're right on time."

"I can't stay long."

"Nonsense," Barbara said. "Alexa will be thrilled to see you. You must have put a spell on my daughter, because she's packed up and left wretched Florida in a hurry. Now that she's finally home to stay, we hope to see more of you."

If this was true and Alexa had moved back, it wasn't because of any spell he'd cast. It likely had more to do with her losing her job. Did Barbara Lattimore know? She seemed awfully upbeat. Jackson hadn't even noticed when she looped her arm around his and steered him from the foyer to a formal dining room. Everyone was seated at a large oval table. Jackson recognized the elderly Augustus Lattimore; his wife, Hazel; Alexa's father, Ben; and her siblings, Jonathan, Jayden, Caitlyn and Dev Mallik. Dev was wearing a paper party hat. He waved Jackson in. "Don't be shy. The cake alone is worth venturing into the lion's den."

Barbara scolded Dev. Everyone laughed and ate cake. It made for a heartwarming scene, but where the hell was Alexa?

Someone tapped him from behind. He glanced over his shoulder and there she was. The mix of anger, confusion and hurt that had clouded his head in the last twenty-four hours receded like fog. Alexa looked worn out and frail. Her brown eyes were dull, but he could make them shine again. Her shy, uncertain smile broke his heart. She was still wearing his necklace. He hugged her and kissed her cheek. "I forgot your key lime pie," she said, contrite.

"Don't worry about it. I'm just happy to see you."

He wasn't the only one happy to see her. Judging by her family's reaction, this was her first encounter with them as well. They cheered her arrival. Caitlyn blew her a kiss. Jonathan demanded to know why she hadn't asked for a ride back from the airport. Jayden wondered why she hadn't answered any of his texts.

Ben Lattimore sat staring at Jackson from his seat at the head of the table. It had been a mistake to gloss over him. A distinguished Black man in his sixties, Ben Lattimore was as intimidating as Jackson knew Augustus once was. This was the man that Jackson would have had to reckon with if he had taken Alexa to prom. The fact that he and Alexa were grown didn't seem to make any difference. The rules were the same.

Jackson stepped forward. "Good afternoon, Mr. Lattimore."

He nodded and looked to his daughter. "You left without saying goodbye. Now your mother says you're back to stay."

"I'm back to stay as long as necessary to help with the case."

Jackson flinched at this caveat. What if the issue resolved itself tomorrow? As he understood it, the matter was simple: if the claim on the oil rights was valid, there was nothing more to be done except maybe negotiate a buyout. Although, the word on the street was that Thurston wasn't open to negotiations.

"What about your job?" Her father continued his interrogation, unbothered that he was shredding the party mood. "Don't you have to return at some point?"

"I'm on sabbatical," Alexa said.

She stood ramrod straight, unwavering even as she lied to her father.

"Is that a thing lawyers can do?" Jayden asked. "I thought that was for college professors."

"Yes, Jayden. It is."

"Don't get me wrong," Ben said, "I'm happy to have my daughter back. Just wanting to make sure you're not jeopardizing your career for us."

"Or anyone," her mother added sweetly.

If that barb was meant for Jackson, Barbara Lattimore had it all wrong. Their daughter's career was in jeopardy, but he had nothing to do with it. She certainly hadn't shared any of the details with him. It was comforting to know that he wasn't in the minority. It looked as if Alexa planned on burying this secret in a Florida sinkhole.

"Could I speak to you privately?" he said.

"Sure." Looking relieved, she asked the others not to eat all the cake and led him out by the hand.

In the foyer, she rushed into his arms. Again, the conflicting brew of emotions receded. Jackson was so in love and so confused.

"Let's go to the garden. It's nice out there."

He squeezed her hand. "I can't. I'm already running late for a meeting. I came here just as soon as I got your text."

"Oh, God," she said, pushing him toward the door. "I don't want you to miss out on work because of me. Go to your meeting and come back later. I'll be here."

"Are you okay?" he asked softly.

"I'm fine."

"How did things go in Miami?"

She manufactured a smile. "Not so great."

"That's okay. Tell me what went wrong."

"Just some misunderstanding with HR about my leave."

"A misunderstanding?"

"Yes. It's resolved. I'm back and free to focus on the task at hand."

It hit him from nowhere, a sucker punch to the chin. Alexa wasn't going to confide in him—not now, not ever.

"It's resolved. Really, Alexa?"

"Yes. Really. God, you sound like the others."

"The others want the truth."

She took a step back. "And you? What do you want?"

"Your trust."

She let out a rusty laugh. "You know I trust you! Why not go to your meeting? We can talk—"

"Let me guess," he interrupted. "Later? We'll talk later. Is that what you were going to say?"

Alexa had gone pale. She nodded slowly but did not utter a word.

"And later, we'll push it back to even later still."

"What's your point? I've been busy and—"

"Busy with work? Is that it?"

"Yes, with work." She reached for his hand and tangled their fingers. "There's nothing or no one else. I promise. My job has been so demanding lately and—"

Jackson freed his hand from hers. He wasn't going to let her lie to his face. "Stop, Alexa. When you're ready to talk, *really* talk, come find me."

Her face fell and Jackson, torn apart inside, nearly faltered. He was this close to grabbing her and kissing away the frown lines. If he caved now, any foundation of trust and respect would be eroded. He wanted a future with Alexa. If she wanted him, it was up to her to make the move.

Jackson arrived at the Texas Cattleman's Club ten minutes late for his meeting with Claire Kennedy. Fortunately, Claire showed up even later. She found him at the bar. He had hoped to sneak in a drink to calm down before the meeting. She'd had the same mindset. She slipped onto the bar stool next to him and ordered a whiskey, neat.

"Jackson Strom, I'm having one hell of a day. Sorry to have kept you waiting."

"Not at all," he said. "I'm honored."

"Are you?" She looked at him. "You seem pissed off."

"I'm having one hell of a day, too."

The bartender served her drink. She raised her glass. "Cheers to that."

Jackson liked how this meeting was going. Claire Kennedy was a small woman with silver hair dyed the same shade of blue as her eyes. No matter how dainty her appearance, he should not forget that she was one of Royal's shrewdest power players.

"I had to fire my nephew this morning," she said with a sigh. "My sister is going to hate me. Want to come over to our house for Thanksgiving this year? It's going to be a riot."

Jackson thought of Alexa taking on her family's case. "Working with family isn't easy."

"He was my accountant. The boy didn't know what he was doing. He only went into accounting to please his parents. And now I'm expected to keep him employed to please them, too."

"It's a vicious cycle."

"I don't have time for that. They should have just let the boy be a magician or whatever else he wanted to be."

"How's his sleight of hand?"

"The hell if I know."

Claire was chuckling now. Jackson knew they'd get along great, whether she hired him or not.

"Your turn," she said. "What's bugging you?"

"I'm trying not to mess up a new relationship," he said. "We're at the tipping point. It could go either way."

"Huh. Nice to know love is still alive."

"I guess that's one way to look at it."

"Let's get to the point of this meeting so we can get you out of here. What do you say?"

Jackson liked her more and more. "Let's do it."

She joined her slender, vein-lined hands on the polished bar top. "My stores need a refresh. We hired a fancy architect and did all the work. Way over budget, if you ask me. Still, it's not enough. Our customer base is aging."

Jackson skipped ahead. He knew what she was about to say next. "You want to attract millennials."

"We need to," Claire corrected. "There's no way around it. It's a matter of survival."

Jackson picked up his glass and gave the amber liquor a swirl. Claire Kennedy's dilemma was inherent to all legacy businesses in desperate need of rebranding. The classic big-box stores that dotted the suburbs were dinosaurs in today's marketplace. Most couldn't keep pace with e-retailers. He tried to think about the last time he'd gone to a home-improvement store. It had been with Alexa. They'd driven a half hour from the lake cabin to reach one. She'd picked up perennials and potting soil. She was determined to revive the front flower bed that curved along the porch. The memory of that afternoon resurfaced. He could see her in a white cotton dress, sunglasses and simple leather sandals. He'd pushed the cart and followed her around the nursery. He'd reached for terra-cotta pots off the top shelves and lifted heavy bags of soil off the ground. Later, he loaded it all into the truck. A solid hour had passed, and it had been heaven.

"Plants."

"Excuse me?"

"You want to attract younger customers? Sell them plants."

"We have a garden section."

"I'm not talking daisies here." Alexa had consulted social media to make her selections. She'd had her heart set on exotic blooms, green plants with odd-shaped leaves or even edible flowers. In the end, she'd had to settle for carnations. He'd tried to lift her spirits by pointing out that carnations were, in fact, edible.

Claire's eyes were narrowed in thought. She was probably thinking he was wasting her time. Meanwhile, he was thinking the red roses he'd sent Alexa were a mistake. He should have sent her carnations.

"You might be on to something," she said finally. "My niece's apartment is like a jungle. She calls the plants her babies, her plant babies. And she keeps fussing over them. She's got apps and a special thermometer and everything. Can you believe it?"

"I can," Jackson said. "The question is, can you?"

Claire made a face. "You're saying I should *get over myself* and *get with the times.*"

She used air quotes for emphasis. Jackson ignored the sarcasm. "That's exactly what I'm saying."

"I don't get it," Claire admitted. "I never enjoyed gardening. Either that or I never gave it a chance. It was the sort of thing I was meant to do. As a woman, I mean."

He understood very well. A woman of her age had likely spent her life pushing against rigid stereotypes. She'd likely been expected to cook, bake *and* grow her own tomatoes. However, his generation had grown up in a digital world and yearned for contact with nature. "Plants are the antidote to tech. They ground us, in a way."

"I suppose," Claire said. "And now you're going to try to sell me on a full-scale social media campaign."

"You know it. A television ad airing weeknights at six is not gonna cut it, Claire." After a pause, he added, "May I call you Claire?"

"Depends. May I call you Jack?"

"No objections."

"All right, Jack." She was nodding and frowning at the same time. "I like this plan. Once we lure them into our store through the lawn-and-garden department, what's to stop them from looking around?"

"Next thing you know, those crazy kids are buying patio furniture."

Claire cackled. "Jack, you're a charmer."

"I think you've charmed me," Jackson said. "Should I even be giving you all this free advice?"

Claire slapped him on his back. "I can't tell you how to run your business, but in my line of work, giving away free samples is always a good idea."

The bartender returned. This time, he handed Claire a key card. "Your room is ready. Anytime is fine."

She slipped the card into her structured purse. "I booked a private meeting room for a video conference after lunch. My new lawyer is located in Dallas, which is a pain. I should have gone with someone local." She asked the bartender for a menu. "You don't mind if we catch a quick bite here, do you?"

"Not in the slightest."

Jackson didn't have to consult the menu. He ordered his usual TCC special, a burger-and-fries combo. Claire ordered a chicken Caesar salad.

"I'm not going to beat around the bush," Claire said. "You're hired. I want to put you in charge of our social media strategy."

"And maybe your niece could give us some insight."

"We could bring her on as a consultant!" Claire exclaimed. "That'll get my sister off my back. I fired her son but hired her daughter. It balances out."

Jackson raised his glass. "Two birds, one stone."

"Efficient. I love it."

Speaking of efficiency. "If you need to prepare for your next meeting, I'm fine wrapping things up. I can take my lunch to go."

"There's no rush. A & C can wait."

"Anderson and Carmichael?"

"You've heard of them?" Claire said. "Their closest office is in Dallas, which makes dealing with them a hassle. Not sure if I'm going to hire them. They come highly recommended."

A sudden jab of anger had Jackson reaching for his whiskey. "I wouldn't recommend them."

"Why not?"

"I know for a fact they don't treat their people right."

"How do you know?"

Jackson couldn't get into that with a stranger when he hadn't even gotten into it with the person in question. "I'm not at liberty to say."

Claire considered him awhile. She then pulled out her phone and dialed a number. "Jenny, cancel my conference call with A & C," she ordered. "I won't be hiring them. I need someone here in Royal, someone I can talk to face-to-face. That's my style. Also, if you could, contact Raul Perez and Miriam Carver. At last week's dinner, I recommended they reach out to A & C for that thing we're working on. Let them know I've changed my mind about A & C. We'll go with another firm. Thanks, Jenny. Want me to grab you lunch? Uh-huh. Okay." She tucked her phone back in her purse with a satisfied little smirk. "There. Now we can enjoy our lunch."

Jackson liked Claire Kennedy well enough before. Now he straight up worshipped her.

Twenty-Three

Moments after Jackson had stormed out, Alexa stood staring at the closed door. Caitlyn entered the foyer, balancing two slices of cake on their grandmother's best china. "Did I miss Jackson?"

"Uh-huh. He left. He's gone."

Her words tumbled like pearls sprung loose from a broken string.

Caitlyn approached, her delicate features bunched up with suspicion. "Are you okay?"

"I'm great. Everything's just great."

Her sister handed her a slice of cake. Alexa ignored the dainty dessert fork and scooped up the piece with her hand and shoved it in her mouth.

"It's good, right?"

"Mmm-hmm." She couldn't taste a thing. She might as well have been chewing on a kitchen sponge.

"It's Dev's favorite."

"Tell him he's got good taste."

"Is something wrong? You're a little off."

"I'm fine, Caitlyn," Alexa said wearily. "Please, just drop it."

"I won't just drop it!" Caitlyn insisted. "Something *is* wrong. Now talk!"

"He's upset."

"Who is? Jackson?"

"Who else?"

"Do you know why?"

"Not really."

Alexa licked frosting off her thumb. Caitlyn cut her a sharp look, which could only be interpreted one way: *Quit playing around.*

"He thinks I'm holding out on him."

"Are you holding out on him?"

"Not really."

"Oh, really?" Caitlyn shook her head. "Seeing how sketchy you've been acting lately, my guess is that you are."

Alexa set her empty plate on the console table next to the flowers Jackson had sent her. She could stuff her mouth, but she couldn't stuff down the truth. "I was fired from the firm. No, wait. Actually, I was asked to submit my resignation. There's a difference, but not much."

Caitlyn screeched. "What?"

Alexa shushed her. "Not a word of this to Mom."

"Of course not! I would never…"

"You two seem as thick as thieves lately."

"Because I'm engaged. It's a magical period that makes your parents treat you like a unicorn. You ought to try it."

There didn't seem to be much chance of that happening. "Whatever. Just don't tell anyone."

"I can keep a secret, Alexa," Caitlyn said. "Now, tell me what happened. How dare they fire you? You're a good attorney."

"I'm an *excellent* attorney."

Her sister reached out and patted her on the shoulder. "Of course, sweetie." Her voice was syrupy, as if she were trying to placate a difficult child, which wasn't too far from the truth. "What went wrong?"

"It came down to a choice between me and the office golden boy. They picked him."

"Why did they have to choose? And how did it come down to a binary choice?"

"Because we couldn't work together."

"Why not?"

"He was making things…uncomfortable at the office."

"Uncomfortable how?"

Alexa realized that she was using coded language to better tuck away the truth. Better to come out with it. "He was making advances."

"He was *harassing* you."

"Yes…that."

Caitlyn's grip on the extra plate of cake tightened until her knuckles turned white. She picked up the dessert fork and stuffed cake in her mouth.

"I filed a complaint," Alexa continued. "Nothing came of it."

"Naturally."

"He's involved with one of the partners' daughter, so there's that."

"Go on."

"He got a slap on the wrist. I was advised to take some time for myself, just until things cooled down. It worked out great because I was needed here. Now they're using my extended absence as an excuse to get rid of me."

"You were gone for just a few weeks!"

"They say my commitment to the firm is in question."

"You're gonna fight back, right?" Caitlyn said between bites of cake. "I mean…you're gonna do *something.*"

"I'm going to put all this business behind me. That's what I'm going to do."

"Is that why Jackson is upset? Because you don't want to fight back?"

"No. That's not it."

Something moved inside Alexa. She and Jackson hadn't even made it that far, but she suspected that it would be an issue when they got there.

"Well, I'm upset!" Caitlyn said. "Women have to speak up. You of all people should know that."

"And I know how disruptive litigation can be. They'll never settle. They'll drag this out in court just to soil my reputation."

"You don't know that," Caitlyn said. "Call their bluff."

It was all well and good for her to say that, but it was Alexa's professional reputation that was on the line.

Caitlyn had finished the cake in a few bites. "When Dad finds out… Whew!"

"He can't find out! No one can find out."

"I knew something was up with you, but I thought you were lonely or just tired of being single. Then Jackson comes along, and you still had that look in your eyes."

"What look?"

"The look of someone who needs help. It was obvious something was chipping away at your self-confidence."

"Nothing was chipping away at anything," Alexa said hotly. "I had it under control."

"I can see that."

"And for the record, I wasn't lonely."

"Uh-huh."

"This is why I haven't told Jackson! I knew he'd react like this."

"You haven't told Jackson *any* of this?"

Alexa stepped back. "Not yet."

"What are you waiting for?"

"Just wanted to sort things out."

"All that time you two were at the cabin, what were you talking about?"

"Things."

"God… Alexa!" Caitlyn shook her head. "No wonder he's upset."

"I didn't want to burden him."

"That's how relationships work," she said. "Look it up. I'm sure there's a Harvard lecture series on the topic."

Alexa fiddled with the miniature queen pendant. "I know how relationships work."

"Sorry, you don't," Caitlyn said. "You gloss over everything with a perfect filter. You do it with me, with him, with everyone."

"I do not." The words barely squeaked past her throat. It was true that she had never let go of her alter ego, Alexandra the First.

"Just talk to him. He's probably imagining the worst."

Defeated, Alexa agreed. "I'll talk to him tonight."

"There's my brave big sister!" Caitlyn pinched her cheek. "Now, I've got to head back. I shouldn't leave Dev alone in the lion's den."

Alexa had no time to waste. She was still haunted by the look Jackson had tossed her on his way out the door. Something was broken between them, and it was up to her to fix it. Caitlyn was right. He suspected she was holding back. Who knew what he was thinking? He was likely imagining the worst.

The funny thing was, she'd only made it through this ordeal because of him. His queen chess piece pendant had worked like a charm to keep her calm and composed even during the most contentious meeting of her life. Knowing that he was waiting for her here, at home, had weakened the blow of getting sacked. Leaving Miami had been the easiest decision of her life. With so much to look forward to, she was running toward her future, not away from her past. That evening, when she knocked on his door, she vowed to clear up any misunderstandings and put their relationship back on track.

Jackson opened the door. No shirt, no tie —no pants,

even. He wore a towel wrapped low on his hips. Her well-rehearsed script was erased from her mind.

"Do you always answer the door like this?"

"I just got back from work and was about to jump into the shower," he explained.

"I could have been anyone."

Oh, great. Having lost her words, she'd stolen Barbara Lattimore's material. What was she going to do next? Correct his grammar?

"I knew it was you," he said. "And you're not just *anyone*."

Alexa followed him into the main room, noting his stiff posture. The tension between them had not dissipated, and she had not helped her cause just now.

She caught him by the arm. He could at least look at her. "I know I've been withdrawn these last few days, but why are you so upset?"

"Alexa, it's more than that."

"I know…"

She rushed to him and buried her face in his chest. His skin was warm. He stiffened for an instant, but only for an instant. The next moment, his hands were in her hair and their kiss went deep. They'd only been apart a couple of days, and yet she craved his touch and missed his kiss. His muscles were taut, and they tensed under her touch. When she tried to loosen the towel, he broke the kiss and searched her eyes.

Alexa started to tear up. "I'm not just anyone."

The words had slipped out in a breath. She was desperate to remind him of what they had. It was a rare connection that spanned years. Nothing she'd done was so terrible that it should jeopardize that.

"You're the woman who's going to do me in."

"That's not true!" she cried, her heart slamming in her chest. "I'm the woman who loves you."

"Alexa…" He drew her to him and kissed her breathless.

Jackson broke away again. His expression was as serious as she'd ever seen it, but there was a glint in his eyes. They'd started as opponents and would likely match wits to the very end. She wouldn't have it any other way.

"We're not in high school," he said. "You have to learn to trust me."

"I trust you!"

"No, you don't," he said. "We're adults. If we're going to be together, we have to communicate."

Alexa nodded. Communication was crucial, vital, but now wasn't the time.

"Make love to me first."

He swore, but then swooped her up and carried her into the bedroom. They made love in slow, rhythmic circles until pleasure swirled inside her, blinded her. He held her trembling body until she calmed down, stroking her back, kissing her eyelids and calling her "my love." Alexa clung to him. If she had to lose everything that she'd worked so hard for just to get to this place, it would have been well worth it.

Much later, Alexa paced the bathroom's marble floor and marveled that it was heated. She wiggled her toes. "So warm and cozy. Are the towel racks heated?"

"Yes, they are."

"Fancy."

"You can thank my interior designer."

Jackson was finally getting around to that shower, and she was joining him. He switched on the water and beckoned her. "Come," he said. "It's warm and cozy in here."

Alexa quickly removed her gold earrings and watch. They were valuable vintage pieces, handed down by her grandmother. To this small pile, she added the gold necklace with the queen pendent. It was valuable, too.

He welcomed her in the shower with a sloppy kiss and slid his wet lips down her neck. She smoothed her palms over his short hair beading with water. If there ever was a place to come clean, this was it.

She held his face between her hands. "I have so many things to tell you. I don't know where to start."

Jackson inched back, brows furrowed. "Start anywhere. I'll make sense of it."

"It doesn't make sense to me." The water stung her eyes now. "I got fired. Can you believe it? *Me*. Fired!"

"All right."

"I didn't do anything wrong," she added hastily. "I *hustled* for those people. Brought in clients. Won cases. Networked like crazy. I did all that and they still chose someone else over me."

"Maybe now it's time to hustle for yourself."

"I knew you were going to say that."

"Well…you know me."

"It's easy to build from success. It's a whole other thing to start from ashes. Failure follows you."

"Babe…it doesn't work like that. I promise it doesn't. Just tell me what happened."

Alexa tried her best to link the events in chronological order in her mind. "I've been up nights just trying—"

Jackson tightened his embrace. "Baby, it's okay."

"I failed at the one thing I devoted my life to. That's *not* okay."

"Darling…" He swept back her damp hair. "Walk me through it. We'll sort it out."

Alexa took a breath and began. She poured out her secrets, wishing each revelation would swirl down the drain and disappear. She told him everything: Theo Redmond and the whole mess at A & C. How she'd been forced out, despite having done her best work for them. How lost she felt now even though, deep down, she was relieved to be free and excited to explore her prospects. She shared her dreams, the ones she hadn't dared articulate: moving back to Royal, for good this time, and starting her own firm. She admitted that all her dreams swirled around him and that he had, in some way, guided her home.

Jackson listened, wiped the tears that had mingled with the shower water, kissed her when she hesitated and did not say a word until she asked him what he was thinking. "You need to sue," he said. "Take them to court."

Oh, God, here we go... "I want to look forward, not backwards."

"You want to avoid conflict."

He had it wrong. She was a litigator. Conflict was her bread and butter. But a lawyer was not supposed to be the plaintiff and victim. It would make her look weak. Plus, she wasn't naive. These sorts of complaints were more often than not settled out of court. She didn't want or need A & C's money. "There's more to it than that. They'll fight, drag it out forever and trash my reputation. The most I'll get out of it is a cash settlement."

"Alexa…" He caught her chin with wet, rough hands. Fragrant steam from the shower thickened around them, a buffer from the world. "They're already trashing your reputation."

"That's not true." That day in Arthur's office, they had come to an agreement.

"Yes, it is."

"How do you know?"

How *could* he possibly know? She'd only just told him about the whole ordeal two seconds ago.

"I wasn't going to tell you this, but here goes."

As it turned out, Jackson had secrets of his own. Those damn roses! A quick call to her office to verify the delivery address had ended with shocking revelations. Sweet-as-cake Patty had *trashed* her. Alexa closed her eyes. Fat drops of water pelted her skin, aggravating her frayed nerves.

"You knew all this time?"

"All what time?" he asked. "I came rushing over to you as soon as—"

"You let me carry on as if nothing had happened."

Jackson released her. "Alexa, I gave you every opportunity to open up to me."

The steam was suffocating. She swiveled around and pushed open the shower door. Cool air slapped her face. Jackson cut off the water. His voice was strained when he called after her. "What are you doing?"

"I need fresh air."

She grabbed a towel off the warming rack and rubbed her body with vigor. All the while, shame and mortification blazed through her. Patty had called her a troublemaker to a random stranger who called to inquire about a delivery. Who else was she bad-mouthing her to? The mailman? The sandwich-delivery guy? Had A & C orchestrated a full-on smear campaign? And Jackson knew! All this time, he knew and was feeling... What? Sorry for her? Nausea swirled inside her belly. How could she ever look him in the eye again?

"Darling, don't worry," he said. "I've already returned fire."

Alexa froze, clutching the heavy bath towel to her chest. "What do you mean?"

"A new client of mine mentioned she was meeting with a lawyer from your firm's Dallas office. She thought they had a good reputation. I set her straight. She dropped them and advised two others to do the same. I hope it goes on like this. I'm not going to rest until their reputation is mud."

He stood naked, hands on his hips—dark, dripping, quite obviously unbothered by the cold air. A pity... All she wanted to do was strangle him right now.

"Jackson, stop talking. Every word you say makes me want to scream."

"Mind telling me why?"

"You're intervening...meddling...stirring things up." She

was babbling now. Outrage and indignation had short-circuited her brain.

"Or just taking action, which is something you've forgotten how to do."

"Oh, shut up! Don't you dare judge me!"

Jackson let out a low whistle. He grabbed the last remaining towel and wrapped it around his waist. She was back to being someone he had to shield himself from. It hurt, but she couldn't let that distract her. He'd overstepped.

Alexa scurried around, looking for her clothes. She found everything where they'd left them, scattered on the bedroom floor. She quickly dressed and was about to storm out when she remembered her grandmother's watch, gold earrings and the necklace.

Jackson was still in the bathroom, apparently too stunned to move. The nerve of him! He was not the aggrieved party here. His brown eyes were muddied with confusion and pain. The look he gave her tore her in half. She wanted to run to him and run away at the same time. The bathroom was still warm, a reminder of how close they'd been only a moment earlier. Was she kidding herself about Jackson? They couldn't manage to sustain momentum. The glimmer of the queen pendant drew her gaze away. Anger zipped through her again. She grabbed the watch and the earrings off the vanity and stormed out without a word, leaving the necklace behind.

Twenty-Four

Tap! Tap! Tap!

The light knock on her bedroom door grew insistent. Alexa ignored it and sank deeper under her duvet. Unless the house was on fire, she had no intention of budging. It was early, barely seven, and her blackout drapes were sealed shut. Even if she hadn't spent most of the night crying, she still wouldn't be open for business. Her mother—and it could only be her mother—would have to learn to respect her boundaries.

A voice broke through. "Hey! Are you in there? It's me!"

Alexa peered out from under the duvet. "Caitlyn?"

The door creaked open. Her sister popped her head through the crack. "Morning, sunshine! May I come in?"

"Does it make a difference what I say?"

"Nope."

Her mother wasn't the only one who would have to learn boundaries. Alexa waved her in. Caitlyn redeemed herself with coffee, a mug in each hand. She pushed the door shut with her foot.

Dressed for work in a light blazer and jeans, Caitlyn was far more chipper than anyone had the right to be. Her career was on track. She had worked as the ranch's office manager since graduating from college. Recently, she'd started a horseback riding program for foster children at the ranch Dev bought. She was quiet and understated yet focused and determined. Alexa could take some career tips from her little sister.

Caitlyn set one of the mugs on the bedside table, right next to the bouquet of roses. Her mother had had it sent up to her room yesterday afternoon. Now the blood-red blooms served only to remind her of the tragic end of her affair.

"I brought coffee, but I have to get to work soon," Caitlyn proclaimed as she moved about the room, opening the curtains. "Now, spill it! How did it go with Jackson last night?"

Seduced by the aroma of freshly brewed coffee, Alexa sat up in bed and reached for the cup. Her sister took in her appearance and froze. "Whoa, Medusa! What happened to you?"

"I don't want to talk about it."

Alexa had tumbled into bed last night, her hair still damp and tangled from the shower. By the feel of things, she was wearing a mop. She sipped her coffee. It needed sugar.

"Want to talk about what happened with Jackson? I expected you to be at his place and was surprised to see your car in the garage."

"Don't you have your own ranch to run? Why are you here so early?"

"I'm stealing a ranch hand for the day. Dad is actually okay with it. Surprised the heck out of me. Now, quit stalling and come out with it," Caitlyn replied.

"And I wish I could paint you a rosy picture, but I can't. Things went from bad to worse."

Caitlyn sat on the corner of the bed, a look of clear exasperation on her face. "How is that possible?"

"Don't do that," Alexa said.

"Do what?"

"Look at me as if I'm to blame, because I'm not."

But you are! her inner voice declared. That voice hadn't shut up once through the night. *This is your fault. Had you been straight with him, you could have spared yourself a ton of grief.*

"Tell me everything," Caitlyn said. "But keep it short. I'll be late for the new kids arriving today."

"Fine! Long story short—Jackson called my office to arrange to have these stupid flowers delivered. The receptionist told him I no longer worked there. When he asked why, she called me a troublemaker and tried to refer him to another attorney. So, in brief, Jackson knew all along that I was holding out on him."

More like, he knew she had lied to his face.

Caitlyn opened round brown eyes. "Yikes! And then what happened?"

"Of course, we had a big fight."

"Why 'of course'? Couldn't you have talked about it? I'm trying to get you two to a space where you use your words to work out conflict."

"Save your efforts," Alexa said. "We had a huge fight… in the shower…which explains my hair."

Caitlyn winked. "A little shower action. I like it!"

"Please, don't."

Alexa set down her coffee mug. She needed both hands to rant like a lunatic. "You're not going to believe what he told me next."

"Go on!"

"He told his client not to do business with A & C because they were mean to his girlfriend. Can you believe that?"

"Honestly? No," Caitlyn replied. "I doubt very much he used those words."

"Okay. I don't know the exact words, but he said something to that effect."

"In his defense, Counselor, it's not like your coworkers forgot your birthday or stole your snacks from the company fridge. They harassed you and treated you unjustly."

"Don't you think I know that?" Alexa cried. "But Jackson's out there trying to singlehandedly destroy the reputation of a well-established law firm."

"He won't have to go it alone for long," Caitlyn said. "I'm ready to join the crusade. I'll order some T-shirts and make signs."

"He overstepped," Alexa snapped. "And I knew this would happen. I *knew* it! Why do you think I didn't tell him? These Royal men are all the same."

"That's not fair. Dev is not like that."

"Dev isn't from here. He grew up on the East Coast."

"My point is—"

"*My* point is, I was right."

"Great! Now, give yourself a gold medal and get past it. There are more important things than being right."

Sure… But none were so satisfying.

"Can you imagine calling an office—or anyplace, really—asking to speak with a friend, someone you know, and getting that sort of response?"

The answer was quite simple: No. It was as rude as rude could get. It was low down and dirty. It was terrible, and she hadn't deserved it.

"After that experience, would you go around recommending that business to your colleagues? Would you do it if the roles were reversed?"

The answer to that was also quite simple.

Caitlyn stood to retrieve a hairbrush and fastener on the vanity. "Sorry. I have to do this. Your hair is driving me crazy."

Her sister brushed her hair into a neat ponytail, all the while doling out standard-issue advice. "Don't give up. Try again. Give him a chance to explain."

Alexa allowed herself to be groomed. It was oddly soothing. Feeling calmer now, her sadness returned. "He says I don't trust him."

"You probably don't," Caitlyn replied. "Let's face it—
you have trust issues."

"I had some issues with this particular matter. I don't
have trust issues in general."

"You don't trust Grandpa Gus," Caitlyn said.

"That's a bold statement."

"You think he intentionally handed off our oil rights."

Alexa let her silence speak for her. She did believe that,
and it had nothing to do with any so-called "trust issues."
She'd studied the evidence, and that was where it led. It was
time her family faced that fact.

"We'll take this up in our next session," Caitlyn said.
"I've got to get to work. I promise to check on you later."

"Okay," Alexa said. "Love you."

Caitlyn dropped the hairbrush. It clattered onto the floor.
To Alexa's horror, Caitlyn dove onto the bed, tackled her and
trapped her in a hug. Alexa froze before nestling into her
sister's embrace. A minute later, though, she wiggled herself
free and clobbered Caitlyn with one of the many decorative
pillows her mother had piled onto her bed, for no other reason than to prove that she hadn't gone soft.

Just minutes after Caitlyn left, another knock on her bedroom door shredded any hope Alexa had of ever falling back
to sleep. And with that hope, she lost any chance of showing
up later at Jackson's door looking sane and serene. No matter
what the future held for them, she was deeply embarrassed
for storming out of his home like a petulant child. She'd left
the man standing naked in his bathroom. Even prima don-
nas had their limits, and she'd exceeded hers.

Another knock, sharper this time, shattered her thoughts.
First thing, she was going to order a do-not-disturb sign for
her door.

"Come in!" she cried.

The door swung open, and Jackson entered her bedroom.

Alexa dug her nails into the palm of her hand to ensure she wasn't dreaming. Impeccably dressed in a tailored herring-bone suit and impeccably groomed, he looked as if he'd walked off a film set. Who let him in? Who let him up? Her family home was a fortress. They were a hospitable bunch, but people didn't just wander in and roam the halls. Her mother wouldn't have that. But there he was, striding into her childhood bedroom—which, for some reason had never looked frillier, with its fringed drapes and not-so-shabby-chic furniture. He stopped at the foot of her bed, hands in his pockets. "Hope this isn't a bad time."

Alexa couldn't think of a worse time. She looked a mess. Caitlyn had fastened her hair in a pouf on top of her head. She didn't need a mirror to confirm that her eyes were blood-shot and her face was puffy with sleep deprivation. Plus, he'd robbed her of the chance to show up at his door looking semi-decent, and she was a little salty about it.

"How did you find my room?" she asked.

"Caitlyn let me in and showed me the way."

"Ah." That explained it. "Why are you here? Shouldn't you be at work?"

"A couple of things," he said. "First, I'm here to offer you the opportunity to grovel and make things right."

Alexa let out a soundless laugh. Now *that* was rich.

"I figured you'd avoid me for a month before coming around to it," he continued. "But I don't have that kind of time."

Maybe it was the matter-of-fact delivery or the hidden challenge in his words, but Alexa was awake…and aroused. Jackson Strom knew how to push her every button, and it was nothing less than thrilling.

"Shows how much you know," she said. "I was going to get dressed, put on makeup and show up at your door later today."

He nodded. "Very well. I saved you the trouble."

She propped herself up on her elbows. He claimed to have two items on his agenda. She wanted to hear it. "What's the second reason?"

He met her eyes. "I came to tell you that I love you."

Warmth spread throughout her body and filled her heart. Jackson Strom loved her. He loved her, and that love was going to hold her steady even when life got incredibly rocky.

"Last night I said a lot of things, except that," he went on. "I'm in love with you, Alexa."

"I love you, too, Jackson."

"All right," he said, his tone gentle. "That settles it."

Alexa fell back onto her stack of pillows, but it felt as if she were falling from the sky.

"Don't get too relaxed. We still have unfinished business."

"You mean item number one on your agenda?"

"Yes, of course."

"Are you kidding me?"

"Alexa, I'm in no mood to kid."

She sat up again and crossed her legs. "Is there any particular way you'd like this to go? Any specific language you'd like to hear?"

He folded his arms across his chest. In her dainty bedroom, he looked solid and strong. "Start by saying sorry."

"I *am* sorry, Jackson. I should not have stormed out the way I had."

Jackson tilted his head, considering her words. "Is that all?"

"What else?"

"Can't help you," he said. "You'll have to puzzle this one out."

She grabbed the same frilly pillow she'd clobbered Caitlyn with a moment ago and hugged it to her chest. "I'm sorry I wasn't completely honest with you. Okay?"

He remained impassive. "You'll have to expand on that."

"It's not that I don't trust you, because I do. With my whole heart, I trust you." Caitlyn's words were bouncing in her head. She had to make that point clear. "I was concerned about how you would react, but mostly I thought I could resolve my issues on my own and leave you out of it."

Jackson was waiting for more, but she couldn't think of anything else to say. Finally, he filled the gap. "You didn't want me to see you fail."

"Can you blame me?" Alexa cried. "We competed as kids, and I always came out on top. But look at us now. My career is in serious jeopardy, and you… Well, you're winning."

He leaned forward and gripped the iron rail of the footboard. "What good is it if I lose you again?"

"Oh, God." She pressed a palm to her forehead. This man was going to break her open, and there was nothing she could do about it.

Jackson straightened up, stripped off his suit jacket and tossed it onto the window bench. He then hunched low to unlace his polished leather shoes.

"What are you doing?" she asked.

He didn't answer. Instead, he joined her on the bed and gathered her in his arms. The old bedframe creaked. Alexa momentarily forgot they were midargument. She nestled closer to him and breathed in the clean scent of his skin. Yesterday, she'd walked away from this. She must not have been in her right mind.

The bed squeaked again. Jackson reached overhead and shook the vintage wrought iron headboard. "What is all this dollhouse furniture?"

"This is my mother's attempt at French provincial decor. She found these pieces at a flea market in Austin. It hasn't been touched since I left for college."

"Oh yeah?" he said. "Where are all of the boy band posters?"

"She stripped those down the day I left."

"How many nights did you spend in here plotting my downfall?"

"Way too many."

"Well, it worked." He kissed her forehead. "I fell for you hard. And I want you in my life. The question is, do you want me?"

She curled a hand around his tie. "Of course I do!"

"It's not that you didn't confide in me," he said. "It's that you didn't even want me to know something was wrong. I kept asking and you dodged the question every time."

"All I wanted was a chance to clean up the mess in Miami before coming back to you."

"That's not how it works," he said.

"How does it work, Jackson?" she asked. "I'm at a loss."

"Just talk to me," he said. "Trust me enough to tell me when you're hurting. I wouldn't have rushed off to fight your battles if that's what you were worried about. I respect you too much."

That had been part of it. Mostly, she had never wanted to be anything less to him than Alexandra the First, the girl whom he had admired at fifteen. Feeling uneasy, she reached for the little gold chess piece at her neck. It wasn't there, and its absence turned her uneasiness into boiling turmoil.

"I want my necklace back," she said. "I miss it."

"In that case…" He reached into the pocket of his trousers and dug out the familiar green velvet pouch. "Here you go, my queen."

Alexa snatched it from him, shook out the gold necklace and fastened it around her neck without his help. The pendant slid into the groove at the base of her neck. She traced its shape with her fingertips and sighed. "Much better." She could breathe again and think clearly. "Is this thing magic?"

"If luck is magic," he said. "The day I ran into you at the TCC pool party was the luckiest day of my life. That morning, I wasn't even sure I wanted to go."

Alexa didn't believe in luck. She put her faith in well-mapped plans. "Okay. Here's what we're going to do. You head back to work. I'm going to reach out to a law school friend. She's an attorney who specializes in employment law. I'm going to sue A & C."

His smile stretched into an I-told-you-so smirk. "Let's ruin them."

God, he was sexy when wicked. "I'm only seeking damages for wrongful termination. It won't put a dent in the firm's business, but they'll remember my name."

"I'm down for whatever you want to do."

"I want you to go to work," she said. "I'll come over tonight looking beautiful and rested, and we'll have the night that we should've had."

"I've got a better plan." He rolled on top of her and kissed her until she was winded again. "Let's play hooky."

She wrapped her arms around his neck, excitement rippling through her. "I've never done that."

"I'm not surprised."

"What would we even do? Spend the day playing pool in some kid's rec room?"

"Actually, we'd drive to the next county to shoot darts and drink beer."

Alexa laughed. How was that any better? "Not my style. I think I'll pass."

He tugged at her earlobe with his teeth. "Don't worry. I'll get you home before curfew."

"Jackson," Alexa whispered. "I'd break any rule for you."

He raised his head and looked at her through lowered lashes. Even so, she could see the emotion in his eyes. "We're in love," he whispered. "Wait until I tell our class Facebook group. They voted you most likely to break my heart."

"When did this vote happen?"

"That day we all played hooky."

"Makes sense."

"Maybe I won't take you home in time for curfew," he said. "Maybe I'll keep you."

Alexa went soft with love. There was nothing she wanted more. *Keep me. Keep me forever.* That was what she wanted to say. Instead, she kissed him and murmured against his lips, "I'm going to crush you at darts."

They did not drive to the next county. Instead, they drove out to North Cove Park, found a sturdy oak tree and got busy carving.

A-JACKS 4EVER <3

* * * *

THEIR MARRIAGE
BARGAIN

SHANNON McKENNA

One

"You have got to be joking," Caleb Moss said, staring at his grandmother. "But I don't find it funny."

Elaine Moss wore an elegant white suit, her back ramrod-straight as she gazed out the floor-to-ceiling window of Caleb's corner office, which overlooked downtown Seattle.

"I'm absolutely serious," she said. "I'm simply not afraid of making unpopular decisions. A skill you need to cultivate as CEO, young man."

"I'm thirty-four, Gran."

"I'm well aware, my love. That's precisely why this is happening."

"By insisting I get married before my birthday? In two months? I can't, Gran, even if I wanted to! Small detail. I don't have a fiancée."

"Find one," Gran said lightly. "You're free to refuse. On your birthday, I'll wish you many happy returns, and pass the controlling interest in MossTech to your uncle Jerome. Who will instantly fire you and hire his lickspittle yes-men. He'll fire Marcus and Maddie, too. But you three are all very gifted. I'm not the least bit concerned about your long-term career prospects."

"And MossTech itself? You don't give a damn about Grandpa Bertram's legacy?"

Elaine shot him a glance. The dart had landed. His grandmother was acutely sensitive about anything that threatened MossTech, their family firm, which specialized in cutting-edge food and agriculture technology. "Of course, I give a damn. But his three grandchildren are his legacy, too. And when you get to my age, things start to look different."

"The world doesn't work this way. It's not the court of Henry the Eighth."

"Thank God for that," Gran murmured. "He wasn't quite the model for harmonious matrimony that I was going for."

"This is not a joke," Caleb growled.

"I agree, one hundred percent," Gran said. "Marriage for everyone. The boys by age thirty-five. Maddie by age thirty. Unfair, I know, but as always, men can afford to dawdle in these matters, while women never can."

"I'm sure Maddie's going to have something to say about that."

"She can carry on until her throat cracks," Gran said. "It changes nothing."

Gran had that look that indicated that further argument was futile. His choices now were full compliance, or war. And with Gran, one had to think long and hard about choosing war. She was always three steps ahead.

"Jerome will take MossTech public," Caleb said. "We'll lose control of the company's moral compass. Grandpa Bertram didn't want that."

"Indeed, he did not. But sometimes you have to relinquish control of one thing in order to maintain hold on another."

"Stop with the cryptic platitudes," he said. "You can't force me to do this."

"No, but even if I were to drop dead of a heart attack this very day, the consequences of not doing it will remain. It's a done deal, my love. I was waiting for paperwork to be finalized to tell you, and for Marcus to come home. Then his return date got pushed out twice, and your birthday is looming, so I'm starting with you, Caleb. You're the oldest. The first fruit to fall."

"But Gran, I can't—"

"It annoys me that Marcus is off gallivanting. It shows poor judgment as a CEO to let your CTO spend his time slashing through some sweaty jungle with a machete."

"It keeps him out of trouble," Caleb said.

"So would marriage," Gran observed. "Nothing like a family to keep an energetic man busy."

"Gran, be reasonable," Caleb urged. "You've groomed us all our lives for this. You trained us to care about MossTech, and now you're just flushing it?"

Gran's lips tightened. "When you're a cunning and devious old man yourself, pulling strings to protect your own legacy, then maybe you'll understand me."

"I can't wait that long," Caleb said, biting the words out.

Caleb's desk intercom buzzed.

"Mr. Moss?" It was his assistant, Sergio. "A Mr. Herbert Riley from Riley BioGen to see you? He's actually not on your calendar, but he says that, um…that Mrs. Moss made the appointment?"

"Hold on, Sergio." Caleb turned to Gran. "We had a meeting with Herbert Riley scheduled tomorrow, and the situation is awkward enough, with you and Jerome trying to annex his company. Why on earth did you call him in here today?"

Gran fluffed up her spiky white hair. "You'll see. Don't make the man wait, Caleb. I know you men like to play at alpha-animal behavior, but I think it's just plain rude."

Hah. Like his grandmother wasn't the reigning queen of alpha-animal behavior.

He hit the intercom button. "Send him in, Sergio."

As CEO of MossTech, Caleb ran a tight ship, but the power dynamic got scrambled when Gran threw her weight around. When she started snapping orders, people got confused about who was in charge. She used to be CEO herself, and she still owned a controlling interest. But that expectant glint in her eyes made him tense. She had a fresh zinger for him.

Sergio opened the door. "Mr. Herbert Riley," he announced. "Ms. Tilda Riley."

Caleb froze. *Tilda?* She was on the other side of the world. No way was she—

She and her father walked in, and Caleb's insides went into free fall.

It had been nine years, three months, three weeks and two days. The relentless calculator in his mind kept grinding out hours, minutes. Even seconds.

She'd been nineteen the last time he saw her. Small, curvaceous, short, even with heels. Her blond head fit under his chin. Heart-shaped face. Hypnotically beautiful green eyes that revealed everything she thought and felt.

The last thing he'd seen in her eyes was shock. Hurt. Heartbreak.

Her eyes showed him nothing now. Her thick blond hair was twisted into a sleek roll, no dangling wisps. No more rose pink lip gloss. Her luscious lips were painted a hot, take-no-prisoners red. She did not smile. Not that he deserved a smile.

Caleb tuned into Gran's voice, belatedly.

"…know my grandson, Caleb Moss, of course? Our CEO?"

"Of course." Herbert Riley, Tilda's father, the owner and CEO of Riley BioGen, shook Caleb's hand.

"Tilda," Gran murmured. "Lovely as ever. I'm glad to see you back in this part of the world. I spotted you at the engagement brunch for Ava Maddox a few weeks ago."

"Yes, it was great to see old friends after so long." Tilda shook Gran's hand, then extended her hand to him politely. It was ice-cold.

"You've been gone so long," Gran went on. "Where were you, anyway? Singapore? South Korea? Taiwan?"

"All over Asia," Tilda said. "Wherever work took me."

Gran clucked. "So far away."

Herbert grunted. "Too far."

"You must be thrilled to have your precious granddaughter home to spoil."

"I am indeed," Herbert agreed.

That gave Caleb a nasty jolt. He turned to Tilda. "You're married?"

Her green eyes snapped onto him. "No," she said coolly.

The awkward silence was broken finally by Herbert Riley. "So, Elaine. We shoehorned this meeting in at your request, and we don't have much time. Why did you insist that Tilda and I meet with you today?"

"Sit down." Gran beckoned them to the couch and chairs. "Shall I ask Sergio to bring coffee, tea? Espresso? A glass of Scotch?"

Command came to Gran as natural as breathing, but Caleb was annoyed to have his office, assistant and liquor cabinet all co-opted by his grandmother in front of Tilda Riley.

He also caught the flash of amusement in her eyes.

"It's early for Scotch," Herbert said gruffly. "Let's get down to business, please."

Caleb belatedly realized that they were still on their feet, waiting for him to join them before they sat down. *Damn.* He walked over with a murmur of apology.

Gran perched on the edge of a chair. "I wanted to meet alone because this must be discussed only with the persons most intimately concerned," she began.

"If MossTech annexes Riley BioGen, everyone in my company will be intimately concerned," Herbert said. "By which I mean, unemployed. Over eight hundred of them."

"I'm well aware of that," Gran said. "I am proposing a solution. Which involves you two young people." She indicated Tilda and Caleb.

"Gran, cut to the chase," Caleb said.

"Don't be rude," Gran murmured. "I'm proposing something different from Jerome's idea. A friendly merger. One that safeguards the jobs at Riley BioGen."

"Your overtures aren't friendly," Tilda said. "You knew Dad was having health issues. You took advantage of his distraction to buy in as a silent partner, and now you're manipulating our shareholders. Threatening a proxy fight. Not friendly, Mrs. Moss."

"That's Jerome's game, my dear," Elaine said. "Not Caleb's."

Tilda's chin was up, her eyes alight. "You did it yourself, or you allowed it to be done on your behalf. For our purposes, I don't see any difference."

"We know how much debt you have," Gran said. "If you don't accept our offer, Riley BioGen will go bankrupt."

Tilda's eyes narrowed. "We can manage our debt."

"I wish to propose another solution, if I could get a word in edgewise," Gran said. "You're a bright girl. What if you could safeguard the eight hundred jobs at Riley BioGen? We would prefer to join forces. Not destroy your company."

Tilda crossed her legs, giving Caleb a distracting view of her shapely calf. "Why suddenly change your tune? What do you want, Mrs. Moss?"

"The most natural thing possible," Gran said softly. "A marriage."

Oh, hell no. Caleb's guts went into free fall again. Tilda just looked confused.

"Ah…" Herbert frowned at Elaine. "Well, in a theoretical sense, of course."

"Not theoretical," Gran said.

Tilda's eyes went huge in the silence. "Wait," she said. "No way. Is this some bizarre joke? Because it's not funny."

Herbert Riley's eyes widened. "Dear God, Elaine. Get someone to help you sort your meds."

"I'll see that she does," Caleb said. "I apologize to both of you. I don't—"

"Do not apologize for me, Caleb." Gran's voice was sharp. "I take responsibility for every word I say."

Tilda let out a brittle laugh. "Wow. Mrs. Moss, thank you. It's a very romantic offer, and I'm deeply flattered, but I'm afraid I must decline."

"Then we'll proceed with the proxy fight," Gran said.

Tilda and her father exchanged horrified glances.

"Gran," Caleb said. "It's one thing to bully me. You can't do this to her."

"Can't I?" Gran asked. "This would solve your problem, too. Wouldn't it?"

"What problem?" Tilda's eyes sharpened.

"You might not be surprised to learn that this isn't even the weirdest idea my grandmother has had so far today," Caleb said through his teeth. "She's informed me that I have to get married before I'm thirty-five. Or else the sky falls."

"Elaine, you're being ridiculous," Herbert said. "This is my daughter's happiness you're talking about. These two hardly know each other. It's insulting."

Gran turned a speculative gaze onto Caleb and Tilda. "I'm paying her the highest possible compliment, Herbert. I wouldn't propose this to just anyone. And I think these two know each other quite well indeed."

Tilda got to her feet. Her face was a hot pink. "Let's go, Dad." She looked up at Caleb. "Call a family meeting, Caleb. It's time to take away Grandma's car keys. Before someone gets hurt."

"Bite your tongue, you mouthy little minx," Elaine snapped back. "Think about it. Look at your balance sheet. Think about your employees. Then we'll talk."

Caleb got to the door in time to open it before Tilda did.

"Sorry," he said softly. "I had no idea. I swear."

But Tilda made no eye contact as she swept out, head high, chin up.

Two

God, what was wrong with her? Why hadn't she whipped out the war file and used it, on the spot? What had held her back? Tilda strode through MossTech's lofty, sky-lit lobby, furious at herself. She'd armed herself with a doomsday weapon, and as soon as she saw Caleb Moss's gorgeous face, she forgot to freaking use it. *Damn.*

"Sweetheart, I'm sorry." Dad's voice behind her was breathless and choppy. "I—I have to sit down for a sec. I'm having a moment."

Tilda spun around, horrified. She'd been so self-absorbed, she'd forgotten how fragile Dad was right now. She took his arm. "Dad, is it your heart?"

"Absolutely not." Dad wheezed. "I just need to, ah…stop. The coffee bar. They have chairs."

Tilda glanced over at the coffee bar, and guided her father's faltering steps into the small café. She settled him at a table that had a soft upholstered chair. She hated to see her father like this. His lips looked tight and grayish.

Tilda kneeled in front of him and squeezed his hand. "Dad, don't be a stubborn idiot. Do I need to call the ambulance? Because if we get this wrong, I'm the one who pays with a lifetime of guilt and regret."

Dad patted her shoulder. "My tough girl," he murmured. "Believe me, I know how a heart attack feels, and this isn't it. I just got light-headed."

"I'll get you some tea. Would you like some pastry?"

"Just tea's fine, honey. Thanks."

Tilda didn't have long to wait at the counter. Soon she was back with a cup of French roast for herself, tea for Dad and some lemon pound cake to offset the adrenaline crash. She'd expected an unpleasant meeting, considering that MossTech had been herding her dad's company like a lamb into the slaughtering pen. She'd been steeled for attack, defense, counterattack. She hadn't been steeled for a marriage proposal.

Though, to be fair, that looked like it had taken Caleb off guard, too.

Wow. Those were some deeply weird family dynamics. She did not envy him that grandmother. No wonder the guy was so monumentally screwed up.

It would have been nice to find him somewhat diminished from how she remembered him, but oh, no. Caleb Moss was still smoking hot.

Nine years had just weathered him a little. Chiseled his gorgeous face with some sexy, expressive grooves and lines. But his big, powerful body seemed more dense and solid. His cheekbones were just as sharp. And those piercing, deep-set eyes. That sexy mouth. So hotly sensual, for a guy who was so cold inside.

It was unfair. False advertising.

His hair had been a long dark mane, back in his wild rebel days. Now it was short, buzzed down to nothing on his neck, barely longer on top. Short hair looked just as good on him. And those eyes. So much like her Annika's.

"Here's your tea, Dad. Earl Grey, steamed milk, two sugars. Have some cake with it." She took a bracing sip of her own coffee. "Feeling any better?"

"Absolutely." Dad gave her a wan smile as he blew on his tea.

"You shouldn't be running around so soon after your surgery," Tilda scolded. "Let me and your team handle things. It's why I came back. To help."

"You are helping. I just wish you hadn't come home to such a god-awful mess."

"It's not your fault, Dad."

"Then whose is it?" Dad set down his cup and took off his glasses, pressing a hand over his eyes.

Oh, to hell with this. She was making this judgment call herself. Tilda pulled out her phone. The call connected with Adam, a junior member of Riley BioGen's legal team.

"Hi, Tilda," Adam said. "See you in Murray's office in a few?"

"No, we'll have to reschedule, Adam. Dad's not well." Her fingers tightened around her father's clammy hand as his eyes widened in protest. She put up her hand to forestall his protests. "I'm taking him to the cardiologist as soon as she can fit him in. She'll let us know if we should go straight to Urgent Care."

She finished the call and slid her phone back into her purse. "Handled."

"I'm not a doddering invalid," her father said as he picked up his cup of tea again. "I could have handled the meeting just fine. Do not hover over me, Til."

"We'll see if Dr. Walensky can see you. I did not haul ass all the way back from the ends of the earth just to lose you now. And Annika is finally getting to know her grandfather. Save your energy for getting better. And for fighting the Mosses."

Dad sputtered his tea and patted his mouth with the napkin that Tilda handed him, shaking his head. "Those Mosses," he said, coughing. "That was surreal."

Tilda was too busy on the phone scheduling the appointment with Dad's cardiologist to comment, but he didn't need to know that at one time, marrying Caleb Moss had been her idea of the pinnacle of earthly bliss. That had been a younger and sillier Tilda Riley.

She slid the phone into her purse. "They're just being their cold-blooded, calculating selves."

"But you are not an asset to be exploited. You are my precious, unique daughter, and these blood-sucking manipulators would do well to remember it."

Tilda squeezed his hand. "Thanks, Dad."

"How is it that you're on Elaine's radar at all?" her father asked. "I didn't know you even knew her."

"I don't, really. Just by sight. She saw me at Ava Maddox's engagement party while you were still in the rehab facility. Ava's getting married to the CSO of Maddox Hill, and she told me there would be kids at the party, so we went. Maddie, Veronica and Elaine Moss were all there."

"Did you notice Caleb's reaction to Elaine's suggestion? Like he was blindsided. But Elaine seemed under the impression that you two knew each other."

Tilda hesitated for just a moment. "We did," she said. "Remember when I interned in San Francisco the summer after I graduated from Stanford? Caleb was doing start-up with a friend of his. Ava Maddox introduced us. We dated for a while."

Her father set down his cup, eyes wide. "You did? You never told me that."

She shrugged. "Why would I? It didn't work out. It wasn't relevant."

"Elaine Moss thought that it was. Is there something you're not telling me?"

The lemon cake felt dry. She washed it down with coffee. "I don't burden you with my romantic disappointments, Dad. I have girlfriends for that kind of thing."

"You are sidestepping me, honey."

"Dad, I'm not trying to—"

"When were you seeing him?" her father demanded.

"What, do you want dates and times? Dad, please."

"The summer after you graduated, you took that job in Kuala Lumpur. Then you called me in May, to tell me I was a grandfather. I about had a heart attack right then."

"Yes," Tilda said.

"Caleb Moss is Annika's father," Dad said flatly.

Dear God. All she needed today. A dose of brutal truth-telling, right after a stiff dose of Caleb Moss himself. A one-two punch. "What do you want me to say, Dad?"

"The truth, which you should've told me years ago. So he abandoned you, and he acts like it's nothing? Not a word today? Is he some kind of ice-cold sociopath?"

"He doesn't know about Annika," she explained. "I never spoke to him again, after we broke up. I found out I was pregnant in Kuala Lumpur. Months later."

"You never told him? Why the hell not? He has a re-sponsibility!"

"I didn't want to see him," she said. "I didn't even want to hear his voice on the phone. Nor did I want that family doing weird power plays over my baby. It's hard enough to be a single mother. I didn't want to have to fight anyone for Annika."

"Elaine knows," her father said.

Tilda was startled. "How could she? I never told anyone."

"Then she guesses. I've known that woman forty years. She's as sharp as a tack."

"I don't see how it's possible," Tilda said.

"What was the problem with Caleb?" Dad demanded. "Was he cruel? Violent?"

"Oh, no, Dad. Just a garden-variety asshole. He dumped me, that's all. Coldly and abruptly. My feelings got hurt. That's all there was to it. Nothing so terrible."

Her father grunted darkly under his breath. "Ungrate-ful son of a bitch. But I couldn't help but notice, honey. You had your weaponized file in your briefcase, to threaten them with, and you never even pulled it out. What's that about?"

Tilda shrugged. "I got rattled," she said. "Distracted. I might still use it. We'll see."

"I don't like to see you get your hands dirty," her father said. "It's a poor use of your energy. You're a brilliant engineer and data analyst. You should be doing research, invention, innovation, your AI algorithm. What's it called again? Far See?"

"Far Eye," Tilda corrected. "And I'm not getting my hands dirty. I'm fighting for survival. We need to get going, if we want to get to Dr. Walensky's office in time."

The cardiologist's exam didn't take long, and they were both relieved when the doctor recommended that Herbert simply go home and relax. After weeks in the hospital for open heart surgery and even longer in the rehab facility, Dad was loath to go near a hospital bed again.

When they got home, Annika and her babysitter had just gotten back from an afternoon science-museum outing. Annika ran to greet them, bright-eyed with excitement, fresh off a virtual-reality museum trip through the human circulatory system.

"It was, like, an amusement-park ride, Mom! We put on a VR helmet, and me and Kaylea got on this big red blood cell, sort of like a big red Frisbee, and then we took a trip through the body, transporting sugar and oxygen into the cells! You have to try it!"

"Oh, I'd love to, honey," she assured her, stroking the girl's hair. "We'll go to the exhibit again together. Maybe next weekend."

Tilda ran upstairs to throw on leggings and a sweater and then got dinner on. Annika kept her grandfather busy with her chatter, and Tilda studied her little girl's animated face over the kitchen bar as she laid out the meal the housekeeper had left for them.

Annika had Caleb's striking dark eyes, strong eyebrows and sharp cheekbones. But even so, a pretty little girl just looked like a pretty little girl, compared to a grown man.

How could Elaine have made that leap? Caleb hadn't been at Ava's party himself to invite comparison. In fact, Tilda hadn't even spoken to Elaine. She barely knew the woman.

When they finished their ice cream, Tilda glanced at the clock. "Bedtime, cutie."

"Can I watch a video first?" Annika wheedled.

"Nope, straight to bed. Get your hair and teeth brushed. I'll come give you a kiss."

After Annika had given her grandfather a good-night hug and run off upstairs, Tilda's dad, who was in the next room, closed his eyes and eased back his head. He looked pale and exhausted.

"Dad?" Tilda said from the kitchen. "Everything okay?"

Dad didn't open his eyes. "I'm just sad that I can't pick up the slack for Annika."

"Meaning what? What slack?"

Dad waved his hand vaguely. "As a father figure. I just don't have the strength."

Tilda dried her hands with the dish towel and marched into the living room. "Of course, you don't. You're on freaking beta-blockers. Your sternum will be knitting for months. But you'll get your mojo back."

"Maybe," Dad said faintly. "Some of it. Not enough."

This kind of talk alarmed her. She sat down on the couch, opposite him, and leaned forward. "We work with what we've got," she said sternly. "You taught me that yourself. You get what you get, and you don't get upset. No moping allowed. Remember?"

Her father's mouth twitched. "That's my girl. The tough babe."

"I need you to be strong for me, Dad. And positive."

Dad nodded. "Yes, of course," he soothed. "I'll try, I promise. No more moping."

Tilda had put Annika in her own childhood bedroom. When she got there, the little girl was curled up in a lump under a flowered antique quilt. She turned worried eyes to her mother. "Mom, is Grandpa okay?"

"He's just tired, because his heart's still healing from the operation," Tilda explained. "And he's taking a medication that keeps his heart rate slow. That takes away his energy. But he'll be okay."

"I hope he will," Annika said. "I want to have a grandpa, at least."

"Hmm? 'At least?' What does that mean?"

"When I was with Kaylea, she was complaining about her family. She has a mom, a dad, a sister, two brothers, two uncles, three aunts, eight cousins, and six grandmas and grandpas."

"Six? Wow!"

"Yeah, she's got extras, because both grandmas married twice. And she complains. She can never get into the bathroom. But I think it sounds nice." Annika snuggled closer. "Kaylea's nice, but I miss my friends from school," she said wistfully.

"I know, honey. I'm sorry I had to pull you away from everything."

"I know. We had to come home to help Grandpa. But tonight, he just seemed so sad. I couldn't even make him smile. At least, I couldn't make the smile stick."

"You are a sweetheart for trying," Tilda said.

Tilda kissed Annika good-night, her throat tight. When she came back downstairs, she sat down on the couch, pulling a big file out of her briefcase.

"Is that the file that could take MossTech down in flames?" Dad asked.

"Yes. Take a look." She laid it on his lap.

Her father seemed reluctant to touch it. "Where did you get this, anyhow?"

"A venture capitalist that I know. I saw him recently at a tech conference in Rio," she said. "We were talking about him possibly financing Far Eye. Weston Brody."

Dad looked impressed. "Really? Brody Venture Capitalists? Far Eye must have some serious potential, if a player like Brody is interested."

"Yes, he liked the project. Then we got to talking. He told me MossTech was coming after Riley BioGen. He offered me this. Said it could bring the Mosses down."

Dad rifled through the sheaf of papers "Orient me, honey. What is it exactly?"

"A journal written by John Padraig, director of a Moss-Tech lab in Sri Lanka, twenty-three years ago. Remember when that MossTech lab blew up there?"

"Of course. A terrorist attack. Naomi Moss, Jerome's wife, was killed. She was a friend of mine, from Caltech. She had a daughter your age. Veronica. It broke my heart."

"Right," Tilda said. "Padraig was a lab director. Moss-Tech was developing a strain of drought-and-pest-resistant millet. It was a perfect host for a toxic mold. A lot of people died, but it was covered up. People paid off, lab reports falsified. All in Padraig's journal."

Her father squinted through his bifocals at the cursive scrawl. "Hard to read."

Tilda fished out a document. "Here's a printed transcript. Padraig thought Naomi was behind it, acting on behalf of Elaine, Bertram and Jerome Moss."

Her father leafed through the pages. "Why does Brody want to hurt the Mosses?"

"I don't know, Dad. He didn't tell me."

"Ah. So why didn't he just do it himself?"

"He'd rather avoid blowback, for his own company's sake. So he's using me."

"Yes, aren't they all," Dad said sourly. "It seems to be a pattern."

"Come on, Dad. He's just trying to help."

Her father let out a doubtful grunt as he flipped through the file. "Naomi was my thesis advisor at Caltech, before she married Jerome Moss. I was half in love with her. She was so principled. She would never have done this. Naomi would have made things right." He patted the file. "Something's off. It rings false."

"So you think it would be wrong to use it against them?"

"If it were true beyond doubt, I'd say, go for it. But is it? Can you be sure?"

Tilda sighed. "I've been trying to decide that ever since Wes gave it to me."

"I'd leave it alone," Dad advised. "Let MossTech do their worst. We'll manage. I just wanted you covered financially, and to have something set aside for Annika's education."

"We'll be fine, Dad. I have skills."

"Of course, you do. You'll land on your feet. As for me, well… Riley BioGen is just a company. Things are born, and then they die. It's the natural order of things."

"I don't want all the people who've worked for you for decades to lose their jobs."

"Me, neither," Dad said bleakly. "But I don't think this file could stop it."

Tilda was silent for a long moment. "I could marry Caleb Moss," she said slowly. "That would stop it."

The papers on her father's lap slid from his hands, and scattered all over the floor.

"No way," he said. "Honey. Tell me you're not serious. You already ran away from this man once. And he doesn't even know about Annika."

"Things are different now. I never intended to marry, anyhow," Tilda said. "Fate already saw fit to give me a child, and she's a spectacular one. I'm satisfied with Annika. I don't need anything more from Caleb other than his signature on a few documents. If he's interested in being part of her life as her father, I'll just stipulate in writing that I have control over all decisions concerning her. So why the hell not? It's just a business move, Dad."

"Wait a little longer, baby," Dad pleaded. "Think about this."

Tilda thought of what Caleb said that night, when she'd offered him her love.

Well. She wouldn't make that mistake again. She pulled out Elaine's card, and entered the number in her phone.

"I'm done thinking," she said. "Time to act."

Three

"Tell me you're kidding," Maddie said. "Please, Gran. Please tell me that."

"I'm afraid I can't," Gran said, her voice resolute. "It's real, and it's already done, my dear."

Caleb kept his back to them as he stared out through the library window at Gran's house. He was so angry, his hands were shaking. "You brainwashed us about MossTech," he said. "And we all bought in to it, like good little soldiers. Protect Grandpa Bertram's legacy! Feed the hungry, protect the soil, safeguard the future! Now you're holding Grandpa's company hostage just to jerk us around?"

"Hostage, my foot," Elaine sniffed. "Such apocalyptic language."

"And seriously?" Maddie said. "The boys get until age thirty-five, and I only get until thirty? How is that fair?"

"It's not, sweetie. Take it up with your higher power. Men have a bigger margin for error when it comes to reproductive timing."

"But I don't even want to reproduce!" Maddie wailed.

"Nonsense. In any case, it's all of you, or none of you. If even one of you defies the mandate, Jerome gets the shares."

"He'll take us public, like he always wanted," Caleb said. "I thought you cared about MossTech's moral compass. Valuing people over profit. Was that all bullshit?"

Gran looked chastened. "Not at all. I care very much."

"So why?" Maddie's voice was getting dangerously high. "Why now?"

Gran sank onto a chair. "At my age, you start taking stock of your mistakes," she said. "My biggest mistake was with your mother. I was too permissive with her. I wanted that fire in her belly to light itself, but it never did. She was as bright and gifted as any one of you three, but all she wanted was to play."

"We're not her, Gran," Maddie said sharply.

"I'm well aware. But I overcompensated with you three, and now I regret it. I was so strict and demanding. Look at you kids now. Driven. Work-obsessed. And single. Not one of you has shown even the slightest urge to start a family—"

"You always taught me that women have a bigger destiny than just making babies!" Caleb's sister raged. "It's not fair to flip the script on me now!"

"I did my work too well. You all should be dating up a storm. You're intelligent, accomplished, attractive. But you hold yourselves back. I can't allow that."

Caleb made a frustrated sound. "And this blinding realization came to you how? In a dream? A vision? A burning bush?"

"Watch the snark, my boy," Gran warned. "It came to me at Ava Maddox's engagement party a few weeks ago."

"I was at that party," Maddie said. "I don't remember any angels with flaming swords."

"That's enough of your sass," Gran snapped.

"Ava's party, huh? So Ava got herself a hot guy to make beautiful babies with, and you're jealous because I don't have one? Do you have any idea how lucky Ava is? She's madly in love, and Zack adores her. But guess what, Gran? I want that, too. I won't settle for something half-assed just to comply with your crazy demands! I want the real thing!"

"I want the best for you, too, but you won't get it crunching numbers eighty hours a week," Gran retorted. "And my epiphany didn't come about from seeing Ava's intended, although he is a sight to behold. My epiphany was when I saw Tilda's little girl."

Caleb's guts clenched at the mention of Tilda's daughter. "What about her?"

"What about her?" Gran said. "You can say that? With a straight face?"

"You've lost me, Gran."

"As soon as I laid eyes on that child, I called my assistant and had her do some research. Annika Ruth Riley, eight years old, born in Kuala Lumpur. After one look at her, I can say exactly what you, Caleb, were doing with Tilda Riley, nine months before that."

Caleb frowned at her, his mind wiped stupid by shock. *"What?"*

"You were in the Bay Area back then, correct? Working on that start-up of yours. And she was at Stanford, as I recall. Bright girl. Graduated very early."

Maddie's hazel eyes widened. "Oh, my God. That's huge, bro. Is it true?"

He opened his mouth, closed it. "I—I don't know." His voice was hollow.

"I do." Gran's voice rang with certainty.

"Come on, Gran," Maddie said. "You can't be sure. Not without a DNA test."

"I'm sure. That child is identical to your mother. My poor Susannah. It was like seeing a ghost. I had to sit down, or I would have fallen down."

They turned to Caleb. "So?" Maddie asked. "Is it true?"

"Is what true?" he snapped. "I only just learned this girl existed!"

"Then I'll be very specific," Elaine said. "Were you rolling around in bed with Tilda Riley nine years ago?"

"We were involved," he admitted. "It ended badly. She went abroad. I haven't heard from her since."

There was a heavy silence.

"That little girl grew up on the other side of the planet. I might never have known she existed." The shaky intensity in Gran's voice made him nervous.

"Don't bite my head off, Gran," Maddie said carefully. "But this child is Annika Riley, not Susannah. Okay? Do not get them confused."

"I am not confused," Elaine snapped. "Don't condescend to me. I have a right to feel cheated about never having met my own great-grandchild."

"We don't even know if it's true," Caleb said. "This is the first I've heard of it."

"You must've made quite an impression, to make her race off all the way to Kuala Lumpur. Nine years, and not a peep? Nicely done, Caleb."

"Yes, she despises me. I could've told you that, if you had given me a heads-up!"

"I couldn't give you time to develop a defense strategy. Sorry for the adrenaline rush, but that was kind of the point."

"Gran, can't you see how sick this behavior is?"

"Oh, twaddle. Clearly, you made a connection with Tilda. Then you backed away. Maybe you should rethink that decision, now that you're older and wiser."

His grandmother's phone buzzed in her purse, and she pulled it out. "Speak of the devil. It's Tilda."

He was jolted. "You have her number in your phone?"

"I did my research. And gave her my card. It's good to leave lines of communication open. Unlike you. Nine years. For the love of God, Caleb."

"Damn it, Gran—"

"Shhh!" She hit the speakerphone button. "Tilda!" she sang out. "Thanks for reaching out."

"Good evening, Mrs. Moss." Tilda's clear voice was velvety smooth. Caleb felt a shiver rush over his skin, as if he'd been stroked.

"Please, call me Elaine. No need for such formality."

"Thanks. Are you with Caleb now? I want to speak to him, but I don't have his direct number."

"As a matter of fact, I am. We were just discussing you. How coincidental."

"Isn't it, though." Tilda's voice was crisp. "Would you pass me to him?"

"Of course." Elaine held out the phone.

Caleb turned off the speakerphone, and put the phone to his ear. "Hello?"

"Hello, Caleb." There was amusement in Tilda's voice. "Let's clarify something, before another word is said. Elaine's proposal seemed to take you by surprise."

"It did," he admitted.

"I see. So should I assume that the marriage proposal isn't valid?"

"Ah…." Caleb paused to gather his nerve. "Why do you ask?"

Tilda made an impatient sound. "Don't waste time being coy. If your grandmother was blathering nonsense, tell me now, and I won't bother you again."

Caleb calmed the tremor in his voice. "What about your daughter?"

"What about her? How is that part of this discussion?"

"Is she mine?"

Tilda said nothing for a long moment. "Yes," she finally admitted.

A shock wave jolted up his spine. He realized that he'd sat down, very hard, on one of the library chairs. His ears were roaring.

"…there? Caleb? Are you still on the line?"

"Yes. Still here." His voice was strangled.

"You never answered my question. So? The proposal?"

"Valid," he said, forcing out the word. "But we have to talk." He caught Gran's gaze, then Maddie's. He'd completely forgotten they were there, both listening avidly to his end of the conversation.

"In private," he said pointedly.

"Tomorrow?"

"Tonight," he said. "The Black Dog Tavern. You're at your Dad's, right? Ten thirty okay? I can pick you up at—"

"I'll meet you at the Black Dog."

He hesitated. "You don't want me to meet her?"

"Annika? Not tonight. She's been in bed for an hour. In any case, you aren't meeting her until I have an idea of what would be expected of me. Or her."

"Nothing bad," he said quickly.

She harrumphed. "See you soon, Caleb. Later."

Caleb put Gran's phone down on the table. He couldn't seem to breathe.

"Caleb?" Gran prompted. "What did she say?"

"None of your business." He strode out of the library and down the hall. Out the door.

"Caleb! Get back here!" Gran's voice faded as he sprinted toward his car.

He might even have time for a shower and shave, if he hauled ass.

Tilda fidgeted in the back of the car, angry at herself for taking her hair down. It was a decision born of frustration, after attempts to put it up ended in failure. Her arms felt boneless, her fingers bloodless. But an updo was an important nonverbal message. It said that she was grown up, formal, guarded. Not a girl to be played with and tossed aside.

She was a professional. A mother. A warrior. And the loose blond curls bouncing cheerfully down her back did not communicate that at all.

She went into the tavern, grateful for the dim lighting. She instantly spotted Caleb in the back. She was intensely self-conscious as she strode toward him. Her face, her hair, her clothes, her mouth, her walk.

Caleb didn't smile as she approached. "Hey, Tilda."

"Hello, Caleb."

He gestured at the seat opposite him. She slid into it, folding her fingers on the table in front of her. "Wow," she murmured. "This is awkward."

"It's not every day that my grandmother offers me up in marriage," he said, a smile flashing across his face. "I apologize for the shock."

"No problem. I'm tough as boot leather these days."

The waitress appeared. They ordered beers, and Caleb indicated the menus. "Do you want dinner? The burgers are good here."

"I'm not really hungry."

They gazed at each other for a minute. "Jesus, Tilda," Caleb said. "Why didn't you tell me?"

She lifted an eyebrow. "Do you remember what you said to me that last night?"

Caleb looked uncomfortable. "More or less, but I'd rather not."

"You said love didn't exist. That I was deluded by my own body chemistry. That what I felt for you was what all virgins feel for the guy who does the honors."

He winced. "I was a huge dickhead."

"Definitely. When I found out I was pregnant, I was half a world away. The longer I waited, the less I wanted to tell you. Annika and I were fine on our own. Now she's getting to know her grandfather. So it's all good."

"I heard about Herbert's heart problems. I'm glad he's better."

"He'd be better still if his company weren't being attacked. Save your platitudes."

"They're sincere," Caleb said. "And since we're being

sincere, Riley BioGen had problems before Jerome started stalking it. At this point, you need us."

"Let's put that debate aside for now," she said. "We have other things to discuss."

"Whatever you like."

The waitress was back with their beers. Tilda took a sip. "So. That grandmother of yours is badass," she said. "Is she always up in your business like that?"

Caleb let out a laugh. "Today, she shocked even me. She ruled with an iron hand when she was CEO. She's never hesitated to share her opinions about our choices. And all that said, today was not normal."

"So she means it, then? Marry by your birthday, or suffer dire consequences?"

"Yes. Me, Maddie and Marcus. We marry, or she gives control of the company to my uncle. Who has a very different vision for MossTech. One we do not share."

"Is there anyone else you've been dating?" she asked. "Other wife candidates? Excuse my bluntness, but we might as well get it out there. No surprises."

Caleb shook his head. "No one. I've been very focused on work lately."

"And you're open to solving our mutual problems by marrying me?"

"Yes," he said.

"She can't mandate more grandchildren," Tilda warned.

"How could she? No one can control that."

"What I mean is, this will be a marriage in name only," Tilda said. "A business arrangement. If we abide by the terms, we get what we want. You get your grandmother off your back, and your company secured."

"And an opportunity to know my daughter," he said.

She was startled by the sudden rush of emotion that clutched at her throat. She loved the thought of Annika having the warmth and security and protection of a father, in spite of the risk involved. She hadn't known how much she wanted that.

She swallowed hard. "Seems fair."

"And you?" he asked. "What do you want?"

"I want my father's legacy protected. I want all of his staff to keep their jobs. Our own people know our intellectual property, our equipment, our research. I want continuity. For the systems we've developed over the last forty years to keep on functioning."

"That sounds fair, and in everyone's best interests. Riley BioGen in top form, with all its trained people in place, is more valuable than a pile of rubble."

"It must be hard to take," she said. "Elaine using Moss-Tech as a game chip."

"It makes me furious," he admitted. "We've quadrupled our bottom line while never compromising our principles. And suddenly, she'd just hand it all over to that conniving bastard, Jerome."

"Sounds like there's no love lost," Tilda said.

"Nope, Jerome isn't very lovable. Particularly not to Gran." Caleb shrugged. "The prospect of a great-grand-daughter is very motivating to her."

"Hmm," Tilda murmured. "That's another thing. How did she know about Annika? I never told anyone you were her father. Not even my dad."

"Evidently, she resembles my late mother as a child," Caleb said. "Gran saw Annika at Ava Maddox's party, and it was like seeing the ghost of her daughter, Susannah. She was very shaken."

"Ah. I see."

"Do you have a photo of her on your phone?"

Tilda pulled up some recent pictures of Annika on her phone, and passed it to him.

Caleb scrolled through the photos, staring at them intently. "It's true," he said. "I barely remember my mother, but I've seen pictures of her at that age. It could be the same person. She's a very beautiful girl."

"She's a wonderful kid. Sweet, funny, bright, perceptive. Very outspoken and opinionated. She senses bullshit instinctively. I doubt she gets that from me."

One of his eyebrows went up. "Are you trying to scare me?"

"Just telling you what she's like. Which brings me to an important point. Married or not, I'm the one who makes decisions involving Annika. Not you, not Elaine. Me."

Caleb nodded. "I'm getting the picture. Marriage in name only, Riley BioGen is treated with kid gloves and Annika is yours. Defensive much?"

She gazed at him with narrowed eyes. "Defensive, very," she said. "Speaking of which. One more thing. An escape route. At some point, we have to be free to divorce."

"Gran's paperwork specifies five years."

"Wow," Tilda mused. "That's very long. I have no intention of having any more children, but you might, at some point. That could cramp your style."

"I doubt it," he said.

"And, of course, we should both be free to pursue other relationships during that term," Tilda said. "Discreetly, of course."

The air buzzed with sudden tension. "Is there someone I should know about right now?" Caleb asked, his voice careful. "Are you seeing someone?"

She shook her head. "Just thinking ahead."

"All right." Caleb scrolled through the pictures on her phone again.

"How does it feel, to see her?" she asked.

"Strange," he said. "I missed so much. I have no idea how she looked as a baby. What her voice sounds like."

Tilda pushed away a rush of guilt. "I couldn't tell you about her, Caleb."

"I understand," he said. "I get how you felt, nine years ago. I pushed you away really hard. I regret that. But I hope to make up for lost time."

"So...you're interested in being her father? For real?"

"Yes." He pushed her phone back across the table. "This is the main thing we have to work out, you and I. The rest is just noise."

She breathed down a rush of emotion that startled her. "I'm glad that you feel that way. It's hard, being the only one who sees how awesome she is at close range. Besides her grandfather, of course."

"I look forward to seeing it myself."

"But get this straight," she said. "It's hard work. And you can't wimp out. Is that clear? Because if you get her hopes up about having a real dad, and then you let her down, I will hunt you to the ends of the earth and tear you into bloody little chunks. Got it?"

Caleb grinned. "I approve of that kind of family-first intensity," he said. "Annika is lucky. No, I won't let her down. Maddie and Gran are on fire to meet her, and they'll never let her down, either."

"Okay, then." She blew out a sharp breath. "Let's have our lawyers meet to get started. What about the marriage license, and all that?"

"I'll have my people take care of it."

"Excellent," she said. "Then I think we're done for the time being."

"I'll walk you to your car," Caleb said.

"I took a car service."

"Even better. I'll drive you home."

She was too fluttery and rattled to think of a reason to refuse. Soon, she was seated in his Porsche. She offered no polite conversation, just sat there in the dark, hands twisted together, wondering if she'd made a colossal mistake.

When they were almost to her dad's house, Caleb spoke up.

"Tilda," he said. "I'm sorry about what I said, that night. I'm not proud of it."

Tilda thought about how long it had taken to put herself back together. The years she'd cried herself to sleep. The anger that had slowly hardened into ice.

"Don't apologize," she said. "There's no repairing what was broken. It's passed and gone. This is just a business arrangement now."

"I see," he said.

"Good night, then. See you soon."

As she opened the car door, Caleb bent over her hand and pressed a soft kiss against her knuckles. She got out of the car and hurried to Dad's front door.

She watched the car's taillights disappear into the night, his kiss burning against her hand.

Four

"I wish I could be there," Marcus said. "But you didn't give me any notice. This is out of the blue."

Caleb moved away from Maddie, Gran and his cousin Ronnie's excited chatter, so he could better hear his brother's voice on the phone. "At least I got through to you before it happened," he said. "It's not like a real marriage. It's a business thing."

"Even so. I look forward to meeting her. You sure this is a good idea?"

"I'm not sure about anything anymore," he admitted.

"Hmmph, it's fun to hear you sounding so rattled, dude. Maybe this will shake things up in your perfect little world."

Caleb snorted. "Right, bro. You know that Gran is coming for you, too, right? Maddie turns thirty before you turn thirty-five, but even so. You'd better start thinking about a solution."

Marcus grunted under his breath. "When hell freezes over."

Hah. If Caleb had been railroaded into this, he'd be damned if he'd let his brother off the hook. But this was not the time for an argument. "We'll talk later," he said. "Gotta go. Things are happening."

"Okay. Congrats, good luck and all that."

Caleb ended the call and turned back to the womenfolk, all of whom had absolutely insisted on witnessing and marking this event. Both Maddie and Ronnie, his cousin, were looking misty-eyed. Lucky Ronnie, being just a niece and not a granddaughter, was exempt from the mandate, but she was engaged anyway, to Jareth, a big shot in the TV world who helped produce her science show.

He'd explained to his sister and cousin that this was just business, no reason to get excited, but they'd ignored him. None of them, least of all him, had any business feeling buzzed about it. He had to play it cool.

But he was about to get married. To Tilda Riley. And meet his own daughter. He could hardly breathe.

The officiant arrived, a thin, stern-faced lady with a curly white helmet of hair. The guy from city hall with the marriage license was here, too. But the bride was late. He'd been informed that this was a bride's prerogative.

He barely kept from jumping nervously when the intercom buzzed. "Mr. Moss, Ms. Tilda Riley, Mr. Herbert Riley and Miss Annika Riley to see you."

"Send them in," he said.

Maddie shone with excitement. She and Ronnie had insisted on dressing up for the occasion. Ronnie wore a snug ice-blue sheath, her dark red hair cascading over her shoulder in perfect curls. Maddie had gone retro-bohemian in a peach minidress that set off her golden brown skin, black curls and long legs. Gran kept it sleek and elegant in a dove-gray suit, her snow-white hair spiked up high.

Gran came over and straightened his tie, giving him an assessing look. "My, you're very smart today," she murmured. "Handsome lad. Opted for Armani, eh?"

Caleb shrugged. "First thing I grabbed when I opened the closet."

Gran's lips twitched. "Nice choice, darling."

The door opened, and Tilda entered, followed by a little girl, and Herbert Riley.

Tilda looked stunning in an ivory suit, with her hair swept up, a clingy stretch lace top beneath the jacket and slim, fitted white pants that hugged her sexy curves. She wore ivory pumps, and had an ivory clutch in one hand and a bouquet of white roses and baby's breath in the other. White ribbon streamers dangled from the bouquet.

The little girl wore a white lace dress and shiny buckled shoes. She had a wreath of roses in her glossy dark hair, and a bouquet like her mother's. Her eyes locked onto him.

He knew that look. Like a researcher peering through a microscope, hoping for statistically significant results.

Tilda smiled at the others, and then turned to him. "Caleb," she said.

"Hey, Tilda." He offered his hand to Annika.

The little girl shifted her bouquet and seized his hand, pumping it. "I'm Annika."

"I'm Caleb," he replied. "Very glad to meet you. I hope we'll be friends."

Annika had a we'll-just-see-about-that look on her face. One he'd seen on Gran's face, and Marcus's, and Maddie's. "I hope that, too," she said politely.

Caleb looked back at Tilda. "Nice flowers. You went all out."

"Annika's doing. Incidentally, that's why we're late. She insisted we stop at a florist for bouquets, and a wreath for her. I put my foot down about wearing one myself."

"It would have looked pretty." Annika's voice was heavy with disapproval.

"Not with a pantsuit," Tilda returned. "With a long, flowing white dress, maybe."

"So you should have worn a flowing white dress, then! It's a wedding, Mom!"

"You both look fantastic." Caleb looked at Annika. "The flowers are perfect. I'm very glad that you both have them. You did well to insist."

"I know. Like, duh!"

"Annika…" Tilda's voice had a warning tone. "'Thank you' would be the appropriate thing to say."

Annika glanced at him, and rolled her eyes. "Thank you."

Then Gran, Maddie and Ronnie descended upon Annika, to fuss and coo, and the little girl was covered with kisses and comments about her beautiful hair, her lovely flowers. That left him and Tilda free to gaze at each other in the charged silence.

"Are you sure about this?" she asked. "You look extremely tense."

"It's a lot to take in," he said. "Meeting her."

"It's not too late to back away," she said. "We haven't signed anything yet. Just those preliminary agreements we signed last week, and the prenup. And you could still get to know Annika."

Caleb shook his head. "We have a lot to gain from seeing this through. If you're still in, I'm still in."

Herbert walked over, his face cold. "Hello, Caleb."

"Hello, Herbert." He shook the man's hand.

"You don't know how lucky you are," Herbert said. "Figure it out fast. And do better by her than the last time."

"Dad! You're embarrassing me!"

"Once you've had a few heart attacks, you don't waste time on mealymouthed bullshit anymore." Herbert didn't break eye contact. "You say it like it is."

"It's fine, Tilda," Caleb said. "You already refused my apology. I'll just offer it to him, instead."

"I refuse it, too," Herbert said. "Do better. These two are my whole heart. Treat them well, or you will hear from me."

"Do you mind, Dad? I was having a private conversation with my fiancé."

Herbert spun around and strode over to the corner window, where he stared out at the Seattle skyline. His back radiated righteous anger.

"Sorry about that," Tilda murmured. "He's a little emotional today."

"It's fine," he said. "I'm sure I'd feel the same, in his place."

"Oh, yes. You'll get there," Tilda said. "In about five or six years, if not sooner. Constantly worrying about her being hurt or used. So. You have that to look forward to."

That gave Caleb a jolt. He glanced over at Annika, who was laughing with Gran, Maddie and Veronica. "I'm still wrapping my head around it."

"Keep wrapping," Tilda murmured. "It's a long, painful process. It ends the moment that you die, and not one second before."

Caleb let out a bark of laughter. "Are you trying to scare me?"

"I don't know. Is it working?"

Caleb shook his head. "I'm not going anywhere."

"Maybe I was trying to take your measure one last time, before swearing vows to you in front of my daughter. In spite of everything, it feels kind of huge."

"Same." He held out his arm. "So? What do you say? Shall we do this thing?"

She took his arm. "Into the jaws of death."

He laughed. "Am I that terrifying?"

She smiled at him. "Just messing with you."

Caleb had expected a brisk exchange of words, followed by a series of signatures on legal documents, but somehow, the event morphed into something momentous, charged with meaning. As they took their places, rare sunshine flooded the room. Tilda stood opposite him, giving him that clear-eyed, searching look. Gran stood next to the officiant. Annika and Herbert stood behind Tilda. Annika proudly held a tiny lace pillow with the wedding bands tied onto it with fraying ancient ribbons. Gran had also insisted on giving Tilda the engagement ring that Grandpa Bertram had given her sixty years before. Opal and diamonds, glittering on her slender hand.

Herbert glared at Caleb, as if daring him to let Tilda down. Maddie and Ronnie flanked him, having declared themselves his groomswomen.

It was unrehearsed and spontaneous, but it seemed somehow inevitable—and powerful.

The ceremony was dreamlike. Caleb was acutely aware of the details. Annika's big dark eyes on him, full of curiosity and hope. Tilda's elegant posture, shoulders back, chin up. Some locks of hair had shaken loose from her coif. They swung loose below her chin. A bolt of light lit the unearthly pale green depths of her eyes. And that look, like she was searching for something in his face, but hadn't found it yet.

Caleb said what he was supposed to say, with a floating sense of unreality.

"...pronounce you husband and wife!" the officiant said in ringing tones. "You may now kiss the bride!"

Oh, damn. Caleb should have specified that she leave that bit out. Frantic, split-second evaluation: to kiss, or not to kiss. He swiftly calculated the embarrassment quotient of either option...and went for the kiss. A businesslike peck on the lips, to save face.

But Tilda's eyes widened in alarm. Her mouth opened, just as he came in for—

Not a peck. A real kiss. And with that contact, the world jolted and reset itself, and suddenly there was nothing but Tilda. Her scent, her skin, her lips. Sweet, hot. Electric.

Caleb leaned back, shaken. Dazed.

After that, hugs and kisses and well-wishes. A stiff nod and handshake from Herbert. An impulsive hug from Annika that made his heart bump. Gran's fierce embrace.

"Watch yourself, lover boy," she whispered.

"Mind your business, Gran," he hissed back. "You've done enough damage."

Gran spun around, undaunted, and clapped briskly. "I now invite you all into the small conference room for a glass of champagne and a brunch buffet!"

"Can I taste some champagne?" Annika asked.

"No, you may not, my sweet. For you, there is fresh fruit juice. But you'll love the pecan caramel cinnamon rolls and the cheesy bacon puffs. Come and see!"

"Don't tell me, let me guess," Tilda murmured into his ear. "This little reception is as much a surprise to you as her initial marriage proposal. Am I right?"

"You nailed it," he said ruefully. "Not that I wouldn't mind some alcohol."

"Agreed," she said, in a heartfelt tone.

In the conference room adjoining his office, a long table was adorned with a white tablecloth and an enormous arrangement of orchids. An ice bucket held bottles of champagne and there was a wide array of appetizing brunch food. Hot steaming savories, fresh bagels and rolls, whipped cream cheese and smoked salmon, an assortment of sweet pastries. As they stepped into the room, a string quintet began to play.

Caleb and Tilda looked at each other and laughed. "Vivaldi's 'Spring'?"

"I'm no expert on music," he admitted. "'Over-the-top' is what I'd call it."

The laughter broke the tension. And the shrill, frenetically bouncing harmonies seemed perfect for the occasion. Surreal, raucous, improbably happy.

He couldn't hear himself think. Which was fine.

He'd rather just feel.

It looked like Annika was having a marvelous time. She'd bonded swiftly with Maddie and Ronnie, and was giggling in the corner with them. They were charmed with her, as well they should be. Her precious Annika was funny and extroverted. A party animal, ever since she was little. Not a trait she'd inherited from her mother. Or Caleb, from what Tilda could tell. He still looked tense. So was she, but the champagne helped.

And that kiss. Oh, dear God.

Repeat after me. Business arrangement.

Say it 'til you mean it, Tilda Riley. Say it with conviction.

She got through a small plate of food and some champagne. The string quintet was now playing arrangements of current pop songs, to Annika's delight. Maddie and Ronnie clapped as Annika announced each song title.

"'Breaking Down Your Walls,'" she shouted. "By Moon Cat and the Kinky Ladies!"

"She's really bonding with Maddie and Ronnie," Caleb said from behind her.

Tilda turned to Caleb and Elaine. "She's good at making friends fast."

"She's a lovely child," Elaine said. "Pleasant and well-mannered. A real delight. You have my compliments."

"Thank you," Tilda said. "She's my treasure."

As the music drew to a close, Elaine lifted her glass, tapping on the side of it. "May I have your attention!" she called out. "I'd like to announce my wedding gift!"

Wedding gift? Oh, dear. She gave Caleb a swift, alarmed glance. Caleb shook his head. "No idea," he whispered. "But brace yourself."

She was in no mood for any more surprises, but Elaine was in full swing.

"I am thrilled to see my oldest grandchild married at last," Elaine said. "A few years ago, I purchased three beach cottages on Carruthers Bluff, between Breakers Bay and Carruthers Cove. My intention was to give them to my three grandchildren upon the occasion of their weddings. At long last, I can begin to unburden myself! Caleb, you and Tilda are now the proud owners of 1200 Carruthers Bluffs Road.

In the fullness of time, Marcus and Maddie will be your vacation neighbors!" Elaine handed Caleb a set of keys. "Enjoy it, with my compliments!"

Caleb looked at the keys in his hands, and then at his grandmother. "Whoa," he said. "Thanks, Gran. But a heads-up would have been nice."

"I'm giving you one now. Along with the house keys."

"Caleb never takes vacations," Maddie said. "A beach house is wasted on him."

"Nonsense. He's a family man now. He'll need a beach getaway. Speaking of getaways, I have organized one for you newlyweds! You two should go to Breakers Bay for a few days, to de-stress. Work out all the details of your new life together."

Tilda started shaking her head. "Mrs. Moss, you know that I can't just—"

"Call me Elaine. Please," the older woman said.

"Elaine, then. I have an eight-year-old. Things need to be organized in advance."

"Which brings me to my next suggestion." Elaine's voice got quieter. "Maddie and Ronnie and I are keen to get to know the lovely Annika. Could she stay with us for a few days while you and Caleb are honeymooning?"

Honeymooning? Tilda almost sputtered her champagne.

Caleb leaned toward her. "Think of it as a business retreat," he murmured. "Gran is getting way ahead of herself. But it might actually be a relief to get away from the craziness. Annika will keep them too busy to bother us while we're there."

"I'll have wine and groceries delivered," Elaine said. "Joshua, the caretaker, is on the tips of his toes, ready to make it all happen for you. If you feel like venturing out for dinner, there is a Michelin star chef at the Paradise Point Resort, just ten miles down the coast. We would be thrilled to have Annika, and honored by your trust. Video-chat with her as often as you like to make sure she's happy. You can be in constant contact."

Tilda disliked being railroaded, but putting her foot down seemed mean-spirited, considering everything. She looked over at Annika, who was currently bending over Maddie's arm to show how far back she could go. Her hair brushed the floor.

"Of course, we've said nothing to Annika yet," Gran assured her. "We would never presume."

Tilda called to her. "Come here, baby."

Annika bounced over, her cheeks bright pink. "Mom, Maddie wants to take me to a Glow Nation show! She knows one of the acrobats, and she can get me backstage! And Ronnie hosts *The Secret Life of Cells* TV show! I never met a TV star before!"

"That's great, sweetheart. Listen up. Mrs. Moss has invited you to stay with her, and Maddie and Ronnie, for a few days."

Annika's eyes got huge with delight. "Oh, wow! Can I go? Please? It would be so much fun!"

"I guess you can, if you're sure you'll be comfortable."

"Oh, I'll be great! They are supernice, Mom. You're going to love them!"

"I'm sure I will, baby. Thank Mrs. Moss for her invitation, please."

Annika flung herself at Elaine and squeezed her waist. Some champagne sloshed out of the old lady's glass and over her hand. Her face softened.

"Oh, you are such a love." Elaine put down her glass and gave Annika a hug.

That hungry flash in Elaine's eyes made Tilda's heart squeeze. It also made her nervous. She wasn't sure she was ready to have other strong-willed adults with unknown agendas having powerful emotions about her baby. Then again, the more people in the world who were willing to genuinely care about Annika, the safer her girl would be.

"Call me Grandmother, or Gran, if you prefer," Elaine said to Annika. "That's what all of them called me. Run over and tell Maddie and Ronnie."

"Thanks, Gran!" Annika hugged Tilda, and for good measure, hugged Caleb, too. He was slow to respond, and didn't manage to hug her back before she scampered away.

"She's a very enthusiastic hugger," Tilda said. "You'll get used to it."

"It's wonderful," Elaine said. "I'll be eating it up with a spoon. Bring on the hugs." She dabbed her eyes with a tissue, sniffing delicately. "I suggest that you go home and pack. It takes three and a half hours to get to Breakers Bay at a brisk clip, with no stops."

Tilda watched Elaine sweep away to talk to Annika, and it suddenly hit her.

She'd just agreed to a romantic beach getaway with her gorgeous new husband.

God help her.

Five

Caleb put his new wife's suitcase in the trunk while Tilda fussed over Annika, who was strapped into Maddie's car. "You have your phone charger? I want you to be able to call me."

"All under control, Mom," Annika assured her. "Relax. I'm good."

"Jammies, right? Underwear? Toothbrush? Your warm jacket?"

"It's all there," Annika soothed. "You'll be fine without me. Have fun, okay?"

Tilda laughed, and watched Annika wave goodbye as Maddie's car pulled away.

"I'm a hot mess," she admitted. "I'm not used to leaving her."

"She'll have fun with Maddie." Caleb opened the door of his Porsche. "Shall we?"

He invited her to find music on the radio as he drove, and Tilda turned the knob until she arrived at a song. "Do you recognize this one?"

Caleb listened. "The string quintet played it this morning, right?"

"Yes. It's one of mine and Annika's favorite alt-rock bands. Moon Cat and the Kinky Ladies. 'Breaking Down Your Walls.' We always car-dance to this one."

She turned up the volume, and they listened to the lyrics for a moment.

Yell and bang on the door
Throw rocks at the windowpane
Your concrete walls are thick
But I always take the blame
And my stupid, stupid love
Waits in the cold, hard rain…

The words were making his jaw tighten up. The song worked for him better as an instrumental arrangement. "The quintet was great," he said, to change the subject. "Gran really knows how to mark an occasion."

"I'll say," Tilda said fervently. "I thought it would be a business meeting, and I find a brunch buffet, a four-foot-tall arrangement of tropical orchids and an orchestra."

"Well, Annika insisted on bouquets, right?"

"Annika is eight. She still wants to be a Disney princess when she grows up. Your grandmother has no such excuse. And the wedding present? A melon baller or a cheese platter would have been fine, but no! Beachfront property!"

"Yeah, I did not see that coming," he admitted. "We never heard a peep about those houses. I guess we had to prove our worth by getting married first."

"Has she been pressuring you about marriage?"

"A few years back, she tried really hard to fix me up. I pushed back. I thought she'd given up. Then she saw Annika at Ava's party, and all hell broke loose."

"Really? Just because she wants a great-granddaughter?"

"It's more than that," Caleb said. "She wants to make old mistakes right."

Tilda looked at him, curious. "What mistakes?"

"I told you how Annika resembles my mother," he said. "Susannah was Elaine's only child. The way Gran tells it, she spoiled my mother rotten. Indulged her every whim. Susannah ran wild. Barely finished high school. A string of bad boyfriends. When she came into her trust fund, she just ran off."

Tilda looked apprehensive. "So...what happened?"

"She got caught in a storm on her boyfriend's yacht. Both of them drowned. Maddie was only eight months old. I was five, Marcus was three."

"That's terrible," she said. "You must've missed her so much."

"Not really," he said.

Tilda looked taken aback. "No?"

"She'd already left Marcus and me with Gran," Caleb said. "I'd been there since I was three years old. Susannah got tired of kids fast, but was too disorganized to prevent herself from having them. Her solution was to bring them home to Gran to raise. She would have dumped Maddie with Gran, too. She just hadn't gotten around to it yet."

"Was the boyfriend your father?"

"No. We all have different fathers, but we don't know who they are. Or even if the guy with the yacht was Maddie's father. Gran said that Susannah's housekeeper at the time seemed doubtful about that. Evidently the yacht guy was a more recent acquisition."

"Well. In any case, it's awful. I'm so sorry."

"Gran wanted to do better with us, so she did the opposite from what she did with Susannah. Surprise, surprise—we're all ambitious workaholics, and she thinks she has to fix it, by brute force. She means well, and that's her saving grace. She's not cruel, just convinced she knows best."

"I can't believe you never told me about your mother," Tilda said. "That's a key piece of biographical info I missed. What did we talk about nine years ago, anyhow?"

"I don't think we were talking much at all."

Tilda snorted under her breath. "I guess not."

"Finding out you're a father changes things," he said. "It

makes you think about the past, and the future. How about your mom? I don't know that story, either. To my shame."

"She died when I was sixteen, on the operating table. They were trying to repair a brain bleed."

"I'm sorry. I can't believe I didn't know that."

"Don't feel bad. I was distracted back then, too. I was also making a big point of trying not to think about it. Her death was still pretty fresh."

"Any other family?"

"No, Mom and Dad were both only children, and I was the only kid they ever managed to have. I remember thinking it was ironic that I should slip up one single time and find myself pregnant, while Mom tried so hard all those years in vain." She kept her eyes straight ahead. "It was a huge shock, but I wanted Annika from the minute I knew she existed. I'm lucky I could make it work."

"But you decided not to tell me."

She twisted her hands together. "Caleb, you do remember what you said to me, the last night we were together, right?"

He looked pained. "Yes, I do. But I'm not that person anymore."

"You said that you didn't love me, and that you never would, because love didn't exist. It was just body chemistry. Sexual hormones. A biological drive to procreate."

"I'm sorry I said any of that," he said. "It was cruel."

"Don't sweat it. It was a long time ago. But when I found out I was pregnant, I was sure you'd think I was trying to trick you or trap you."

"I wouldn't have seen it that way," he said.

"How do you know? You said yourself that person doesn't exist anymore. And the guy who told me my glands were tricking me into reproducing for the sake of the species? I'm pretty sure that guy would've seen it that way."

"I know you told me not to apologize again, but that apology still stands."

Tilda looked down, twisting Gran's pearl-and-opal ring. "Thank you," she said. "I accept your apology, if it helps. You don't have to keep making it."

They fell into an awkward silence. When he looked at Tilda again, she was yawning. She laughed, embarrassed, when she caught his eye.

"Sorry," she said. "Haven't been sleeping very well. Lots on my mind."

"We've got a couple of hours to go," he said. "Take a nap. Put the seat back. Here, I'll do it for you." He pushed the button, and the seat smoothly reclined.

"Tell me if I snore," she said.

She dropped off almost immediately, which was good, since he was having a tough time. He was good at organizing, management, strategy, risk analysis. He knew how to run a sprawling, global agri-tech company. That was his comfort zone.

This stuff was not comfortable. Tilda, Annika. His mother. She'd been dead thirty years. Hell, she'd never really bothered mothering him to begin with. And his father had never made himself known at all.

Gran and Grandpa Bertram made up for it, though, and he was grateful, but the blank spot remained. He had an idea of who his mother had been, what she looked like, where she'd come from, but his father was an unknown. No pictures, no mementos, no stories to tell. Just chromosomes.

Annika deserved better. Every child did. And he'd been such a dick, he'd managed to convince Tilda that her baby would be better off growing up without knowing him.

He could have passed on his own hidden wound, never even knowing he'd done it, all of it happening below the level of his conscious mind. He used to get angry at his mother for not loving them enough. Now he was angry at himself in the same way. It didn't feel good.

They were almost through the coastal range, the road

twisting through towering fir trees, when Tilda woke. She opened her eyes and stretched just as they rounded a hill, and the vast expanse of the ocean spread out before them.

"Oh, my," she said. "How beautiful. How long have I been asleep?"

"Couple of hours. We're almost there."

"I can't believe I conked out on you like that. Sorry you had to drive all this way to the tune of my snoring."

"You do not snore," he lied. "The exit should be around here."

Just then the sign came into view. A smaller road branched off from the larger highway, which headed down toward the coast. Carruthers Bluff Road.

Caleb turned onto it. "Six more miles," he said.

The road wound through the trees until it reached the top, and meandered along the crest. The terrain on either side was rugged, and rocks towered everywhere, set off by long, vivid green grass. The sun was low on the horizon, and the clouds were a mix of gray and stained pink, rimmed with glittering gold on the edges. Steep hills overlooked the long, broad beach. The foaming surf surged and then retreated, leaving huge swaths of wet sand that caught the mellow evening light.

Caleb slowed down at the mailboxes, and turned into 1200. The driveway was another few miles of spectacular rock formations and wind-twisted trees. Then an expanse of green, dotted with big trees, and a shingled gray house. It had a widow's walk on the second-floor balcony that faced the sea.

The view was stunning. Coastal mountains plunged steeply down to the beach and stretched out for miles in both directions.

Caleb parked the car. They got out, both awestruck.

"It's marvelous," Tilda said softly.

"The caretaker texted me info," Caleb said. "Nearby restaurants, hiking paths, supermarkets. He says he left us dinner, so we don't have to go out hunting for it tonight unless we want to. Let's go explore."

They went inside and wandered through room after room, calling to each other to take a look at this or that. The downstairs was one large room, with high ceilings and exposed beams. Enormous windows opened onto a veranda that faced the ocean. The furnishings had a rustic, weathered look. Natural fabrics, earth tones, woven seagrass mats, Pendleton-wool accent pillows. Sunset made the room glow. They found a hot tub on a side porch, and it released an inviting puff of steam when they peeked under the lid. There was porch furniture on every side and a barbecue on a big back patio, sheltered from the wind.

The kitchen was modern. Dark granite-topped counters, a big central island and an enormous fridge, discreetly hidden behind rosy cherrywood cabinet doors. Two sinks, two ovens, two stove tops and…wait—yet another fridge, this one exclusively for drinks. Wine, champagne, prosecco, sodas, mixers.

Tilda read the note from the caretaker. "The food this guy left sounds great," she said. "Lobster bisque, straight from the Mermaids Perch Café, down in Breakers Bay. Fresh bread. Breaded oysters, ready to panfry. Salads and sides and desserts. Red wine, white wine, champagne. You really had no idea this place existed?"

"None. Gran said she bought the properties a few years ago."

"I was wondering," she said. "Since you have this cool business approach toward marriage, why didn't you just go with one of those women Elaine picked out before?"

Caleb gave her a quizzical look. "I never even considered any of them."

"Why?" she asked.

None of them was you. Caleb fished for something to

say in place of the unsayable truth. "The marriage mandate is new. So is knowing about Annika. Maybe I'm not quite as cold and businesslike as you might think."

Her face went pink. She turned away. "I see."

"I'll get our bags. We can go and check out the upstairs."

When he came inside with their suitcases, Tilda was kneeling at the hearth. "There's a fire all set to light," she said.

"Great. We'll have a fire after dinner. Shall we look at the upstairs?"

She followed him up. He left the bags in the hall as they opened the doors to the various bedrooms. The first was a smaller room with dormer windows and skylight, with a single bed built into a niche in the wall, a window right in the niche.

"This could be Annika's room, when she's here," he said.

Tilda gave him a cautious smile. "I'm sure she'd love it."

Each bedroom was beautiful, with its own stunning view and comfortable bathroom, but the master bedroom was the largest. French doors opened onto the widow's walk, and the bed was made up with velvety linens, a cloud-soft comforter and a fluffy heap of white pillows.

"I'll put your bag in here," he said.

"Good heavens, no. It's your house, Caleb. Take the master bedroom."

"Take this room. I insist."

"Caleb—"

"One gallant gesture. Let's save our big fights for more important issues."

He went out to grab her suitcase. When he came back, Tilda had folded her arms over her chest. "Do you anticipate a lot of fights over important issues?"

Caleb weighed his options swiftly before he told her the truth. "Yes."

"Why is that?"

Caleb flipped on a beaded lamp on the vanity. "Because you're strong, and proud. And still pissed at me."

"If you feel that way, I'm surprised you went forward with this," Tilda said.

"So it'll be complicated. We'll figure it out." He kept his voice light. "Take it easy. Let's take a few minutes to settle in and then maybe wander around. Look at the grounds."

"Sounds good," she said. "See you in a few."

He got his suitcase, carried it into another bedroom and sat down on the bed, willing his heart to slow down, his back to stop sweating. *Take it easy.* Right.

But, hey. He was a Moss. He'd been in training all his life. He could do complicated.

Six

As soon as she was alone, Tilda sat down on the bed and called Annika.

The call connected, and Annika's face filled the screen. She had flames painted around her eyes and held up an enormous, dripping ice-cream cone that was visible in the view screen.

"Hey, Mommy! Banana and chocolate fudge!"

"Looks delicious, honey. Where are you?"

"At a street fair in Fremont, with Ronnie and Maddie! I got my face painted!"

"I see that. It looks fabulous. Get some pictures of it and send them to me, okay?"

"You bet!"

Maddie's face appeared in the screen next to Annika's. "Hey, Tilda! Did you guys get to the honeymoon cottage?"

"We did, and it's gorgeous," she said. "You're going to love it here."

"If I ever qualify for my part of it," Maddie said, laughing. "A very big *if*. Ronnie and I have been having the time of our lives with our fabulous new niece." Maddie gave Annika a kiss. The little girl giggled.

"Thanks for showing her such a good time," Tilda said.

"Oh, no, the pleasure is all ours."

"I second that!" Half of Veronica's smiling face appeared in the view screen on the other side of Annika. "Next stop, the movies."

"We're gonna see *The Terror of the Titans*!" Annika announced.

"Great! Make sure you behave, honey. I'll call you tomorrow."

"Okay! 'Bye, Mommy!" Annika's smiling face froze on the screen, then disappeared.

Tilda felt bereft. It was silly, of course. Annika was having a wonderful time with her newfound extended family. No need to worry. And that left her feeling oddly lost.

The constant busyness of single motherhood was hard, but one of the plus sides was that there was never any time to dwell on her own problems. She couldn't stop for an instant, with Annika to look out for.

Suddenly, she was alone in a luxurious beach house, with this sexy, intriguing man, and no one needed her shoes tied, or her hair braided, or her sandwich wrapped.

And she was married to the guy. It made her light-headed.

Damn. She was stalling, like a teenage girl. She was a grown professional woman, and this was just a business retreat. Caleb had said so himself.

Grow up, already.

He was outside on the front deck, leaning on the railing, when she came downstairs. The man looked damn good from behind. And every other angle. She'd liked his long hair, but his short, severe haircut accentuated the sharp points of his jaw, the well-shaped ears, those stunning cheekbones.

She took in his broad shoulders and gorgeous legs, all thick and ropy with muscle. The taut, cut, ripped details, all hidden under his sweatshirt. She remembered it so well. The pattern of his chest hair, his scent, his taste, his texture. They were burned into her memory.

She joined him at the railing. The cool wind from the ocean lifted her hair and cooled her heated face.

He looked over at her. "All settled in?"

"Yes. It's a beautiful room. And the widow's walk is to die for."

"The caretaker's text says that if you hike up past the swing, you'll find a path. It connects with a public hiking path that follows the crest of Carruthers Bluff. From there, you either go left and hike down to Breakers Bay, or go right and hike down to Carruthers Cove. Do you like hiking?"

"I love it," Tilda said. "Whenever I get a chance. It relaxes me like nothing else."

Caleb looked pleased. "Me, too. I'm surprised I didn't know that about you."

Tilda started to speak, and promptly shut her mouth. As if she'd been thinking about hiking trails nine years ago. The only thing she'd wanted to explore back then was his muscular, virile body. All their athletic energy had been spent rolling around in bed.

"Tomorrow, we'll hike down to Breakers Bay or Carruthers Cove. We'll walk on the beach, explore the town, get lunch and hike back. It'll be quite a walk. You up for it?"

"I'm up for anything."

He smiled. "Yeah? How about dinner?"

"Sounds great," she said.

It didn't take long to get dinner organized. In no time a spectacular meal took shape. Caleb panfried the oysters and heated up the lobster bisque, while Tilda set the table and laid out the many sides that were packed into the fridge.

"White wine work for you?" she asked. "There's a sauvignon blanc."

"Sounds good," he replied. "I prefer a white with fish."

She set out a vast array of goodies: artichoke fritters, shrimp salad, smoked swordfish, roasted peppers, sautéed greens with bacon. "There's food for ten people."

"Blame Gran for the excess, and don't forget to cut up some lemon wedges."

"I'm not blaming anyone. I'm not complaining. I love fresh seafood."

Caleb carried a big platter of crispy, golden breaded oysters to the table. Tilda ladled up two bowls of lobster bisque and poured out the chilled wine.

"The oysters look great," she said. "When do CEOs have time to learn to cook?"

Caleb sipped his wine. "Remember how Gran wanted to compensate for past mistakes? My mother never learned anything practical. She couldn't even make coffee. So Gran made a big deal about us learning practical skills. Laundry, ironing, lighting a fire, changing a tire, changing the oil in the car. And, of course, cooking."

Tilda laughed as she popped an artichoke fritter into her mouth. "These are great," she said. "Did you skin rattlesnakes, too?"

"No, but I'm glad that you weren't around to suggest it, knowing Gran."

"What else do you know how to cook?"

Caleb loaded some roasted peppers onto a chunk of fresh bread. "All kinds of stuff. We got formal instruction. Classes, tutors, workshops."

"Lucky you," Tilda said. "I just improvised, and hoped for the best. I still do."

"We learned the classic sauces," Caleb said. "Soups, salads, main dishes, roasts, grills, baked dishes, cold dishes. French cooking, Italian, Chinese. Maddie loves Mexican and Thai, anything with hot peppers and cilantro. Marcus specializes in barbecue. I like all of it. Every style, every continent. By the way, I make a great linguine with clams, and this is the perfect place to get fresh clams. You into it?"

"Lay it on me. You had all this culinary prowess when I met you? I never knew." She wound a slice of swordfish around her fork and ate it with a sigh of pleasure. "This is so good."

But Caleb looked appalled. "Wait," he said. "I never cooked for you when we were together?"

"Never," Tilda said. "We went out, or we ordered out."

Caleb shook his head. "It was a really weird time in my life." He sounded bemused. "We should make a point of cooking together while we're here."

She laughed at him. "Why? As a trust-building exercise, for our business retreat?"

"No, I just think it would be fun. Here, try some of this shrimp. It's good. Super fresh."

Tilda thought about that. The affair with Caleb had been fiery, intense. She'd been madly in love. Nothing she experienced before or since had come anywhere close.

Yet, at no time would she have called the time they spent together "fun."

It was too much for that. Too fraught. She remembered that feeling all too well. High on adrenaline, walking on a tightrope. Barely believing it was real.

Until it wasn't. She'd fallen off that tightrope, lower than she'd ever imagined falling. At least not since Mom died.

Finding she was pregnant had shocked her out of her stupor. She'd pulled herself together for Annika.

But it had not been much fun. Not by any means.

"What?" he asked. "What's that look on your face?"

She put on a smile. "Sorry. I just don't associate you with, ah…fun. I guess."

Caleb looked embarrassed. "I was a self-absorbed asshole back then."

"So what's changed?" Tilda asked.

He looked startled, and Tilda laughed in embarrassment. "Sorry, that came out wrong. I didn't mean to imply that you're still a self-absorbed asshole. It's just a straight-up question. If you have changed, then why?"

"I'm not sure," he said. "Just time, I guess. I haven't had

any great illuminating events. Just work. I threw myself into MossTech after my start-up went to hell."

"Yeah, I heard about that."

"Yeah, BioSpark was a spectacular fail. I had to make up for that mess. Prove myself all over again. And I've been working like a bastard ever since. Haven't really taken a breath since you last saw me. How about you? Have you changed, since then?"

"I must have, but I haven't had the time or leisure to think about it."

Caleb served her some oysters, and put a wedge of lemon on her plate. "I admire you for coming back here to defend your dad's company."

She considered that as she squeezed the lemon on her fish. "It might've been better if you hadn't attacked him to begin with."

"Agreed, but one picks one's battles with Uncle Jerome. And Gran threw in with him at the last board meeting, a few weeks ago. She and Jerome together have enough shares to dictate the company's direction. There was nothing I could do."

She harrumphed. "This happened after Elaine saw Annika at Ava's party?"

Caleb shot her a cautious look. "Yes. I suspect that Gran's prime agenda might have been to ensure access to her great-granddaughter, and you and I getting married was a happy afterthought for her. But she took it, and ran with it. And here we are."

Tilda tried an oyster. It was exquisitely fresh, tasting of the sea, juicy in its crunchy golden breading. "By the way, I called Annika," she said. "She's partying up a storm with Maddie and Ronnie. She had her face painted, and was eating an ice-cream cone bigger than her head. Next comes the movie. Superheroes in space."

"I knew Maddie would come through. I'm glad they're having a good time."

"Your grandmother has made Annika's extended-family dreams come true, with a wave of her wand," Tilda said. "Since she's offering something that Annika genuinely wants and needs, I'm inclined to be forgiving. However, Elaine doesn't have to strong-arm us. She could just, you know, ask."

"Really? You would've been willing to open up to her and give her what she wants, just like that? With our history?"

Tilda thought about it. "I don't know," she said. "And it doesn't matter now. But if she tries to shove my girl around, she'll have one hell of a fight on her hands."

"Annika is lucky to have such a fierce mother," Caleb said.

Tilda studied him, sipping her wine. "You really are different now."

"God, I hope so," he said. "It would be depressing if we hadn't grown at all."

They polished off the oysters. When they were full, she packed the leftovers into the fridge while Caleb demonstrated his ability to load a dishwasher. He dropped in the detergent tab and set the machine to run, giving her a grin. "See? For real. I know how."

"Look at you, the ultimate Renaissance man," she said, laughing. "You cook, you wash dishes, you run a vast global agri-tech corporation. If only you could skin a rattlesnake. But I guess a girl can't ask for everything."

Caleb grinned as he pulled out the pastry boxes from the fridge. "We forgot this."

"Oh, horrors. What an oversight." Tilda opened one. "Lemon cheesecake with butter cookie crust." Then the other. "Chocolate with caramel swirl. Be still, my heart."

He leaned on the kitchen island and watched as she cut

two small slices of each dessert. She pushed a plate in his direction. "So?" she said.

"You first," he said.

It made her self-conscious, but she took a bite…and shivered. It was melting, decadent, dark, chocolatey goodness. A sticky swirl of caramel. A crunchy hint of sea salt on top.

"Good?" His eyes were mesmerizing.

"Shockingly," she said.

"Now the other one."

"Why me?" she protested. "Take your turn."

His lips curved. "I like to watch."

Seven

Whoa. Too much, too soon. He'd meant those words at face value. Only after they came out of his mouth did he realize how seductive and flirtatious they sounded, and how involuntary the instinct to seduce her was. He dialed it way down as they finished the desserts and went to sit by the fire, but he was rattled. There had been a time, years ago, when he and Marcus had challenged each other to take risks. They had specialized in extreme sports for a while. Hang gliding, freestyle skiing, skydiving, dirt biking. The riskier it was, the more they'd liked it.

He didn't flinch at professional risks, either. He'd risked everything on BioSpark. It would've been a wild success if his former business partner and ex-best friend, Jack Daly, hadn't torpedoed their start-up by selling their professional secrets to a competitor.

He tried not to think about that too often. But he did know how to lean into risk.

This was different. His palms sweated, his belly churned. A classic stress reaction, out of proportion to a glass of brandy by the fire with a beautiful woman. His body was somehow convinced that this situation was life-or-death. There was no reasoning with it.

Tilda was curled up in an armchair by the fire, brandy in her hand, with that keen, switched-on look in her light green eyes. Like he was an interesting problem that she needed to solve.

Well, yeah. He was problematic. Ask any of his ex-girl-friends.

He knew how to give satisfaction, up to a point. He could be charming and attentive, and he could please a woman in bed. But in the end, he always ended up disappointing them. He'd left a trail of angry, hurt, confused women in his wake.

Tilda among them.

Building the fire gave him something to do. He couldn't look at her right now. Eye contact felt like a current of electricity. He took his time with the kindling, the paper.

"Caleb, can I ask you a personal question?" she said.

"If you can't, then I can't imagine who can."

"Nine years ago, your grandmother wanted you to work in the family company, but you said no. You didn't want to be under her thumb."

"That's true," he said.

"I was surprised when I heard that you were working at MossTech," she said. "I wouldn't have expected you to ever back down. Now look at you. Top dog."

He was quiet for so long that Tilda fidgeted in her chair. "I didn't mean to pry," she said. "It's just curiosity. No judgment."

"Long story," he said.

"I'm not in a hurry," Tilda said. "What happened to Bio-Spark? It was going so well. Who was that guy you were working with? Jack…?"

"Jack Daly," Caleb said.

"Right. You two were the darlings of Silicon Valley. On the cover of *WIRED*. Profiles in *Rolling Stone*. Both of you smoking hot, brainy sex symbols. BioSpark was the hottest property around. What happened?"

After years, the story still made him sick with anger. "Jack Daly happened."

Tilda sensed the tension. "You don't have to talk about—"

"Jack was passing our proprietary secrets to a rival company," Caleb said. "That company released an almost identical product, days before our IPO. The scandal broke, and they made billions. And we went down in flames."

"Ah. So what happened to Jack?" Her voice was careful.

"Prison, but he didn't stay in for long," Caleb said. "His lawyer got him out, on a technicality. I'm lucky I didn't end up in prison for malfeasance myself. I don't know what he's doing now. I don't care, either. As long as he does it far from me."

There was an awkward silence. "I'm so sorry it ended that way," Tilda said. "So…that's why you ended up going back to MossTech?"

Caleb thought about it. "I don't know. I was in a very dark place for a while. It was lucky for Jack that he was safe in prison. I couldn't touch him there."

"And now that he's out?"

"Oh, he's safe from me now. I have better things to do than go after him. Besides, he's going nowhere. He can only operate in the criminal underworld if he operates at all. Our paths aren't likely to cross again."

"I hope they don't. So, then? Your family persuaded you?"

"Maddie and Marcus persuaded me. MossTech's general manager retired, and Gran wanted me to take the job. I did it to keep busy. Then I decided to take MossTech into the third millennium. Marcus and I made Gran an offer. She'd step down, I'd be CEO, Marcus would be CTO and they'd let us run things. Or we'd start our own company."

"And Elaine actually thought it was worth it to step down?"

"Oh, she carried on about how we were a couple of arrogant, ungrateful little punks. But it was the only real way to safeguard her legacy. Jerome was livid."

"So Maddie is, what? Chief financial officer?"

"She will be later this year, when Benson retires. She is now in all but name."

"Where does Ronnie fit in?"

"Ronnie was working for the R-and-D department. Then she got called by a producer friend of hers to write and narrate educational videos for kids. The producer saw the potential, and Ronnie ended up going the show-biz route. Our celebrity science whiz."

"Supercharged overachievers. All four of you."

"You're hardly one to talk," he said. "Besides, it's not our fault. We were warped by fate. Now Gran's trying to undo the damage. Which brings us both here."

She laughed, lifting her glass. "Here's to making the best of your own individual wreckage. It's all any of us can do, right?"

"True thing." They clinked glasses, breaking eye contact. He turned away. Too much voltage.

"When did you find out what Jack was doing?" she asked. "If you don't mind me asking."

"It's okay. It was all starting to fall apart right during the time we were together. Near the end."

Tilda fell silent. He finally looked over his shoulder. She looked startled.

"Holy shit, Caleb," she whispered. "For real?"

"It's not that earthshaking a revelation."

"Something that traumatic was going on with you, and you never said a word?"

"It wasn't about us," he countered. "And there were legal reasons to keep my mouth shut. My lawyers said that I shouldn't talk about the—"

"Bullshit. Your business partner betrays you, and you don't tell your girlfriend?"

"I felt humiliated," he admitted. "We'd been friends since high school. We went to Stanford together, came up with BioSpark together. We were going to take over the world. Then he screwed me over. I didn't want anyone to know. Least of all you."

"When did you find out?"

"You mean, when did I have absolute proof that it was Jack? I'd been seeing things for weeks that made me suspicious, but I couldn't believe it was him."

"Yes, but when was that day? When did you know for sure?" she persisted.

"The day that you left," he said reluctantly.

Tilda leaned forward, frowning. "Left, meaning…?"

"Left, meaning, left me," he clarified. "The day you left for good."

"Let me get this straight. You're saying that the day that I declared my love to you…*that* was the day you found out Jack betrayed you?"

"Yes," he confirmed. "The timing was, ah…not ideal."

"Well," she said. "It explains why you were acting so strangely those last few weeks. I thought that it was me. That you were bored with me."

For several seconds, they just listened to the fire crackle.

"God, no," he said finally, his voice rough. "Never. You were perfect."

She let out a low, bitter laugh. "Hardly."

"Please be clear," Caleb said. "I'm not claiming this as an excuse. I let my anger at Jack bleed out onto you. It was a dick move. I regret what I said that night more than anything I've ever done in my whole life."

He looked at her, and was horrified to see that her eyes were wet. "Oh, no," he said, alarmed. "I'm sorry. We shouldn't dig up old stuff—"

"No," she said sharply. "No, it's good that you were finally straight with me. Nine years too late, but it's a step in the right direction."

"But…you're crying," he said helplessly.

"And?" Her chin went up. "Sometimes I cry. So?"

"Okay," he said carefully. "As long as I'm not the one making you cry."

Tilda set down her brandy glass. "I can't make any guarantees. Emotions are unpredictable, if you let yourself really feel them. They do whatever the hell they want."

"Sounds chaotic," he said.

"Oh, it is. Or you can just flatten them out. Not care about anything. I've made my choice. You have to make yours. I just hope you can make some space for Annika. She needs a dad who can genuinely feel something for her, and caring takes real courage."

He had no idea how to respond to that. "I… I'm not sure if I know what you—"

"Never mind, Caleb. I'm just babbling. Excuse me. It's been a long, intense day. I'll just take myself and my ridiculous, chaotic feelings up to bed. Good night."

Tilda strode away, head high. Her hair swung and bounced at the small of her back. He heard her quick, light footsteps on the stairs.

He sat there alone, staring at Tilda's empty chair. Confused. Bereft. Rattled.

One single damn day with her, sipping wine, sharing desserts, talking by a fire, and already he felt the risk factor, ratcheting up, up, up.

Into the stratosphere.

Eight

Tilda was shy when she came downstairs the next morning, after storming off in her big head-tossing huff last night. She'd spread out all her feelings at his feet, to be freshly trampled on. Had she learned nothing from her past experience with this guy?

But when he turned around from the stove, he showed no sign of discomfort.

"Buttermilk pancakes," he said. "I was about to call you. Blueberries, or plain?"

"I love them with blueberries. Look at you. Showing off."

"You want to see me show off, try my crepes with crème Chantilly. Coffee's in the pot, cream is on the bar, syrup's on the table. We have to fuel up, big-time. We have a long walk ahead. So? Breakers Bay, or Carruthers Cove? Breakers Bay is a three-mile hike one way, and Carruthers Cove is almost two miles longer."

"I'm sure they're both great, but I love the looks of those huge rocks on the beach down at Carruthers Cove," she said. "I vote for that direction."

"Fine by me. The caretaker said there's a great place to eat on the boardwalk in Carruthers Cove. They're famous for their fried-calamari platter."

She laughed. "I'll have to shop for a new wardrobe, if we keep this up."

"He also said there was good shopping. For your new wardrobe."

She laughed as she accepted a plate with a stack of fluffy, golden-brown pancakes, dotted with juicy splotches of piping-hot blueberry goo. The scent was mouth-watering.

"There's sausages on the platter," Caleb said, pouring more batter onto the griddle.

"What a treat," she said. "I usually do yogurt with granola for breakfast."

"Enjoy my culinary bounty. As a trust-building exercise."

She poured on syrup, added butter and took a bite, sighing with delight. "It's amazing," she said. "How very unsurprising."

"Glad to hear it," he said, sitting down opposite her with his own plate. "It's fun to cook again. How about Annika? Is she a pancake lover, or a waffle lover?"

"She likes both, but I think waffles have a special place in her heart," Tilda said.

"I have a waffle iron at my house. I can indulge her."

Tilda laid her fork down, and dabbed her mouth with the napkin. "Um. About that. We haven't really discussed that whole issue yet," she said in a halting voice.

"Where you're going to live, you mean?" Caleb asked, in a measured tone.

"Yes," she replied.

"Were you staying with your dad because he needed the support after his heart surgery, or because you haven't found a place of your own yet?"

"Both, I guess. I love hanging out with Dad, but he's better now, slowly but surely, and he has a housekeeper who comes in every day. And I don't want to settle down in my childhood home. It feels like going backward."

"I see. We haven't talked about this because I didn't want to spark off knee-jerk resistance. But I have a big, comfortable house. Lots of room. Big lawn, right on the lake. Not far from Gran and Maddie, or your father."

Tilda opened her mouth, but Caleb held up his hand.

"Don't answer. Now is not the time to decide. You're the boss, of your life and Annika's. No pressure."

She nodded, and finished her pancakes, feeling shy.

The feeling evaporated after they went outside. There was actual sunshine, and the air was sweet and fresh. The world seemed dewy and sparkling. Caleb swiftly located the faint deer path above the swing. It wound through the rocks until it intersected with a bigger trail, which they followed along the crest of Carruthers Bluff. At one point, the trail crossed the road they'd driven in on the day before.

It was a beautiful walk. After an hour or so, the trail diverged, and they followed the path heading down to Carruthers Cove, to the sweeping expanse of beach, where huge rock monoliths reared up from the water, with seabirds swooping and wheeling above them. The roar of the surf filled her ears, and the tang of salt spray was on her lips.

They rolled up their pants, took off their shoes and waded in the icy surf, trying to dodge the frothy waves when they swirled up too close. They looked into tide pools, admiring the rainbow-tinted marine life clinging to the rocks beneath the crystalline surface.

"Annika would love this," Tilda said, as the translucent green tentacles of an anemone closed stickily around her finger. "She isn't sure yet what kind of scientist she wants to be. Marine biology, robots, space? Fun things beckon from every side."

"I thought she wanted to be a princess," Caleb said.

"And why not? She doesn't have to choose. She gets it all, if I have my say."

"Amen to that. We'll bring her with us the next time we come."

She walked faster, pulling ahead of him, not trusting the expression on her own face. What a fabulous fantasy. But she'd given in to it before, and she'd paid a very high price for it.

The dangerous moment passed, and they wandered up the main drag of the attractive, touristy town of Carruthers Cove, past hotels and seafood restaurants, antique and trinket shops, ice-cream parlors, boutiques, art galleries.

At one point, they came upon a street artist, and Caleb insisted on giving the guy thirty bucks to do Tilda's portrait. The guy was talented, and with a few bold strokes of his colored ink pens, he did an expressive rendition of her face. She looked otherworldly—hair flying around, eyes huge and green, lips intensely red. She demanded a portrait of Caleb as well.

She liked the result. Caleb was smiling, and the artist had caught his dimples.

Caleb rolled up the portraits into the cardboard tube the guy provided, and stowed it in his knapsack. By then, they were well and truly hungry.

The restaurant the caretaker had recommended wasn't far, and the exercise had given them an appetite. The grilled prawns, oyster stew and fried calamari and cuttlefish hit the spot. For the first time, she felt like she could talk about Annika as much as she wanted to. While talking to friends, or even to her dad, she took care not to rattle on too long about her kid, but Caleb didn't seem to get bored by it. He actively drew information and stories out of her. No detail was too small for his interest.

Nine years ago, their conversations had been fun, stimulating, but she'd often felt overwhelmed. Like she was sparring with him. Fighting to maintain her balance.

But not now. She told him about Annika's babyhood. The colic, the hernia operation, her first tottering steps. The language delay that had worried her, and then suddenly Annika had started chattering. She showed him photos on her phone, the ones Maddie had sent, of Annika's street-fair face-paint job. She sent her photos to his phone.

It was wonderful.

After lunch, they got ice-cream cones and headed back to the beach. The walk up the hill took longer than it had coming down; they were slowed by a dense fog. A big cloud squatted right on top of Carruthers Bluff, so thick they could barely see the path a few feet ahead of them. Fortunately, the hiking path was clear and well marked.

It had gotten cold, and the damp sank into her clothes, beaded on her hair, settled into her bones. The fog created an eerie, muffled stillness. Her field of vision was narrowed down to just Caleb, a few steps ahead, constantly looking back to check on her.

Caleb turned to her. "This is where we leave the trail and go down to the house."

Tilda glanced around, impressed. "You're sure?"

"I memorized the landmarks, and gauged how far it is from the trail to where the hiking trail crosses the highway."

Tilda's teeth chattered. "Good for you. All I see is fog. Lead the way, trail-finder."

"Actually..." Caleb hesitated. "I propose something else. Could you go a little bit farther? There's something I want to show you. I think it will be worth seeing."

"In this fog? Is there any point? Let's come back and look at it later."

"No, what I hope to see will only be visible now. If we wait, it'll be gone. We don't have to, though. I know you're cold and damp."

Tilda crossed her arms over her chest, trying not to shiver. "Okay, but afterward, I want a cup of hot chocolate by the fire. With a shot of something alcoholic in it."

"Deal," he said. "Follow me."

A hundred feet down the path, Caleb stepped off onto a barely visible trail. It wound through big boulders, zig-ging and zagging up the rocky hill. The fog was so thick, she could barely see an arm's length ahead of her. She was literally feeling her way.

"Are you sure about this?" she asked him.

"Almost there," he said. "Hang in there."

She scrambled on, straining to see, irritated at herself for agreeing to this madness, when what she really wanted was a hot shower, a hot drink, some dry clothes and a crackling fire. These macho athletic types always had something to prove.

Caleb materialized from the mist, holding out his hand. "Come on. We're here."

His big hand clasped her wrist and pulled her up the last few steps with effortless ease. Up, up...and suddenly, she was in another world.

The air was clear. The clouds were below them, being torn up by the wind, and blown out into wild, pink strands, great shredded layers of gray, pink, gold and blinding white. Breakers Bay was a bowl full of clouds, and on the other side, Carruthers Cove was another. Bolts of sunshine sliced through the clouds. One landed directly on them. Another hit the ocean, turning the water a pale, glowing green.

They floated over a sea of pink clouds. No earth to be seen, except for the ground beneath their feet. It was all sky, everywhere she looked. Celestial. Unearthly.

It brought tears to her eyes. The wind was shifting, and the tips of a stand of tall pine trees now sliced up out of the clouds on the next ridge. Ragged holes revealed moving layers of clouds below.

Caleb was grinning. "Was it worth it?"

"How did you know it would be like this up here?"

"I didn't. I just hoped it would. Yesterday when we drove in here, the clouds were starting to clear. I saw this hill poking through the clouds, the sun hitting the very top. I thought, that would be a hell of a view, looking down on the clouds. So on our way down, I took note of the pathway leading up there. But this exceeds my wildest expectations."

They locked eyes. "I know you're tired," he said. "But it was now or never."

"Yes," she said softly. "Thank you. It's sublime."

"There's rock up here, like a bench. Let's sit for a minute and take it in."

She took his hand. Soon they were sitting together, gazing out at the shifting clouds. It was so huge. The feelings, the sensations, the heart-shaking beauty of it.

"You're shivering," he said. "I shouldn't have insisted."

"No, it was so worth it. I'll remember this until the day I die."

Caleb pulled off his fleece jacket and laid it over her shoulders. The heat penetrated her own damp jacket and sent a rush of startled pleasure through her body.

"But you'll get cold," she protested. "That wind is sharp."

"I'm fine," he assured her. "I'm perfectly warm without it."

She looked away, shivering. The stunning view changed constantly as the wind moved the clouds. First the ocean, then a blaze of sunshine. Then shadows again.

"Maybe we should head down," she said reluctantly. "We need light for that path."

"Yes, you're right." He stood. "I'll go first. I can help you down."

"No need," she told him. "I run, I hike, I work out. I'm pretty agile."

At that moment, she stepped on a loose rock, but before she even started to wobble, he'd grasped her waist, steadying her. He was rooted to the ground like an oak.

"I know you're strong, but you've walked for hours, and you're tired and chilled," he said. "Indulge me. Please."

His low voice was caressing. *Indulge me.*

That was all it took. In an instant, her fantasies were full-blown. She saw herself indulging him to the point of madness. Making him writhe and moan and beg.

Damn it, grow up. Don't read too much in to every word, every look.

Funny how every time she repeated that to herself, it got less and less convincing.

Nine

Caleb stayed close, though it was clear that Tilda didn't need his help. When the fog cleared, he was careful to stay ahead of her. To hide the look on his face.

He didn't want her to see him like this. Hopelessly turned on. He didn't want her worrying about having to fend him off.

They got to the house, and he was able to fake being normal again as he unlocked the front door. "I'll get that hot chocolate going."

"Maybe we should grab a hot shower first, to warm up?" She followed him in and shrugged off his coat. "Thanks for lending me this. Very gallant of you."

"It was my pleasure, but let me remind you. There's a hot tub out there, all steamed up and ready for us. Want to try it out?"

Her expression was wary. "I, ah… I didn't bring a bathing suit."

Who needs one? He swallowed it back. "Leave on your underwear. Or you can have it all to yourself. Either is fine with me. You really need to warm up."

"Oh, please. You're cold, too. Let's both try out the tub. I can share."

"Great. Grab a robe and towel, and I'll meet you down there."

Caleb waited until Tilda was up the stairs, and sprinted up to his room. He tore off his clothes, yanked on swim trunks and pulled on a robe, spurred on by an urgent need to be safely in the hot tub before Tilda got there. She did not need to see his erection.

In the kitchen, he yanked out a champagne bucket and filled it with ice from the bag in the freezer. He uncorked some prosecco and grabbed a couple of champagne flutes.

Outside, the wind off the ocean was cold, but a gratifying puff of steam came out of the tub when he pulled off the top. The only light was what filtered through the house from the kitchen, which suited him fine. The less ambient light, the better.

He tossed his robe onto a chair, and stepped into the hot tub with a sigh. Damn. Very nice. He even spared a charitable thought for Gran.

A few minutes later, the sliding door opened. The tub's motor was a quiet one. Just a mellow, pleasant burbling hum.

Caleb kept his eyes closed. Or seemed to, anyway. He was human, so he peeked as Tilda tossed off her terry-cloth robe and stepped into the water, noting her toned, curvy body, her taut nipples jutting against the cami top. The lush flare of her ass.

Tilda sank into the water up to her chin. "Ahhh. I think I'll stay here forever."

He opened his eyes. Her face was pink. Her lips curved with pure bliss.

She was so beautiful, it made him ache with a yearning for something that he couldn't even name. Sex, of course, but this hunger went beyond sex. His first instinct was to distract himself, so he turned to the prosecco. "Care for a drink?"

"Sounds nice. Thank you."

He poured and passed her the champagne flute. "Can I ask you something personal?" he ventured.

"I'll tell you anything while sipping prosecco in a tub of bubbling water."

"When you were in Malaysia, and you found out you were

pregnant, why didn't you come home? I would have thought that you'd want familiar surroundings."

Tilda sipped her drink. "I didn't want to stress my dad. His health wasn't great. Also, I found out very late. My cycle is irregular, so I can go months with no cycle, particularly when I'm stressed. Which I was, after we broke up."

"Yes, I imagine you would be."

"Anyway, I put it all down to stress for a long time. Changes in my body. Mood swings, weight gain, puffiness, nausea. I actually thought I had gotten some tropical disease. Finally, I went in for tests, and the doctor said, 'Congratulations. In less than four months, you're going to be a mother.'"

"Wow. That must have been a shock."

"Oh, my God, yes. Then, as I was freaking out, I felt her move. This fluttering. It was miraculous. I was still panicked, but at the same time, I fell in love. I was so lucky, that I could get good care, and the help I needed, so I could keep working."

"And you never told your father about me?"

"It wasn't his business," she said.

"I bet he had strong opinions about that. I would have."

"Yes," she admitted. "We've argued about it for years."

"Well, he knows now," Caleb said.

They were both quiet for a few minutes, listening to the bubbles.

"It was good to talk to you about Annika," she said. "My own kid is the most fascinating thing in the universe, but only to me. Even my dad's eyes glaze over if I overdo it. I bet if Mom were alive, she'd be there for it, but she's gone. Today was the first time I felt like I was talking to someone as invested as I am. And you hardly know her."

"I regret that," he said. "I wish I'd been there for all of it."

"That's surprising," she said slowly. "What you said that night we broke up…it made me think procreating was the last thing in the world you would ever want."

"It must have seemed that way," he said. "But I'm older now. Less of an idiot. And I know how it feels not to know my father. It's not great. You have to work so hard to convince yourself that you don't care, that you have nothing to prove. I don't want my child to feel that way. I've got no clue how to be a father, but I'm here for it. The rest of my family is, too. You saw how excited they were."

"I appreciate that. Annika is thrilled. She tried to get me to talk about who her father was. It's been harder and harder to put her off. Now I don't have to."

He worked up the nerve to say it. "No. Neither of us has to."

Tilda sipped her wine, her eyes questioning. "Meaning?"

He groped for the right words. "Those blank, empty places in our lives," he said. "Maybe some of those empty places can be filled."

Tilda put down her glass on the deck behind her. Her eyes were apprehensive.

"Sounds like a dangerous proposition," she said. "Dangerous to me, at least."

"I don't see why," he said.

"This arrangement could be very good for Annika," she said. "But as for myself, I don't think I could make myself vulnerable to you again."

"You wouldn't be here if you weren't sure that you were safe with me."

"Just to be clear," she said. "We're talking about sex now, right?"

He considered her words for a moment. "It's in the air," he ventured. "And I don't think it's just me."

"No. It's not just you," she said. "But I process these things very differently than you."

Caleb chewed on that statement, trying to decipher it. "Meaning what?" he asked. "You know that I'll always respect your wishes and feelings."

"Like you respected them nine years ago?"

His jaw clenched. "Damn it, Tilda. I can't take it back. Forgive me, already."

"I want to let it go. But I can't be sexual with you and not get wound up about it. You know me. The chemistry, the hormones, the endorphins. They hijacked me then, and they'd hijack me again. There I'd be, in trouble again. But worse, this time."

"Please don't throw that conversation we had nine years ago in my face."

"I'm not. I'm just being clear. I'm sorry it feels like an attack."

He leaned back. "I won't bother apologizing again. But I'm just as attracted to you now as I ever was. And I sense that the feeling is mutual."

"Busted," Tilda said. "There's attraction, yes. We're already married. Already parents, for God's sake. So why not just go for it, right? As a trust-building exercise."

There was a gleam of humor in her eyes, so he even dared to laugh. "The only way we'll find out if it's safe to be intimate with each other is to be intimate with each other," he pointed out. "Otherwise it's all just theoretical."

Tilda laughed out loud. "Nice maneuver, Moss. Very slick."

"I do my best. Can't blame a guy for trying." He reached out and clasped his fingers with hers. She didn't pull away, so he tugged. Not hard enough to budge her if she didn't want to be budged. Just a gentle invitation to drift in his direction.

"That walk today," he said. "I sensed a real opportunity. When we were up above the clouds, I got this crazy feeling."

"What feeling?" she whispered.

"Like anything was possible," he said. "Anything in the world. Like maybe we could start out fresh. Try this whole thing again, from the top. Do it right this time."

"Yeah?" She drifted infinitesimally closer. "Just like that?"

"I know it wouldn't be easy. We'd have to do the work. We'd have to be brave. Willing to push through the hard parts. Crawl up steep hills. Blind in the fog."

"It's a risk," she said softly. "We could lose the path. Fall off a cliff."

"It's risky," he agreed. "But I want to step out on top of the world with you. I felt like I could see to the ends of the earth with you. Like we could take off and fly."

She was right next to him now, her fingers woven through his, her eyes dazed. "You seductive bastard," she whispered. "Dangling pretty fantasies in front of me."

"It's not a fantasy," he said. "I'm for real. I mean what I say."

"How can I believe you, with our history?"

His heart was thudding so hard, it deafened him. "Let me try to convince you," he said. "Let me make it up to you."

She shook her head. "I can't even imagine what that would look like."

"So let's find out," he coaxed. "Incredible opportunities come along only a few times in any person's life. You were an opportunity like that for me, but I was too stupid and self-absorbed to see it. I'm hoping that maybe, I might get another shot. I will not screw this up a second time. I swear it."

"Don't swear anything," she said swiftly. "It's way too soon for that."

"No, it's nine years late. But maybe not too late. That's what today made me hope." He tugged her closer. Gently. Hopefully.

Tilda touched his cheek with her fingertips. He took that as license to do the same to her, freshly amazed by how soft and fine her skin was.

Their lips met for an instant. He couldn't have said who initiated the contact. It didn't matter. He wound his fingers into the damp silkiness of her hair, tasting her soft lips, open

to his. Her fingers dug into his shoulders, pulling him closer.
Their eyes locked.

"How about you, Tilda?" he asked hoarsely. "What do you hope for?"

"I can't think far enough ahead to hope," she said. "All I can see is you."

He pulled her closer, and kissed her hungrily.

Ten

Oh, God, he felt good. Solid and hot and strong and *good*.

That voice in her head that was pleading for sanity yammered away, but it sounded shrill and ineffectual. This was just too perfect to resist. The strong grip of his big hands. His lips, ravenous and beseeching all at once.

Her hair fell down, floating around her like a cape on the surface of the water before sinking, clinging to her neck and shoulders as he pulled her onto his lap. She was sitting on his stiff erection, and she wanted to wrap her legs around him and drag him closer. Press into him right…there. Where she ached for him the most.

His touch was like magic. He'd always been so good at this. He cradled her bottom, sliding his hand up her thigh. Each flirtatious flick of his finger was an invitation. His tongue probed and danced with hers as he stroked between her legs, letting her imagine the possibilities, and remember how good it was to open up to him. To take him inside. All of him, that big, gorgeous body all over her, inside her, moving, lighting up all her sweet spots. Driving her wild with helpless pleasure.

She was already at the brink. Damn the man. Teasing her. Making her squirm and writhe. Tilda covered his hand with her own, and pressed it against her mound.

Caleb groaned as his finger slid under her panties, seeking out tender secret flesh. She was primed. The whole damn day had been foreplay. It barely took a few moments of his expert caresses until her tension wound up to the breaking point…and broke.

She lost herself in a million flying pieces.

Afterward, she found herself wrapped in his arms. "So hot," he groaned. "So damn good. Feeling you come. I could do that all night."

She lifted her head, trying to calm her quivering throat enough to speak, but Caleb kissed her before she had the chance, peeling the wet cami top down over her breasts, her arms, to her waist, tugging it and her panties down.

The garments floated off her ankles. He lifted her, and she felt the edge of the tub against her bottom. Caleb sank down on his knees in front of her and pressed hot, seductive kisses against her thighs. He gave her that smoldering gaze. Part entreaty, part challenge.

"I want to taste you again," he said.

The tone of his voice unraveled her. Raw need, echoing her own. Her legs opened to him, and Caleb kissed the inside of her thighs. Caressed her with his fingers, opening her tender folds as he pleasured her with his clever, skillful tongue.

Every detail felt so vivid. The grip of his hand, the tender swirl and flick of his tongue against her most sensitive flesh. The sting of the wind against her feverish skin.

She made helpless sounds, head thrown back, watching the moon disappear behind the clouds as the pleasure built. A star floated into sight, then disappeared as the cloud swept over it. Pleasure tore through her like a flash flood. Huge, wrenching.

Afterward, she opened her eyes. The moon glowed softly behind the clouds. She felt so open. Laid utterly bare.

A memory echoed in her head. His voice, cold and distant. Words that had been burned into her mind. *It's not love, Til. Just chemistry. Sexual hormones. That's all.*

Tilda pushed away the memory, and slid down into the

pool. Caleb floated back, giving her room to sink down into the water's warm embrace.

"I wasn't ready for this," she whispered.

"Me, neither," Caleb said. "On a practical note."

Tilda blinked at him. "Meaning?"

"I don't have condoms. I can't say I didn't hope to get lucky. I'd have to be dead not to hope. But I figured, if you were interested, you'd bring them, or send me out to get some. Bringing them myself seemed presumptuous. Didn't want to be that guy."

"You've given this quite a bit of thought," she murmured.

"Guilty as charged. I'll go right now, if you want. Just say the word."

The wind moaned around the sides of the house, rushing in the trees outside.

"While we're talking about this, we might as well be thorough," he said. "I got a physical not long ago. Blood work. No STDs. Haven't been with anyone since that."

"Same here," she said. "It's been a very long time since I've dated anyone."

"Good to know. I can go out." He hesitated. "Or not. Up to you."

It wasn't so much a question of whether she would take the bait. There was no question. The question came down to *how.* She pulled her floating underwear and cami from the water, and wrung them out. Laid them on the wooden deck.

The challenge was to take what she wanted, and keep her balance. To get what she craved, without automatically giving him what he'd never wanted from her.

But she was afraid unwanted emotion and intensity would spill out, like before. Unrequited love. He'd rejected her before. She couldn't bear it again.

Keeping the upper hand with a smart, seductive, strong-willed man—it was a lot to ask of herself. And it's not like she was some femme fatale with loads of practice.

But she was a stronger, tougher person than she used to be.

She had this. Caleb Moss wouldn't even know what hit him.

Tilda stood up. Water sluiced over her body. She lifted her arms to squeeze the water out of her hair. Always a good look. Arms up, chest out. Boobs at maximum lift.

Caleb watched in fascination. He cleared his throat. "So, ah…" His voice trailed off. "It looks like you're about to make all my wildest dreams come true. Correct me if I'm wrong."

"Come inside," she said. "There's a nice thick rug in front of the fire."

She climbed out, back straight, taking gliding steps. She shrugged on the robe. The whirlpool function went silent. She heard the sloshing of water as Caleb got out behind her. She kept her head high as she opened the sliding door. Firelight was good. The dimmer, the better.

Caleb crouched to build the fire up while she toweled her hair with the hood of her robe. He laid some blankets and pillows over the rug. Tilda finger-combed her hair out as he positioned the largest piece of wood in the hottest part of the fire.

"That should last a while," he said.

"Good." She let the terry-cloth towel fall open. "Get down on the blanket. Take off the bathrobe."

Caleb shrugged it off, reclining on his elbows, magnificently naked.

So fine. As gorgeous as she remembered. He'd always been fit and strong, but he'd put on more muscular bulk since she'd seen him. And his erection was as stiff and enthusiastic as it has ever been. The only difference was in his eyes. Like he wanted something he'd never wanted before. But now was no time to get sappy. Not during her stern sex-goddess routine. *Upper hand, Tilda. Upper hand.* She tossed off the robe.

Caleb made a helpless sound. "God," he muttered. "This might kill me."

"Don't die. I have big plans for you. They require lots of manly vigor."

"I'm up for it," he assured her.

"I see that," she murmured. "You look…eager."

"Oh, you have no idea." His voice was rough and shaky.

Tilda straddled him, letting him look up at her. Savoring the moment.

Caleb sat up, grasping her hips, and pressed hungry kisses against her mound, nuzzling the swatch of blond hair that decorated it.

Tilda dug her fingers into his hair, and gave in to pleasure. His hands slid up inside her thighs, caressing her as he worked her with his tongue. So…sweet.

But pleasure was making her knees weak. Not tonight. She sank down, astride him. At least down here, she didn't have to fight gravity.

A flush was burned into Caleb's face as she trailed a teasing finger down his body, following the arrow of silky dark hair down to his groin. Stroking up the underside of his penis. Feeling his smoothness, his hardness. Making him shudder and moan.

"Tilda," he said roughly. "I'll fulfill any fantasy you want, but if I'm inside you, I can't guarantee I won't come. I'm too turned on for that. So if you don't want me to go out and look for latex, we'll have to confine ourselves to—"

"Not necessary," she said.

"No?" He frowned in puzzlement. "Meaning?"

"I told you about my irregular cycle. I regulate it with the pill. We're covered."

"Oh. Well…wow." He sounded stupefied. "That's—that's awesome."

"Of course, the pill has a certain failure rate as a method of contraception," she pointed out. "As we both well know. It's all a gamble." She gripped his shaft and gave it a slow, twisting stroke. "Still want to play?"

"God, yes," he moaned, forced out the words. "Please."

So far, so good. He seized his erection, holding it up for her.

She'd walked this emotional tightrope up to now, but as she nudged him inside and sank slowly down over his stiff, unyielding shaft, she realized that her act was about to fall apart. She rose up, sank down, and then she was moving, helplessly. Ravishing waves of surging pleasure, carrying her away. All of her fantasies about controlling the situation, keeping the upper hand, protecting herself emotionally—all bullshit.

Caleb had that same look on his face that she felt on her own. He made the same breathless sounds. Their hands clutched. They gasped for air in tandem as he pumped into her. She felt so soft. Yielding. Her body glowed with welcome. Every slick, gliding stroke was a fresh delight.

That huge sensation rose up inside her, and then crashed down on top of her. Like a vast, endless wave, wiping her out. Sweeping her under.

Caleb didn't want to move. Tilda's hair was across his face, and with every inhale, he got the sweet, subtle honey scent. Their bodies were still joined, her weight draped trustingly over his. Skin-to-skin. Relaxed, sated, satisfied.

Nothing could be better. But such moments were fleeting, and this one was no exception. Tilda stirred, and lifted her head. She smiled, but her eyes were guarded again.

For a moment, while making love, he'd felt her guard go down. His own had gone back up, too, mirroring hers. They both stood to lose too much now, if they got this wrong. Tilda was capable of cutting him off completely if he screwed this up. She'd done it before. Not that he had any right to complain about that, but there it was.

"You good?" he asked, because a guy couldn't be too careful.

Tilda laughed. "You have to ask?"

"I never make assumptions."

"Well, fine, then." She folded her hands on his chest and leaned her chin on them. "As trust-building exercises go, it was truly stupendous."

He narrowed his eyes. "Don't toy with my fragile male ego."

She smacked his chest. "You know perfectly well it was amazing. Sex wasn't ever the problem for us."

True enough. He'd been her first lover, but even that first, slow, careful time, his heart in his mouth, he'd managed to please her. It had made him feel like a god.

Tilda sat up, sliding off his body. She tossed back her hair, and ran her hands teasingly through his chest hair. "Look at you," she murmured. "Keeping it tight. You're even more ripped than nine years ago. You must work out like a maniac."

Caleb's body stirred at her touch. "I don't really care about how it looks," he admitted. "But if I don't run and lift pretty hard, I can't unwind enough to sleep."

"I'm not complaining," she assured him. "You look great."

"So do you," he told her, his eyes wandering over her. "Stunning."

Tilda looked down at herself. "Different. Having a baby will do that."

"You were stunning then," he said. "And more stunning now." For some reason, it was important that Tilda understood the depth of this truth. Tilda the girl had been radiantly pretty, but the woman… She was complicated, dangerous, fascinating.

Maybe she had been all along, and he only saw it now. Who knew?

His stomach rumbled. They looked at each other and laughed.

"We forgot about dinner," she said. "Want to raid the fridge?"

It was an awesome idea. They put on their bathrobes and descended upon the fridge, pulling out yesterday's leftovers and more that they'd never even gotten around to last night. A big wedge of aged pecorino cheese, some shaved honey ham, thinly sliced pepper-rolled roast beef. Fresh vine-ripened tomatoes. A big fluffy flatbread went into the toaster oven, and came out fragrant with the scents of olive oil and rosemary, and a smoky, roasted eggplant spread to dip it into. They chose a red Italian wine, a Nero di Troia, and it tasted like a sultry summer afternoon, heavy with flowers, herbs, humming bees.

They got a little goofy from the wine, and by the end of the meal they were feeding each other delicious bites. That buzzed, on-the-edge-of-reason feeling was ratcheting up, and conversation had slowly subsided into charged silence.

Caleb had just eaten a bite of the caramel chocolate, and had a sticky strand of caramel on his fingertips. Tilda leaned forward and pulled his finger into her mouth, licking off sweet goo. The hot, wet suction of her mouth drove him wild.

"Oh, God. Tilda, don't," he begged. "Unless you want sex again right now."

A last, teasing lash of her tongue, and she jerked the sash of his bathrobe loose. Reaching inside, she grasped his penis and sank to her knees, pulling him into her mouth.

It felt so…incredibly…good. The luscious pull and glide, every skillful swipe and swirl of her tongue, made him shudder and gasp. He wouldn't survive this intact. He never wanted it to end. Deep, hot, wet, rhythmic. Sweet pulsing agony.

Pleasure thundered through him, flattening him.

He was still gasping for breath when she got up. Before he could even focus his eyes, she was pouring herself a glass of water.

"Tilda," he groaned. "My God."

"I know," she agreed. "Let's take this upstairs. To bed."

She grasped his hand and pulled him out of the kitchen and up the stairs into the master bedroom She didn't turn on the light, just tossed away her robe and slid into the bed, lifting the cover for him in silent invitation.

Caleb got into the bed. Her body was so warm, the texture of her so smooth, silky. He rolled over on top of her, and it felt so inevitable, the sinuous way her body arched and opened, the way her legs clasped around him. They cried out together as he sank his stiffened shaft slowly into the wet clasp of her body.

This was followed by deep, gliding strokes. Her legs hugged his waist, squeezing as they writhed together. She couldn't see the hope he didn't dare to feel, written over his face.

Darkness kept him safe.

Eleven

It was late when Tilda finally opened her eyes. The morning sky was soft gray. Tilda rolled over to study Caleb's sleeping face. She felt soft. Open. No way could she hide her feelings, in this state. She could only keep up the tough-babe stance for so long.

The truth felt naked. She was just as in love with him as she'd ever been. But logic suggested that if her emotional intensity had repelled him nine years ago, it would repel him again. Eventually. Nothing had changed, really. Except for her own intensity.

Now she wanted even more from him. Now she wanted not just for him to love her, but for him to love Annika, too. The stakes kept getting higher.

He'd assured her that he'd changed. But he'd been extremely turned on at the time, and men were men. Who knew how he'd feel once the novelty wore off?

Chilled by her own thoughts, she slipped out of the bed and tiptoed into the shower. When she emerged, she rummaged for a sleep T-shirt, wishing she'd brought something sexier. But she'd been telling herself a very different story when she packed. The chatter in her head had been filled with trepidation. *Not a chance, girl. Not even in the privacy of your own head. You'll get dinged so hard your head will spin.*

"Hey." Caleb's lazy morning rasp sent a sweet shiver up

her spine. "What are you doing? Putting on clothes? For God's sake, why?"

She smiled at him. "Good morning to you, too."

He held out his hand. "Come back to bed."

How could she resist those dimples? The shirt came right back off.

It was a long while before they got back into the shower. Longer still before they got back out of the shower, which proved to be a fresh source of sexual stimulation. At long last, they were both shampooed, dried, dressed. Extremely ready for breakfast.

In the kitchen, Caleb got to work, and soon he was browning ham with onions and peppers, beating eggs and grating a chunk of cheese. It all smelled divine, so Tilda left him to it and made coffee, clearing off the table from last night's bacchanalian feast.

Soon, he set a tempting ham, cheese and veggie omelet before her.

"I was thinking," he said, as he sat down opposite her with his own plate. "After breakfast, we tell the caretaker to send up the cleaning crew, and drive down to the fish market in Breakers Bay. We'll pick up pasta and clams for tonight's linguine, and some fresh parsley. I think we have everything else we need."

"Look at you, enjoying one amazing meal while already planning the next," she teased. "Who knew you'd be such a foodie?"

"Just thinking ahead," he said. "Things don't turn out perfect just by chance. You have to plan."

Her phone on the dining room table began to buzz. Annika. Tilda hit the talk button. The screen showed Annika wearing a fuzzy wool hat and an orange life jacket. Behind her was a boat railing, and rippling water.

"Hey, honey!" Tilda said. "Where on earth are you?"

"We're on a boat!" Annika said excitedly. "We're going

to see orcas! There's a pod of orcas out here, and Gran and Maddie and Ronnie are taking me to see them!"

"Wow, how exciting!"

"Hey, Tilda!" Maddie appeared on the screen, her color high, the wind whipping her wild curls. "Did you get my photos of Annika's face painting?"

"I did, thank you. Caleb and I both enjoyed them."

Elaine's smiling face appeared. "Hello, Tilda! I expected to see you and Caleb out and about at this hour! But there you are, in the kitchen, having…what did Caleb cook up for you? He's quite the chef, isn't he?"

"He certainly is. He made a fabulous omelet," she admitted, turning the camera around to show them first Caleb's culinary prowess, and then Caleb himself. He smiled and waved at the phone over his coffee cup.

"So it's brunch, then? I see!" Elaine's smile widened. "At twelve twenty in the afternoon? My, what a luxurious morning."

"Yeah, and your hair's still wet, Mom! Did you guys, like, just get out of bed? We've been up for hours! Since six o'clock!"

"Good for you, baby. Tell me about this pod of orcas you're going to see."

Having steered Annika onto a less dangerous subject, they heard all about the orca expedition.

Then Ronnie appeared on the screen. "Hey, exactly when were you two planning on coming back to the city?"

Tilda and Caleb exchanged swift glances. "We hadn't set a time yet," he hedged. "A few more days, at least. Why do you ask?"

"I want to host a family dinner to celebrate my engagement to Jareth," Veronica said. "He has to fly down to LA the day after tomorrow, and he won't be back for weeks, so it has to be tomorrow and I'd rather you two were there. We'd be welcoming Jareth and Tilda both into the family."

"We could be back tomorrow night," Tilda told her. "I should be getting back, anyway, to pull Annika back down to earth, or she'll be ruined for normal life."

"So… I can on count you two?" Veronica persisted.

Caleb hesitated. "Okay," he said reluctantly.

"Great! Eight o'clock, at my dad's house. Be there. Maddie and Aunt Elaine will bring Annika here directly. See you tomorrow night!"

Tilda set down the phone. "Well," she murmured. "Reality calls."

"Too soon. I wish she'd texted me, so you and I could've discussed this in private," Caleb said. "We just got here. It's awesome. I'm not ready to leave."

"Me, neither. Sorry. I didn't think it through. I got rattled."

"By Gran's teasing?" He smiled. "You'll get used to that. You'll get a mega-dose tomorrow night, for sure. Might as well start building up immunity."

"I still have to convince myself that I'm not crazy for letting you seduce me," Tilda said. "I don't need to field other people's opinions, too."

"Hey, this was Gran's evil plan all along," Caleb said. "She's on our side."

"God help us," she said fervently.

"The only way to survive is to present a united front. We maintain our privacy inside that space, just you and me all alone. On the outside, we just smile and wave."

It was the most seductive thing he could've said to her.

Damn. On one hand was an opportunity to roll around in bed with the most desirable woman he'd ever known in their magical beach hideaway. On the other, a tense, uptight, potentially hostile family dinner at Uncle Jerome's house. Gee. Tough choice.

But the deal was done, so Caleb would make the best of the time they had left.

The trip to Breakers Bay was fun. They grabbed fresh clams, freshly baked bread and more decadent pastries, against Tilda's desperate protests. No rules, no limits. This kind of prolonged erotic activity required very heavy fuel.

They got back to the house. The cleaning crew had left the kitchen spotless, so Caleb promptly got to work putting the clam sauce together, to Tilda's amazement.

"Dude, you're obsessed! You just cooked a couple hours ago!"

"Like I said, just thinking ahead. I figured we'd hike down to the private beach this afternoon." Caleb dumped the clams into the pot where the garlic was sizzling, and they hissed madly, sending up a cloud of steam. He stirred the rattling clams around, and sloshed some sauvignon blanc into the pot. "When we come back up, we'll be cold, damp and hungry. All we'll have to do is boil up some linguini and toss the clams with some parsley and oil, and voilà. Dinner."

Once the clam sauce was organized to his satisfaction, they ventured outside, and took the path down the cliff that led to the private beach. It was blocked off on both sides by big jutting spits of sharp, unforgiving rock, which created a sheltered sandy cove about an eighth of a mile long. The trail was well-kept, and when they reached the cliff, a steel staircase that led down to the beach was bolted to the rock itself.

Caleb lay out the blanket near a big rocky outcropping. They wandered around for a while, exploring the beach, the rocks, even a sea cave, with foaming white surf constantly rushing inside and then retreating, leaving the rocks black and gleaming.

They curled up on the blanket together, leaning back against a big, smooth rock, with Tilda between his legs, her back to his front. He stared up at seagulls wheeling and screeching against the white sky, as the surf churned its endless, mesmerizing rhythm. Tilda's warm, flower-scented hair was beneath his chin.

Tilda, lying in his arms. So improbable. Like a unicorn had laid its head on his lap. He didn't deserve this miracle, after being so stupid. But who cared? He might get lucky. Whether he deserved her grace or not. He could only try.

Fog finally broke the spell. Moisture was beading on the gilded strands of her hair. "Hey, Til?" he said. "We're inside a cloud. We're going to get waterlogged."

She looked up. "Hmm? Sorry. I dozed off."

"I didn't let you get enough sleep last night, hmm?"

"You sure didn't." She stretched luxuriously in his arms. "I hate to go," she said lazily. "It's another world, down here. Wonderful, even in the fog. Like we're the only people in the world. We could be shipwrecked. Lost in time."

"I'm glad we're not," he said. "It's great that on the top of the cliff is a nice house with a fire already laid out, and hot chocolate in the kitchen."

"What outrageous luxury," Tilda said. "A private beach. The mind boggles."

"Tell me that the next time Gran pisses me off," he said.

At the house, he made a fire while Tilda made hot chocolate. She brought him a cup and got down on the floor, close to the crackling fire. "I don't want to trade this for a goddamn Moss family dinner party," he told her, rebelliously.

She sighed. "Me, neither. Sorry. So do you not like this Jareth?"

"He's given me no reason to dislike him," Caleb said. "He's a smiling mask."

"Maybe that's their united front. And he's just smiling and waving."

He grunted. "I wouldn't blame him. But in any case, his precious studio business in LA isn't a good enough reason to cut our trip short."

"Well, I didn't want to hurt Veronica's feelings. And I

should get back to Annika. Uncle Jerome is the one who wanted to annex Riley BioGen, right?"

"That's right," Caleb said.

"I see," she murmured. "Is he liable to be unpleasant?"

"He'll probably behave," Caleb said. "Jareth is a rich, powerful guy. Uncle Jerome is impressed by that. He won't want to appear in a bad light in front of Jareth. I wish I could say 'don't worry, you'll love him,' but it would be a lie. He's difficult."

"Well, he'd better mind his manners in front of Annika." She sighed. "I don't want this to end," she said wistfully. "It's so perfect here."

"It doesn't have to end," Caleb said suddenly.

She looked up at him. "Hmm?"

"I mean, this particular trip will end, but enjoying each other like this? Having fun? It can just keep on going, and we'll just follow along. See where it goes."

"I know you like planning, but please," she said. "Don't try to plan."

"For how long?"

"I'll let you know when I know."

She shivered, and he put his arms around her. "You cold?"

She cuddled closer. "A little. I was thinking about that hot tub, actually. Since we're leaving tomorrow, it would be a shame not to enjoy it again, right?"

Caleb was on his feet so fast, he almost spilled his hot chocolate.

"Best idea ever," he said. "I'll grab the towels."

Twelve

"Are you sure you don't need to go back to your dad's house?" Caleb asked.

"No. I'm anxious to see Annika, and I don't want to be late. I packed a cocktail dress for the coast, in case we ended up going out. It'll be fine for tonight."

They exchanged smiles. Once passion broke free, it had reigned supreme. There had been no time left for such mundane things as going out to eat.

"I've never had such a good time in my life," Caleb said. "I'm still buzzed."

"Same," Tilda admitted. "And Annika did fine without me this weekend. Your people really know how to show an eight-year-old girl a good time. But I would've started feeling pulled in two directions soon enough."

Caleb shook his head. "Gran certainly wasn't a barrel of laughs when the three of us were growing up," he observed. "She was stern as hell. Hard work and duty. Hup, hup, hup."

"She had primary parenting responsibility. You can afford to be the fun, indulgent adult if someone else is setting the boundaries. The primary adult never has that luxury."

"All things I'll be learning now," Caleb said.

"It'll be a gentle lesson. Annika is a sweet, affectionate little girl. Smart and fun to be with. It won't be hard for you to get the knack."

"I can see that," he said. "I'm looking forward to getting to know her."

They pulled through an electronic gate on Lakeside Avenue. Caleb's house was a severely elegant modern design, a series of huge, interlocking glass cubes, with decks and patios on every side. Tall, mature trees shielded the house, and the lawn was wide, velvety green turf. The lake glimmered below, reflecting shimmering city lights.

She got out of the car and gazed at it. "Wow," she murmured. "Stunning."

"I wish you'd seen it first in the daylight," he said.

"I'll admire it tomorrow. Did you find this already built? Or have it built to order?"

"To order. Drew Maddox designed it six years ago. I met him while Ava was doing the publicity for BioSpark. He was designing houses for himself and all of his friends, and I was lucky enough to snag him during that brief phase of his career."

Caleb opened the front door and ushered her in. "There's no time for the tour. We're going to be fashionably late as it is, with our late start."

"It was worth it," Tilda said demurely.

The air ignited as they remembered the scorching interlude that had delayed them. Caleb backed away. "Stop looking at me like that, or we won't get to Jerome's at all."

Tilda laughed. "Just tell me where to get dressed. I won't be long."

"Come to my room." He led her through an open-plan kitchen and a big living room dominated by a central fireplace. "Upstairs there's a bedroom and office suite for you, but I'm hoping you'll sleep in my room. I asked my assistant to prepare a room for Annika. Let's see how it turned out."

The stairs led to an open loft with a railing. He led her down the passageway and pushed open a door, then flipped on the lamp.

Tilda smiled in delight. The bedroom had long windows on two sides and a four-poster bed with a puffy deep blue comforter with a print of the night sky. Stars, galaxies. Crocheted pillows in the shapes of the planets were heaped at the head of the bed. There were bookshelves, a big desk and a tilted drafting table. The bedside lamp was in the shape of the moon, with all of its craters and bumps and scars faithfully reproduced. The ceiling lamp was the sun, and the solar system dangled around it. There was a framed poster from *The Secret Life of Cells* television show, personally signed by Veronica Moss.

"Ronnie sent over a signed set of her *The Secret Life of Cells* books," Caleb said. "I told my assistant to decorate for a bright, science-loving kid. And to leave plenty of space for Annika to fill. She can pick out her own stuff as her interests change."

Tilda switched off the light, and let out a startled laugh as the lamp projected a starry sky map onto the ceiling. "Oh, look!"

He slid his arms around her waist from behind. "Glad you like it. And now, ah…"

"Yes, yes. I know. We have to hurry."

Caleb's huge bedroom was also beautiful. The mellow gleam of bamboo flooring and the pattern of the huge circular rug were so harmonious. Besides the king-size bed, there was a couch and armchairs. Huge picture windows with subtle, understated wooden vertical blinds opened out onto a terrace, with a lake view.

"Bathroom is that way," Caleb pointed. "Feel free. Use anything you find."

Tilda took a quick shower, then tugged on thigh-high black lace stockings and wiggled into the crimson dress, decorated with glinting jet-black beads. It had a frilled, bias-cut tulip skirt with black beaded fringe that swung just above her ankles. Black velvet shoes with ankle straps completed the outfit. She twisted her hair into her I-mean-business updo, and decorated it with hair sticks adorned with chunky black crystals.

It took a couple of minutes to put on her game face. Red lipstick, eyeliner and mascara. She'd gotten enough sun at the coast to have some color. After putting on black crystal drop earrings, she was ready.

When she emerged from the bathroom, Caleb was already dressed in an elegant black suit and a gray silk shirt, no tie. His eyes widened as he looked her up and down.

"Is this good for the occasion?" she asked.

"Stunning. But that's how you wear your hair when you're going into battle."

She put her hand to her hair. "You don't like it?"

"I love it down," he admitted. "But it's sexy to see it up, knowing that I'm the one who gets to take out the pins. Wrap it around my fingers."

His deep voice was a velvety caress against her sensitized nerves. Tilda wrapped her black beaded shawl around her shoulders. "Am I going into battle, then?"

Caleb shrugged. "I hope not."

Jerome's huge house was on Queen Anne Hill. Caleb told her on the way that the mansion had been a wedding gift from a nineteenth-century timber baron to his daughter.

They walked into the wood-paneled entry hall, lit by a belle epoque chandelier, and a familiar shriek of happy excitement hit her ears. Annika ran to greet her, closely followed by Maddie, Ronnie and Elaine.

Tilda knelt down and hugged her girl. "I missed you so much, baby."

"Me, too, Mommy." Annika's face shone. She was wearing a new flouncy pink dress and her hair was curled into tight ringlets.

"Tilda! My, you are looking well." Elaine's smile widened

as she looked Caleb up and down. "Both of you do. What lovely color. So the beach was pleasant?"

"Marvelous," Tilda said. "Everything about it was great."

"I had so much fun with them, Mom," Annika said excitedly. "And Ronnie and Maddie and Gran were so nice to me!"

"I'm glad you had such a great time, baby." Tilda smiled her thanks to them.

"But I'm glad you're back." Annika wrapped her arms around Tilda's waist and squeezed. "It's better when you're with me." She let go of Tilda, and gave Caleb a quicker, more cautious hug, but this time she hung on long enough to let him hug her back. Gran, Maddie and Ronnie exchanged delighted glances.

Jerome greeted Tilda coldly. He was a tall, handsome man in his late sixties, with thick hair that had gone silver and strong bone structure. Not unlike how Caleb would look at that age, though Jerome's mouth was tight and sour. He greeted Caleb more coldly still.

Ronnie led Tilda over to a tall, well-dressed man who stood with his arm on the fireplace mantel like a model in pose. "Tilda, this is my fiancé, Jareth," Veronica announced. "Jareth, my new cousin-in-law, Tilda Riley."

Jareth's white teeth flashed amid a carefully trimmed dark beard. "How do you do, Tilda," he said. "It's been a pleasure to talk to your lovely daughter. She is a walking example of our prime target audience for *The Secret Life of Cells*, so it's been a very illuminating experience."

Annika tugged at her hand. "Mom, Mom! You've got to see Uncle Jerome's library! It's, like, huge! He collects books, and he's even got stepladders to get to the books on top, just like in the *Beauty and the Beast* library in the cartoon!"

"Really?" Tilda laughed as she caught Ronnie's eye. "Annika and I have always agreed that the Beast's library would be irresistible to us. Can I see it?"

"Of course." Ronnie gave Jareth a smile. "Excuse me. Come this way."

They left Caleb telling Maddie and Elaine about Breakers Bay, and followed Ronnie through the house. Annika scampered ahead through one stunning room after another. It was like a museum, decorated with priceless nineteenth-century antiques, massive flower arrangements, stunning art, ceramics and sculptures.

The library was breathtaking. Perhaps not quite as big as the one in the cartoon Beast's enchanted castle, but still stupendous, with the advantage of being a real room. It had towering ceilings, and one side had stained glass windows between banks of books. The end of the room was dominated by a huge family portrait over the fireplace. The central figure was a seated man, dressed in the style of the 1950s. His wife stood behind him, a toddler in her arms, and a boy of maybe ten years old stood next to them. There were other portraits on the wall opposite the stained glass windows. Tilda nodded toward them. "Is this the Moss family portrait gallery?"

"Yes. The big one at the end is of my grandfather, Horace Moss, and my grandmother, Maud. The older boy is my uncle Bertram, Elaine's late husband, and the baby is my father, Jerome. Then, here…" She led Tilda farther down the room and pointed. "My uncle Bertram again, when he graduated from college. He looked a lot like Dad."

"They're all dark." Tilda scanned the wall. "Where did you get that incredible red hair? Your mother?"

Ronnie's smile faltered. "Yes, she had red hair. They say I look exactly like her."

"Is there a picture of her here?"

"There is a portrait, but it's not here. It's hanging in Elaine's library."

Tilda sensed Ronnie's discomfort. *Yikes.* "I'm sorry if I—"

"Oh, no. Don't be," Ronnie reassured her. "It's a long tale. Lots of drama. I'll tell you sometime, in private, over drinks. Lots of drinks. But not tonight."

"Sure. I didn't mean to put you on the spot. The room is just beautiful."

"Yes, this library saved me, when I was a kid. My favorite place in the house."

"Oh, there you are! Sweetheart, we have a problem. Can you come?"

They turned as Jareth hurried in. "What is it?" Ronnie asked.

"I'm not sure what the issue is, to be honest, but Jerome is having one of his meltdowns about something you did or didn't do involving the antipasti. He sent me to collect you. Please, deal with it. If you'd excuse us?" Jareth flashed his teeth at Tilda.

"Sorry," Ronnie said. "I've got to take care of this."

"Of course," Tilda replied, as Jareth led Ronnie away.

Elaine had followed Jareth into the room in the meantime. She stood with Tilda and watched them go.

"I don't like the sound of that one bit," she said.

"The sound of what?" Tilda asked.

"Him ganging up with Jerome against Ronnie. Even if it's something silly like antipasti. It doesn't bode well."

"You don't like him?" Tilda asked.

Elaine harrumphed. "I don't dislike him. He's fine on paper. He looks good, he sounds good, he works hard, he has money of his own. It's hard to put my finger on it. But I wish Ronnie had a man who can hardly believe his luck. A man who wonders if he can ever possibly deserve her." Elaine looked up at the portrait of her husband with a misty smile. "My Bertram was like that with me. As I was with him. For fifty-two years."

"That's wonderful," Tilda said. "How lucky."

"Oh, it was, and we were," Elaine said. "But Jareth has no trouble believing his luck. In fact, I suspect that he thinks that Veronica is the lucky one. He has no idea of the treasure he has in his hands. History, repeating itself."

Tilda wasn't sure what to say. Elaine just gazed wistfully up at the portrait.

"At least Jerome likes him," Elaine reflected. "It's a miracle that Ronnie found someone that Jerome approves of. The poor girl has been trying to please that man all her life, but there's no help for it. She'll always be punished for someone else's sins."

"Whose sins?" Tilda asked, unable to help herself.

Elaine waved her hand. "Oh, my, I have been babbling, haven't I? Portraits do that to me. I wander down memory lane and get lost. Oh, look. My Susannah. I have this exact photograph hanging in my library, too. It's my favorite."

Tilda looked up, and gasped.

This portrait was a large and striking black-and-white photograph, stark and gorgeous. It depicted a beautiful young woman, dark-haired and willowy. She wore a short white dress, and she was perched on a swing, a secret half smile on her face.

It was Annika. Or how Tilda imagined that Annika might look in ten years.

"Uncanny, isn't it?" Elaine asked.

"Amazing," Tilda whispered. "It gives me chills."

"Oh, yes. Come sit down." Elaine beckoned Tilda to one of the plush leather couches and sat next to her, pulling an envelope from her purse. She shook a handful of photographs into her hand. "I picked the ones when Susannah was about Annika's age. The resemblance is even more striking that way."

And it was. Tilda leafed through the photos, unnerved. "It could be her," she said. "Other than hairstyles, clothing. It's like Annika time-traveled."

"You can imagine how I felt when I saw her at Ava Maddox's engagement party," Elaine said. "I got light-headed for a moment. Had to sit down and have a stiff drink."

For a brief, painful instant, Tilda sensed the depths of the grief behind Elaine's reaction. It made her heart quail to imagine it. A parent's worst nightmare. Mourning the loss of one's child.

She took Elaine's hand impulsively, squeezing it. "I'm glad you have Annika now," she said. "I hope it helps."

Elaine looked away, dabbing her eyes with a tissue. "Oh, yes. She is a treasure. Words can't even express."

Maddie and Annika appeared at the door. "Time for dinner, Mom!" Annika announced. "They sent us to get you guys."

Tilda and Elaine shared a laugh as Elaine tucked her photos away.

Dinner was pleasant. Elaine's graciousness made up for Jerome's stiffness. The younger Mosses had no trouble carrying on an animated conversation, and Annika had plenty to say on every subject. Maybe too much, for such a young and recent arrival. But explain that to an exuberant eight-year-old who had just been spoiled all weekend by a new great-grandma and two doting aunts. It was hardly Annika's fault.

After dessert, Jareth stood, holding up his dessert wine. He tapped the glass with his spoon. "Attention, everyone! As you all know, Veronica and I have recently decided to make our engagement official. Show them the ring, Ronnie!"

Ronnie held up her hand, adorned by a large and protruding square-cut diamond that flashed brilliantly in the candlelight.

"I would just like to say to everyone in this room how pleased I am to be associated with such an accomplished family," Jareth went on. "Every element of this group is formidable in its own right. Together, you are a force to be reckoned with, and I feel both proud and humbled to add my small part to that."

They toasted, drank, applauded.

"Let me also say," Jareth went on, warming to his subject, "the women in this family are legendary for their beauty. I am privileged to have one of those famous beauties as my arm candy."

"No," Annika said. "Actually, you'll be *her* arm candy."

Everyone looked at Annika, startled.

"Excuse me?" Jareth said.

Annika shrugged. "Well, she's the TV star, isn't she?"

"Annika!" Tilda hissed to her daughter. "Pipe down!"

"No, no," Jareth agreed swiftly. "Annika is absolutely right. Ronnie is the star, and I am proud to hitch my wagon to such a brilliant one. Cheers, everyone!"

Glasses clinked as everyone toasted.

Jerome set down his glass with a thud. "The rules for children's behavior have changed since my day. I would never have had a child her age at the dinner table. She'd be asleep in her bed. Not being encouraged to share her opinions so boldly."

Tilda bristled. "I'm glad Annika speaks her mind. It's good practice."

"Just because you're eight doesn't mean you don't have opinions," Annika said.

"Case in point." Jerome's mouth twisted unpleasantly.

"You still don't like it when I share my opinions," Ronnie said, her voice ringing out. "And I'm twenty-nine years old."

"Ronnie!" Jareth said, under his breath. "Don't make a scene."

Tilda turned a chilly smile on Jerome. "I encourage Annika to speak her truth," she said. "Will it get her into trouble? Yes, probably it will. Is it worth it? God, I hope so."

"I foresee a clash of parenting cultures ahead of you."

Jerome's teeth showed. "You might have to modify your progressive notions if you're going to fit into this family."

"No, she won't," Caleb said. "I agree with her approach. I respect Annika's thoughts and opinions. And I'll always encourage her to stand up to bullies."

Not a fork clinked. Everyone was holding their breath. Jerome stood up.

"Oh, God. Dad, please. Just don't," Veronica begged.

"Bullies, Caleb?" Jerome said. "Is that what I am?"

"For God's sake, Jerome. You are embarrassing us," Elaine snapped.

"That's something, coming from you," Jerome said. "Using the terrible prospect of me taking control of Moss-Tech as a weapon to terrify your idiot grandson into getting married on your schedule? It's as stupid as it is offensive."

Elaine sighed. "Here we go again. Jerome, you misunderstand—"

"And you!" Jerome pointed at Caleb. "It was a shock, to hear you were married. I would have expected to be on the guest list for an event like that."

"We just signed some papers in my office, Uncle."

"Never mind. Your rudeness no longer surprises me."

"Dad, stop it!" Veronica sprang to her feet, jostling the table. She knocked over a glass of wine and Jareth scooted his chair back with an exclamation of disgust, dabbing at his stained trousers with a napkin.

"Ronnie!" he said sharply. "This is no time for an ugly scene!"

"Oh, so I'm the one with the bad timing?"

"Ronnie, please—"

"I might have known you'd ruin this for me," Ronnie said to Jerome. "All I asked was for my fiancé to get to know my family. How hard could it be, to pretend to be normal for a couple of hours? Some small talk, some food, some wine, a toast at the end, best wishes for the happy couple, and boom, you're done. You can go back to being hateful and critical and making sure I'm as miserable as possible. I thought, with all of them here, and Jareth, too, that you'd behave. I overestimated you. Again."

"Ronnie, you're making it worse!" Jareth protested.

"It couldn't possibly be worse," Ronnie shot back as she stalked out of the dining room.

Jareth stood, dabbing at the wine stain on his lap. "I apologize for her outburst."

"No apologies necessary," Caleb said, as Jareth hurried out. "Not for Ronnie, anyhow."

Jerome glared at Elaine. "And you!" he snarled. "Ruining my plans for Riley BioGen. Months of work for that merger, thrown away without a thought."

"Don't expect my sympathy," Tilda said. "Riley BioGen is my father's life work."

Jerome snorted. "Don't be childish. It was nothing personal."

"It's pretty goddamn personal to me," Tilda told him.

"Clearly, considering what you're disposed to do," Jerome said. "Selling yourself, to save Daddy's company? Is that standard procedure for you?"

"Jerome!" Elaine's voice rang out. "Tilda is the mother of Caleb's child. You will be respectful to her. I insist on it."

"Yes, the precious great-granddaughter. And you claim her, just like that? No questions asked?"

"Not another word about Annika," Caleb said in a warning tone. "Don't speak to her, or about her."

"You don't even remember what Susannah looked like, do you, Jerome?" Elaine's voice was low and sad. "That really shouldn't surprise me, but somehow, it still does."

"What does Susannah have to do with anything?" Jerome roared. "You're making no sense!"

Elaine turned to Tilda. "This may seem strange, but don't

take it personally. We're female, so Jerome is convinced that we're all scheming liars. No woman escapes his judgment."

"I don't care what his psychological problems are, he can't speak this way in front of Annika," Caleb said. "Or Tilda."

"I'm not a baby, Dad," Annika said. "I can handle it."

That startled everyone into silence for a moment. Elaine's furious scowl melted into a smile. "'Dad,' is it?" she said. "Well, just look at that. Isn't that lovely."

But Jerome wasn't finished. "Don't preach at me, Elaine. You've been fighting me ever since you married Bertram."

"Fighting to keep you in check! Particularly for the last twenty-three years, which is how long you've been sulking. And I am sick of it."

"I'm not the one jerking people around with controlling shares of MossTech!"

Elaine sighed. "I'm doing it for the sake of the future, Jerome. Whereas you're just punishing us all for sins of the past."

"Shut up, you sanctimonious old hag! You scheming—"

"Don't yell!" Annika jumped up, her mouth quivering. "You need to take a time-out!"

Maddie hid her face in her hands. "A time-out," she whispered. "Oh, yes. I love it. So perfect."

Annika grabbed Caleb's hand, then Tilda's. "Mom? Dad? I don't like it here."

"Agreed," Tilda said. "Good night, everyone. This is our cue."

Thirteen

The three of them beat a hasty retreat, leaving the raised voices yammering behind them in the dining room. Caleb grabbed Annika's suitcase and booster seat from the entry hall, where Maddie had left them, and they hurried out to Caleb's car.

Caleb got the booster in place and helped Annika strap herself into the back seat. Annika was trembling with nervous tension. He gave her a kiss on the top of her head.

"Hey," he said gently. "Thanks for sticking up for us, back there. That took real guts. Jerome can be one scary guy when he gets mad."

"Why was he so mean?" Annika's voice still shook.

"It's hard to explain," Caleb said. "But I don't think all that is about us, not really. It's been there a long time. We just happened to be there when it came out."

"Poor Ronnie," Annika said. "She was always there, when she was little. And he was probably always mean."

"Yeah," Caleb agreed. "Probably."

He got into the driver's seat and pulled out of the driveway. When they were through the gate, Tilda reached over, patting his leg.

"I'm glad you included Annika in our united front," she said. "That felt good."

"I'm glad, too," Caleb said. "We needed her. She was our secret weapon."

"You bet I was," Annika agreed.

"You went a little overboard, though, honey," Tilda scolded gently. "Next time, hang back and let the grown-ups fight if they want to. Don't intervene."

"But you said some stuff to him," Annika argued. "And so did Dad."

"That's different," Tilda said. "The rules are different for grown-ups."

"But that's not fair!"

"Nope, it sure isn't. But it's still the rule."

Annika chattered for a while, but the intensity of the evening, followed by her busy, exciting weekend, had worn her out. In less than five minutes, she was fast asleep.

Once on the highway, Caleb took Tilda's hand, and he felt invisible doors between them open, in his chest, his head. Maybe he was just fooling himself, but damn, he'd made that bad call nine years ago, and he'd paid a terrible price for it. This time, he'd learn from his mistakes.

He was trusting this feeling, wherever it took him.

When they got home, he gave the keys to Tilda and let her wheel Annika's suitcase inside while he carried their sleeping child. He dictated the alarm code to Tilda, and carried the little girl through the house and up the stairs, Tilda close behind.

She opened the bedroom door and snapped on the bed-side moon lamp to its lowest setting, a delicate crescent. She turned down the comforter, and pulled off Annika's pink ballerina shoes, tucking the comforter around the girl when Caleb laid her down.

"You don't want to get her into her pajamas?"

"She can stay like that tonight," Tilda whispered back. "The dress is soft and stretchy. It'll be as comfy as a night-gown."

Then Annika's eyes fluttered open. She looked around, blinking, and smiled when she saw the moon lamp, and the starry sky comforter. "Where are we?"

"This is your bedroom at Caleb's house," Tilda told her.
"Cool."

"It is, but you can explore it tomorrow. Sleep now, baby."

Annika nodded, snuggling down into her pillows, but she reached out and seized Caleb's hand. "Dad?" she whispered. "Why is Jerome so mad at everybody?"

Caleb considered all the ways he could answer that loaded question. "He got his feelings hurt, a long time ago. And he never got over it."

"Why didn't he just talk to the person who hurt his feelings? That's what Mommy always tells me to do."

"He couldn't," Caleb replied. "She died before he had a chance. It was really sad."

"Oh." Annika considered that. "Well, I'm sorry. But he made Ronnie cry."

"Yes, he did," Caleb said. "Don't worry. You won't be seeing very much of him."

Annika nodded, and then reached up to her mother for a hug. After a brief hesitation, she lifted her arms up to Caleb, too.

He was blindsided by how that felt. That rush in his chest, like a flock of startled birds taking off all at once as he hugged her back.

They left the room. Tilda blew Annika a kiss, and left the door open.

They looked at each other in the passageway.

"You absolutely have to tell me that story sometime," Tilda whispered. "Jerome, and Veronica's mother. You guys all keep dancing around it. Those maddening hints."

"Sure, but not tonight. Jerome has taken up enough oxygen for one night."

"Good point," Tilda said.

"Would you like a drink?"

She shook her head. "Thanks, but all I want right now is to get these heels off."

His eyes dropped to the sexy shoes. "Then let's go get you comfortable." He led her down the hall and opened the bedroom door. "I'm sorry if they hurt. They look great."

Tilda sat on the bed, and got to work on the ankle straps. "Yeah, well. Sexy shoes are always a devil's bargain."

Caleb turned on the bedside lamp, to just a dim, mellow golden glow. He kneeled down in front of her and nudged her hand away, undoing the buckles himself. "There's another walk-in closet next to mine for your stuff, by the way."

Tilda laughed. "Really. His-and-hers walk-in closets? How luxurious. And hopeful, too. Now that's what I call thinking ahead."

"Drew Maddox's idea," he admitted, sliding off her shoes. "I would never have thought of that on my own, but I'm glad that he did." He took her narrow, elegantly arched feet in his hands, his calluses catching on the sheer fabric of her black stockings. The beaded fringe of her dress swayed and clicked, draping over his cuffs as he massaged her feet.

She clutched the edge of the bed with a shuddering sigh. "You're good at this."

"You inspire me," he said.

Tilda reached out, cupping his face. Her fingertips trailed delicately over his cheekbones, down to his jaw.

Caleb turned his head, pressing her hand to his lips. Kissing it. Then he leaned forward, kissing the tops of her thighs. The beaded fabric was a barrier to the warmth of her skin, but he had to keep it slow. Sliding his hands up, down, back up, gently over her calves. The swaying beaded fringe draped on his forearms.

Finally, he dared to lift the skirt, baring her knees. High enough to see the band of lace holding up the stockings on her upper thighs. The mysterious shadows and heat of her beautiful body pulled at him. Beaded fringe draped out over her pale thighs.

He ventured higher, until he brushed a fingertip over the

lace of her panties. A teasing fingertip. He was an artist, stroking delicately with a paintbrush. Up and down, over her sensitive flesh. A slow, seductive invitation.

Tilda placed her hands on his shoulders, her fingers digging into the fabric of his shirt. "Caleb," she whispered. "Oh, my."

"More?" He kissed her thighs, first one, then the other, while brushing his fingertips over the tender folds beneath her panties. Pushing back against the grinding ache of need in his own body. It had to wait.

"You seductive bastard," she whispered. "Hold on a sec. Don't go anywhere."

She gently pushed him back and slipped away, making her silent way over to the bedroom door. She opened it, listened for a moment, then closed the door. Locked it.

She approached the dresser with the mirror and took off her earrings, then pulled out her hair sticks. Caleb walked over and stood behind her, watching her pull out the pins, and release the coil of hair. It tumbled, unwinding down her back.

She shook it out over her shoulders, into a wavy golden cape. That sultry, flirtatious glance, the curve of her secret smile, emboldened him to step forward, and slide his fingers into her warm, thick mane. Hot, silky, perfect.

"I'm sorry about tonight," he said. "The Mosses did not come across well. If that had been a test, we would have failed it. Good thing you and I are already married."

Tilda's mouth twitched. "Every family has its problematic uncle, right?"

"I think the Mosses have taken the problematic-uncle thing to a whole new level."

She laughed at him. "It's not fair to do a dysfunctional family one-upmanship game with me. My family is too small to compete."

"Lucky you," he said, with feeling.

"I'm sorry for Veronica, though. Hope it doesn't scare her man away."

Caleb grunted. "We'll see."

"It almost sounds like you're hoping it does," she commented. "You and Elaine. What have you got against the guy?"

"Annika nailed it. Jareth's in love with himself. Veronica can't possibly compete."

"She's like a sister for you," Tilda said. "It's hard to think that anyone is good enough for a woman that you love." She shot him a teasing glance. "Just ask my dad."

"Please, let's not," he murmured, burying his nose in her hair. The soft, warm weight of her head against his shoulder felt so good.

"To be fair, it was Annika and I who set Jerome off," Tilda said. "We lit the fuse."

"He would've lit the fuse himself if you hadn't. He was itching for a fight. I should have foreseen that. Kept you two away from him."

"We're tough," she told him. "Don't worry about it."

"But I discovered something about myself," he told her. "Something surprising."

"And what would that be?"

"Watching you hold your ground, like a boss. Huge turn-on. Huge."

Tilda laughed at him. "And here I was, afraid I'd embarrassed you. Driving a wedge into the family at the very first gathering."

"My heart was galloping. It was like watching Wonder Woman do her thing."

She twisted to look up at him, her eyes solemn. "It was only because I had my secret magical talisman," she said. "The one that confers superpowers."

"Yeah? And that is?"

She spun around, placing both of her hands on his chest,

looking into his eyes. "Our united front," she said. "If someone strong has your back, you can face anything."

Her words sliced through him, like a laser flash. The blazing truth in them, and the power. The potential. Shaking, breathless hope that this magic could actually be for real.

And they were kissing. Desperately. Every time they came together, he devolved into a seething vortex of hunger. Ravishing her mouth, hands all over the lithe, strong perfection of her body. He fumbled for the zipper of her dress, and worked it down, hands shaking as he peeled the sleeves over her arms, the bodice down over her chest.

The pale, lush globes of her breasts were showcased by the sexy black lace bra The weight of the beaded fringe made the dress hit the ground with a soft thump. He didn't speak. He would only stammer. Kisses were better.

Tilda struggled to get his shirt unbuttoned, but he couldn't stop kissing her, and finally she let out a frustrated sound and batted his arms away.

"Help me with those damn cuff links," she directed.

Yes. He wanted to feel her in his arms, skin-to-skin. Caleb kicked off his shoes and peeled off his socks. They wrapped around each other, her hands busy with his belt.

Tilda jerked down his pants and his briefs with them. He shook them off his ankles. That left nothing but her black bra and panties, quickly discarded. But not the stockings. The stockings stayed. He spun her to face the mirror. "So beautiful," he said.

Tilda shivered as he pushed aside her hair, kissing the nape of her neck. He nudged her legs apart and petted her sleek little triangle of dark blond curls as he kissed her throat with hypnotic slowness. Then slowly moved lower, to between her thighs. Caressing tender folds, the secret, liquid heat, the sweet spots. The slower the build, the bigger the payoff.

She stiffened in his arms, crying out softly, as pleasure

pulsed heavily through her body. Oh, yeah. He could not get enough of this. Not ever. He could spend the rest of his life just pleasing her, reaching for that blinding flash of perfection.

Tilda's eyes were still closed as she reached behind herself, clasping the hard shaft of his erection. Their gazes locked in the mirror. Her eyes were dilated, dreamy. Her full, rosy lips were flushed, still parted. "The bed," she said.

The bed worked for him. Tilda bent to toss back the covers, and he must have made some helpless sound at the sight of her in that position.

Tilda glanced over her shoulder at him. Her eyes had a hot glow of desire through the wild locks of her tousled hair. "Like this?" she asked. "Do you like this view?"

He tried to speak, but could only nod and stare at the stunning spectacle of Tilda on her knees, flaunting her shadowy curves with that tempting smile.

He clasped her hips, stroking them. "This works for you?"

"*You* work for me," she said. "It works, if it's you. It hardly seems to matter how."

He was humbled at her generosity, dazzled by her beauty. His eyes caressed all the gorgeous details—her back, the shape of her spine, the dimples of the small of her back. All the graceful curves, gleaming like a pearl in the dim light, painted by shadows. That seductive, mysterious smile of hers pulled at him like a tow chain.

She was slick and welcoming as he reached around her, sliding his fingers down between her legs as he sank inside her plush depths…and they were off. More, more. More astonished pleasure, more panting excitement. Every plunging stroke. So wet and tight.

He wanted it to last, make her come over and over before he let go, but their joined bodies surged and heaved, out of control. She rocked back to meet every deep thrust.

She crested first, and the demanding pulses of her orgasm dragged him right along after her. His own climax roared through him, shaking the world to shattered pieces.

Afterward, he rolled over, reluctantly sliding out of the hot clasp of her body.

She rolled over, cuddling closer. After barely a moment, she let out a regretful sigh, and gave him a swift kiss. "Excuse me," she murmured.

"What?" He jerked up, disoriented. "Something wrong?"

"Not at all." She slid off the bed, peeled off her stockings and picked up her dress, draping it neatly over one of the chairs. She grabbed a few things out of her suitcase and headed for the bathroom, toiletries case in one hand, pajamas in the other.

She came out a few minutes later from the bathroom in a puff of scented steam, dressed in gray boy shorts and a cami top. "Where do you keep your pajamas?"

"Left closet, second shelf of the dresser," he told her. "Why do you ask?"

She disappeared into his closet, coming out with a pair of his pajamas, and tossed them in his direction. They hit him in the chest.

"What's this?" he asked.

"Your days of sleeping naked are over. At least when Annika is in residence."

"We can't just lock the door?"

"I can't have a locked door between me and Annika. Not in a strange house, after such a weird evening. She could wake up, be scared. The bedroom door stays open."

He put on the pajamas. As he pulled Tilda into his arm, he felt it again, like he had in the car. Invisible doors, opening up. Light streaming in. Walls coming down.

Making room for Tilda, for Annika. For something deeper, richer. More real.

It felt like flying.

Fourteen

Herbert Riley set down his teacup on its saucer. "It sounds like you know what you want to do with Far Eye," he said. "You need a partner. Why not partner with the biggest and the best? MossTech would implement Far Eye quickly, and on a more massive scale than any other scenario." He patted Tilda's hand. "Just weigh the emotional costs and benefits. You're getting closer with Caleb. That's good. But don't give this property to MossTech unless they know its value, and compensate you properly."

Tilda took a final sip of her own tea, and set the cup down on the coffee shop table. "I just don't want to make any of my professional decisions based on emotion," she said. "That never turns out well."

"Never?" Her father raised a teasing eyebrow. "Seems like some of your emotionally based decisions are turning out fine. I haven't seen you look like this in years. Annika, too. Having a dad agrees with her."

"Yeah, Caleb seems to enjoy being a father. It seems too good to be true."

"You and Annika are the only parts of this equation that are too good to be true," Dad said sternly. "And I hope he realizes it. He should be on his knees in front of you, giving thanks for his good luck."

A vivid image of the last time Caleb had been on his knees before her flashed through her mind. Her face got hot. "He's behaving well," she assured her dad.

He grunted. "If you say so. It's hard to believe that anyone's good enough for my precious girl. Or my granddaughter, either, for that matter."

"Caleb picked Annika up from her after-school program today," she said. "Their plan was to go to the farmers' market to shop, because, of course, the stuff delivered from the grocery store wasn't special enough for their lofty foodie tastes. He's teaching her to cook. She made a great apple crisp the other night. Yum."

"Sounds delicious," her father said. "Father-daughter bonding. Very nice."

"It is. She's practicing for when you come over for dinner."

Tilda walked him outside to the street, and they firmed up dinner plans before he got into the car she'd called for him. Then she went to her car and headed home.

Home. Wow. So far, so good. Things were going so well. Even after that crazy scene a couple of weeks ago at Jerome's. She could casually invite her dad over to dinner. That showed how well it was working. She'd started to feel like she wasn't just playing house with Caleb. It almost felt like they were a real family.

Tilda slowly wended her way through Seattle rush-hour traffic, the only thing about the Emerald City that she disliked. She loved the rest of it: the cool air, the constant clouds, the luminous greens and blues and grays. Mountains and water on every side.

Tilda parked next to Caleb's Porsche, and went in. As she hung up her coat, her eye caught the trio of pen-and-ink sketches done by the street artist in Carruthers Cove that had a place of pride in the entrance hall. They'd gone back to the beach house with Annika and gotten her daughter's portrait done as well. Caleb had insisted on framing all three and hanging them up. Another marvelous weekend. Different, but also great.

Annika's high, excited voice came from the kitchen, as did fabulous cooking smells. Some rich combo of curry, butter and chicken. Music was playing. Another fresh hit tune by Moon Cat and the Kinky Ladies.

Tilda set down her purse. As she got closer, she could make out the words.

"…won't listen to me," Annika complained. "I'm supposed to be project leader for the diorama, but Patti wants to draw an Argentinosaurus, and Tyler goes nuts for gigantic nine-foot insects, and Kira wants to do saber-toothed tigers! And Poonam was supposed to do the background, because she's good at drawing, but she drew flowers! Like, there were no flowers back then! Flowers didn't evolve for another fifty million years! And I'm, like, make up your mind, guys, because this diorama's going to be all over the map!"

"Yeah, it's a dilemma," Caleb agreed. "Drop those beans in the steamer. My advice is to rethink the project itself. If you can tweak the structure to make it work better for your team, they'll invest more energy."

"Like, tweak it how?" Annika sounded dubious.

"You've been thinking about a single point in geologic time," Caleb said. "That's the simplest way to organize the project, but it rules out a lot of interesting plants and animals. Widen your scope. Do a longer timeline, with room for everyone's favorites."

Annika was silent for a moment. "Hmm," she said doubtfully. "We'd have to make it bigger. Sounds like a lot of work. Especially for me, 'cause I always end up helping everyone."

"Get used to that," Caleb said sagely. "It won't get any better. Put it to them that way. It's more work for everyone, but Poonam gets her flowers, Tyler gets his insect, et cetera. Your real job as project leader is not the diorama. It's to get the best out of your team."

Tilda leaned against the kitchen entryway. "Spoken like a true CEO."

Caleb smiled at her. Annika ran over to give her a hug.

"Hey, sweetheart," she said. "Smells great."

"Yeah, chicken in butter sauce! With steamed rice and green beans from the farmers' market, and Dad made a special dressing."

Caleb poured her a glass of wine, and passed it to her. "We've been thrashing out the thorny issues of team leadership as we cook."

"I'm just like Dad, that way," Annika informed her. "Cooking makes me think better." She busily stirred the chicken in its bubbling pot of fragrant sauce. "It's a great time to work stuff out. You just let your mind run free while you cook stuff."

"Sorry to say it, but that never worked for me," Tilda said, sipping her wine. "If I let my mind run free in the kitchen, I'd lose a limb."

"That's just because you hate cooking, Mom."

"Oh, you mean, you've noticed?"

"I don't mean you're bad," Annika said earnestly. "Just not real enthusiastic."

"Food's done," Caleb told them. "The table is set. Let's eat."

The meal was fabulous. Delicious chicken in a spicy, fragrant butter sauce, fluffy Thai rice, lightly steamed green beans from the farmers' market tossed in tangy dressing with herbs and toasted pecans. Fresh fruit salad. A scoop of peach ice cream. Annika was so proud to have helped. She loved the thought of having inherited a talent for cooking from her father. It made her feel connected. Tilda was moved at the sight of her precious baby, basking in the focused attention that Caleb enjoyed giving her. It was so great, it scared her.

Please, please, don't let this be too good to be true.

"Mom, tonight's the premiere of season three of *The Se-*

cret Life of Cells!" Annika announced. "I've been waiting for weeks!"

"Really?" Tilda asked. "What kind of cells? Human cells?"

"We have a long way before we get to humans. I think tonight is plankton."

"Wow, exciting," Tilda said. "An hour-long deep dive into pond scum."

"Plankton, not pond scum," Annika scolded. "We wouldn't exist without single-celled plants, Mom! And Ronnie makes it interesting."

"Of course, hon," Tilda soothed. "I was teasing. I'm sure it'll be great."

"It starts in five minutes. I'll turn on the TV. I love the opening sequence, when we see the magnified cells swimming around, and then you go inside the cell. So cool."

Annika disappeared into the TV room, and Caleb lifted his glass. "You cold, hard math types," he murmured. "Give single-celled organisms the respect they deserve."

She clinked his glass, laughing at him. Look at them, joking around, teasing each other. Eating dinner together. Watching a show together.

They settled on the TV-room couch, all three of them. There were armchairs, but Tilda curled up on one side of Annika, and Caleb sat down on the other side.

Tilda enjoyed the show, but with a strange sense of double vision. She was never quite able to believe this was real. A family for Annika. All the love, attention and support she gave her daughter, doubled. More than doubled, if she factored in Caleb's quirky relatives.

She didn't just want this for Annika. She wanted it for herself, too. But she kept bracing herself. This gift seemed freely offered, but she couldn't stop feeling like someone was going to slap her hand if she actually reached out to take it.

Aw, hell. She'd try to enjoy it while it lasted. Be in the

moment. After all, nothing lasted forever. Change was the only constant.

She focused on Ronnie's show, which was no chore. The show was well written and entertaining, with excellent production values, and Ronnie herself was funny and engaging.

When the credits were rolling, she turned to Annika. "Time for bed, pumpkin."

"Can I stay up another hour? Kaylea stays up until ten thirty every single night."

"Not a chance," Tilda said. "Go do your jammies and teeth. I'll come up in a few minutes to tuck you in and say good-night."

"'Night, kiddo," Caleb said, kissing her cheek. "Thanks for being my sous chef."

"Will you help me with the prehistory timeline for the new diorama tomorrow?"

"Certainly," he said. "It would be my privilege."

When Annika had disappeared upstairs, Tilda grabbed the bag she'd left by the couch and pulled out her laptop. She sat down on the couch next to Caleb, grabbed the remote and turned off the TV, looking at Caleb. "Have you got a moment?"

"For you? Of course."

Tilda inserted the thumb drive that contained the outline of her project. "I have something to show you. An idea I've been playing with for years. Last year, by chance, I found exactly the right mix of scientists and engineers to help me take it to the next level. I've named it Far Eye."

Caleb leaned forward, peering into the screen. "What does it do?"

"It's an AI program for forecasting, for farmers," she said. "It connects with satellite pictures to track trends, analyze weather patterns, ocean currents, et cetera. It helps farmers plan far enough ahead to mitigate droughts, floods or fires, smoke and smog cover, potential for armed conflict, climate change. But it needs more development. I've been talking to some venture capitalists about it."

"You wrote the algorithm yourself?" Caleb asked.

"Yes. I was evaluating various options before Dad's heart attacks, trying decide whether to partner with Riley Bio-Gen's R-and-D department, or to find investors and develop it myself. Then the merger drama happened, and then…us. And I got distracted."

"What did the venture capitalists say?"

"There was real interest," she told him. "I would find investors for sure. The question is, do I want the life of a tech entrepreneur, or the life of a researcher and data analyst. I vastly prefer being a researcher and analyst. But I wanted your thoughts."

Oh, that look in his eyes. Full of tenderness, wonder. Heat.

"You would trust me with this?" he asked.

"Yes," she said. "You'd never steal my intellectual property. Besides, you haven't even seen it. You might not like it."

"I'd love to check it out."

"Then go for it." Tilda passed him the computer. "I'm running up to say good-night."

Annika was in bed, reading. She cuddled up as Tilda slid into the bed next to her.

"Mom, you're not mad about me doing stuff with Dad, and not with you, are you?" Her voice was anxious. "You know, cooking, and the diorama? I know biology isn't really your thing, so I asked Dad for advice. You're not jealous, are you?"

The question startled her. "Oh, no, baby. It's wonderful that you have these special things with him. You and I have our own special stuff. We have Moon Cat and the Kinky Ladies, and our robot kits, all kinds of stuff. And you know who wins out the biggest?"

"Who?" Annika asked.

"Me," Tilda announced. "I get a spectacular dinner served me every night, and my lunch leftovers are just as amazing. I've been eating like a queen since you started learning to cook. Now I'm hopelessly spoiled. I've forgotten how to scramble an egg or cook a pork chop. Keep it up, girl, if you want to keep eating. Keep it up."

Annika giggled, and snuggled closer. Tilda reached across her to snap off the light.

"Mom?" Annika's voice was very small.

"Yes, baby?"

"Do you think…that Dad likes it?"

Tilda felt a strange tension grip her. "Likes what, honey?"

"Oh, you know," Annika whispered. "Being a father. He's been supernice, but I know it can be boring. All the stuff you have to do. School runs, lunches, homework. And it's not like I can talk to him about grown-up science stuff, or anything. Not yet, anyway. Maybe it's boring to him. Do you think he'll get tired of it?"

The question made Tilda's heart hurt. She hated that her girl had to feel that kind of insecurity. It took a moment to breathe down the clenched-throat feeling.

"I can't speak for him, or make promises on his behalf," she said. "I only speak for myself. But I think he does like it. From what I can see, he likes it a lot, and he damn well should, because he is insanely lucky. You are an awesome, lovable kid."

Annika hid her face against Tilda's shoulder. "You think?"

"I do think," Tilda said. "I can't say for sure what'll happen, but I have high hopes. And you're a Moss now, as well as a Riley, no matter what happens. That whole family wants you, baby. They're not stupid. They know a diamond when they see one."

She could see Annika's smile in the dim glow of the moon night-light. Her eyes were wet. "Thanks, Mom."

"I love you, sweetheart. And remember. No matter what happens, we are going to be fine. We've got this."

"Yeah. Okay. I love you, too. G'night."

The instant she was out of Annika's line of sight, she pressed her hands against her eyes. She was fighting to get her face presentable before she stepped onto the walkway, in full view of Caleb on the couch below. She squared her shoulders and was ready with a smile when he looked up. She sat down next to him. "Did you look through it?"

"Insofar as I could. You'll have to explain how the AI works. Using small words."

"Ha," she scoffed.

"I understand just enough to sense how brilliant this is. It's groundbreaking. You need to talk to some good IP lawyers about protecting your interests, if you're actually considering developing this with MossTech."

Tilda gave him a misty smile. "Yeah," she said softly. "I'm glad you like it."

He cupped the back of her head and kissed her. The laptop almost slid off his lap. He caught it without looking at it, then placed it on the coffee table, never breaking the kiss.

When she came up for air, she was smiling.

"What's so funny?" he asked.

"You and your quirky turn-ons," she teased. "Scolding your mean uncle does it for you. Now it's predictive atmospheric science algorithms. You have some freaky kinks."

He pulled her onto his lap, letting her feel his erection. "God, yes. Statistical analysis, meteorology, soil dynamics. Makes me stiffer than carbon nanotubes."

She swatted him, laughing, but he trapped her hand and kissed it.

"No, seriously," he said. "It does turn me on. Seeing you do your thing, seeing you crush it. Seeing you trust me with your work, your daughter, yourself. I want to be good enough for that. I want to deserve it."

Her breath caught. She slid off his lap and tugged him to his feet. "Come on upstairs. I'll make sure that Annika is asleep. We'll go into your bedroom and lock the door, and I'll show you exactly what you deserve."

Caleb looked intrigued, but wary. "What does that mean?"

"Do you trust me, Caleb?"

His dimples carved deep around that gorgeous smile. "Yeah."

"Then what are we waiting for? Off we go to your bedroom."

"Our bedroom," Caleb said.

Tilda looked over her shoulder. "What?"

"Not my bedroom. *Our* bedroom."

That hot, shaky feeling in her chest was making her soft and gooey. "Um...right."

They lost no time getting up the stairs.

Fifteen

Tilda woke up to feel Caleb patting her shoulder. "Hey," he said gently. "Til? Sorry to wake you, but isn't that your ringtone?"

Tilda jolted awake. The faint sound was coming from downstairs, the opening riff to "Breaking Down Your Walls." "You could hear that?"

"I sleep more lightly than you," Caleb said. "You should check it, right?"

"Absolutely. Thanks for waking me." She slid out of bed and hurried down the stairs, Caleb on her heels.

The phone was on the kitchen bar. She snatched it up. The call was from Dad. She answered it. "Dad? Are you okay?"

"Til? Is that you?" Dad sounded confused.

"Yes, it's me. Are you okay? Are you sick?"

"I'm fine, and no, I'm not having a heart attack, honey. I just got back from my bridge game with Arthur and Trix and Sylvie. And someone broke into my house."

Tilda gasped. "Good God! Are the police there yet?"

"They're on their way. I'm fine. Just shaken. I shouldn't have bothered you at this hour. I came home, and the place is just…it's just destroyed."

"Dad, you're inside the house now? Do you even know if the thieves have left?"

Caleb gestured for her to put the call on speakerphone. She hit the button, and her father's shaky voice blared out, loud and distorted.

"...don't have to worry, honey. I've been through the whole house. There's no one here anymore. They've been and gone."

"Dad!" she wailed. "That was not for you to do! That was for the police to do!"

"Well, it's done, in any case. They took my laptop, my tablet, the TVs. They neutralized the security system somehow. Deactivated the video cameras."

"I'll be right over there, Dad."

"Oh, no, honey. Don't bother. The police are on their way, and there's nothing you can do. I guess I just needed to talk to someone. Sorry I woke you."

"I'm coming over," Tilda said. She looked up at Caleb. "Could you cover Annika here while I drive to Dad's house?"

"I'll take you there," Caleb said.

"But Annika—"

"I'm already calling Maddie." Caleb's phone was at his ear. "Hey, Mads?" he said. "Yeah, I know. Sorry, but Tilda's dad's house was robbed. He's in shock. I want you to get over here and watch Annika so that we can... Yeah?... Thanks. See you in a few." He ended the call. "She'll be here in fifteen. I'll drive you there. Go get dressed."

"Thanks," Tilda said. "We're on our way right now, Dad. Take it easy."

"I'm all right, hon. But I'll be glad to see you. Looks like the police are here. I'm going to talk to them. See you when you get here."

Tilda put down the phone. Without a word, Caleb pulled her into his arms. His strong hug felt so good, reinforcing all the lovely things he kept on saying about trust.

She was starting to let herself lean on it. Expect it.

Even, God forbid, need it.

She stepped away, wiping her eyes. "Thanks," she said, sniffling. "For calling Maddie. And offering to drive me. It'll be really great to have you there with me."

"You wouldn't be able to keep me away," he said.

Maddie arrived not long afterward. She'd thrown on sweats, and had wild bed head. The big, square black glasses she wore seemed both nerdish and stylish.

Tilda embraced her as they passed in the doorway. "Thanks," she whispered.

"Anytime," Maddie assured her. "Call and let me know how he is."

They made good time, with the streets empty. They didn't speak, but when Caleb's hand was free, he held hers. "You can relax," he urged. "The police are there. He's safe."

"I know. But this was all he needed," she said. "After the heart attacks, and then the merger business. I thought things were looking up, and smack, another blow."

They pulled up behind a police cruiser, then went inside and found Dad at the kitchen table, hunched over a tumbler of Scotch. He looked up, his face bloodless. His hands, wrapped around the glass, were shaking.

She hugged him and pulled up a chair. Her father looked up Caleb. "Who's with Annika?" he demanded.

"My sister is with her," Caleb said. "Don't worry."

Tilda took Dad's ice-cold hand. "When did you realize what had happened?"

"The front door was open when I came home. The alarm was deactivated."

"And you walked right inside." Tilda couldn't control her tone.

Her father gave her a look. "You already scolded me, so let's move on. I went in to assess the situation. Then I called the police. They took the electronics. Tore open all the drawers and cabinets. Made a huge mess." He met Tilda's eyes. "And they took the safe."

Tilda's stomach dropped. Wes Brody's file. The nuclear option. She'd left it at Dad's house for safekeeping, never dreaming something like this could happen.

"Did they open it?" she asked.

"No. They just took the whole thing," Herbert said. "Pried it right out of the wall."

"Is there a tracking device in it?" Caleb asked.

"There was," Herbert said. "The thieves removed it. They must have been familiar with the model. They left the tracking device on my desk."

"Thieves like that usually have a specific agenda," Caleb said. "What was in the safe?"

"Oh, the usual. Emergency cash. Deeds for the house. Life-insurance policies. Personal things. A few pieces of your mother's jewelry. I meant to give them to you, but it kept on slipping my mind. And now they're gone forever."

Caleb looked at each of them in turn, stood up and cleared his throat. "Excuse me," he said smoothly. "I'll let you two talk in private."

He walked out, and her dad gazed after him. "The man can read a room," he said. "I'll say that much for him."

"Come on, Dad. You can say a lot more about him than that. Things have been good lately with him. With me and Annika. I told you."

"So you did, honey, so you did," Dad said. "That's wonderful. But someone now has your nuclear option. We have no idea who, but that person is not our friend."

"To anyone but the Mosses themselves, the file would be meaningless," she said. "No one else would ever connect the dots. And the Mosses don't know about it. Nor will they. I never told them. You never told them. The only person we told was your lawyer."

"Murray would never say a word," Herbert said. "Still, it's strange. Such a slick operation, and poof, the file is gone. I wish we'd destroyed it ourselves."

"We've done nothing wrong by just having it," Tilda assured him. "We chose not to use it, because we didn't trust its contents. We are in the clear, Dad."

The police detective came in to talk to her father again, effectively ending that conversation. She and Caleb stayed with her father for the better part of the night. When dawn was near, Herbert urged them to go home and get some sleep.

"You young folks run along," he said. "I imagine you have to work today."

"I'll work from home today," Caleb said.

"I'll head home with him and get my own car," Tilda said. "Then I'll come back here with Annika. I don't want you to be alone."

"Don't be ridiculous!" Herbert protested. "I won't have Annika sleeping in a place with no functioning security system, covered with fingerprinting dust."

"Come stay at our house, then," Caleb offered.

Herbert looked taken aback. "Oh, I couldn't intrude. I'll stay in a hotel."

"It's the perfect solution," Caleb said. "Let the cleaning service deal with the mess. Until it's all in order, stay with us. I have a guest room. Annika would love it."

"Please, Dad?" Tilda said. "I'd feel so much better if you did. Please."

Herbert threw up his hands. "Oh, fine. But you're both overdoing it."

"I'll run upstairs and pack some stuff for you," Tilda said.

Forty minutes later, she was driving Dad's car, with Caleb in his own car ahead of her on the road. At Caleb's house, her dad was quickly persuaded to crash in the guest room.

Tilda finally sat down in the kitchen, and Maddie poured her a cup of coffee.

"Thank you," Tilda said. "Your help tonight meant so much to me."

"Don't mention it. You're family now." Maddie turned to Caleb and gave her brother a stern look. "I hope you're not going into the office."

"Just a quick call to Sergio, to ask him to organize a

board meeting as soon as possible. I have to tell everyone about Far Eye."

Maddie's elegantly shaped eyebrows climbed. "And what is that?"

"An incredible AI tool for agricultural planning that Tilda is developing," Caleb said. "You'll grasp the math better than me. I wish Marcus were here. He'd go nuts."

"Can I look at it?" Maddie asked.

"Be my guest." Tilda slid the computer toward Maddie.

Tilda lifted her coffee cup, but Caleb put his hand on her arm. "I was thinking we could go curl up in bed. Take a nap. You've earned it."

"Annika has school," she said. "I have to get her ready for—"

"Don't worry," Maddie assured her. "I've got Annika covered. I'll get her breakfast, and pack a lunch, and drop her at school. It'll be fun. We're great pals."

"Thank you," Tilda said.

"Tell her I'll help with the geologic-ages timeline after she gets home from school today," Caleb said. "Her grandpa can help her, too."

Tilda followed Caleb up the stairs. She felt so strange. That feeling in her chest. Soft and open. Strange, that she should feel that way after a robbery.

"You're being so sweet to me," she blurted. "I don't know what to do with it."

Caleb held out his hand. "How about you just go with it?"

Okay. She took his hand, and followed him.

Sixteen

"That's it," Caleb concluded, looking around the board-room table at his various family members. "Look over the files. Once you've had time to review it, we'll meet to discuss it again. For my own part, I'm ready to set up a meeting with Tilda's legal team right now. Far Eye would be the best investment we've ever made."

"I'm sure she'll make us pay accordingly," Elaine said. "Through the nose."

"As well she should," Maddie pointed out. "It's an incredible tool. She could make a fortune with it. Why shouldn't we pay a fair price for this opportunity?"

"Excuse me for pointing out the obvious, but aren't Riley BioGen's assets already the property of MossTech?" Jerome asked.

"Not this," Caleb said. "Tilda hasn't been on Riley BioGen's payroll for years. She consulted for them. Far Eye is hers. She didn't use their resources to develop it."

"Well, now," Jerome murmured. "Isn't that convenient."

"What are you insinuating?" Caleb's voice was getting sharper, in spite of his teeth-clenching determination not to let Jerome needle him.

"Since the entire Riley family is living with you, including your father-in-law, you might be losing that perspective that only healthy distance can give."

"Oh, Jerome," Elaine said, impatient. "Don't be a pill. It's exhausting."

"Herbert stayed for three days," Caleb said, through his teeth. "Until his house was habitable again. He's been gone for over a week. I don't know what you're getting at."

"So I am the only one here who can see the huge conflict of interest staring us in the face?" Jerome glared at each of them in turn. "Far Eye is his wife's pet vanity project. Quick, fling open the company coffers!"

"You're being unfair," Elaine told him. "It's hardly Caleb's fault if he is married to someone with unusual talent. Tilda is an asset in herself. So her relationship with Caleb disqualifies her from contributing? How does that make sense?"

"It's not that simple," Jerome said. "I will need time to study this proposal."

"Of course," Caleb said. "Take the time you need. But Tilda won't wait forever."

"We'll all study it," Elaine said. "Give Tilda my compliments."

"I will." Caleb glanced pointedly at Jerome. "She deserves them."

"Well, then? Have we covered everything on our agenda?" Gran asked. "Yes? Excellent. Then I must scoot. I have a tea date, with my lovely great-granddaughter."

"Caleb, would you please meet with me in my office?" Jerome said.

"Sorry, but not today. I have a tight meeting schedule this afternoon," Caleb replied. "I'll have Sergio call your office to schedule you in as soon as possible."

"No, actually." Jerome's voice was harsh. "It's urgent that we speak. Now."

The room went quiet.

"Really, Jerome?" Elaine said. "Shouldn't I be aware of it, too?"

"My thoughts exactly," Maddie said.

"Ditto," Ronnie chimed in. "Just tell us, Dad."

"No," Jerome said. "The rest of you aren't invited. I need Caleb, alone."

Gran's meaningful look said Caleb would be in for some serious grilling later.

"Fine," Caleb said, teeth clenched. "Your office, in ten. But it has to be quick."

After Jerome and Veronica left the boardroom, Gran turned to him. "We'll talk this over after my tea date with Annika. Goodbye, my loves." Gran swept out, with a fluttering wave, in a wafting cloud of Chanel and attitude.

Maddie walked alongside Caleb to the elevator while he called Sergio and told him to push all of his meetings to later in the day. He stepped into the elevator with her.

"I appreciate your support for Far Eye," he said to her.

"Oh, it's not a favor. It really is brilliant on its own merit," Maddie said. "I can't quite follow all of it, but what I do understand gives me the shivers."

"My feelings exactly," he said.

"You know, Uncle Jerome surprised me today," Maddie said. "He always did love to piss on everyone's parade, but he's never been one to turn down an obviously great business opportunity. Something else is going on in his head."

"I'll find out," Caleb said. "Knowing Uncle Jerome, it won't be anything good."

"You'll tell me what's up?" Maddie asked, as the elevator opened.

Caleb held the door. "If there's anything to tell."

She gave him a stern glance. "Gran and I will come over for the debrief."

He let out a sigh as the elevator rose. His sister, born to bust his balls. Now Uncle Jerome wanted his turn. Ballbusting was one of the Moss family's many genetic gifts.

Jerome's assistant, Yvette, announced him, and he walked into his uncle's lair. Although Jerome was no longer CTO, a job Marcus now held, his uncle had stayed on at MossTech in an advisory capacity. Jerome had insisted on keeping an office in the middle of the action. Caleb and his siblings just tried to keep the man from digging in his heels and making trouble. Jerome was constantly trying to bully Ronnie into using her shares to give him a controlling edge. So far, Ronnie was holding firm, at the price of her father's enduring rage. Not that Veronica had ever gotten much tenderness from Jerome, even in the best of times.

"As I said, I'm pressed for time," Caleb told him. "What's on your mind?"

"I have bad news for you," Jerome said. "You should be sitting down for this."

No, he should not sit. He should back away from this raging train wreck of a man. But it was part of Caleb's unspoken job description as CEO to wrangle him. "I'll remain conscious, whatever you throw at me."

"What if someone told you that your bride was plotting to destroy your company?"

It took a moment for Caleb to recover his voice. "I would call whoever had the bad judgment to say it a lying son of a bitch," he said. "Then I'd tell him to go to hell."

Jerome grunted. "About what I figured you'd say."

"Whatever you've got, spit it out," Caleb said.

Jerome held up a thick folder. "Here. Hard proof that Tilda Riley is acting in bad faith. Come take a look." He shook the contents onto his desk.

Caleb hesitated, sensing a trap. Every step he took toward that file felt like a betrayal, but he had to know what the hell Jerome was driving at.

It was a thick sheaf of photocopied pages of handwritten text. A messy, scrawling cursive script. He stared at it, jaw aching with tension. "What am I looking at?"

"The file that could destroy MossTech," Jerome said. "A file that was in your wife's possession."

"My wife's...then what the hell are you doing with it?"

"Sharpen up, Caleb. What part of 'the file that could destroy MossTech' did you not understand?"

Caleb clenched his teeth. "You're bugging me, Uncle. Give me the abridged version, please."

"This journal was written by John Padraig, director of one of our labs twenty-three years ago. It appears to be evidence of a scheme to cover up a scandal in Sri Lanka, where Naomi was working when she died. A toxic mold overgrowth in a strain of drought-resistant millet. Sixty-two people died, twenty-eight of them children. This file implicates all of us. Me, Naomi, Elaine and Bertram. Padraig accuses us of cold-blooded murder. Attached to the journal are lab results that presumably prove his claims. Padraig says that the victims were silenced, intimidated, bought off—by us. That no one was ever held accountable. It's all bullshit, of course. It was Padraig who did the cover-up. We didn't even know about it until afterward. Raimund Oswalt was CTO back then. He told us what really happened."

"Why did this Padraig wait twenty-three years to accuse you?" Caleb asked. "Where was this guy, all this time? Why didn't you face down his accusations years ago?"

"He's dead," Jerome said. "In the same bombing that killed Naomi. Almost certainly a retaliation for what he'd done to the victims. Raimund told me that she and John Padraig were having an affair at the time, but according to this journal, he certainly wasn't loyal to her. He was setting her and all the rest of us up to take the fall for this horrific mess. Screwing over her company, while enjoying what pleasures he found along the way. Like someone else I could name."

"You'd better not name anyone," Caleb said in a warning tone.

"Face reality," Jerome said harshly. "Even though none of it is true, this file could still destroy us. And your wife has been holding it to your throat while she's been rolling around in bed with you. There was a Post-it note stuck on top of it, addressed to her." Jerome snapped his fingers in Caleb's face. "Wake up!"

"How did you get this file?" Caleb's hands were clenched and shaking. *Easy, now.*

Jerome snorted. "Does it matter?"

"Yes, it damn well does!"

"Judge me if you want to," Jerome said. "It was in Herbert Riley's home safe."

"That was *you*?" Caleb was freshly horrified.

Jerome looked unrepentant. "That's the difference between you and me, Caleb. I've always been willing to do what was necessary for MossTech. You aren't."

"But how did you even know to look for it?"

"From their conversations with their lawyer. They talked about their 'nuclear option.' I had to know what that option was, Caleb. To disarm them."

Caleb was appalled. "You hacked their phones? That's insane!"

"No, that's war," Jerome corrected. "I've been sweating blood for this company for fifty years. I will not let that snotty blond tart trash it out of spite."

"You've been spying on them since when?"

"Oh, stop with that tone of voice," Jerome snapped. "If you had half a brain, you'd have been monitoring them yourself. Be grateful I handled it."

Caleb backed away from him. "Aside from the fact that your behavior is illegal and despicable, Herbert Riley has had two heart attacks in the past six months. Your thieves could have literally scared that man to death. You would have murdered him."

"I should weep bitter tears for Herbert Riley? He was plotting to destroy me!"

Caleb fought for patience. "This file in Herbert's safe does not prove that the Rileys planned to destroy us. Owning a knife doesn't mean you intend to stab someone."

"Oh, please! That's all you've got? They held our death warrant in their home safe, for what, Caleb? For laughs? For fun? Because they could?"

"It was not in their best interests to use it," Caleb said grimly. "So they didn't. End of story. A happy ending."

"Happy ending, hah! You are so goddamned innocent. Your precious Tilda is just waiting for a payout on her clever but still undeveloped idea. As soon as the money hits her account, she'll shoot us down. She's just holding off on the killing blow because she means to cash out first. Being no fool. Unlike you."

"Your logic is questionable, Uncle," Caleb said. "Her payout would be much bigger if she stuck with MossTech, and she knows it. You're just assuming that everyone is out to get you. As usual."

"And you're being stupid and soft," Jerome snarled.

"Do not touch her, Uncle," Caleb warned him. "If you do anything to damage her, I'll expose everything you've done. Instantly."

"As usual, you're up on your moralistic high horse, and I'm the only one willing to do the dirty work. You should be down on your knees, thanking me for warning you before it's too late."

Caleb headed for the door. "We have nothing more to say to each other."

"Are you going to run to the little wifey and tell her everything?" Jerome snarled. "You'll get run over like a goddamn train. It hurts to look at you."

Caleb slammed the office door on his uncle, so angry he could hardly see.

What had Tilda and Herbert planned to do with that file? He wasn't going to be able to take a deep breath until he knew what the hell was going on. If it was bullshit. If it was true. Who was actually responsible?

But no matter what he learned, he would not let that bitter old man muscle in between him and his wife.

Tilda put her feet up on the footrest on the patio as twilight set in, and she watched Maddie play Frisbee with Annika on Caleb's lawn. The lake rippled in the breeze. Any other day, she would've joined them, but she was exhausted. She'd taken advantage of Elaine's after-school tea date with Annika to work on the future of Far Eye, and the day had devolved into a never-ending series of video calls, sounding out Far Eye team members about possibly coming to Seattle to work at MossTech with her. She would need every one of those brilliant women to make this project work. Her experts in meteorology, botany, statistical analysis, soil dynamics and climate science. Far Eye's magical secret sauce.

But, as usual, it was complicated. Meng was reluctant to be that far from her ailing father, Mariko hesitated to disappoint her boyfriend and Sidra had just signed a contract with a firm in Bangalore. Only Julia Huang had said that she'd be on the next plane whenever Tilda gave the word. The others were going to take some serious persuading, and serious compensation, too, to make it worth their while. Nothing was ever simple.

Annika leaped up and grabbed the Frisbee out of the air, and landed on her butt, rolling head over heels and shrieking in excitement. Maddie promptly piled on and started tickling her. The two of them rolled around on the grass like puppies.

"I simply can't get used to it." Elaine's soft voice came from behind her. "She looks so much like Susannah at that age. It just knocks me back. Every damn time."

She turned to see Elaine sipping a glass of white wine, smiling at the spectacle.

"Annika has such a good time with Maddie," Tilda said. "She's the ideal fun aunt."

"Annika is good for Maddie, too," Elaine said. "She's been working so hard. But since Annika burst on the scene, well… I haven't seen Maddie giggle and laugh and play like that since she was eight years old herself. It's lovely to see."

Tilda thought about her own long-ago capacity to laugh and play. She'd lost that playful quality, the belief that dreams could come true, around the time Mom died. Then she'd fallen in love with Caleb, and suddenly it seemed as if dreams might actually come true after all.

Then, of course, what happened had happened. Disillusionment, heartbreak, yada yada. The double whammy of shock, to find herself pregnant. The terrors of single motherhood. Who had time for playfulness? She'd been hanging on by her fingernails. For years.

But as Annika grew, Tilda had started thinking about her little girl's future. The whole world's future. Far Eye was an anxious mother's attempt to predict, control and plan for that scary, uncertain future. It processed countless constantly shifting variables, to offset the dangers of extreme weather and global warming, to push back against soil degradation, so that farmers could continue to produce food for everyone. Far Eye made it possible to predict and adjust for the random cruelty of fate. That protected the whole world.

It wasn't perfect, but it was better than nothing. And damn, a girl could try.

Her phone rang. Panic stabbed in deep when she saw the name on the display.

Wes Brody? Oh, God, what was she going to tell that guy?

Of all the variables she'd been trying to control lately, this was one she'd hoped would disappear.

She got up, giving Elaine an apologetic smile. "Sorry. I have to take this call."

She went inside the house, continuing to the farthest room

on the main floor, Caleb's study. A gorgeous cube of glass seemingly suspended over waving tree boughs.

She shut the door, and hit Talk. "Hey, Wes."

"Tilda." Wes's voice had lost all its warmth. "How's your project going?"

She hesitated. "It's complicated."

"No shit," Wes said. "I've heard. You're married, huh? To the CEO of MossTech? What the hell kind of game are you playing with me?"

"I'm not playing a game," she told him. "And I wasn't under the impression that I was obliged to use the file at all costs."

"You made it sound like you had every intention of doing so."

"I'm sorry if we miscommunicated," Tilda said. "It ended up being in Riley BioGen's best interests to agree to a friendly merger, and I—I—"

"And you decided to make a personal merger, too? Sweet. I didn't want to drag my own company through the mud, since you seemed willing to do it for me. But if you want something done right, do it yourself. So here I am, in Seattle. And MossTech is going down."

"Oh, no. Please, don't do that."

"Really?" Wes demanded. "Why not?"

Tilda watched the breeze ruffle the lake surface. "Can we talk in person?"

"I'm staying at the Cartwright Hotel. Right near MossTech. My room looks out over their office complex. You know it?"

"Yes, I've seen it. Wes, it's more complicated than—"

"There's a restaurant and bar downstairs. Be there in an hour. Tell me why I should hesitate. Entertain me."

Movement caught her eye through the window. She saw Maddie, out on the lawn, teaching Annika how to do a cartwheel. Elaine had strolled onto the lawn to watch them, laughing at their silliness. A beautiful little tableau.

She swallowed over the dry, painful lump in her throat as she watched them. These lovely moments were so fragile. So easy to destroy.

"I'll be there," she said.

Seventeen

Annika barreled into Caleb, squeezing him around the waist as he walked in the door. "I told Gran and Maddie I'd help make dinner! Will you help me grill the steaks?"

"Whoa, hang on. Let me get my bearings. Didn't you go out for tea with Gran right after school? Are you still full of pastry?"

"Yup. It was awesome! Lemon scones and hot chocolate!"

"Lucky you, but I'm guessing you haven't looked at your homework yet today."

Annika's face fell. "There's not a lot. A couple worksheets, some spelling words, some easy math problems. I could do 'em with my eyes shut."

"Go take care of it," he told her. "And keep your eyes open. Then we'll talk about dinner. Go on, run and get it done."

Annika scampered off willingly enough, but he regretted putting her off. He liked their rapport, but Tilda was always reminding him that he had to maintain firm rules, for Annika's sake. In any case, he couldn't be present for Annika while Gran and Maddie bore down on him with that look in their eyes. Like an oncoming train.

He couldn't tell them about Jerome's bombshell. Not until he talked to Tilda.

"Smoothly done, Caleb," Gran said briskly. "We needed a private moment for the debrief. So? Enlighten us. What was the bee in Jerome's bonnet?"

"Yeah, I have eyewitnesses on that floor who say that you came out of his office looking all steamed up," Maddie said.

Caleb shrugged. "More of the same. He doesn't trust her, and he doesn't trust the project. I don't think he's grasped its value yet. And he's still offended about playing the ogre of the melodrama, with your marriage-mandate crap."

Maddie and Gran just waited. "That can't be all there is to it," Gran said.

"Caleb, come on," Maddie urged.

"Nothing. I had another tense, unpleasant conversation with Jerome, that's all. As usual." He looked around. "Where's Tilda?"

"She had to run out," Maddie said. "A meeting about Far Eye. She said to go ahead and eat without her. She didn't call you?"

Caleb pulled out his phone. No missed calls. No texts.

"Well," Maddie said, faltering. "She ran off pretty quickly. She's probably still driving."

His phone buzzed. Caleb checked, expecting Tilda's name on the display.

Jerome. Again? For the love of God. "Excuse me," he growled. "Gotta take this."

He made his way to his office, and shut the door before he answered. "What is it?"

"Not that there's any point in asking, but do you know where your wife is?"

"Back off," he snarled. "Not another word about Tilda."

"I'm watching a livestream of her, as we speak. Want to take a look?"

"You have someone following her? You sick bastard! Stop creeping on my wife!"

"I imagine she told you she was out shopping? Doing errands, drinks with a girlfriend? It's a lie, Caleb. I'm watching her right now. Want to see what I see?"

"I want you to get the hell out of my business!"

"I sent you the file. With photographs. A link to the livestream. Open it if you're curious. See if your wife is where she said she'd be. Happy viewing. Lovesick idiot."

Jerome ended the call, and Caleb stared down at the laptop on his desk. He reached out, woke it up by touching a key, and the screen lit up.

He entered his password, and opened the email app. There were two messages from Jerome, one with zipped files attached. He opened one. Snaps of Tilda, getting out of her car. On the street, walking. In front of the Cartwright Hotel. Tilda sitting alone at a table in a dim restaurant, looking at her phone. Tilda standing, as a blurred silhouette of a man joined her. Tall, broad-shouldered, wearing a black hoodie.

In the next shot, they sat across from each other. Tilda leaned toward him, an earnest expression on her face. The man was good-looking. He looked intense.

Caleb open the second email, which contained only a link to a livestream.

He opened it. The investigator had hidden a phone among the leaves of a plant. The video camera's lens was framed by long green fronds. Tilda was still talking.

Caleb pulled out his phone, and dialed Tilda's number. Saw Tilda react as she heard the ringtone and pulled out her phone. She gave the man an apologetic glance as she held it to her ear. "Hey. Caleb?"

"Hi," he said. "Thought you'd be home by now."

"Me, too. Something came up. I had to meet someone about Far Eye."

"Yeah. Maddie told me. Julia Huang, right? Did she fly in from Hong Kong?"

Caleb watched closely, as Tilda hesitated.

"Ah, yes," she said. "I may be a while. Go ahead and have dinner without me. Oh, and Maddie is taking Annika home with her tonight. They're going to the Pythagorean Dream exhibit at the Pacific Science Center tomorrow morning."

"Got it. See you later."

"I'll miss you," she said. "Later."

The connection broke. Caleb watched Tilda slide the phone back in her purse, and then lean back toward her companion.

Getting back to her real business. Inconvenient distraction handled.

Caleb realized he was clenching his smartphone so hard, he'd probably damaged it.

It took a second to find her train of thought. She hated being dishonest with Caleb, but now was not the time to come clean about Wes's file.

Tonight, when she got home. She'd tell Caleb everything tonight.

Wes was on his own phone, too, when she closed her call. "...yes, four extra-large towels," he said. "Bring them up right away. Room 408, yes. Thank you."

He put his phone on the table and shoved his fingers through his dark, damp hair. He had a sheen of sweat on his tense, masklike face.

"Did you just go running?" she asked him.

"Yeah," he said. "Had to unwind. Sorry to inflict myself on you like this without showering and changing, but I figured that was better than making you wait."

"It's fine," she said. "Does it work? To unwind you, I mean?"

He shrugged. "Not really, but it's better than nothing."

"I remember your workout schedule in Rio. Every morning at ten, in the hotel gym. Two hours without fail."

"It has to happen the same time every day, or it doesn't work for me," he said. "We all have our coping mechanisms.

But yours wins the prize, Tilda. Marry your sworn enemy, and to hell with our agreement?"

"Wes, be reasonable. I was sure I was going to war with the Mosses, but when I got here, things changed. And my father thinks the file is misleading. He thinks Naomi wasn't capable of what Padraig accuses her of. And even if it were true, why go after the younger Mosses now? They weren't threatening me."

Wes's eyes were cold. "You should have told me you were in love with the guy."

She waved away his comment. "I wasn't when we spoke in Rio. I hadn't seen him for nine years. But imagine that you were me, and that you found a way to save your father's company and safeguard eight hundred jobs and forty years of hard work. Would you throw it away out of spite? A friendly merger was the best option. So we took it."

"You and I made a deal." Wes's voice was hard. "Remember?"

"So don't finance Far Eye," she said. "I'll find someone else."

Wes's eyes sharpened. "You're handing Far Eye over to the Mosses? He's that good in the sack, huh?"

"Wes, I will not discuss my personal—"

"So good, you'll just hand him your ten-billion-dollar idea. And for what? To be nestled in the bosom of the Moss family? Poor, motherless girl, safe at last? You're in for a nasty shock, Tilda."

"Screw you, Wes."

"You already have. Whatever fantasy of domestic bliss you had with Moss, it's over. Those bastards are going down hard."

"But this happened twenty-three years ago!" she protested. "The younger generation who run the company were children then! Whatever your reasons, you're punishing the wrong people. What have you got against Caleb, and Maddie, and Marcus?"

"I'm not confiding in you. You've thrown in with the Mosses."

The look in Wes's eyes made it clear that there would be no reasoning with him. His anger ran too deep.

So this was it. The end of MossTech, and Riley BioGen along with it.

"Have you already given the file to your journalist friends?" she asked.

"I have meetings tomorrow," Wes said. "Warn them if you want to. There's nothing that can stop this now."

"Then I guess there's nothing left to say," she said.

He shook his head.

"So why did you ask me to come here at all?"

"I wanted to tell you one last time that you're betting on the wrong horse," he said. "But you're in too deep. You had your chance to save yourself. You blew it."

Tilda stood up, grabbing her purse. "Do what you have to do, Wes."

"Count on it," Wes said.

Her eyes swam with angry tears as she walked out. She was an idiot. She should've planned for the worst, but she'd been too busy playing house with Caleb.

She drove straight to her father's house. Dad looked alarmed when he flung open the door and saw her wet face. "Honey? Are you okay? What did that bastard do to you?"

"Not Caleb. It's Wes Brody. I met with him."

"Ah." Her father pulled her inside. "He's angry because you never used his file?"

"So he'll ruin them with the original." Her face crumpled. "So it was all for nothing, Daddy. If MossTech goes down, so does Riley BioGen."

Dad pulled her into his arms. "Oh, honey, it's okay. We'll live."

"But Caleb will hate me now," she whispered.

"Why would he? You're not to blame. You two will get through this. That much talent and brainpower put together will eventually be a wild success."

"I'm just afraid it'll all go to hell. And now Annika loves him, too…" She melted into silent sobs against his chest.

When she calmed down, he herded her into the kitchen. "Shot of whiskey?"

Tilda let out a soggy laugh and dug for tissues, blowing her nose. "Thanks, but I have to drive home. I'd better not."

"Herbal tea, then? One of those weird things you bought and then left here in my tea drawer? Green tea, white tea? That weird stuff with pepper in it?"

Dad urged her to stay the night after she finished her tea, but she declined. "I have to tell Caleb what's going on. Annika is at Maddie's tonight, so we can hash it out in private. But thanks, Dad. I'm sorry I couldn't save Riley Bio-Gen for you."

"You did everything you could. You are a brave warrior, and I'm proud of you."

Dad's pep talk helped, but by the time she pulled into Caleb's garage, the comforting certainty that they'd get through was gone. All she felt was nervous dread.

Tilda opened the door and looked around. No noise. No TV, no music. The studio door was open, but the lights were off. "Caleb?" she called out. No response.

She went upstairs and opened the bedroom door. There he was. Asleep.

"Caleb?" she whispered. "Are you awake?"

He didn't reply. It was past 1:00 a.m., but they were often up that late, enjoying each other. But Caleb didn't move.

She thought about waking him. They desperately needed this talk. But she hated the thought of jerking him out of a sound sleep to give him ugly news like this.

Okay. Tomorrow. Annika would still be with Maddie.

She would tell him at breakfast. A heads-up, before whatever nightmare Wes devised landed on their heads.

Tilda got into her pajamas without turning on the light and brushed her teeth. She slid into bed and tried cuddling up to him, but his back felt like a wall. She rolled away and just stared at the ceiling, rehearsing tomorrow's speech.

A million miles from sleep.

Eighteen

Tilda jerked awake from an ugly nightmare, heart galloping from a dream about drowning in the open sea, wreckage all around. She looked to see if she had woken Caleb.

She was alone.

This was the first time since she had been in Caleb's house that she'd woken up alone. Usually, they got up early and luxuriated in kisses, cuddles and more, if there was time. Much, much more. All of it meltingly delicious. This was the first time she hadn't gone to sleep in his arms, and woken up the same way.

He knew.

In a sickening flash, she understood. That was why he'd shut her out last night. And why he was gone this morning. But how could he know?

She got up, unsettled, and looked around the house for Caleb. He hadn't made coffee. Another first. There was a note on the bar:

Gone running

No signature, no sweet talk. No punctuation, even. Unlike his usual tone.

She knotted her hands into fists, and pressed them against the hollow feeling in her belly.

Gone running. Like Wes. Caleb had said that before they

got together, he had started every day with a hard, two-hour workout to blow off steam.

Since she'd moved in, they had found many marvelous ways to blow off steam.

Caleb knew. And he was furious.

She went upstairs, and took a shower, trying to think. Wes was manically intense about his two-hour workout. He would want back into his groove as soon as possible.

She wondered if he kept his file in a room safe. But room safes were too small for that big file. No way would Wes haul it around while he lifted weights or jogged.

Oh, God, what the hell was she thinking? Her mind raced as she blew her hair dry, then put on her makeup. She had to look sharp. Like a woman who had every right to be wandering around a nice hotel. Hopefully, Wes's meetings with journalists would be in the afternoon. She had to act fast. No time to second-guess herself.

This mess wasn't her fault, but she was the one person who might be able to fix it.

Wronging one person to do right by another was questionable, but she'd abandoned the nuclear option in the first place because her father had convinced her that it was wrong to use it. Which meant that logically, it was wrong for Wes to use it, too.

But damn. Who died and made her judge of what was right and wrong?

She was on shaky moral ground, but too bad. She had to just stagger onward. Better to be scared to death but fighting for something she cared about than sitting around on her butt, dabbing at her wet eyes with a tissue, being so, so sorry. Screw that garbage.

Not on her watch.

Jerome's name flashed on Caleb's phone display.

Damn. Again?

Caleb reluctantly slowed to a walk. He peeled his phone

out of the Velcro strap that held it to his arm. He needed to stay calm to have this conversation with Tilda. Jerome hammering on his ragged nerves would not help.

He entered the kitchen side door. The phone had stopped, thank God. But a couple of seconds later, it started again.

"Tilda?" he called out. "You up?"

No response. Caleb hit Talk. "What the hell do you want now?"

"Do you know where your bride is?" Jerome's taunting tone made his skin crawl.

"None of your goddamn business," Caleb responded.

"She's up to her usual mischief. Want to know where? I sent fresh pictures."

Caleb stared sightlessly out at the lake, which was covered in a sullen misty gray this morning, and dismay seeped into his bones. "You just never stop, do you?"

"Not when my life's work is at stake," Jerome said.

"I told you to let this go," Caleb said. "Stop following her. Stop spying on her. Whatever our issues are, we'll work them out without your help."

"She's at the Cartwright again," Jerome said. "Evidently, whatever she got last night wasn't enough. She's back this morning, bright and early, for a second helping."

"Fuck you." Caleb closed the call and blocked the number.

Though he'd blocked Jerome's number, like the day before, it was now impossible not to walk into his office and open up the laptop.

Still more photos in Jerome's message. Tilda walking into a Circuit Security store, Tilda getting into her car. Her hair was loose and wild today. Not her smooth, upswept hairdo. She wore a silk blouse and an elegant pantsuit. High-heeled boots. Dark red lipstick. Like she was meeting the dark-haired guy for breakfast.

Pictures of her walking through the revolving door of the

Cartwright. Heading straight to the elevator, as if she knew right where to go.

He was out the door in moments, keys in hand. He knew just where to go, too.

And he was going to raise pure, holy hell when he got there.

Nineteen

Tilda strolled casually up the hotel corridor. Wes wasn't in his room. The housekeeper was servicing it. But the master key card was chained to the laundry cart, also inside room 408, so she had to keep loitering in the corridor, pretending she had legitimate business. The card reader-writer that she'd bought at the Circuit Security store was in her purse, ready to catch the number on the master key.

Finally, the heavy cart loaded with cleaning supplies and linens lumbered out of room 408. A tired-looking middle-aged woman was pushing it.

Across the corridor, another housekeeper asked the first woman something in Spanish. Tilda pretended to babble something into her cell phone, sidling up to the dangling master key. She had to be within a couple of inches for the field to activate the capacitator.

The housekeepers wrapped up their conversation as the light on the reader-writer device in Tilda's purse flashed green. *Yes.* She turned and strolled back into the alcove by the ice machine, still talking, to swiftly program her key card. With that, she could get into his room, but she had to wait for the housekeepers to get busy in the next rooms. Time was ticking. Wes could be back anytime. Tilda stepped into the elevator, and rode up and down. She stepped back onto the fourth floor—

As Wes came out of the stairwell in sweaty workout clothes, looking at his phone.

Oh, God. Tilda darted into the first open door she found. The two housekeepers were changing sheets on a bed. The women looked at her, then at each other, bewildered.

Tilda laughed nervously. "Oh, no! Sorry! I must've gotten the wrong room. My bad." She backed out, smiling, just as Wes's door closed…with Wes now inside his room. *Shit.*

She walked by his room, slowing down as she passed Wes's door. Any minute now, the housekeepers would come out, see her lurking and get suspicious.

She heard a hissing sound. A shower. Wes must have just gotten into it. She couldn't cruise this corridor forever. The housekeepers knew her face. It was now or never.

Now.

Tilda held up the cloned key card…and the door lock turned green.

She pushed the door open slowly. The bathroom door was closed, thank God. She tiptoed in. Both beds were made. One had an open suitcase lying on it.

She reached in, rummaging. Among the clothes, she saw a stained, yellowed accordion file. She pulled it out. Inside was the original journal. A sheaf of lab printouts.

Tilda put the file under her arm, and walked out, closing the door delicately behind her. She headed toward the elevator, tucking the file into her big shoulder bag. Heart in her throat.

She stopped short, deciding against the elevator, and turned around. The stairwell gave her the option of leaving through a side door downstairs. Much better. She started to scurry, in spite of herself. *Slow down. Don't run like a rabbit. Or a thief.*

This was necessary. And right. But damn, it did not feel good.

Room 408. Weston Brody.

Caleb had pinned down Jerome's PI, who had been parked

outside the hotel, and pried the name and room number of the dark-haired man out of him. The elevator opened onto the fourth floor. Caleb forced himself to move. His legs felt like lead. Until last night, he'd been drunk on euphoric certainty. Flying so high, natural laws didn't even apply to him anymore.

The spell had been broken. He was falling fast, and the rocks down there were sharp.

A room door started to open. He ducked into the alcove near an ice machine. There was a security mirror up high that allowed him to see around the corner.

Tilda. Her image was distorted in the mirror, but it was her, shoving something inside her shoulder bag. She looked up and down the corridor. Her eyes looked shadowy and worried. If she headed toward the elevator, she would walk right past him.

They had to confront each other. Spying, sneaking, this wasn't who they were. They had to have this out. Even if it destroyed his world.

But Tilda didn't go to the elevator. She spun around and headed toward the stairwell at the other end of the hall. Caleb stepped out into the corridor. If she looked back, she'd see him…but she didn't. Something clutched his throat like a claw. Grief. Rage. Hurt.

No. He didn't dare confront her, the way he felt now.

The stairwell door closed. He stared at it until the red emergency exit sign was burned into his retinas. He tried to gauge which way to move, but every direction led to a void.

Caleb stood outside of room 408. Someone was taking a shower in there. As he listened, the hissing sound stopped. He knocked on the door.

"Hey." A man's deep voice. "Is this housekeeping? Do you have the extra towels?"

"Yes." Caleb got the word out somehow.

"Good timing." Brody opened the door, and focused on

Caleb with a puzzled frown. Big guy. Handsome, muscular, wet. Tight, cut abs. Lantern jaw. Dark eyes. Lots of dark, messy hair. He wore a towel around his waist.

Brody opened his mouth, but Caleb punched him before the words got out. He knocked him back onto the floor.

The guy fought back hard. They writhed around, grunting and cursing. The towel fell off. Brody was fighting naked, but he gave as good as he got. Caleb blocked a finger stab to the eye, then a knee to the groin that sent him reeling back. *Smack*, a right hook to the mouth. Pain throbbed through him in sickening waves.

"What's your goddamn problem?" Brody bellowed. "I've got nothing to steal!"

"Yeah?" Caleb snarled. "What about my wife?"

Brody's face changed. "Wait. *You're* Caleb Moss?"

"That's right." Brody blocked the next punch, but Caleb elbowed his ribs, hard enough to make the other man stumble away, coughing.

"Hold on!" Brody gasped out. "You think I'm sleeping with Tilda? You're nuts!"

"Nice try." Caleb lunged at him.

Brody retreated, hands up protectively. "Wait. I call a truce, for one goddamn second. I'm happy to beat you to death if you really want me to, but let's make sure we know why. What makes you think I'm sleeping with Tilda?"

Caleb wiped blood from his mouth and nose. "I know you are."

"You don't know a damn thing. Sure, I would have taken any opportunity, if she gave me one. But Tilda never gave anyone a break. And now I see why. She was hung up on a brain-dead caveman like you. God help her."

"I just saw her. I knock, and here you are, naked." Caleb beckoned with his fingers. "Beating each other to death is the only way this plays out today."

"Saw her where?" Brody pinched his nose, which

streamed with blood. "She's never been up here. I saw her last night in the bar. Not in my room."

"Don't try," Caleb growled. "I watched her come out your door five minutes ago."

Brody froze…and sucked in a horrified breath as he looked at the suitcase on the bed. "Oh, no." He lunged for the suitcase and rifled through it. "Oh, *shit*!"

He let out a furious roar, and flung the suitcase off the bed with a swipe of his arm. The suitcase hit the desk, knocking over a lamp. "She took it," he snarled.

"Took what?" Caleb asked.

"My file!" Brody roared, his face distorted with blood and rage.

Caleb's insides went heavy and cold. "The original file," he said. "So she got it from you? The one about Naomi, and the lab in Sri Lanka?"

Brody looked at the blood on his hands. He grabbed sweatpants from the floor, pulled them on. "Right. The file that proves that Mosses are murderers. Tilda met with me last night. Tried to convince me you guys were all sweetness and light. I underestimated her. But she won't feel so triumphant when they haul her off in handcuffs."

Caleb gaped at the other man, aghast. "But—but you can't—"

"Sure I can." Brody laughed harshly. "If you still want to fight, let's do it. There's nothing I'd like better than to beat you to a pulp, Moss. It's the only satisfaction I'm going to get today, so come on." He motioned with his fingers. "Bring it."

Caleb shook his head. "Sorry to disappoint you, but I read this wrong."

Brody laughed bitterly. "Ya think? It's funny. You came in here convinced that you were the one being screwed over by Tilda. But no. That honor goes to me."

Caleb backed toward the door. "Don't go after Tilda," he said.

Brody slammed the door in Caleb's face. Caleb staggered down the hall toward the exit. Just as miserable, just as ashamed. Just as scared of what might happen next.

But now the stakes were even higher. And he'd just waded in, fists flying, and made the situation even worse.

Freaking brilliant move.

Twenty

Tilda pulled into the garage behind Caleb's house. Caleb's Porsche was gone. So he planned on avoiding her altogether today.

She went inside, and wandered from room to room. It was windy, and had started to rain, splattering the glass and turning the greenery outside to a wavering blur. "Caleb?"

His studio was also empty, but his computer was open. She touched the keyboard to close it, waking up the screen.

The image she saw made her gasp.

Herself, walking into the Cartwright. That picture had been taken this morning.

She shook herself out of her paralysis, and closed the picture. It was one in a list of jpegs in a folder. She clicked the others. Her, in the revolving doors at the hotel. Getting into the elevator. That file had forty pictures. And there were other files, other folders.

The oldest were from almost two months ago. Two days after they came back from the coast. There were eighty pictures in that folder. Tilda clicked on one. Her and Annika, stepping out of a mall. Annika was laughing, a big cookie in her hand.

That gave her a jolt. A stranger had been following her around, taking pictures not only of her, but also of her little girl. All this time, Caleb had been talking about trust, bonding, their united front. And a spy with a camera has been monitoring her movements.

All day. Every day. That was the bond she'd risked breaking the law for.

That was how far Caleb's trust went.

Tilda felt detached, floating. She closed the files, exited the windows of the laptop. She didn't have time for the luxury of shock and hurt. She had a lot to do, and it was better done while Caleb wasn't here, distracting her with God knew what disingenuous bullshit.

Time to finish what she had started.

She retrieved her and Annika's suitcases from the storage area, and did Annika's room first, collecting all her clothes and books, her computer and her schoolwork. Then she went to Caleb's bedroom, and got to work on her own things, packing haphazardly.

She hauled the suitcases out to the car, and went back into the living room. She kneeled at the fireplace, and built a heap of kindling around crumpled paper. She lit it, and fed the blaze until a small fire crackled on the hearth, then loaded on larger pieces of wood. She needed a big, hungry, devouring flame, capable of reducing the shadows of the past to dust and ashes. She wanted this damn file wiped off the face of the earth forever.

She didn't even turn her head when she heard Caleb's car. His presence for the upcoming ritual was no longer relevant to her. She didn't turn when she heard the door open, either. Or when she heard his footsteps behind her.

"Tilda," Caleb finally said. "Please. Look at me."

He had no right to make requests, but her head turned in spite of herself.

She stopped breathing for a second. He looked awful. His face was blood-smeared, his sweatshirt blood-spotted. His lip was split. She could tell from his swollen nose that both his eyes would blacken in a day or so.

"Dear God," she said. "What concrete piling did you crash into?"

"The guy in room 408," Caleb said.

She tried to stay cool, detached, but her muscles contracted, in spite of herself. "So you followed me to the Cartwright Hotel? And attacked Wes Brody?"

"I thought you were having an affair with him," Caleb said.

Oh, ouch. That stung, even in her flash-frozen state. She turned back to the fire, and carefully placed another log on the crackling flames. "Do you still think that?"

"No," he said. "I know it's not true."

"Good. I'm in no mood to try to persuade you. Nor do I care, to be honest."

"Tilda, I never—"

"Really? At no time did it occur to you to just ask me for the truth, before you physically attacked a complete stranger?"

"It was stupid," he admitted. "Brody told me about the file, when he realized you'd taken it. He was really upset about it."

"Stolen his file," she corrected. "I stole it, Caleb. Call it like it is."

"How the hell did you get into his room?"

Tilda turned away so he wouldn't see her face. "I bought a card reader. Followed the housekeeper's cart. Got close enough to copy the master key with it. Programmed a new one for myself."

"I had no idea you could pull off something like that."

She snorted. "You had no idea about a lot of things." She lifted up the file. "This is a journal, written by John Padraig, the manager of the lab in Sri Lanka twenty-three years ago. This, along with the lab tests in the file, implies that Jerome, Elaine, Naomi and Bertram covered up a mass poisoning event. Toxic mold, which developed in an experimental strain of drought-resistant millet. I met with Wes at a tech conference in Rio a few months ago, to talk about funding Far Eye. He's a venture capitalist. I've known him for years."

"Yes," Caleb said. "Now that I hear it in context. I've heard of him."

"Everyone has," she said. "He was the one who told me that MossTech was making a move on Riley BioGen. He offered me a copy of this file as a potential weapon. Said I could use it to fight the hostile takeover."

"And when were you planning on using it on us?"

"Never," she said. "I let the idea go, after our first meeting." Her voice felt as if it came from far away. "I never liked the idea. Dad convinced me to drop it, but he didn't have to try that hard. Naomi had been his thesis advisor at Caltech. He said he didn't believe she'd sign off on something like that. She would have made things right. Dad even defended Jerome. He said, he's an ass, but not a killer. So I didn't use it. I married you instead. I trusted you." She swallowed, hard. "But you didn't return the compliment."

"Tilda, I'm sorry that—"

"Don't." Tilda turned back to the fire. "In any case, I don't have it anymore. It was stolen during the home invasion. You don't have to worry about me using it on you out of spite. Clearly, you'd believe anything of me."

"That's not true," he said.

"Wes had been waiting for MossTech to bite the dust, and it didn't happen, so he came to take matters into his own hands," Tilda said. "I met with him. Hoping to persuade him to back off." She opened the folder, and shook out the journal and the lab printouts into her hand. "He was beside himself. I had no idea that he had such a personal stake in making the Mosses pay."

Tilda placed the loose papers on the fire, and watched the flames surge eagerly to consume them. When those were burned, she opened the journal and laid it facedown on the flames, which changed color as they curled around the edges of the journal, slowly devouring it. The cardboard cover curled and blackened, slowly shrinking, twisting.

They watched in silence until it was entirely gone. Just blackened flakes.

"The only one left now is the copy stolen from my dad's safe," she said. "God knows where that is."

"No, that's gone, too," Caleb said. "Jerome had it. He'd arranged to have it stolen."

Tilda let out a startled laugh. "Whoa. I did not see that coming. How long have you known about that?"

"I found out yesterday afternoon, after the board meeting."

"I see. Well, I'm sure Jerome destroyed that copy. The only question that remains is, who looks after my daughter when I go to jail for stealing Wes Brody's property."

"Tilda, I'm sure that he won't—"

"Why wouldn't he? He's furious with me. And it is a crime, after all. Theft, corporate espionage, I don't even know what possible charges I might be facing."

"I had no idea that he—"

"You have no idea about anything," Tilda interrupted. "But if I have to go to jail for any period of time, you'll have to pull yourself together and help Dad look after Annika."

"I'll never let that happen," he said.

Tilda got up, brushing her hands on her pants. "Grow up. You still think you can control everything, but it's just a fantasy, Caleb." She headed for the door.

"Tilda." Caleb followed behind her. "If you're so angry, why burn the file at all? Why not just spank us with it, like Brody wanted you to?"

Tilda pushed the front door open and paused in the doorway. "I want this to be over," she said.

"But we don't have to be," Caleb said.

Tilda just stared at him. "You are kidding, right?"

"I've never been more serious." Caleb said.

Unbelievable. After what he'd pulled. The man must be delusional.

She shook her head and walked out the door, toward her car. "When the police come, tell them I'm at my dad's. I prefer to wait for my arrest there."

"Wait, Tilda. Can't we talk about—"

"I'm done talking." She looked over her shoulder. "I'm going to pick up Annika at Maddie's house. She'll go with me to Dad's."

Caleb stopped short, stricken. "But, Annika…"

"Oh, don't worry. I don't intend to forbid you to see her, or anything stupid and vindictive like that. She'll need you, if things go sideways for me. Be ready to step up."

"I'll put our legal team on it. You did this for MossTech. You won't face it alone."

"Not your problem anymore," she told him. "Goodbye, Caleb."

She got into the car, and started up the engine, trying to keep her face a stony mask, but that didn't last long.

By the time she got to Maddie's, she'd pulled it together. She managed to smile and chat as she waited for Annika to gather her things, chattering about the Pythagorean Dream interactive exhibit, how fabulous it was to bake lemon cupcakes with Maddie, and the joys of lemon butter cream frosting and rainbow sprinkles.

Tilda thought she covered her turmoil well, but Maddie gave her a worried look after their goodbye hug. "Everything good?" Maddie asked, under her breath.

"Sure," Tilda assured her. "All good."

Maddie would know soon enough, but she didn't have to hear it in front of Annika.

She got Annika strapped into her booster, cupcakes on her lap. Annika always had a lot to say when she'd seen a science exhibit, but she soon fell silent.

"Mom?" she asked carefully. "This isn't the way to Dad's

house. Why are there suitcases in the back? And our computer bags?"

"Actually, honey, we're going to stay with Grandpa." Tilda tried to keep her voice bright, upbeat. "He needs the company. He can't sleep well, and he's been stressed, after the robbery. I decided that you and I would just chill with him for a while."

They drove in silence for several minutes before Annika spoke up again. "You broke up with Dad, didn't you?"

Tilda struggled for control of her voice. "I, ah, I do need some space, yes."

"Is it me?" Annika's voice was small. "Because he decided he doesn't want me?"

"Oh, no! No, it has nothing to do with you! He adores you! All of them do, baby. It's a personal thing between your dad and me. You are not the problem. And I'll make sure that you get plenty of time with him and all the other Mosses. They would never be able to manage without you."

Annika's face crumpled. "I just wanted us to be a family," she whispered.

Tilda pulled over. She couldn't drive with her eyes blinded by tears. She climbed out and got into the back seat, scooting close to wrap her arms around her girl. "I wanted that, too, baby," she murmured brokenly. "I'm so sorry."

Her father was startled to see them, but he rose to the occasion, canceling his bridge game and asking his housekeeper to make dinner for three. His eyes silently demanded an explanation, but not yet. She just couldn't.

Annika and her grandpa played cards while Tilda hauled the suitcases upstairs and got Annika's room ready. She was putting out Annika's toothbrush and pajamas when her phone rang. It gave her a sickening rush of alarm to see Wes Brody's name on the display.

She headed for her room, closed the door and sat down on the bed. "Hey, Wes."

"I wasn't sure you'd answer me," Wes said. "Congratulations. I underestimated your determination. Hats off. You won. I lost. Well done, you."

"I'm sorry, Wes," she said. "I really am."

"I suppose you've destroyed the file?"

She hesitated, suddenly wondering if Wes was setting a trap for her. "I'd rather not talk about that," she said. "Not without a lawyer present."

Wes snorted with bitter laughter. "I hope you're proud of yourself. That was my last chance to blow the whistle on those murdering bastards."

"They aren't. They really aren't. They're good people, Wes."

"I know you believe that," Wes said. "I'm pissed, but I'm still sorry for what those bastards will do to you. Your husband just kicked my naked, just-out-of-the-shower ass."

She winced. "I'm so sorry. Should I expect the police anytime soon?"

She waited for a long time before Wes spoke. "I haven't reported this. You've destroyed the file, anyway. There's no getting it back. And you aren't the one I wanted to punish, not even after what you pulled. Besides, you'll get your punishment from the Mosses. They'll destroy you and your family. Like they destroyed mine. You'll see."

"No, I'll be keeping my distance from them," she said. "I'm single again. As of today."

"Seriously? That dude struck me as very invested. Judging from my black eyes, and cracked ribs. And loose teeth."

"Invested, yes, but in all the wrong ways," Tilda said. "He had a PI tailing me. Ever since we got married. I saw evidence on his computer. Thousands of photos."

Wes whistled under his breath. "Yikes. Well, I can't say I'm surprised. The guy's a Moss, after all. So you stole my file, compromised yourself and risked prison, all to protect these ungrateful clowns, and you don't even get true love as a reward. Damn, girl. If I were anyone else, on any other day, I'd feel sorry for you. As it is, not so much."

"I understand," she said. "Goodbye, Wes. Thanks for not calling the dogs on me."

Wes broke the connection. Tilda let the smartphone fall to the bed.

A knock sounded on the door. "Honey? You okay?" Dad's voice.

"I'm fine," she said, forcing out the words. "Come on in."

Her father came slowly into the room. He opened his mouth to speak, and then closed it again as he looked at her face. There was absolutely nothing that anyone could say.

So he just sat down next to her on the bed, put his arms around her and held her tight.

Twenty-One

Buzz. Buzz. Buzz.

Even through his earbuds, Caleb could no longer ignore the door buzzer. He spun in his chair, and thumbed off the pounding metal rock music. Dull numbness was the goal. If he couldn't think, he couldn't feel.

At least not as much.

He approached the front door. There was no hiding in his transparent house. That was the down side to all that glass.

Maddie was outside, in classic fighting pose. Arms folded, chin up, her bright, pale green-and-gold eyes daring him not to open his door.

Caleb opened it. "Hey. What's up with you?"

"Don't pretend that you care," she said. "It's an insult to my intelligence."

Caleb sighed. They gazed at each other in charged silence.

"You look awful," Maddie said. She lifted her smartphone, and snapped a swift picture of him. "I'm sending that to Gran and Marcus, if you don't shape up right now."

"Of course, I look like hell," he said. "I told you, I'm sick. It's probably contagious. Viral pneumonia. We'll talk when I've recovered."

Maddie's eyes narrowed. "Bullshit. Move aside."

She shoved him out of the way and walked in. "You've been ignoring my calls," she said. "Gran's, too. Even Marcus's texts, from the jungle, or desert, or wherever the hell he is."

"You told Marcus?"

"Of course, we told him! We're worried! Your team at work is worried, too."

"They have no reason to be. I'm working remotely. Everything's covered."

"They'll be covered when you put on a suit and tie and get your sulky ass back to MossTech to do your damn job!"

"Mind your own damn business, Maddie." He couldn't give the words the punch they needed, but he tried.

"Would you rather have this conversation with me, or with Gran? Think about it."

That didn't bear thinking about. He followed Maddie to the kitchen as she opened the coffee maker. "Gross," she murmured, prying out the hardened grounds. "You haven't made fresh coffee in days. No wonder you're a wreck. Where's your cleaning service?"

"I told them to stay away. Didn't want them here while I was sick."

Maddie snorted as she spooned fresh coffee into a filter. "Sick, hah," she muttered.

"Shut up, Mads—"

"Never." She sloshed a pot of water into the chamber of the coffee maker. "I will bust your balls until one of us leaves this world. Be grateful for my sisterly devotion." She pushed the button, and searched through his cupboards as the machine gurgled and hissed to life. She took down two coffee mugs. "You haven't been eating."

"Maddie, I'm fine," he insisted. "Just let me sulk. It's not like I do this often."

"Never, is more like it. I've never seen you take a sick day." Maddie pulled the milk out of the fridge, and sniffed it, wincing. "Black coffee, today. There are eggs in here. Can I make you some?"

"No, Mads. I do not want to eat."

She slammed the fridge door closed, and turned her back

to him. He realized, belatedly, that she was shaking. *Oh, God.* She was crying. *Oh, no. Please, no.*

"Maddie," he said carefully. "Hey. What is this about?"

"You can't fall apart on me, Caleb." Her voice shook. "I need you to be strong. Gran is a tough old bat, and she loves us, but her wires are crossed lately. Veronica is awesome, but she's swamped with her own problems, and Jerome runs over her like a tank. And Marcus… I can't get a grip on him, even when he's home. All he cares about is work and his next adventure. The only one I can count on is you. And you're slipping."

"I'll try to keep it together for you."

"Dude, I think you need Tilda for that," Maddie said. "You have got to fix this."

"I tried," he said bleakly. "I've tried everything. But I seem to have crossed some sort of invisible line with her. She won't take my calls, or answer my texts."

"Keep trying! It's been a week since whatever happened. I wish you'd tell me."

"It's private. And I can't stalk her, Mads. Not the way you stalk me."

Maddie sniffed loudly. "Maybe not, but damn. Much as I hate giving Gran any credit, when it comes to Tilda, Gran was right on the money. Tilda's smart and strong. She could even stand up to Jerome. And I've never seen you like you were with her."

"Don't," he said grimly. "Please. It really doesn't help."

"You were transformed," Maddie went on, merciless. "Playful. Having honest-to-God fun with Tilda and Annika. Your own little girl. It was so sweet. We were melting. It was so perfect for you."

"You're forgetting something, Maddie," he said. "She's perfect for me, yes. No doubt about that. But maybe I'm not perfect for her."

Maddie looked rebellious. "Well, make yourself perfect,

dude. Or she'll fly to the other side of the world and take Annika with her. That'll suck for everyone."

Silence followed that dispiriting thought. The coffeepot stopped gurgling, its carafe filled, and Caleb poured out two mugs and passed one to his sister.

She blew on it. "There has to be a way forward. That's why I'm here. I have an idea."

"Yikes," Caleb murmured. "Scary."

"I suppose it's a good sign that you're being snarky again. Feels more normal."

"I aim to please," he murmured. "So? Let's hear your idea."

Maddie winced at the bitterness of her coffee. "Well, I got a call from Yvette."

"Jerome's assistant?"

"Yes. She swore me to secrecy, so before telling you this, I'm swearing you to secrecy in turn, okay?"

"That's not really how secrecy works, Mads, but whatever. What did Yvette have to say?"

"She's worried about Jerome," Maddie said.

Caleb laughed out loud. "And she wants us to worry about him, too? When pigs fly."

"No, listen. This is interesting. Yvette found a box in his office. Things that belong to Herbert Riley. Passports, insurance policies, real-estate deeds, jewelry. Yvette's no fool. Jerome's doing something shady, and she wants to protect him from himself."

"And protect her own job, while she's at it, I expect."

"Maybe, but let's assume nobler motives, shall we?"

"Yeah? So what does this have to do with me?"

Maddie rolled her eyes. "Make him do the right thing! Demand their stuff back! I'm sure he'll be glad to be rid of it. It's an opportunity to talk to Tilda. It also excuses her from the unpleasant necessity of confronting Jerome and reclaiming her things. Spare her that, for God's sake. Jump on it!"

"I can see it now. 'Tilda, here are the documents, jewelry and cash that my uncle stole from your dad in a terrifying home invasion. Will you be my valentine?'"

"Cut the snark," Maddie snapped. "At least it's a conversation starter, and it looks like you need one. This is your life, Caleb. The only one you get. So fight for it!"

The gears started grinding in his mind. "Did Yvette call from the office today? Is she there now?"

"I'll call and make sure." She looked him over. "But you're not going anywhere before you shower and shave."

An hour later, he was at Yvette's desk at MossTech, asking to see his uncle.

Jerome was stone-faced when he walked in. "To what do I owe this pleasure?"

"I want everything you took from Herbert Riley's home safe," Caleb informed him. "I also want a written apology from you, and a blank check for the damages."

Jerome's eyes narrowed. "Deep in the pocket of the little woman, eh?"

"You have no idea what Tilda risked to protect this company," Caleb said. "She stole the original file, at great danger to herself. And she burned it in front of me."

Jerome huffed. "Finally, some good news."

"So?" Caleb said. "Where is it?"

"I shredded the file, if that's what you mean," Jerome said.

"Everything else you took," Caleb said. "And the apology. And the check."

"I'll be damned if I'll write a blank check to that conniving little—"

"Be damned, then. Do it, or else I call the police."

"Don't scold me, boy," Jerome growled.

"Write it on your letterhead. Date it, sign it. Write the check. I won't hesitate. In my current mood, I would enjoy seeing you paraded through MossTech in handcuffs."

His uncle dragged his feet, bitching all the way, but he knew when he was cornered. He wrote out the check, and scrawled the requisite declaration, shoving it across his desk with bad grace and slapping an envelope on top. "There," he snarled. "Satisfied?"

Caleb looked it over. It said what it needed to say, and not one word more. He cosigned it himself before folding the sheet of paper and tucking it and the check into the envelope. "Where are Herbert's things?"

"The box on the table. Good riddance. Now get the hell out of my sight."

"With pleasure," Caleb replied.

A brief glance in the box showed that it was just as Yvette had said. Documents, insurance policies, certificates, cash. A few time-worn jewelry boxes. A laptop computer and a tablet. He tucked the envelope inside the box and picked it up.

"You're pathetic," Jerome said. "A dog bringing a dead duck to his master's feet."

"Not exactly the metaphor I'd choose, but call it what you like, Uncle."

He left Jerome sputtering, and caught Yvette's eye as he went past her desk outside. She gave him a grateful smile when she saw the box in his arms, and then Jerome's furious roar sent her scurrying back into his office.

Caleb politely evaded everyone who tried to corner him, and headed to his car.

He'd parked a block past the Cartwright Hotel. He looked into the restaurant as he passed, and saw a man at the bar. Broad shoulders, hunched over his drink. Dark hair, spiked up and messy. The guy he'd fought in room 408. Brody was still in town?

Curiosity got the better of him. Caleb made his way into the restaurant. Sure enough, it was Brody on the stool. He had the dark, shaggy beginnings of a beard.

The place was deserted. Caleb set the box down and sat near Brody. "Hey."

Brody turned his head. His bruises had faded, as Caleb's had, but he still had dark marks under his eyes, a scab on his lip and his cheekbone.

The other man's mouth twisted when he saw Caleb, as if he'd tasted something bitter. "You," he muttered. "All I needed today."

"I thought you'd be gone," Caleb said.

"I already had a plane ticket to Tokyo, leaving tomorrow morning," Brody said dully. "So I went up to the Olympic Peninsula. Some hiking. To clear my head."

"Did it work?"

Brody gave him an unfriendly look. "No."

The bartender approached them. "Can I get you something?"

"He was just leaving," Brody said sharply. "He has no time to drink."

Caleb waved away the bartender. "Can I ask you a question?"

"You can try. I might tell you to go to hell."

Caleb nodded. "Why do you care so much about taking MossTech down?"

"You wouldn't understand if I told you," Brody said. "You're an idiot. That woman risked jail time for you and your family. She's in love with you. Sucked for me, but hey. You should've trusted her. But like an asshole, you hire a PI to follow her day and night. She's better off with her heart broken than with a paranoid sleazebag like you."

Caleb stared at him. "I didn't do that," he said blankly. "That wasn't me."

Brody snorted. "Don't lie. She saw the photos on your computer. You are so busted. If I were her, I would've dumped you, too. Anyone with a brain and spine—"

"It wasn't me!" Caleb's voice got louder. "My uncle did that, not me!"

Brody's eyes widened. "No shit. What a freaking tool." Brody gulped his drink. "My family doesn't do that crap to me. Because they're dead. Ironic, if you think about it. I try not to. But it takes a lot of drinking. So piss off. Leave me to it."

"Ironic how?" Caleb demanded. "What do you mean? What the hell did we ever do to you?"

Brody's bloodshot eyes narrowed. "I don't want to have this conversation right now," he said. "Get lost."

"Fine. I'm gone," Caleb grabbed Herbert's box. When he got out on the street, his phone buzzed in his pocket. He pulled it out. Text messages, from Maddie.

Tilda coming over to bring Annika to Gran's at 5 pm.

Just sayin.

He bolted toward the car, electrified. He didn't dare to hope.

Hope was too dangerous.

Twenty-Two

As soon as Annika scrambled out of Tilda's car, she bolted across the grass, shrieking as she leaped into Maddie's arms. It was a tribute to Maddie's athleticism that she wasn't knocked over onto Elaine's lawn. She staggered back, laughing. Annika clung to her in a big arms-and-legs monkey hug, and then bounded over to give Elaine a more decorous greeting.

The older woman smiled at Tilda over Annika's head. "I'm so glad you came by," she said. "We've been pining away without regular doses of our precious Annika-girl."

Tilda heard the subtext loud and clear. *Don't you take our darling away from us.*

Good thing she'd had the presence of mind back at the beginning to retain the deciding vote on all matters concerning Annika, but she didn't want to tear Annika away from her newfound family. That would be awful.

But seeing them hurt her? She wasn't sure if she could endure this kind of discomfort on a regular basis.

She'd been considering Portland, maybe, or Spokane. New surroundings, but close enough for Annika to have frequent visits, both with Tilda's father and with the Mosses. Maybe that would be survivable.

But one thing at a time. "Nice to see you, Elaine."

"Come on in," Elaine said. "Can I offer you coffee, tea, a cocktail?"

"Oh, no. I'm supposed to meet a friend, and I'm late. Another time."

"But I need to speak to you, my dear. It won't take long."

Tilda slung Annika's backpack over her shoulder and followed her up into the entrance hall. She laid Annika's bag on the ornately carved wooden bench in the entry hall and followed Elaine into the library. "Elaine, I don't want to be rude, but I don't—"

Caleb was standing there. He looked thinner. His eyes seemed to burn in his face.

Tilda turned on Elaine. "You set me up."

Elaine lifted her hands. "Don't you glare at me. It's not like I could stop him from coming here."

Tilda backed toward the door. "You are not doing this to me."

"Please, Tilda." Caleb's voice was rough. "Five minutes. That's all I ask." He looked at Elaine. "Privately," he said pointedly.

"Oh, of course." Elaine marched out. The heavy door fell shut.

Tilda felt as if she was in a spotlight. Stammering and stupid. "I can't be manipulated this way. I didn't sign up for this. Being monitored, spied on."

"Can I just say my piece?" Caleb asked.

She waved her hand. "Fine. I'm listening."

"I'll start with this, then." He gestured at a file box that was lying on the table.

"Yes? And this is…?"

"The contents of your father's safe." Caleb opened the box and took out an envelope. "Herbert's documents and cash, laptop, tablet. Your mom's jewelry."

"Oh, wow," she said. "I've been putting off dealing with that. I'm so glad I won't have to, now. Thank God, Dad wasn't there when they broke in."

"Yes," Caleb said. "I'm sorry. For all of it." He held out the letter. "Here."

Tilda took the envelope. "Is this a new trap? I'm not interested in playing games."

"No games. This is exactly the opposite of that. Just open it."

Tilda pulled out a piece of paper. A check fluttered to the floor. Caleb picked it up as she unfolded the paper. The handwritten words were terse and brief.

I, Jerome Philip Moss, formally apologize for organizing the robbery that took place at the home of Herbert Riley on October 6 of this year.

Jerome's signature was scrawled below that, and then, in Caleb's handwriting, was "witnessed by Caleb Horace Moss." Then the date, and Caleb's bold, jagged signature.

She stared at it for a few minutes, speechless. "Is this for real?"

"Absolutely," Caleb said.

"How on earth did you coerce him into this?"

"I threatened to turn him in to the police," Caleb said.

Tilda finally managed to speak. "I assume he's destroyed the copy of Brody's incriminating file by now?"

"Yes," Caleb said. "But he kept the rest of the safe's contents in his office, in plain view. His assistant got nervous and told Maddie. Maddie told me."

"Well, good. I'm glad to have Dad's stuff back. But what's the point? Is this just to punish your uncle?"

"It's an insurance policy. Against anything Jerome could ever pull on you. You could punish him with it now, or just keep it, secure in the knowledge that Jerome won't mess with you again. Not while you hold this on him."

"He could steal it back," Tilda said. "It's his specialty, after all."

"He couldn't," Caleb said. "I cosigned it. To make that fly, he'd have to make both me and the document disappear. That's a stretch, even for Jerome."

She shivered. "I wouldn't want to put it to the test."

Caleb held out the check to her. "I appreciate the sentiment."

She flinched at the brief brush of his fingers. "What's this for?"

"Damages. The TVs, the cleaning bill, the new home-security system, a top-of-the-line safe. Don't economize. Go hog wild. Jerome can afford it, and he deserves for this to sting. Maybe he'll even learn something."

Tilda tucked the envelope into her purse. "Thank you," she said. "Dad will be relieved to have his things back. Losing Mom's jewelry really upset him."

"It's the least I could do," he said.

The long silence between them felt brittle. It could shatter like a delicate crystal.

Caleb took a step closer. "I don't want to stop at the least I can do." His low voice shook. "I want to offer the very best. To you. To Annika."

Tilda's throat tightened. "Caleb, I can't live like this. Being spied on. I don't want that. For me or for Annika."

"I know," he said. "I know that. I'll never—"

"You have no right to say that you'll never." The words burst out of her. "You had me followed by a private investigator. That's a deal-breaker for me. And it started right after our trip to the coast, after all that bullshit you spouted about trust."

"I didn't hire an investigator," Caleb said. "Jerome did that."

"Jerome is easy to blame," she said. "An all-purpose villain. I saw those files on your computer."

"Jerome sent them to me," Caleb said. "I'll show you the dates of the emails. The first one was the night that you met with Brody at the Cartwright. I had no idea you were being followed before that. I would never have allowed it if I had known. I swear it on my honor."

"Why was Jerome doing it in the first place?"

"He knew about Brody's file," Caleb said. "He'd been monitoring your phones."

"Ah. So he hacked us, tailed us and then robbed us. Wow."

"But he knew your file was a copy," Caleb said. "He wanted the original, so he kept watching you. I found out about the file right after that board meeting. I came home, intending to ask you about it." He stopped, swallowing. "But you were gone."

"Yes." Tilda's voice hardened. "Gone to save your company from disaster."

"I wish I'd known where you were going," Caleb said.

"I wish you'd trusted me to tell you!"

"So do I. But Jerome sent me a livestream of you, talking to Brody in the bar."

Comprehension rocked her. "Were you watching it when you asked if I was meeting with Julia Huang?"

"Yes," he admitted.

"Another trap, Caleb?"

"I didn't mean for it to be. I was just trying to understand."

"Well, you failed," she said.

They gazed at each other, a long, searching look. Caleb took a step toward her.

"Nine years ago, I didn't believe love existed," he said. "I thought it was just sex, hormones, ego gratification. But in the last few weeks, you convinced me. What we have is real. As deep as the ocean. Nothing is more precious to me. You, me. Annika."

"I felt that way, too," she whispered, sniffing.

"Jerome messed with my head. And don't get defensive,

Til, but if I'd known about Brody and his file, Jerome would never have been able to get to me."

She crossed her arms. "So it's my fault, now?"

"God, no. You took a huge risk for us, and I appreciate that. I'm just saying, very respectfully, that I'm not the only one here who has difficulty with trust. This mess happened because of a lack of trust on both our parts."

Tilda turned away from his intense gaze. It took a minute, to find the words.

"I was afraid to show you that file," she said. "I didn't want to throw off our equilibrium. It didn't seem necessary, once I decided not to use it. I didn't know Brody had a personal stake in bringing down MossTech. He never told me. It seemed irrelevant."

Caleb nodded, saying nothing.

Tilda clenched her shaking hands. "Okay," she said. "I accept my responsibility, if it makes you feel better. I, Matilda Jane Riley, formally apologize for withholding vital information from you, causing you great distress and embarrassment, which ultimately resulted in a sleazy fistfight in a hotel room with a naked man. Give me some paper and I'll write it down. You can cosign it, if you want."

"No," Caleb said. "That's not what I want."

"Then what the hell *do* you want?"

"You, Tilda," Caleb said. "You, forever. For always."

Tilda's heart thudded. "If this is about Elaine's mandate, and the controlling shares, I'll keep my side of our bargain," she told him. "I'll stay legally married to you for the stipulated period. You don't have to do cartwheels just to save your company."

"I don't give a damn about the company." To her shock, Caleb sank to his knees and took her hand. He produced a ring box from his pocket, and held it up.

The ring inside was stunning. Interlocking bands of white

gold, forming a striking geometric design with different colored gems. Luscious, gorgeous. One of a kind.

She couldn't speak, so Caleb spoke up, hesitantly. "Annika helped me pick it out. It was fun, jewelry shopping with her. She talked a mile a minute. Had really strong opinions. I meant to give this to you before, but things got crazy."

Tilda's throat tightened.

"Prepare yourself, because this is going to sound strange," Caleb said. "Matilda Jane Riley, I love you. With everything I've got. Everything I am. It's all yours. Will you do me the immense honor of divorcing me?"

She realized, after a moment, that her mouth hung open. *"What?"*

"Let's take our lives back." Caleb's voice was urgent. "By brute force. After we sign the divorce papers, I'll resign from MossTech, and we'll leave this bullshit in the dust. We'll take Annika and run away. Anyplace you want. Someplace sunny, a city you like—France, Italy, Spain, Greece, Ireland, Iceland. I'll find a job there. Put your team together and develop Far Eye. We'll live together in sin, until death do us part. Or maybe we'll get married again, later on, when it's no longer anybody's goddamn business but ours."

"But—but your job—"

"Screw my job. I'll find another one. I get headhunted a dozen times a week. And there's no rush. We could take a long anti-honeymoon. Spend weeks or months lolling on a beach somewhere. Hiking, sailing, whatever you want to do."

She was laughing through her tears. "To celebrate our divorce?"

"To celebrate our independence," he corrected. "Sweet, sweet freedom. It is a shame, about that awesome house at Breakers Bay, but whatever. We'll buy another one."

Tilda's eyes were wet, but she couldn't stop laughing. "You're nuts."

"For you, yes. I wish I had divorce papers ready, just for

the satisfaction of signing them this minute. But that takes time to prepare. I couldn't wait one more second."

"You'd do that for me? Walk away from MossTech? Let Jerome take over?"

"I won't trade my happiness for MossTech," Caleb said. "Will you wear my ring?"

Tilda nodded, blinking away tears.

Caleb slid the ring onto her ring finger. He pressed her fingers to his lips, a slow, reverent kiss. When he rose to his feet, his eyes were wet, too.

He pulled her into a tight hug. "I can't believe it," he whispered against her ear. "I was afraid you'd melt away. But here you are."

"Right where I want to be." She clung to him, and the hot contact set off a cascade of delicious shivers that rippled through her entire body. So sweet. So good.

"Think up some destinations. I'll set up a meeting with my lawyer to draw up divorce papers." He laughed. "That sounds strange. It'll be hard to explain to people."

"Like your grandmother, for instance."

Caleb's smile dimmed. "Yeah, she won't be happy, but it's her own damn fault. She drove me to it. She'll be glad for us, though, once she gets over being furious."

"Jerome will be thrilled," Tilda said. "He'll rub his hands together in glee."

Caleb shrugged. "An unintended side effect, but nothing's perfect. We're just lucky to get out of this mess intact. And together."

"You think nothing can be perfect?" She laughed at him. "I beg to differ, Caleb."

"You're perfect. It's the rest of the world that leaves something to be desired."

"Hah! I'm hardly perfect. But we could rethink the divorce. Unless you're ditching MossTech for your own personal sake. If you sincerely want that, then fine, I'm on board. But if you're doing it just for me, to make a point, you're off the hook."

Caleb gave her a narrow look. "What do you mean?" he asked carefully. "That if I stayed on at MossTech as CEO, you'd stay married to me? For real?"

"Yes," she told him. "Don't get me wrong. I still want the honeymoon. The lolling on beaches and all that. Don't think for a second that you're cheating me out of that."

Caleb's eyes went soft with wonder. "Really?" he said. "You'd stay in this Moss madhouse with me? After everything that's happened?"

"If we're both safe inside that united front that you talked about," she told him. "If we're straight with each other. If we can trust each other for real. Forever."

His smile had widened into a grin. "You're sure?"

"It would be a damn shame, to let Jerome win," she said. "I know when you're serious, Caleb Moss. You're the most serious, focused, driven man I've ever known."

He quirked up an eyebrow. "I, uh, hope that's a good thing."

"Oh, yes. Trust me," she murmured, stroking his chest and looking seductively up through her lashes. "Very good. Best I've ever known, actually. It's a quality that I miss. I can't wait to experience it again. At our earliest opportunity."

"Anytime," he said. "Anywhere. How about now? Here? I'm up for it. Literally."

"I bet you are, you sex fiend." She laughed at him. "In your grandmother's library, hah! I'll wear your ring, but I hereby formally refuse your request of divorce, Caleb Horace Moss. You're legally stuck with me."

"Oh, hell yes." He pulled her into his arms.

Their lips met, and the pent-up emotion broke loose. It was like they were fighting their way closer to each other, straining together toward that beacon of hope that burned, hot and desperate at the core of their beings. Every kiss got them closer. So perfect, poignant, real. His caressing hands left trails of sweet, shivering awareness—

"They're kissing! And hugging!" Annika's voice, squeaky with excitement, broke through the dreamy fog of arousal. Tilda looked around to see her daughter's wide brown eyes, peeking in through a crack of the opened library door.

"Annika! Do not intrude on a private moment!" Elaine scolded in a hushed tone, but Tilda saw her delighted smile as she tugged the door smartly shut.

Tilda leaned her forehead against Caleb's chest. "Oh, my," she whispered. "Busted."

"So it's a done deal?" His hot kiss to the side of her neck made her melt and shiver.

"Signed and sealed," she told him. "From the moment I first saw you. Took us long enough to get here, though."

"Too long, but here we are. Home at last. And I'm never letting go of you again. We belong to each other, Til. I'm yours. You're mine."

Tilda wrapped her arms around his neck. "Forever and always," she whispered, as their lips met.

* * * * *

COMING SOON!

We really hope you enjoyed reading this book.
If you're looking for more romance, be sure to
head to the shops when new books are
available on

Thursday 4th
August

To see which titles are coming soon, please visit
millsandboon.co.uk/nextmonth

MILLS & BOON

THE HEART OF ROMANCE

A ROMANCE FOR EVERY READER

MODERN

Prepare to be swept off your feet by sophisticated, sexy and seductive heroes, in some of the world's most glamourous and romantic locations, where power and passion collide.

HISTORICAL

Escape with historical heroes from time gone by. Whether your passion is for wicked Regency Rakes, muscled Vikings or rugged Highlanders, awaken the romance of the past.

MEDICAL

Set your pulse racing with dedicated, delectable doctors in the high-pressure world of medicine, where emotions run high and passion, comfort and love are the best medicine.

True Love

Celebrate true love with tender stories of heartfelt romance, from the rush of falling in love to the joy a new baby can bring, and a focus on the emotional heart of a relationship.

Desire

Indulge in secrets and scandal, intense drama and plenty of sizzling hot action with powerful and passionate heroes who have it all: wealth, status, good looks…everything but the right woman.

HEROES

Experience all the excitement of a gripping thriller, with an intense romance at its heart. Resourceful, true-to-life women and strong, fearless men face danger and desire - a killer combination!

LET'S TALK
Romance

For exclusive extracts, competitions
and special offers, find us online:

f facebook.com/millsandboon
🐦 @MillsandBoon
📷 @MillsandBoonUK

Get in touch on 01413 063232

For all the latest titles coming soon, visit
millsandboon.co.uk/nextmonth

Nadine Gonzalez is a Haitian American author. A lawyer by profession, she lives in Miami, Florida, and shares her home with her Cuban American husband and their son. Nadine writes joyous contemporary romance featuring a diverse cast of characters, American, Caribbean and Latinx. She networks on Twitter but lives on Instagram and increasingly on TikTok! Check out @_nadinegonzalez. For more information, visit her website, nadine-gonzalez.com

Shannon McKenna is the *New York Times* and *USA TODAY* bestselling author of over thirty romance novels, ranging from romantic suspense to contemporary romance and even to paranormal. She loves abandoning herself to the magic of a story. Writing her own stories is a dream come true. She loves to hear from readers. Visit her website, shannonmckenna.com. Find her on Facebook at Facebook.com/authorshannonmckenna or join her newsletter at shannonmckenna.com/connect.php and look for your welcome gift!